FIRST
GIRL
GONE

BOOKS BY L.T. VARGUS AND TIM MCBAIN

THE VIOLET DARGER SERIES
Dead End Girl
Image in a Cracked Mirror
Killing Season
The Last Victim
The Girl in the Sand
Bad Blood
Five Days Post Mortem
Into the Abyss
Night on Fire

THE VICTOR LOSHAK SERIES
Beyond Good & Evil
The Good Life Crisis
What Lies Beneath
Take Warning
Silent Night

FIRST
GIRL
GONE

LT VARGUS
TIM MCBAIN

bookouture

Published by Bookouture in 2020

An imprint of Storyfire Ltd.

Carmelite House
50 Victoria Embankment
London EC4Y 0DZ

www.bookouture.com

ISBN: 978-1-83888-833-6
eBook ISBN: 978-1-83888-832-9

PROLOGUE

Kara kicked at the wood chips beneath the park bench, flinging flecks of red every which way. Something about the activity jarred her out of a daze, highlighted the level of boredom she'd now achieved.

Christ. This was how she was spending her Christmas break? Sitting on a park bench, kicking wood chips?

The street was dead. This part of Salem Island always was.

Even the air itself seemed lifeless. Overcast sky the gray shade of a stone. No sun. No breeze.

Kara checked the time on her phone again, wondering what was taking Maggie so long. She should have been here by now.

She felt his presence before she saw him. Bodily responses communicating the signs of danger one by one.

A prickling of the hair on her arms.

A chill climbing up her spine.

Her breath hitching in her throat.

Someone was watching her. Someone in the shadows.

Kara locked her eyes on her feet. Searched out of the periphery of her vision.

There was a darkness there. A hulking shape across the street. A man. His broad-shouldered silhouette framed in the doorway of one of the boarded-up shops.

And he stared straight at her.

She fidgeted on the bench. Wished she could keep still. Convey no emotion. Like playing dead.

The last half hour flashed through her mind. She'd wandered down here after the fight with her mom. Stormed out of the house and then circled through town, killing time, smoking cigarettes, cutting through lawns. Waiting for Maggie to come pick her up. So, where was she?

She glanced up, eyes seeking and finding him at last. He turned his head the other direction, overselling the nonchalance.

That chill in her spine grew colder, shooting up her back and hovering between her shoulder blades.

He looked like he could be in witness protection, covered up to the point of ridiculousness. Chunky sunglasses screened much of the face behind sheening black plastic. A Detroit Tigers hat rode low over his brow. His hand rose to cover his mouth, index finger and thumb pinching at his top lip like a crab claw.

She froze. Watched.

After several heartbeats, he spun away and walked off in the other direction.

She held her breath as she watched his figure grow smaller, breathing again only when he disappeared around the corner. Relief.

Her shoulders sagged. Tiniest puffs of laughter exited her nostrils in a staccato hiss.

It was nothing, of course. Just some rando out for a friendly afternoon stare with his best pair of Kim Jong-il sunglasses on.

Her trembling hands peeled the soft pack of cigarettes out of her left hip pocket, adhered the crooked tube of tobacco to her lips. Then she fumbled back into the pocket for the matchbook. Struck one. Brought the flame up under her chin.

She inhaled. Tasted the sweet breath of tobacco smoke. Right away the nicotine calmed her—maybe it was the habit more than the chemical itself.

She texted Maggie.

Hurry up. I'm freezing my ass off.

When the Marlboro was about half gone, she stood, her heart still hammering away inside. Weird. She hadn't even been that scared. Not really. She'd tell Maggie about it later, and they'd laugh. Kara the paranoid.

She crossed the street. Stepped up on the curb on the other side. The library was only a few blocks away. She could loiter inside until Maggie texted her back and avoid dying of hypothermia. She made sure to avoid the doorway where the creep had stood, reassuring herself in a little whisper that she was overreacting, though she didn't quite believe her own voice.

The cigarette smoldered between her fingers, mostly gone now. She held off on hitting it again, not quite wanting to let it go as she approached the corner where the man had disappeared.

She chewed her lip. Couldn't help but picture the man in the black sunglasses lurching out from behind the wall of the donut shop like a mountain lion leaping for her jugular.

She held her breath as she rounded the corner.

Nothing.

He wasn't there.

Just another sleepy street on Salem Island.

She crossed to the next block. Jitters still running up and down her limbs.

She lifted the cigarette butt to her lips and hit it. Tasted the caustic tang of melting plastic. She'd burned it down to the filter now.

Shit.

She flicked it toward the storm drain, the cherry detaching upon impact.

She swallowed, and her throat clicked.

He lunged out of the bushes. A ski mask now covered his face, his arms outstretched.

He gripped her around the shoulders. An awkward hug. Forceful. Kara screamed. Threw an elbow into his gut. Heard a *woof* of breath knocked out of him.

Now she stumbled into a run. Choppy steps. Half-falling.

He leapt after her. Fell flat on the concrete.

His right arm shot out and hooked her ankle. Tripped her at full speed. Thunked her head-first on the cement.

Dark. Stars. All of reality seemed to suck down into a tunnel. The world around her grew smaller. Smaller. A little circle cutout. Dark around the edges now.

He rolled her. Lifted her torso. Hands snaking under her armpits. Each finger pressing into the soft flesh there. And he dragged her face up.

She could hear a choppiness in his footsteps. Hurried and uneven.

Her head lolled. Neck slack.

She watched through slitted eyelids as her limp legs dragged over the concrete behind the two of them, but she couldn't feel them. Couldn't feel much.

When he tried to shove her into the backseat of a sedan, she lurched. Clawed for his eyes, for his masked face.

Missed.

He dropped her. The back of her skull thumped down on the asphalt.

Things got far away again. Distant. Quiet. That black circle around the edge of things cinched tighter.

"Enough already," he hissed between his teeth.

He knelt over her. Picked her head up and slammed it down again. A solid connection of skull and concrete that shot bolts of lightning through her vision.

The last circle of light retreated. The darkness became total.

CHAPTER ONE

Misty sobbed in the seat across from Charlotte Winters' desk, tears tinted with mascara gathering along her jaw.

"Jesus H," Allie said. "The waterworks came on like she flipped a switch."

The observation was true enough, Charlie thought, even if it was phrased in Allie's typically rude fashion. The girl never knew when to keep quiet.

Misty hadn't managed a word yet. She'd just walked into Charlie's office, sat down, and started bawling.

Now her face wrinkled up like a Halloween mask, and violent sobs shook her from the center of her torso out. The little pot belly quaked, the shoulders and legs seeming to throb a beat later.

Charlie was so taken aback by the abrupt blubbering that she froze. Lips parted. Watching Misty cry. Not sure what to say or do.

She stared at a strand of clear snot collecting in the center of Misty's top lip, threatening to rush down into her mouth.

"Get her a Kleenex before I puke, for God's sake," Allie said.

Charlie nudged the box of tissues closer to Misty, thanking the universe for the millionth time that no one could hear Allie's running commentary.

She hadn't seen Misty Dawkins since high school graduation. They'd been friends back then. Maybe not close, but the kind of friend you paired up with in biology lab and ate lunch with in the cafeteria.

Charlie studied her. Misty looked mostly the same, with her small elfin chin, freckled nose, and kind brown eyes. She spotted a few strands of gray here and there, but Misty's dishwater-blonde hair hid it well. None of these observations told her why her old friend was in her office or why she was crying. She suspected the two were related.

"Just breathe," Charlie said, her voice finding that soothing tone two notches louder than a whisper. "Take your time, and tell me what you need."

Misty nodded, her shoulders rising and falling with a deep breath.

A crying woman wasn't what Charlie had expected when she arrived at A1 Investigations this morning. Her stomach grumbled, and she couldn't help but think longingly of the bagel going cold in the other room.

"It's probably the standard," Allie said. "Missing cat or cheating husband. No offense, but my money is on the cat."

Misty smeared a wadded tissue across her cheeks, which had now gone red and splotchy beneath the smudge of makeup.

"I'm sorry, Charlie. I guess I didn't expect to see you here. I was all prepared to say my piece, and then I came in here to find you instead of Frank, and it just… How long have you been back in town?"

"A few months," Charlie said, trying to find a comfortable position in her chair.

Misty's eyes fixed on a photograph on the wall. A snapshot of Charlie, age eight, her twiggy arm slung around the shoulder of her twin sister. The water of Lake St. Clair sparkled in the background, dotted with boats. Misty got the same sad look on her face people always got when they looked at old photos of Charlie's sister.

"I bet your family is glad to have you back home."

"Yeah." Charlie's chair creaked like an ancient ship as she leaned back. Eager to avoid any further questions about her family, she flipped the question back at Misty. "What about your family? How's Kenny?"

The furrow between Misty's eyebrows pretty much answered that question. Charlie should have known better, really. Kenny Barnes, the guy who'd knocked Misty up while they were still in high school, had always been kind of a loser.

"Oh, he left way back, when Kara was five. Got together with a gal down in Columbus. They have a four-year-old now. He sends money when he can. Child support, you know. Tries to call Kara on her birthday and at Christmas."

Charlie noted the phrases Misty had used: "Sends money *when he can...*" and "*Tries* to call Kara on her birthday..."

She was the same old Misty, alright. Still too damn nice for her own good and making excuses for people who didn't deserve it.

"That's why I'm here, actually," Misty said, the words coming out strangely high-pitched and tight.

And then she burst into tears again.

"Damn it," Allie muttered. "I should have known it would be a deadbeat ex."

Charlie did her best to block out Allie's voice so she could focus on Misty.

"I don't know what to do, Charlie. I'm so scared," Misty wailed.

Tugging another tissue free from the box, Charlie leaned across the desk and handed it to Misty.

"Why don't you start by telling me exactly what happened," Charlie said.

"It's Kara. She's missing."

Charlie flinched at the word "missing," and goosebumps prickled over her forearms. Her own twin sister had gone missing when she was eighteen, and she'd never been found. The jolt of alarm Charlie got when she heard about disappearances was an old tic she'd never been able to shake. But she'd gotten good at covering the reaction, and Misty hadn't seemed to notice.

Charlie took a deep breath.

"How long has she been gone?"

Misty's hands clenched around the handles of her purse.

"Two days. We had a fight… an argument. And she stormed out of the house. I haven't seen her since."

"What about her friends?"

Misty shook her head.

"I've called everyone. No one knows where she is."

A montage flashed in Charlie's head of the early days of her sister's disappearance. The panicked phone calls. The frantic searching. She didn't have to imagine what Misty was feeling because she'd been through it all herself.

"Have you talked to the police?" Charlie asked.

Misty nodded.

"They took down a report, said they'd 'look into it,' whatever that means. That's why I need your help."

Charlie sighed. She could see the anguish in Misty's eyes and remembered that feeling, the way not knowing gnawed at your insides until they were raw. But the reality was, a missing persons case wasn't in her wheelhouse, not with the resources she'd be working with. A1 Investigations was equipped for run-of-the-mill stuff: cheating spouses, insurance claims, worker's comp fraud, bail jumpers, and, yes, the occasional missing pet.

Folding one hand over the other, Charlie gazed across the desk at her old friend.

"I'm really sorry you're going through this, and I know how worried you must be. But I'm not quite sure how I can help."

Misty blinked, letting loose a tear that slid down the side of her face.

"You guys are the best. Everyone says so. My cousin hired Frank when she was going through her divorce. He's the reason she got sole custody of the kids."

Charlie fiddled with the corner of her notepad. She hated this. Hated having to turn an old friend away when she was scared and desperate, but she didn't know what else she could do.

"That's what I'm trying to say, I guess. Divorces, marital issues… those are the kind of things we're equipped to handle," Charlie said, trying to sound apologetic. "Don't get me wrong, we're very good at what we do, but this sounds like something that'd take manpower and hours way beyond our capability."

"If it's an issue of money, I'll pay. I will pay anything to get my daughter back." Misty opened her purse and started to pull out her wallet. "Some of it might have to go on credit cards, but—"

"No, Misty. It's not about the money."

"Then I don't understand. You're a private investigator. You find things. So why can't you try to find my daughter?"

Eyes closed, Charlie frowned. Misty wasn't hearing her.

"I'm trying to tell you that this is something better left to the police. They've got the resources to handle a case like this. We don't."

Misty stared at her wordlessly. The silence stretched out long enough that Charlie felt obligated to fill it with something.

"The police will find your daughter. Everything will be fine, you'll see."

Brow furrowed once more, Misty swung her head from side to side.

"I can't believe this. When I walked in the door and saw you sitting behind the desk, I thought it was the answer to all of my prayers. Because if there was one person who would understand, one person who would listen and take me seriously, it would be you."

"Misty—"

"No! How can you tell me everything will be OK after what happened with your sister?"

The comment hit Charlie like a punch to the gut. Everyone in town had an opinion on the disappearance of Allison Winters, but the one thing they could all agree on was that the Salem Island police had botched the investigation. And it was true, wasn't it? They'd never found her sister. Never brought her killer to justice. And Charlie's family had never gotten any closure.

The lump in Charlie's throat kept her from speaking, and she wasn't sure what she'd say anyway, so she kept quiet.

"How can I trust them to find my Kara after that?" Misty asked. "Besides, they've already written her off as a runaway. I saw it on their faces the second I mentioned that she'd run off a time or two in the past. Little sidelong glances at each other like I'm too dumb to know what they're thinking. They gave up on her right then, I could see. They don't care that this time is different."

With a final sniffle, Misty snapped her purse shut and got to her feet.

"Well, if you won't help me, then I guess I should be moving on. Someone out there'll take my money. But thank you for your time anyhow."

Charlie found her voice at last.

"You said she's left before, but this time is different," she said. "Why? What's different about it?"

Pausing near the door, Misty squinted at Charlie, like the question might be a trap.

"Her phone. It goes straight to voicemail. Like it's turned off or something. If you knew Kara, you'd know that means something is wrong. She *never* turns her phone off. It's always glued to her hand."

Charlie plucked a pen from the mug on the desk and flipped to a fresh sheet of paper on her notepad.

"Does this mean you'll take the case?" Misty asked, and Charlie could hear the hope in her voice.

"It can't hurt for me to do some poking around," Charlie said, ignoring Allie's tongue clicking in disapproval.

Misty clutched her chest, and for a moment, Charlie thought she was going to start crying again.

"Oh, thank the Lord. Thank you, Charlie. And I meant what I said before, I can pay. I'll pay whatever it takes."

"We'll worry about that later. For now, let's get some of the basic questions out of the way." Angling her face back at her notepad, Charlie asked, "The other times she ran away… how long was she gone?"

"Usually it wasn't even a full day. She'd stay overnight at a friend's and be back the next day. Maybe a weekend at the most, but…"

Misty chewed at her lip. Charlie waited.

"Well, one time she was gone for four days, but that was because I confiscated her car keys."

Charlie waggled the pen between her fingers. Clicked and unclicked the tip.

"And you said this time you had a fight? What was that about?"

"Not really a fight. Just a little argument. You know how teenagers are," Misty said, fiddling with the zipper pull on her bag. "Kara got into some trouble this past summer, right after her seventeenth birthday. She'd been drinking, and, well… she got into an accident. And then she left the scene. It was kind of a big mess, but thankfully her lawyer was able to get the charges brought way down. I mean, there was talk of sending her to juvenile detention, but the judge agreed to six months of probation and some community service. So she may have dodged a bullet as far as all that, but she's lost a lot of privileges at home. I mean, she knows how I feel about drunk driving. I won't tolerate it."

"Right," Charlie said, making a note to look further into this blemish on Kara's criminal record.

"Anyway, for Christmas break, a bunch of the seniors were going on a cruise. Miami, Key West, and Cozumel. We told Kara she could go if she got her grades up at the end of last year, which she did. But then she pulled the stunt over the summer, and Chris and I discussed it—that's my husband—and we decided that we just couldn't reward that kind of behavior. We have other kids, and we don't want them getting the idea that we'll look the other way with this stuff. So we told her she couldn't go."

"And I'm guessing Kara wasn't too happy about that?"

Misty let out a sad laugh.

"I think she thought I was bluffing. It was all paid for, and we're way past the cancellation window. We told her a month ago it wasn't happening, but I guess it didn't hit home until Wednesday."

"What happened on Wednesday?"

"That was the day everyone was getting on the bus for Miami."

"And she couldn't have tried to get on the bus anyway?"

"I still have the tickets for the bus and the cruise, not to mention she wasn't going to get far without her passport, which I have locked up. And I called one of the parent chaperones for the trip, just to be sure. No one has seen her."

Charlie jotted this down, turned to a fresh page on her notepad, and slid it across the desk to Misty.

"I want you to write down the names of anyone Kara might have seen or spoken to after she left the house. Friends, boyfriend, co-workers if she has a job."

Pen in hand, Misty scribbled down names and phone numbers.

"I'll need to come by your house later. Take a look through her things and talk with the rest of your family, if that's OK."

Fresh tears glistened in Misty's eyes, and she lifted a hand to wipe them away.

"Of course. Anything you need," she said, passing the notebook back. "I meant what I said before. I was never scared any of those other times she left. Not once. You know how they say a mother knows these kinds of things? Knows it in her bones? Well, it must be true. It has to be. Because I'm scared, Charlie. I've never been so scared."

Charlie took down a few more details, and when they finished, both women stood. Misty crossed around the desk and threw her arms around Charlie, gripping her tightly.

"Thank you, Charlie. You have no idea what this means to me."

"Well... you're welcome," Charlie said awkwardly.

Misty seemed to swallow another surge of emotion, and then her eyes went to the photograph of Charlie and her sister again.

"I always admired Allie. She was such a free spirit."

Charlie nodded. People were always saying things like that about Allie.

The glass on the door rattled as Charlie closed it behind Misty. She sank back into the crumbling wooden chair, and one of the slats jabbed into her spine. It was like the damn thing had elbows of its own.

"So… Misty Dawkins…" Allie said. "She got fat."

"Don't be a dick," Charlie said.

"See? That's why I'm never having kids," Allie continued. "Seen it a hundred times."

"Stop."

"You pop out some crotch fruit, and your hips and thighs stay doughy until the end of time."

Charlie's silence only seemed to egg Allie on.

"Hey, you're the one who talks to her dead sister instead of having real friends. Perfectly normal, perfectly healthy, right?"

Charlie closed her eyes, trying not to listen to her sister prattle on.

For a dead girl, she sure never shut up.

CHAPTER TWO

With Misty Dawkins gone and the office empty once more, a cold feeling settled over Charlie—that bone-deep chill that belonged to the deepest, darkest parts of winter. Even as she worked—setting up interviews with Kara Dawkins' friends and family and running basic background checks—her mind lingered on Allie's disappearance all those years ago. Creeping gray memories flashed through her mind.

She saw Allie as a cackling toddler, cookies crammed into her sticky little fists. She'd pushed a dining room chair into the kitchen to commandeer the sweets in the highest cupboard for her and Charlie. So long ago now.

Next, she saw Allie as a teenager, perpetually smirking, her hair chopped short and dyed pitch-black for that one year—the year she hated everything, as Allie herself later described it.

Allie would have been sixteen that year. Only two years before she'd disappeared, and yet she'd changed so much in such a short time after, changed and changed again. Every year seemed so much longer at that age, the personality shifts coming hard and fast every three months or so.

And then, jumping to the time after Allie had vanished, Charlie saw the empty bed where Allie was supposed to be, her sister's half of the room taking on a hushed reverence during the time she was missing. A quiet place, somber, it felt more like being in church than a bedroom, felt terribly empty without her.

They searched for nearly three weeks, and during that time, everyone kept holding on to the hope that she was still alive. That's what they kept saying, anyway. "She's out there somewhere."

Until her sister's foot washed up on one of the public beaches. No one pretended she was alive after that.

Charlie saw the funeral, all the people draped in black. Uncomfortable. Muted. Her mother sobbing the whole way through. The visitations. The service. The wake. Rituals stripped of meaning, reduced to a blur of strangely formal images in her memory.

Each of these memories conjured ancient feelings, awakened them, brought them back fully fleshed out, just as intricate and potent as they were back then. The level of detail in each one bewildered Charlie. Together they overwhelmed her.

Charlie moved to the coffee machine in the corner of her office, the too-hot burner there slowly cooking decent coffee down into a thick gloop. She poured herself a cup. Drank. The coffee still tasted good enough for now—only faintly burned—but the scalding liquid couldn't touch the cold feeling that had settled over her. Maybe nothing could.

The investigation into Allie's disappearance had focused heavily on a local hermit, Leroy Gibbs, who did odd jobs around town, but the evidence was circumstantial, and despite a media frenzy upon his arrest, the charges were eventually dropped due to a lack of evidence. The crime was never solved, the wound never closed. And while the town moved on and mostly forgot as the years crept by, the Winters family never recovered.

The grief killed Charlie's father rapidly, taking him out by way of a stroke just two years later at forty-nine. It drove her mother to madness, a series of mental breakdowns that shuffled her in and out of the hospital and on and off various medications.

It was during Allie's funeral that her voice first made an appearance. Charlie couldn't stop staring at the closed casket.

"You think it's in there?"

Charlie's gaze swept to the right, to where she'd heard the voice. There was nothing there but a table with an antique-looking lamp and a vase of tulips.

"The foot, I mean," Allie's voice clarified. "*My* foot. Can they embalm just a foot? Do they put makeup on it? I hope they gave it some polish at least. Nice pop of color."

Charlie blinked, certain she was going crazy but feeling completely calm about it.

The voice never left after that. Her sister was her constant companion now, sarcastically commenting on everything that happened.

Whether Allie's presence was psychological or supernatural, Charlie couldn't say, but she was in no hurry to fix the problem. Even if Allie only existed in her imagination, she didn't want to lose her again.

Charlie went to take another sip of coffee but found her mug empty. She moved to the kitchenette in the room beyond the office. Rinsed her mug. The warm water felt good on the tips of her fingers.

She still couldn't believe she was back here on Salem Island, working in the office her uncle Frank had set up decades ago: A1 Investigations. He'd worked the standard private investigator jobs for all those years—cheating spouses, background checks, a touch of surveillance now and again. With him out of commission due to cancer and her stepping in, it was as though she'd inherited the family business by default—the prodigal niece returning to fulfill her destiny—even if Frank was still hanging in there for now, going through chemo treatments, looking quite hairless at the moment.

But this wasn't Charlie's destiny. She wasn't supposed to be here, didn't belong here at all.

With what had happened to Allie and her parents, Charlie had taken her first opportunity to flee Salem Island. She'd planned to get far from here and managed to accomplish it pretty well, making it the full 2,395 miles from the east coast of Michigan to the Pacific Ocean.

She'd worked the last eight years as an investigator for a law firm in Seattle. There she did *real* investigative work—nothing like the menial cases Uncle Frank worked around Salem Island. Corporate fraud, pollution cover-ups, political espionage, hacked elections, embezzled charity money, all the sordid trappings one would expect in a world as corrupt as this one.

Approaching these through the civil side rather than through criminal law, her law firm never really achieved justice so much as they made some small group of the crooks pay. They couldn't stop these crimes. They couldn't even slow them down, but they could sock each bully in the nose a couple times, bloody them up, and make them pay a few million in punitive damages. Justice? Not really. Vengeance? Yes. That blurred line between vengeance and justice made sense to Charlie, fit the way she saw the world. It made it something like her dream job to be part of it.

But eventually things in Seattle went bad. Things always went bad in time, didn't they?

And now she was back on Salem Island, back where her family had come apart at the seams, their insides pulled out and put on public display. Maybe you could never really get away from something like Allie's disappearance. Maybe it followed you.

Even now, years later, Charlie suffered recurring nightmares of finding Allie's body, kneeling down on a patch of bare earth in the woods, fingers scraping at the rich black soil. Sometimes it was Allie's face that emerged, eyes closed as though she were only sleeping, peaceful if a little colorless. But usually it was her sister's bones that emerged, white and stark against the dark of the dirt. Some part of her believed, way down deep, that justice would still be served for her sister in this small way, that she could find her way to Allie's remains, someway, somehow.

Alas, reality offered no such satisfaction. No body found. No resolution.

In real life, justice was lopsided. Halfhearted. Usually unattainable. Even in the best-case scenario, it occurred in shades of gray. Maybe the real thing couldn't exist in a world like this one.

Still, she couldn't help but wonder what it would be like, to get that closure in Allie's case, to dig up her bones. She wanted it so deeply, but could it offer any satisfaction after all this time?

The body could be found, perhaps—the *what* finally known definitively, but even then the *why* would still linger. No explanation. No meaning ascribed. Wasn't that what every family of a victim truly sought? The why. The reasoning. Some sense of meaning they could hang their emotions on.

So many times over the years, Charlie had driven past Leroy Gibbs' place—a ramshackle farmhouse near the water's edge. She repeated the ritual every time she was back for the holidays, dredging all those memories up to the surface again, and again, and again. Here was the main suspect—a quiet type, bearded, with fierce eyes—never fully cleared so much as deemed not guilty due to a lack of real information. Here was the house, the place where perhaps her sister had met her end. Could the woods nearby be her resting place, even now?

She didn't know. Couldn't know.

And the not knowing became a second wound to go with the one Allie's absence made, one that festered, one that rotted from the middle out. Like one of those spider bites that went necrotic and ate the flesh away, Charlie thought. The not knowing ate at the meat of you, stripped you down to the bone.

The grief hurt. The loss ached. But the not knowing? The not knowing killed you.

Charlie ripped her hand out from under the hot water pouring out of the faucet, realizing only after she'd scalded herself that she'd zoned out into ghostly memories once again, letting the water run over her fingertips, the heat growing and growing until the hurt shook her awake.

She spritzed cold water on her reddened fingers to stop the burn from getting worse, then shook her hand. The pain held for a moment and receded.

Back out in the main office, she adjusted her clothing as though that might help refocus her on the task of the day: the Kara Dawkins case. She needed to pull herself together. Do her job. A girl was missing, after all. Misty Dawkins' crying face flashed in her memory to remind her of that grave reality.

And suddenly it struck Charlie that Allie had been curiously quiet during this whole trip down memory lane. No sarcastic remarks. No crude jokes. Nothing. Maybe that was where the cold feeling came from: Allie's absence.

The quiet of the office seemed to swell to fill the space until it seemed hollowed out, desolate, cavernous, freezing.

Yes. Charlie was alone. Quite alone.

CHAPTER THREE

In the car that afternoon, Charlie planned her approach to the case. She'd dug through Kara's social media accounts for the rest of the morning, scanned hundreds of pictures, posts, and comments. She'd started to get a real sense of the girl's personality in the process: sarcastic yet sensitive. When she wasn't smiling in her photos, she was making silly faces or posing for comedic effect. And she was witty, too. Several of her tweets had made Charlie laugh out loud.

She'd also checked out the GPS records for the Dawkins family's vehicles, which Misty had given her access to. These days, much of Charlie's job came back to checking GPS logs. Everyone agreeing to track their own movements with technology certainly made a private detective's life easier. Alas, there was nothing out of the ordinary in the Dawkins' logs—school, work, grocery store. Kara had been grounded from driving for months, and much to Charlie's chagrin, she had apparently abided by the rules of her punishment.

That led to the question of how to proceed: should Charlie start talking to Kara's family, or focus on her friends first? She had some time to figure it out. She had to swing by Frank's first, take him to his chemo appointment.

She pulled into the Wendy's drive-thru on the way, ordering a Spicy Chicken Sandwich, French fries, and a Dr. Pepper.

"Nothing for you?" Allie asked. "You know how Uncle Frank is about his food. He'll take off a finger if he catches you bogarting his fries."

"I'm not hungry," Charlie said.

"Oh, right. Your hospital phobia. Time for some real talk, sis. You need to get over that."

That was easy for Allie to say. She hadn't been there to witness the way their father had withered away after his stroke, rapidly losing every physical, mental, and bodily function, one by one. Hadn't had to deal with their mother's neuroses on top of everything else—every time one of the doctors came into the room, her mother had a new ailment of her own to complain about. "I think I'm having heart palpitations," or, "I was looking in the mirror this morning, and I'm sure this mole on my shoulder didn't look like this before." Or Charlie's personal favorite, "What are the symptoms of Lyme disease, because I think I might have it."

Hospitals made Charlie uneasy now. The smell. The noises. All of it gave her a queasy feeling in the pit of her stomach. But this particular hospital was the very one where she'd watched her father die. So Allie could take her "real talk" and shove it up her non-corporeal ass.

The line of cars moved along in the drive-thru until Charlie was at the window. The girl who passed her the food looked like she was probably in high school, and that brought Kara Dawkins back into the forefront of Charlie's thoughts.

Where are you, Kara?

Frank's house was a small white cottage on the tip of a peninsula that jutted into the St. Clair River. Gravel crunched under the tires of the Focus as Charlie rolled down the driveway and parked next to the garage.

He'd lived here as long as Charlie could remember. When they were kids, she and Allie used to ride their bikes over here almost every day in the summer. They'd swim off Frank's dock all morning until he called them in to eat lunch, and then they'd go right back into the water, cramps be damned.

Charlie knocked on the door and waited for Frank to let her in. Salem Island was a small town, the kind of place where everyone knew their neighbors. Most people left their doors unlocked when they were at home. But not Frank.

"A little bit of paranoia goes a long way," he always said.

When Frank opened the door, she again found herself surprised by his appearance: no hair, no eyebrows. She thought it was the latter she couldn't get used to. He gave Charlie a squeeze and took the proffered bag of food.

"Oh, baby. Am I glad to see you," Frank said, eyes sparkling.

"It's good to see you too," Charlie said.

Frank raised a nonexistent eyebrow.

"I was talking to the food."

A classic Uncle Frank joke, and Charlie was stuck between amusement and annoyance that she'd fallen for it yet again.

While Frank dug in, Charlie sat on the plaid couch that had been in his living room for decades. There was a good chance it was older than she was.

"How's the cheating spouse racket going?" Frank asked before shoving a handful of French fries into his mouth.

"Fine," Charlie said. "Actually, we got a new case today. Something different."

"Wait, wait. Let me guess." Frank screwed up his face like he was really thinking it over. "Missing pet. But not a cat or a dog. Too obvious. I got hired to hunt down a missing cockatoo once. You lookin' for a bird?"

"No. This is the real deal. An old friend of mine from high school came in. Misty Dawkins. Her daughter is missing."

Frank nodded.

"See? I know there are people who look down on what we do, think we're just a bunch of paid snoops. But what we do has value. It's important to people. Even the missing cockatoos." He aimed a ketchup-stained finger at her. "Never forget the human side of these cases. Whether the case is big or small, it matters to someone."

Frank knew Charlie had mixed feelings about trading the more upscale cases she'd worked at the law firm for the domestic cases that made up the bulk of his work on Salem Island.

"I know," she said, bobbing her head up and down.

But Frank was on a roll now.

"It's the damn truth. Sure, sometimes things have a tendency to lean toward the sordid, but our ultimate goal is truth and justice. People need that. *Society* needs that. Heck, if the chemo hadn't knocked me on my ass, that's what I'd be doing right this minute. Fighting for another little piece of truth for someone. What else am I gonna do, watch Ricki Lake?"

"Ricki Lake hasn't been on TV for years."

Frank waved this away.

"You know what I mean." He took a bite of his sandwich and followed it immediately with a long pull on his drink.

Charlie gazed out the windows that looked over the small backyard, which sloped down to the water. She could see two yellow kayaks and an old metal canoe overturned on the shore for the winter. Beyond that was the giant willow tree with a rope swing hanging down from its branches. She wondered how many times she and Allie had swung out on that rope and let themselves drop into the water. How many afternoons had they sprawled on the L-shaped dock, sunning themselves on top of their towels, hair tangled in wet ropes after their morning swim? She remembered doing underwater handstands, pretending they were synchronized swimmers. Contests to see who could hold their breath the longest. A lump formed in Charlie's throat.

"Ah, don't get all nostalgic on me, sis," Allie said.

But it wasn't just nostalgia for Allie that was getting to Charlie. It was Frank, too. Her uncle had always been larger than life. To start, he was six foot five. The tallest man ever, Charlie had thought when she was a kid. And the strongest—he used to carry a card in his wallet that declared he had the strength of ten men, which Charlie had taken as something official until she was nine or ten. She looked at him now, wiping fast-food grease from his mouth with a napkin. He'd lost so much weight, and the lack of hair and eyebrows only added to the frail appearance. He looked withered and gaunt. Like a tree that someone forgot to water.

He'd maintained a positive attitude since he'd been diagnosed with chronic lymphocytic leukemia. Hadn't uttered a single complaint throughout the weeks of chemotherapy. And his doctors were still optimistic. But for Charlie, the fear had started to creep in. There was no cure for CLL. The best they could hope for was remission, and that was only if he made it through chemo, which was taking its toll. If they didn't start to see some progress soon, then what? She'd read up online, of course. If Frank's cancer didn't go into remission the first time around, his doctors would likely recommend more chemo. And despite his lack of complaints, Charlie wasn't sure the old man could take it.

The lump in her throat shifted into something sharp and painful. She wasn't ready to say goodbye. Not to Frank.

She blinked, struggling to keep the tears in check.

"You OK over there?" Frank asked, wadding the foil wrapper from his sandwich into a ball.

Charlie covered by coughing into her hand. She didn't want Frank to know she was worried. She had to stay positive, for his sake.

"Yeah, just a tickle in my throat," she lied.

"Go drink some water, ya turkey."

She did as he said, using it as an excuse to get herself under control. She pulled her designated glass from the cupboard and filled it with water. Frank had a whole set of collectible McDonald's glasses circa 1977. She and Allie always used to fight over the Mayor McCheese glass when they were kids, so Frank had scoured the local thrift shops, garage sales, and flea markets until he found another. And even though Charlie was past the age where drinking out of a specific cup was important to her, her hand instinctively went for the one with the anthropomorphic cheeseburger.

"That one's mine," Allie said.

Charlie didn't bother to ask how she could tell the difference between two identical glasses because she knew Allie was only trying to annoy her.

"I'm serious. The copyright symbol on mine is partially worn off," Allie insisted. "Put it back."

Ignoring her, Charlie filled the glass and drank. When she was finished, she set the glass in the sink and glanced over at Frank, who was collecting the trash from his meal and placing it in the paper bag it had come in. He would be OK, she told herself. He was strong. If anyone could kick cancer's ass, it was Frank.

"Do you still have that card? The one that claims you have the strength of ten men?" Charlie asked.

Frank smiled around the straw in his mouth.

"Of course."

He leaned onto one hip and reached into his back pocket, rifling through the various cards in his wallet until he found the laminated rectangle of cardstock.

"Can I see it?"

He held the card out then snatched it away when she tried to grab it.

"Depends."

"On what?"

Frank took another swig of Dr. Pepper.

"On what you meant by *claims* I have the strength of ten men. Are you suggesting the card is fraudulent?"

Charlie rolled her eyes.

"Of course not," she said with mock earnestness. "Can I see it now?"

"See, I saw that roll of the eyes there. I'm not sure I care for your attitude."

Charlie blew out a breath.

"Come on. We're gonna be late if we don't leave now."

CHAPTER FOUR

They had to drive forty minutes north to Port Huron for Frank's infusions. The cancer treatment center in East China was closer, only twenty minutes away, but Frank's insurance wouldn't cover treatments there. And paying out of pocket wasn't an option when each treatment cost thousands of dollars.

In the car, Charlie put on the playlist she'd made especially for Frank, full of his favorites: Led Zeppelin, The Allman Brothers, Creedence Clearwater Revival. When "Travelling Riverside Blues" came on, Frank sighed.

"Did I ever tell you about the time I saw Zeppelin at the Grande Ballroom in '69?"

"Yes," Charlie said. "Like a hundred times."

Frank didn't seem to care. There was a faraway look in his eyes as he gazed out the side window.

"They were all completely wasted. So drunk they could barely play. Robert Plant was slurring off-key. The crowd was furious, and rightly so. It was a disaster of a set, but they made it through, somehow. They walked offstage at the end of the night to the crowd booing. But then they came back for an encore, which was rare for them. They didn't usually do that. But they came back and played 'Whole Lotta Love.'"

"And they killed it."

"Everyone went apeshit! The whole audience, screaming their heads off. It was like they redeemed the whole night with that one song."

At the hospital, Charlie parked near the door to the outpatient wing. The rock salt scattered over the parking lot and sidewalks to melt the ice and snow sparkled like diamonds.

Frank tightened the scarf wrapped around his face.

"Colder than a polar bear's asshole out here," he said, shivering theatrically.

Everything was brightly lit inside the treatment center. The lobby area was all glass on one side, with tropical plants and a small water feature. But despite the attempts to make the space inviting, Charlie felt her insides clench as they walked through the doors. It was the smell, she thought. A lingering odor of disinfectant and floor wax.

The infusion room was a long, narrow space with a series of chairs and IV machines along one wall. Frank took his place in a sort of industrial-looking recliner. A nurse scanned his ID bracelet and then hung a bag filled with the special chemo cocktail on the IV pole before hooking the tubing up to the port-a-cath on Frank's chest.

Charlie pulled one of the smaller plastic chairs from the other side of the room to sit closer to her uncle. They played a few rounds of Rummy, and then Frank pulled out his wallet and handed Charlie the card she'd asked for earlier.

It was a simple laminated rectangle of white cardstock. The black lettering read, "This card certifies that FRANK J. WINTERS has the STRENGTH OF TEN MEN."

Underneath the writing was a row of ten tiny musclemen flexing their miniature biceps.

Charlie smiled and flipped the card over to see the seal that read, "Council of Extraordinary Strength."

"Where did you even get this?"

"What do you mean? It says right there, 'Council of Extraordinary Strength.'"

Chuckling, Charlie had a sudden flashback to the time she was seven and tried to get her dad to admit that Santa Claus wasn't real.

"Seriously, though," she said. "Did you buy it at a carnival or something?"

"A carnival?" Frank scoffed, swiping the card from her fingers. "You've got some nerve, questioning the validity of my credentials."

She considered asking if he'd made it himself, but she didn't want to push it. And maybe part of her didn't really want to know.

Frank dozed on the way back to Salem Island, which wasn't surprising. Treatment days tended to wipe him out.

He stirred as soon as Charlie took the turn into his driveway, straightening in his seat and unbuckling his seatbelt. Charlie followed him inside, nervously watching him totter over the icy ground. Breaking his hip in a slip and fall was the last thing he needed right now.

Frank took his usual place in a beat-up leather recliner. Marlowe, a black cat with oversized fangs, slinked into the room and hopped onto Frank's lap.

"You want me to get you anything before I go?" Charlie asked. "Something to drink? A sandwich?"

Frank shook his head.

"No, but thanks. You're a doll."

"I thought I was a turkey."

"Oh, you're definitely a turkey," Frank said, grinning.

He'd been calling her that since the time she and Allie were fishing off the end of his dock, and Charlie lost her balance and fell in the water. She was probably six. It was early May, and the water was still pretty cold. As Charlie climbed up the dock ladder, her hair and clothes dripping wet, she could already hear Frank laughing.

"Why are you swimming with your clothes on, turkey?" he'd asked.

Charlie had been furious.

"I'm not a turkey! I'm a girl!"

That had only made him laugh harder.

She knew he was picturing that now, could tell by the smirk on his face.

"I'm gonna head out, then," Charlie said.

As she reached for the doorknob, Frank called out, "Hey, turkey. Your missing girl… how old is she?"

"Seventeen. Still in high school."

He nodded, absently patting the top of Marlowe's head.

"Any siblings?"

"A younger brother and a stepsister who's about the same age."

"Listen to the sister. Talk to everyone, of course, but keep this tidbit in mind all the while: when it comes to high school kids, the siblings always know more than the parents."

CHAPTER FIVE

Charlie met up with Misty Dawkins at her house, a small gray ranch in a subdivision of nearly identical modular homes where the old Salem Paper Mill had once been.

Misty opened the front door, and Charlie paused on the threshold to kick snow off her shoes before entering. There was a Christmas tree in one corner of the living room, and stockings hung over a gas fireplace on the far wall.

"Sorry about the mess," Misty said, bustling past her six-year-old son, Tyler, who was sprawled on the carpet watching cartoons. "I just need to pop in the kitchen for a sec and make sure my chili isn't burning."

A man and a teenage girl sat at the round dining table off the kitchen. Misty picked up a wooden spoon and gestured at them.

"This is my husband, Chris, and my stepdaughter, Rachel."

They exchanged greetings while Misty lifted the lid off a pot, releasing a cloud of steam. She stirred then gave the wooden spoon a few taps against the pot before replacing the lid. She slid into the seat next to her husband and gestured that Charlie should sit as well. Chris closed his laptop, and Rachel shut her math book, leaving her pencil between the pages to mark her spot.

"OK, what can you tell me about the days before Kara left? What she did, who she saw, anything unusual that might have happened."

"Since the kids are on break, the girls have been watching Tyler for us during the day," Misty said. "As far as I know, everything's been normal. Up until Kara realized she really wasn't going on that trip, things had been fine with her."

Charlie looked over at Rachel, who was fiddling with the sleeve of her shirt.

"What do you think? Had she seemed normal to you?"

Rachel nodded.

"Yeah, I mean, she complained a lot about having to meet with her probation officer. She said it was Christmas break, and she should get a break from everything."

"What day was that?" Charlie asked.

Misty gripped both sides of her head with her hands.

"The day before we had the fight. Tuesday. And she's had an attitude about her probation requirements this whole time, so that was certainly normal. I kept telling her she should be thanking her lucky stars it was *only* probation."

"And how often did she see her probation officer?"

"Once a week or so. Sometimes her officer would show up for random check-ups, but usually they'd meet up at her lawyer's office. Kara could walk there after school, and her lawyer wanted to be sure she was keeping up with the requirements. I was so grateful that he kept her out of jail, and now this." Misty started to tear up again. "I thought the worst was behind us."

"Would you happen to have her probation officer's name and number?"

"I have it written down right over here," Misty said, scooting her chair out and moving to a small notepad on the counter.

She scribbled the information down on a Post-it and handed it to Charlie.

"And her lawyer?"

"Oh, that would be Will Crawford, right here in town. I'm sure you remember Will."

"Of course," Charlie said.

Another classmate. Will had been a grade ahead of her and Allie.

Charlie glanced down at her notes. She had a solid list of friends to talk to, plus Kara's father, probation officer, and lawyer.

"This is a good start," she said. "Is it OK if I take a look around Kara's room before I go?"

Rachel raised her hand, as if she were in math class instead of sitting at the dining room table in her own house.

"We share a room. I can show you."

CHAPTER SIX

Rachel hovered in the doorway while Charlie entered the room. There were bunk beds against one wall, and Charlie could guess which bed belonged to which girl with a single glance.

The bottom bunk—Kara's—had a purple feather boa wrapped around one bedpost. The wall next to the bed was adorned with rows of Christmas lights, and Polaroids of Kara and her friends had been clipped to the wire strands.

The top bunk, Rachel's space, was more low-key. There was a Beatles poster, a print of Van Gogh's *Starry Night*, and a single photo. Moving closer, Charlie saw that it was a black-and-white strip from a photobooth. Charlie took in the miniature photos, top to bottom: Kara and Rachel with their tongues out, Kara wearing Rachel's glasses, Kara and Rachel holding their noses up like pigs, and lastly, Kara and Rachel smiling sweetly, arms slung around each other's shoulders.

"You two are close?"

Rachel took a step into the room.

"It's hard to share a room with someone for eight years and not be close," she answered. "She's probably my best friend."

There was a dresser and desk on the opposite side of the room from the beds. The top of the dresser was cluttered with makeup, lotion, jewelry, and more photos. Clearly Kara's stuff. In contrast, the desk beside it was neat and orderly, with a laptop, notebook, and some pens and pencils in a cat-shaped mug.

Charlie noticed as she studied Kara's photo collection that Rachel was not in any of them. Nor did she remember seeing any photos of

Rachel on Kara's Facebook or Instagram. An uncomfortable feeling wormed in her gut. She knew she should leave it, but something wouldn't let her.

She gestured at the Polaroids.

"Looks like Kara has a lot of friends."

Rachel smiled, but there was sadness in her eyes.

"Yeah."

"How well do you know them?"

"We… don't really hang out with the same people."

Charlie felt a familiar twinge in her gut. She was getting the strongest reminders of herself and Allie in this room. Was it the bunk beds? The way the two girls' spaces were so different? Kara with all of her friends and Rachel with… her computer?

She and Allie had always been close. They were twins, after all. And yet the older they got, the more Charlie had felt like they were drifting apart. Except that wasn't quite right. It wasn't so much a drifting apart as Allie pushing her away, at least in public. At home they'd been closer than ever. It was at school that Allie had seemed to want nothing to do with her.

Charlie understood Allie's need to be separate sometimes. There were times when being a twin felt like everyone viewed you as only one half of a person. But it was the push-pull of it that stung, even now. The way Allie could fall right back into BFF mode at home after ignoring Charlie at school all day. Charlie shook these thoughts away, wary of getting sucked into a black hole of nostalgia.

"Is the computer…?" Charlie gestured at the laptop.

"It's mine," Rachel said. "But Kara uses it sometimes. For school, usually. Though most of the time she talks me into typing up her reports for her. She says it's because I'm faster at typing, which is true, but…"

"But she also likes getting people to do things for her?" Charlie guessed.

Rachel looked surprised but nodded.

"I had a sister like that," Charlie said, thinking of the time she constructed an entire diorama for Allie's history class. "Can I check the search history real quick?"

"Sure," Rachel said.

Charlie opened the browser and checked the history for the days leading up to Kara's disappearance. Searches for "makeup tutorials blue eyes," "best tanning spray," "SpongeBob memes," and "clubs in Cozumel" were obvious enough. Charlie scrolled further down the list, but nothing gave an indication of where Kara might be now.

"Does she ever use your dad's laptop?" Charlie asked.

Rachel's head shook from side to side.

"No, that's his work computer. It's strictly off-limits because one time Misty was using it to play Bejeweled, and she accidentally downloaded spyware. Dad got really mad and banned any of us from touching it."

Charlie chuckled.

"And aside from that, is this the only computer in the house?"

"Yeah."

"Do you know if Kara ever talked to people online? People she didn't know in real life, I mean."

"I don't think so. She would think that was… I don't know, dorky or something," Rachel said, then tilted her head to one side. "But maybe if it was the right kind of person."

"A cute guy, you mean?"

A shy smile spread over Rachel's face. "Yeah. Pretty much."

"Does she have a boyfriend?"

"No. At least I don't think so." Rachel looked like she was about to say more but stopped herself.

"What is it?"

"It's just that Kara has a big heart, but sometimes she trusts the wrong people. And lets them get away with treating her like crap."

Rachel went quiet then, her eyes on the photostrip of Kara pinned to the wall.

"She acts like she's invincible."

This comment struck Charlie as odd, at least without some sort of context.

"How do you mean?"

Rachel startled slightly, as if she'd forgotten Charlie was even there.

"I... don't know. Just things she does sometimes."

She was trying to pass it off as nothing, but Charlie wasn't buying it.

"What kind of things?"

When Rachel started chewing her lip, Charlie knew she was onto something.

"If you're hiding something, I need you to tell me what it is. Keeping Kara's secrets right now isn't helping her. There's a chance she's in trouble, and I'm not talking about the kind that gets you grounded. You understand?"

A tear spilled down Rachel's cheek. Her voice came out a whisper.

"She's been sneaking out after her curfew. Not every night. Usually on weekends." She wiped the wetness from her face and sniffed. "I figured it was to go to parties or to hang out with a guy or whatever. I told her it was stupid. That if she got caught, she could end up in juvie."

Charlie only nodded, waiting for Rachel to continue.

"She kept saying she had a plan."

"A plan?"

"To get out of Salem Island. For good. She's always hated it here. But it got worse after the trouble she got into. I don't know why she hates it so much, really. I figure Salem Island is probably mostly the same as everywhere else. It's not perfect, but it isn't so bad," she said, shrugging.

Charlie thought Rachel was right and wrong at the same time. Salem Island wasn't so different than any other small town. But

Charlie knew the feeling of wanting to escape it. Some places had more ghosts than others.

"And you have no idea where she went those times she snuck out?"

Rachel shook her head.

"She outright refused to tell me where she was going or what exactly her big plan was. And that was weird. Because she tells me everything."

"OK," Charlie said, with a nod of her head. "Just one last question. If you had to guess the first person Kara would have called or gone to after she left the house on Wednesday, who would it be?"

Charlie's gaze followed Rachel's to the photos on Kara's wall. The girl seemed to scan the faces, trying to decide who Kara trusted most.

"Probably Maggie."

"Last name?" Charlie asked, getting out her pen.

"Stahl."

The pen scratched over Charlie's notepad. She took a business card from her pocket and handed it to Rachel.

"If you think of anything, even something small, please let me know. You never know what detail might help."

Staring down at the simple card with Charlie's name, phone number, and email address printed in neat black letters, Rachel swallowed. Her brown eyes flicked up to meet Charlie's.

"Do you really think she's in trouble?"

"I hope not." Charlie tucked her notepad back in her bag. "But I intend to find her either way."

CHAPTER SEVEN

When Charlie returned to her car after talking to Kara's family, she shut herself inside and sat for a minute, not moving. A thousand memories of Allie flashed through her mind. Being in that bedroom had felt like ripping off a scab—a familiar injury reopened.

After a couple minutes, Charlie started the ignition and headed toward town, trying to push away the negative feelings. Kara wasn't Allie. This case had *nothing* to do with Allie. Continuing to compare the two girls wasn't helping. It was only clouding her thoughts, dredging up old feelings that helped exactly no one.

She'd made arrangements earlier to talk with Kara's friend, Maggie Stahl—a prospect that seemed all the more critical after what Rachel had said about Kara sneaking out at night—but that interview wouldn't happen until the following morning. In the meantime, there was another lead she could pursue.

Downtown, Charlie pulled to the curb in front of an old Victorian house and parked. It had been converted into offices sometime during Charlie's absence from Salem Island. The place had been in bad shape when Charlie was growing up—peeling paint and a sagging porch roof—but someone had really put some work into it, restoring the exterior to its original condition. The sign out front listed two businesses: Judy Walenski, CPA and Will Crawford, Attorney at Law.

"Well, well, well…" Allie said. "You didn't even have to look up his address or anything. You dirty dog."

"Shut up."

The wooden steps out front creaked under Charlie's feet as she climbed the porch and opened the door. The ground floor had been split into two separate spaces, and there was also a stairway leading to a second floor. Charlie spotted Will's name next to the door on the left and entered.

A middle-aged woman with a Bluetooth earpiece in her ear sat behind a desk in the waiting room, having what sounded like a conversation with a child.

"Then you're ready to put the clothes in the dryer," she was saying. There was a pause. "I don't know. It's different every time. Start with sixty minutes and go from there. And don't forget to empty the lint trap."

She sighed and held up a finger in Charlie's direction.

"The pull-out screen thing. Yes," she said, rolling her eyes. "OK. Love you. I'll see you in a bit."

Pursing her lips, the woman shook her head and ended the call.

"Sorry about that. My thirteen-year-old is going bowling tonight, and now he's in a panic because his favorite shirt is dirty. A year ago it was a fight just to get him to shower regularly. Now he's obsessed with cologne and body wash." She sighed dramatically. "Now, what can I do for you?"

"I'm here to see Will… er… Mr. Crawford?" Charlie said, her nervousness making it come out more like a question than a statement.

The woman smiled pleasantly, ignoring Charlie's awkwardness.

"Do you have an appointment?"

"No, I—"

Just then the door beyond the woman's desk opened, and a man in a suit came out. It took a beat before Charlie realized it was Will. She'd still been picturing him as a tall, gangly eighteen-year-old with red-gold hair that hung in his eyes. And definitely not wearing a three-piece suit.

His hair was still on the long side, especially for a lawyer, though it wasn't quite the surfer-esque mop it had once been. But it was the eyes that really gave him away. They were bright hazel. Intense. Perhaps retaining some mischief even after all these years.

Will stopped short in the doorway, staring at her. At first she thought he was only trying to place her, but she saw the recognition on his face. It was a beat before Charlie realized he wasn't seeing *her*. He was seeing Allie. The Allie that could have been. Because Allie was the one everyone remembered, and it would have been that way even if she hadn't disappeared. If Allie had lived, Charlie probably would have gone her entire life being mistaken for her.

Finally, he seemed to find his voice.

"Charlie. Wow."

"Hello, Will," she said, feeling suddenly self-conscious. Like she was imposing. Why hadn't she called first? "I was hoping you had a minute."

"Of course." He gestured that she should follow him into his office. "Come on in."

Will's office looked like something out of a TV show. Barrister-style bookcases lined either side of the room, each one filled with leather-bound books. On the back wall, Will's credentials hung in large gold frames. The walls were midnight-blue, the ceiling coffered.

Will took a seat behind a large mahogany desk. As Charlie slid into the velvet wingback opposite him, she couldn't help but notice that his chair sat much higher. She wondered if it was on purpose. To make him seem more dominant or imposing or something.

"Nice office," she said, glancing at a pair of antique-looking brass sconces flanking the window. "I kind of feel like I'm a contestant on *The Apprentice*."

Across from her, Will's mouth popped open. He was quiet for a moment, and she worried she'd hurt his feelings.

But then he burst out laughing.

"You know, I used to have a much more casual office. Fewer books. Way less desk," he said, pointing at the carved behemoth he was sitting behind. "Simple. Minimalist. But Marcia, that's my assistant you saw out front, she suggested hiring a designer to come in. She said that my clients have certain expectations. And she was right. Business has more than doubled since we put in fancy bookcases and moody lighting. Everyone wants something that looks like a TV procedural or something."

He hooked a thumb at the wall. "Most of those are fake, by the way. The books. If you try to pick one up, the whole row comes with it. It's just an empty shell with book spines stuck on."

"I don't know if anyone's told you," Charlie said, "but you're not supposed to brag about being illiterate."

Will flashed a good-natured grin.

"What I'm trying to get at is that so much of litigation is about the theatrics, especially in the courtroom. But it applies even in the privacy of your office. It was an incredibly valuable lesson to learn. About life and about people. All the world's a stage, right?"

"Are you quoting Shakespeare now just to prove to me that you *can* read?"

"Shakes-who-now?" Will asked, feigning seriousness.

It was his favorite kind of joke, pretending to be stupid.

"Anyway," he said, "what brings you to my humble establishment?"

"I'm here about Kara Dawkins."

The smile on his face turned to a frown.

"What about her?"

"She's missing. Her mother hired me to find her."

"Missing?" he repeated. "For how long?"

"Since Wednesday afternoon."

"Shit. Hold on one second."

He lifted his phone from the desk, swiping and tapping at the screen. Charlie heard a number being dialed as Will pressed the phone to his ear.

"Amanda? Hi, it's Will Crawford." He paused. "I'm calling in regard to Kara Dawkins. Yeah. Well, apparently she's missing."

Will nodded as the other person spoke.

"Wednesday... I know that." He sighed. "I know that, too. No, that's why I called. Can you try? OK, thanks."

He hung up then looked apologetically at Charlie.

"Sorry about that. That was Kara's probation officer. I wanted to be sure she knows what's going on. Otherwise this could really screw up her deal."

"A girl is missing, and that's what you're worried about?"

"Hey, if you knew what it took to keep her out of juvenile detention... Did her parents tell you she resisted arrest?"

"No."

"They wanted to charge her with assaulting an officer, which was bullshit. She's five foot two. Probably 100 pounds soaking wet. She was just a scared kid who panicked. Struggled when they tried to put the cuffs on. No punches or anything. Anyway, my point is, wherever Kara is, I consider it part of my job to make sure things don't go to shit in the meantime. The last thing I want is her getting back here and ending up in juvie because she screwed up her probation."

"Would that happen? If she ran off and came back, would they really lock her up?"

"They could lock her up even if she didn't run off."

"OK, wait. You're saying that—worst-case scenario—if someone kidnapped her or something, the court would still penalize her for violating her probation?"

"They could, if they wanted," Will said, nodding. "Especially if a judge was feeling particularly salty that day."

"That's ridiculous."

"That's justice. Or so the courts would have you believe." He leaned back in his chair. "The whole thing is a racket. Do you know what Kara's blood-alcohol was at the time of her arrest?"

"No."

"Point-zero-three."

Charlie frowned.

"But the legal limit is point-zero-eight."

Will held up a finger.

"Not if you're underage. Then the limit is point-zero-two in Michigan. It's essentially zero tolerance for minors."

"But she *had* been drinking," Charlie pointed out.

"Look, I'm not saying what Kara did was right," Will said. "She's underage and had alcohol in her system. She should have been charged with minor in possession, sure. But a BAC of point-zero-three for a girl Kara's size means she likely had a single drink—maybe less—over the course of an hour. If you had a glass of wine right now, would you be OK to drive in half an hour?"

"Yes."

"See? We're not talking about someone chugging a fifth of Popov and hopping behind the wheel. Kara had been drinking, but she was not *drunk*. There's a difference, and it should matter."

"OK, so why doesn't it? To the legal system, I mean."

"Because the whole DUI system is essentially a business. When they first started doing widespread breath tests, the American Medical Association was asked to come up with a blood-alcohol level that would signify impairment. Their number was point-one-five. And now we're at point-zero-eight. Why? Because now they don't even have to make a case of whether you're actually impaired. It's all down to the number. Pass/fail. And the lower they make it, the more people they catch in the net, and the more money they make from fines. It's all about generating cash for the city."

Will leaned back in his chair, swiveling slightly from side to side. "There have actually been articles about how Uber and Lyft are hurting local government coffers because DUI arrests are down. I'm not making this up. I mean, that should be a good thing, right? It just shows that this isn't a system that's primarily concerned with keeping people safe. If it were, they'd figure out comprehensive ways to actually prevent people from driving drunk. They'd be glad that rideshares are lowering DUI rates. But I'd put money on us seeing a push to lower the legal limit again very soon to compensate for the fact that the money isn't flowing like it used to. They tried back in 2013 to get it lowered to point-zero-five. It's a joke. The whole system is punitive and corrupt."

Sighing, Will closed his eyes.

"Sorry… as you might be able to tell, I'm just a touch obsessed with this particular subject. People like to label me pro-drunk-driving, but that's not it at all. I'm all for keeping drunks off the road. But I am absolutely opposed to the justice system being used as a money-grab. And Kara is a perfect example. She should have been charged with a much lesser crime. She would have paid a small fine for the underage drinking, been on probation, taken some classes. But suddenly, because she happened to be behind the wheel at the time, the judge wants to throw the book at her."

"You don't think the zero-tolerance system is a way to try to discourage underage drinking?" Charlie asked.

"Oh, that's what groups like Mothers Against Drunk Driving like to claim, but I don't buy it. How is it discouraging underage drinking? At best, it *might* be discouraging underage drinking *and driving*, but I doubt it even does that. You remember being that age. Would the zero-tolerance law have kept you from drinking?"

Charlie considered this.

"Probably not."

"Exactly. This is a girl who did what probably over half the kids her age have done, and she's looking at jail time? Who is that supposed to be helping? Certainly not Kara. And I don't think society at large needs to be protected from someone who had one beer, no matter her age."

"Did you try to get the charge reduced from a DUI to minor in possession?" Charlie asked, more out of curiosity than anything.

"I did," he said. "It didn't work, which was no surprise. I've had a dozen or so cases like this over the years with no success arguing that point. I know other defense attorneys who have tried the same. And I don't know of a single case where it's ever worked."

"Because no judge wants to look weak on underage drinking," Charlie said, reasoning it out.

"Pretty much. Justice is blind, but the blindfold tends to slip when it's a topic that might come up during re-election."

"Have you always been this cynical?" Charlie asked. "Or is that something they teach you all in law school?"

Will smiled.

"Cynicism 101. Great class. But I'm guessing you didn't come all the way over here so I could rant about the state of our judicial system. You had questions for me about Kara?"

Charlie had been so wrapped up in Will's commentary, she'd totally forgotten that she hadn't yet asked about Kara's last meeting with her probation officer. She couldn't deny that Will had a natural charisma—he always had—and she imagined he did very well in the courtroom on account of it.

"Kara's mother told me she met with her probation officer here the day before she disappeared."

"That's right."

"Can you tell me about it?"

"I didn't usually participate in the meetings. I just wanted Kara to have somewhere close to school so she could get to the meetings with as little fuss as possible."

"And did she ever mention being involved with anything or anyone who might give me something to go on? A person she might have gone to if she were in trouble?"

"Even if she did, I wouldn't be able to tell you." He pointed at her, an amused twinkle in his eye. "And I know that you know that."

"Attorney–client privilege. Yeah. Doesn't mean sometimes people don't slip," Charlie said. "Thanks for answering my questions, especially considering I barged in here without scheduling an appointment or anything."

"I'm always happy to take walk-ins when it's an old friend."

As she got up to leave, Will came around the desk, and Charlie stepped forward, for some reason thinking he was going to hug her. Instead, he extended his hand.

"It's good to see you, Charlie."

Charlie's face flushed, and she felt her hands go clammy in an instant. Will's fingers were cool and dry by comparison. She wondered if that was another lawyer trick, always seeming calm and collected.

"You too," she said and slipped through the door.

CHAPTER EIGHT

Charlie pulled the zipper of her parka all the way up, using the collar to shield the bottom half of her face from the icy breeze coming off the lake. It was almost fully dark now, just a sliver of salmon-colored light on the western horizon. Against the bright splash of pink-orange, Charlie could just make out the silhouette of the decaying Ferris wheel on the far side of the island.

In the car, she slid out her phone and got back to work, checking more potential leads off her list. A couple of quick phone calls to both Kara's probation officer and biological father had failed to turn up anything useful. In fact, Charlie was starting to grow concerned at just how unconcerned everyone else seemed to be. The probation officer predicted that Kara would turn up within the next day or so, at which point she wanted to be called immediately. Meanwhile, Kara's dad said it was "normal kid stuff" and he was sure Kara was "just fine." Something about the "just fine" in particular made Charlie shudder.

On her way back to the office, Charlie stopped off at Town Square Pizza and ordered a large with mushroom and green pepper. She watched Marco, the owner, assemble the pie in lightning speed. In less than a minute, he'd stretched the dough, ladled on the sauce, spread the cheese and toppings, and slid the whole thing into the oven to bake. Marco had been running the place almost single-handedly as long as she could remember. Aside from the fact that his waxed handlebar mustache had gone gray, he even still looked mostly the same.

Roughly ten minutes later, Marco pulled the pizza from the oven and put it straight into the box before slicing it. He handed it over to Charlie, thanking her and wishing her happy holidays.

She kept forgetting Christmas was less than two weeks away. Holidays hadn't really been a thing since Allie died. Charlie had come back for visits now and then, but the magic of Christmas, the joy felt gathering around the table for Thanksgiving, those things were over. Her mother hadn't put up so much as a sprig of mistletoe in the years since Allie disappeared.

The heat coming through the cardboard box warmed her hands as she made the trek to her car. Inside, with the door shut, the smell of the fresh-baked pizza overwhelmed her. She suddenly remembered that she hadn't eaten lunch.

Lifting the lid, Charlie pulled a slice of pizza from the box. It was still steaming, but she judged it not quite hot enough to burn her mouth.

She bit into the chewy crust and gooey cheese. The taste instantly brought back a dozen memories from childhood: a picnic in the park with her dad and Allie, a sleepover at Candace Mitchell's house in seventh grade, impromptu pizza parties when the staff of the school newspaper stayed late to meet a deadline.

"This is classy," Allie said. "I mean, nothing screams 'you've made it' like eating pizza in your car."

"Go away."

"I'm just saying… if you want to rub elbows with the upper echelons of society, you have to think about these things."

"What are you talking about?" Charlie asked. "Who exactly am I supposedly wanting to rub elbows with?"

"Uh, Will Crawford," Allie said, as if the answer were obvious.

"That wasn't a social call. I was asking him questions about Kara Dawkins."

"Yeah, one teensy whisper of his name, and *WHOOSH*! You're parked in front of his office."

"Whatever." Charlie made a dismissive sound. "Anyway, Will isn't like that. He's not a snob."

"He's a lawyer now. You saw that office. Pretty lux."

"He basically said himself that it was all for show," Charlie reminded her. "Underneath the suit, he's the same old Will. I guarantee it."

"You know what else is underneath the suit?"

"No. Stop."

"Big ol' hog leg."

"I said stop."

"His plonker, as the Brits might say. His kielbasa sausage. His anaconda, which may or may not want some, depending upon the bun situation."

Charlie closed her eyes, trying to ignore her sister.

Allie leaned close and whispered, "Charlie, I'm talking about his penis."

CHAPTER NINE

Charlie hovered over the coffee machine the next morning in the dark. Bleary-eyed. Her hands splayed on the kitchen counter, arms holding up her top half as though she'd crumple back to sleep on the spot without their support.

It was too damn early. Too early to turn the lights on. Too early to be doing any of this, but here she was.

The gurgle of the coffee machine thrummed through the thin laminate countertop and shuddered through her fingers and palms. A strange vibration. Not unpleasant.

Her half-awake mind tried to tumble through all she now knew about Kara Dawkins. Cogent thoughts coming to her in fits and starts. She seemed to gravitate back toward one detail over and over.

Kara had been sneaking out at night. Charlie's mind replayed the moment over and over: Kara's stepsister Rachel standing in their shared room, shoulders slumped, a frightened look passing over her face as she gave up the secret.

Yes. Something there, Charlie thought. Something meaningful. If morning intuition was worth anything, figuring out where Kara had been going after dark would lead to a break in the case.

And then her eyes drooped closed and her mind wandered, making that intuitive leap from Kara to Allie once again, half-dreaming and half-remembering. The pictures opened in her head. Blooming. Becoming.

It started with the memory of one of the photos in Kara's room—Kara and another girl her age, posing in front of the giant clown head at Poseidon's Kingdom. The marine-themed amusement park had once been a big attraction for summer tourists on Salem Island. There had even been a dedicated ferry that took people back and forth between Detroit and the park. This was mostly before Charlie's time, of course. The park had closed when she and Allie were six or seven. It was abandoned now and had been for decades. She knew it as a sprawling maze of paved pathways peppered with crumbling rides, the whole place overgrown with weeds and rogue trees.

It was closed to the public, of course, off limits in the way that meant that every kid on the island between the ages of twelve and eighteen had snuck in at least once. Almost instantly, Charlie was overcome by a memory of her and Allie standing in the very same spot as Kara in the photo. They were probably fourteen or fifteen, and she remembered pausing to gaze up at the giant red lips of the monstrous clown. Allie jumped up to slap her hand against the grinning teeth as they passed through the mouth and into Zinky's Funhouse. They followed the labyrinthine path through the Hall of Mirrors, just as they had a hundred times before. If not for the myriad of holes in the roof, they'd have needed flashlights. Instead, the sun glinted through the Swiss cheese ceiling above, giving them just enough light to make their way.

The mirrors were dusty and spotted now, some of them broken, but there were enough intact to still make it a disorienting experience. Charlie could half-remember what it had been in the park's heyday: bright lights shining against the gleaming mirrors, the sound of kids laughing and shrieking competing with the organ music blaring from the speakers.

"Do you remember playing Bloody Mary when we were younger?" Allie had asked.

"I remember you trying to get me to play."

Allie snorted out a laugh.

"Yeah, I forgot you were such a chicken."

"I just don't believe in stupid urban legends."

"Well, Heather told me that she and Laura played Bloody Mary in here once. And they *saw* her."

With a scoff, Charlie said, "Heather also thinks that if you swallow gum, it stays in your stomach for seven years."

Charlie was walking just ahead, running her hand along the mirrors on the right side. She turned back and saw a mischievous glint in Allie's eye.

"Then let's do it," Allie said.

"Do what?"

"Play Bloody Mary."

"It's a stupid kids' game."

"Then there's no harm in it, Charles," Allie said. "Unless you're scared."

"I'm not scared, I just think it's dumb," Charlie said.

Allie was silent for the next several seconds, long enough that Charlie actually thought she'd won the debate.

And then Allie said, "Bloody Mary."

Her voice was low, and she drew out each syllable of the name.

"Allie, seriously—"

"Bloody Mary."

Charlie's mouth opened, ready to protest. But that's what Allie wanted. Better to turn the tables on her sister, she thought.

She didn't drag it out the way Allie had. She said it loud and proud, as if daring the specter to appear.

"Bloody Mary!"

Her voice ricocheted off the glass-paneled walls, echoing down the passageway. She chuckled at her own boldness.

"See?" She glanced over her shoulder. "It's all just—"

In the corridor behind her, she saw a dozen different reflections of herself, but none of them were her sister.

The hallway was empty.

She spun around.

"Allie?"

No answer.

Charlie realized that this had been Allie's plan all along. Get Charlie all worked up with the talk of Bloody Mary and then abandon her in the mirror maze on her own.

"Another laugh riot," Charlie said, deadpan.

She took several steps back the way she'd come. What she couldn't figure out was how Allie had vanished so quickly.

"OK. The joke's over now. I get it. Ha. Ha."

Charlie took another step, and then another.

"Allie?"

The mirrored wall behind her suddenly shifted, a hidden door springing open. A ghoul lurched out from the darkness, its hair long and matted, blood running down from the eyes. It howled like a banshee.

Bloody. Fucking. Mary.

Charlie screamed and stutter-stepped away from it. Her hands flailed at the mirrors as though she might find a way through them. She stumbled, coming down hard on her butt, her teeth clacking together.

She scrabbled backward, finding herself trapped in the dead end of the maze. Backed up against a mirror.

The high-pitched keening coming from the thing's mouth turned to laughter.

Still giggling, Allie ripped the mask from her head and tossed it to the ground. Charlie's eyes went wide, her emotions rapidly shifting from pants-shitting fear to relief to embarrassment to anger.

Allie bent over at the waist, laughing so hard now she was gasping for breath. She struggled to get the words out.

"You should… have seen… your face."

Charlie gritted her teeth together, furious at herself for falling for the prank.

"And the… flailing!" Allie said, mimicking Charlie's frantic movements.

"I hate you."

Allie sunk to the ground across from her sister, silent laughs still spilling out of her. She held up a hand to indicate she couldn't quite speak yet but then tried anyway.

"... peed a little." Allie's voice sounded pinched, like she was forcing the words out through a pinhole.

"What?" Charlie asked.

"I think I just peed my pants a little bit."

"You *think*?" That got Charlie laughing too. "You either peed, or you didn't."

Allie nodded, tears streaming down her face.

"OK, I definitely peed. Happy?"

Now they both laughed.

When they'd composed themselves, Allie stood and helped Charlie up.

"Come on. I'll show you how the hidden door works. There's a bunch of them, all connected by a series of passageways that run alongside the maze."

Allie walked up to the door she'd come out of, running her hand along the right side of the mirror, which triggered a small latch. The door creaked open.

Charlie poked her head into the space beyond. It was dank and smelled of mildew.

"I can't believe we never knew about this before," Charlie said. "How'd you find it?"

"Will Crawford told me about it. I guess he's really into exploring this place. He said he's found all sorts of crazy stuff he doesn't think anyone else knows about."

The sharp smell of the coffee hit then, bringing Charlie back to the present—dark roast, her favorite. Her eyelids fluttered. The fragrance alone seemed to wake her up a notch or two.

She poured herself a cup. Added a glug from the carton of half-and-half, the fridge light sending two flares over the kitchen floor as she got the creamer out and then put it away.

As she took that first scalding sip, her eyes sensed a slight movement where her laptop lay open on the counter next to her—a notification pop-up. It could wait. She took a few more sips, getting about half the coffee down, feeling the caffeine seep into her bloodstream, start working on her brain.

Then she figured she better check the notification. She fiddled with the touchpad one-handed, not willing to part with the coffee just yet.

The notification was for a new email, but the subject line was blank. She navigated to her inbox and opened the message. It was short, just two cryptic lines that seemed like they could be swallowed up at any second by the white space dominating the rest of the screen:

FOLLOW THE WHITE RABBIT.
FIND HER.

Was this a message about Kara Dawkins?

Goosebumps rippled over Charlie's skin, the flesh surrounding her body seeming to contract all at once like a strange membrane tightening around her.

The "sent from" box showed Charlie's own email address. Like she'd sent it to herself, which didn't make sense.

Spoofed. She didn't know where she'd learned the term, but she remembered that spammers and other scam artists could fake an email address, make it look like it was sent from someone it wasn't. Obviously, this person was set on remaining anonymous.

FOLLOW THE WHITE RABBIT.
FIND HER.

There was something menacing about that. Almost taunting. If it really was connected to the Kara Dawkins case, it made the whole thing seem much more ominous.

CHAPTER TEN

Kara's friend Maggie had agreed to meet Charlie in front of the high school that morning. Arriving a few minutes early, Charlie got out and gazed up at the two-story rectangle of beige brick, another surge of memories flooding her mind. She couldn't go anywhere in this town without drowning in the past.

The time they were sitting under the big maple tree at lunch and a seagull swooped down and stole the top bun off Liane McIntyre's burger.

Avoiding pep assemblies by hiding in the girls' bathroom with Zoe Wyatt and Jennifer Siskey.

The day Mara Snerling leaned over a Bunsen burner in chemistry class and set her hair on fire.

These memories didn't stick in her head like some of the earlier ones had. The prospect of talking to Maggie, of finding out where Kara was sneaking off to at night, proved too strong to be pushed out of Charlie's thoughts for long. She was close now, perhaps minutes away from fresh answers in the case, and the excitement thrummed just behind her eyes.

Charlie milled around for a few minutes, eventually peering through the glass of the front doors. The school looked the same as it always had inside. Beige terrazzo floors with banana-yellow lockers set into the brick walls.

An older Honda Civic pulled to the curb, and Charlie swiveled toward it. A girl with long hair in an unnatural shade of purplish-red climbed out of the driver's side, lighting a cigarette.

"I thought all the cool kids were into vaping now," Allie commented.

Charlie's first thought had not been about the coolness factor of smoking cigarettes but wondering where a girl of seventeen or eighteen even got cigarettes when the legal smoking age was twenty-one.

Allie scoffed.

"Oh, please. We got our hands on much worse at that age. It wasn't even hard."

Charlie reached the bottom of the steps and called out.

"Maggie?"

The girl swung around to face her, blowing out a cloud of smoke. She wore dark eyeshadow and had drawn-in eyebrows.

"Yeah. You the private detective or whatever?"

"That's me. Charlie," she said, extending a hand.

Maggie popped the cigarette between her lips and held it there while they shook.

"Thanks for meeting me here," Maggie said. "My stepdad is sort of a wannabe militia-type, and he'd be all, 'Why'd you bring a cop into my house?'"

"I'm not a cop."

"Yeah, I know that. But he's an idiot."

Charlie noticed that in lieu of a coat, Maggie was only wearing a black hooded sweatshirt.

"Do you want to sit in the car to do this?"

"Nah," Maggie said, ashing her cigarette on the ground. "I don't smoke in the car. Is it cool if we walk and talk?"

"Sure. Whatever you want."

Maggie pushed off from where she'd been resting her shoulder against the car and headed toward downtown. Charlie followed.

"How close are you and Kara?"

Taking a drag, Maggie shrugged.

"I wouldn't say we were really friends at all until this year. I moved here in the middle of last year, and I don't know, we didn't hang out with the same people, I guess."

"When did that change?"

"I'm guessing you heard about Kara's DUI?"

"I did."

"The same night Kara got busted, I got an MIP. Minor in possession."

Charlie nodded.

"It was the same party. Anyway, we met during community service. We had to volunteer at the senior center, serving food and stuff. And, I don't know, I guess you could say we bonded."

"And when was the last time you saw or talked to Kara?"

"We talked Wednesday."

That got Charlie's attention. "What time?"

Resting the cigarette between her lips again, Maggie drew her phone from the pocket of her hoodie. She swiped at the screen a few times.

"Around four. She sent me a few texts after that, but I was in the shower and didn't see them until later."

"Can I see?" Charlie asked, gesturing at the phone.

Maggie passed her the device.

Charlie looked at the last few exchanges between the two girls.

MAGGIE: *OMFG NO HE DID NOT!!! That's hilarious tho.*

KARA: *ikr? So are you gonna come get me or what?*

MAGGIE: *Yeah, I just gotta do my stupid chores first, or stepdouche will freak.*

KARA: *Ew… he treats you like a slave, I swear. Do you have to wash his nasty skidmark underwear again?*

MAGGIE: *Lol, stop yer gonna make me throw up.*

KARA: *So what time?*

MAGGIE: *4:30. Soup bench.*

KARA: *K.*

KARA: *Almost smells like chicken noodle today.*

KARA: *Where r u?*

KARA: *Hurry up. I'm freezing my ass off.*

Charlie glanced up from the screen.

"You two had plans to meet up?"

"Yeah," Maggie said, taking one last drag from her cigarette and then tossing it to the sidewalk.

"Where's the—" she glanced back down at the screen to read it again before handing the phone back "—soup bench?"

"It's the bench all the way on the other side of the town square." Maggie pointed at the park up ahead. "Always smells like soup over there. Usually French onion. Sometimes it's more like beefaroni. Either way, it's gross."

"And did you have plans after that?"

Maggie sighed.

"She'll kill me for telling you this, but whatever." The girl reached up and ran her fingers through her hair. "We were gonna try to hitch a ride down to Florida."

"Hitch a ride? Like with someone you knew or hitchhiking with strangers?"

Maggie's eyes went wide.

"Uh, with someone we knew," she said. "If I was ever in the mood to get rape-murdered by a psychopath, then maybe I'd hitchhike with a stranger."

"Well, I'm glad to hear that," Charlie said, laughing a little. "So what happened Wednesday afternoon?"

"I was late. Not by a lot. Fifteen minutes, maybe. And by the time I got there, Kara was gone." Maggie thrust her hands in her pockets. "I figured she bailed on me."

"Did you leave right away?"

"No, I waited around a while. I thought maybe Kara ran inside the gas station for smokes or something. When she didn't show, I went over to Trevor's house. He was the one driving down to Daytona Beach. But he'd already left. I was so pissed off that they'd left me behind that I sort of forgot about Kara for a while. Until the next day when her mom called me all freaked out, anyway."

Charlie considered this, and a new idea came to her.

"Is there any chance Kara caught a ride with them anyway?"

"No."

"You're sure?"

"Yeah, because I called to bitch Trevor out for leaving without me. I asked if Kara was with them, but he said no."

A pang of disappointment hit Charlie then. Kara sneaking off to Florida would have been such a clean and simple explanation for her disappearance. Her parents would have been angry, sure, but they also would have been relieved to know where she was and that she was safe.

Charlie was nearly at the end of her list of questions for Maggie. She'd left the most important for last.

"Kara's stepsister says she's been sneaking out at night," Charlie said. "Do you know where she might have been going?"

"I have no idea," Maggie said, but there'd been a beat of hesitation before she answered, and her voice had gone up in pitch, like she was nervous.

"Maggie, you heard how panicked Kara's mom was. I need you to tell me what you know."

Chewing her lip, Maggie relented.

"Fine, but when you find Kara, promise you won't tell her it was me that said anything?"

"OK."

The girl let out a long sigh.

"Well, a while back, I wanted us to get jobs together at Taco Bell. But Kara kept saying no, and I kept bugging her about it because she's always talking about getting out of here, and I figured what better way than to make some money?" Her shoulders scrunched into a shrug. "Then one night, we smoked a bo— a cigarette together and got to talking about it again, and she told me she already had a job. I asked where, but she wouldn't say more. Said part of the job was keeping everything confidential."

"Why would she have to keep it a secret?"

"I don't know, but a few weeks later, I overheard some guys at school talking about seeing her at the club."

"The club? Like the Lakeside Tavern?"

It was the only bar in town that Charlie could imagine someone referring to as a club, as they occasionally had live music. It was a popular tourist destination in the summer because of its location near the marina.

Maggie frowned.

"Maybe. My stepbrother washed dishes there for a while, and I know they paid him under the table. I guess that could be why she had to keep it a secret?"

"Did you ask her about it?"

Closing her eyes, Maggie shook her head.

"No. I was kind of mad about it, actually. I kept talking about us getting a job together, and then it turned out she had some sweet gig she wasn't letting me in on? Pissed me off."

Charlie lapsed into silence, pondering this new development. A secret job? It would certainly explain the sneaking out, but it also begged a whole slew of new questions.

"So, is that it? Are we done?" the girl asked.

"Yeah, just one last thing," Charlie said, remembering the cryptic email she'd received earlier that morning. "Does 'Follow the white rabbit' mean anything to you?"

Hugging herself against the cold, Maggie asked, "Like, from *Alice in Wonderland*?"

Charlie smiled.

"Never mind."

They'd come to a stop near the bench where the two girls were supposed to meet, and Maggie's eyes went to the empty seat.

"You know, I wasn't worried at first," Maggie said. "But this isn't like her. She never goes this long without texting me back. What if something bad happened because I didn't show up on time?"

Charlie saw the fear in the girl's eyes. She knew from experience how it felt to blame yourself for something like that. How many times had she wondered what might have happened if she'd been pushier about asking Allie where she was going or who she was hanging out with?

"This wasn't your fault," Charlie said. "And don't worry. I'll find her."

"Don't make promises you can't keep," Allie said, and Charlie tried her best to ignore it.

Charlie sniffed the air and frowned.

"It really does smell like soup over here."

Maggie had started to walk away, and she paused now and turned back, a half-smile on her lips.

"I know, right?"

CHAPTER ELEVEN

Charlie sat down on the "soup bench" and let her eyes roam the area. The texts Kara had sent to Maggie suggested she'd been here the afternoon she disappeared. Perhaps even sat in this very spot. This was, at least in terms of Charlie's investigation, Kara's last known location. A prickle of unease accompanied that thought.

She jotted down a few notes. Kara had begun texting Maggie at 3:57 p.m. on the day she disappeared. The timestamp for the final text Kara had sent Maggie was at 4:36 p.m. Her comment about the bench smelling "like chicken noodle today" indicated that Kara had been in the park at that time. And by approximately 4:45 p.m., when Maggie arrived, she was gone.

Charlie glanced up again, her gaze moving from the playground at one corner of the park to the Shell station across the street.

"You were here. Right here. Where did you go?" she asked in a whisper.

She sat a few more seconds, thinking. Observing. Looking out at the same view Kara would have looked at.

Find the trail, Charlie told herself. *Figure out where she went next.*

The talk with Maggie had been productive—more than she'd dared to hope. She now knew where Kara had gone after she left her house. She knew what her plans had been. And she knew that Kara possibly had a job she hadn't told anyone about. Charlie was getting somewhere.

Tucking her notebook into her bag, Charlie stood.

"Where are you going?" Allie asked.

"To see if anyone around here saw Kara that afternoon."

An electronic ding announced her arrival at the Shell station. She went to the candy aisle and grabbed a Snickers. She wasn't hungry, but she'd found that clerks and cashiers were more likely to brush her off as a nuisance if she waltzed in and started asking questions. Being a paying customer often got better results. The routine shifted the roles, put the worker in the mindset of serving the customer.

The man behind the counter was thickset with a black beard that tumbled halfway to his belly button.

"Just the candy bar?" he asked.

"Yep," Charlie said, handing him a five-dollar bill. "Well, that and a quick question for you."

He made a face that told her to go ahead with it.

"My little sister has been missing for a few days, and I know she comes in here sometimes," Charlie said. "In fact, she might have come in here on Wednesday, which was the last time anyone saw her. Were you working then? Around four-thirty?"

That was another thing she'd learned. People on the street were much more likely to help you out if your story was personal.

Squinting, the man turned around to consult an employee schedule posted on the wall. He jabbed Wednesday with a finger.

"Yeah, I was here."

"Great! Would you mind taking a look at this picture of her?"

She brought up a photo of Kara on her phone and held it out to him.

He leaned in, wrinkling his nose. The way he kept squeezing his eyes down to slits made Charlie think he needed glasses, which probably didn't bode well for asking whether he'd seen anyone hanging around in the park on Wednesday.

While he studied the photo, Charlie took a good look at the TV screen behind the counter, displaying the store's security camera feed. The top two quadrants showed the gas pumps out front. The bottom two were interior shots—one positioned at the far end of the store, the other focused on the cash register. Charlie blinked at her own tiny likeness. Too bad none of the exterior cameras offered an angle wide enough to see the park.

The cashier gave the photo of Kara a thorough examination before shaking his head.

"Nope, sorry. Doesn't look familiar to me," he said, handing over her change.

"And you didn't happen to notice anything unusual that day, did you?"

"Nah. To be honest, every day in here bleeds into the next."

"OK," Charlie said, depositing her wallet and the Snickers into her bag. "Thanks, anyway."

As she walked to the door, Charlie checked the view of the park through the windows of the gas station. Most of the glass was blocked by merchandise—motor oil on one wall and two-liters of Faygo on the other. Even if the guy's eyesight was fine, he wouldn't have been able to see Kara from here.

Charlie spent the next few hours canvassing the area around the park, showing Kara's photo to employees in the other businesses on the block. She hit the copy shop, café, and salon, and then she moved on to houses, rousing retirees and housewives in the hopes they'd seen something. No one remembered seeing Kara in the neighborhood.

Her breath came out in plumes as she walked back to where she'd parked outside of the school. A fresh dusting of snow crunched underfoot.

When she reached her car, she climbed inside and sat in the quiet for a moment. The frustration was starting to build again. She knew she should focus on the positive. It hadn't been an entirely fruitless morning.

Charlie's notebook sat open in her lap, and when she looked down, her gaze snapped to the line in her notes where she'd written,

"Secret job?" She considered what Maggie had said about her brother being paid off the books. It didn't surprise her at all—she recalled it being somewhat of an open secret that the bar paid a lot of high school kids under the table. But she didn't remember anyone being particularly tight-lipped about working there.

Also, dishwashing didn't pay much, and Kara's stepsister had said Kara had some scheme to get off the island for good. Charlie couldn't imagine a minimum-wage job fitting the bill. Maybe a waitressing job, but the Lakeside Tavern served alcohol, which meant the servers had to be eighteen.

Allie chimed in then.

"Maggie said that when she got to the park, and Kara wasn't there, her first thought was that Kara had gone to buy cigarettes."

Charlie picked up her meaning right away.

"She would need a fake ID."

"Exactly."

Charlie felt a momentary surge of triumph, but it faded just as quickly. It was something, sure. If Kara used the ID to get a waitressing gig at the Lakeside, that might be a reason to be secretive about it. To hide it from her parents.

"It's wafer-thin," Charlie said out loud, more to herself than anything, but Allie never passed up an opportunity to butt in.

"I'm afraid it's all you've got."

The only way to know for sure would be to go to the Lakeside and ask around for herself.

CHAPTER TWELVE

Charlie had hoped to beat the dinner crowd to the Lakeside Tavern, but after taking Frank to and from another chemo treatment, it was early evening by the time she arrived. The sprawling building overlooked Lake St. Clair and the marina, and Charlie admired the way the setting sun turned the lake metallic orange as she approached the door.

The place had started as a small bar, but the owners had built it up over the years, putting in restaurant seating, an area with pool tables and a small stage, and a roof deck with a tiki bar. Charlie visualized Kara working here, sporting the green polo that most of the servers seemed to wear, a tray loaded with giant steins of beer balanced on her palm. She asked herself if it fit, if that picture seemed likely. Maybe.

It was warm inside, and Charlie undid her jacket as she passed a gangly teen wiping a rag over a four-top. The place looked about the same as she remembered it. The walls were dark wood paneling lined with local memorabilia and framed newspaper clippings of notable events chronicling the island's past. Beside the large, U-shaped bar, there were four pool tables and an old-school jukebox with neon lights aglow. Overall, it had a rustic, homey feel.

Charlie edged closer to the bar and ordered a Negroni. The bartender was young and shockingly tall—over six and a half feet, she'd guess. He probably spent most of his free time getting asking by strangers if he played basketball. Despite his size, his movements as he mixed the drink were fluid, and he was surprisingly gentle about setting her drink on a cocktail napkin and sliding it over to her.

"Can I ask you a quick question?" she asked.

He neatly quartered a lime with a serrated knife and grabbed another before glancing her way. "What's that?"

"Do you know if a girl named Kara Dawkins works here?"

He scrunched up his face into something like a wince.

"I'm bad with names. Brain's like a sieve for that stuff. Hold on a sec." He dropped his knife to the cutting board and called out to a waitress folding napkins at the other end of the bar. "Hey, Lindsey. Come here for a minute."

The girl crossed the room, her blonde ponytail swinging from side to side.

"What do you need, Glenn?"

"You know a…" The bartender glanced back at Charlie. "Shit, what was the name again?"

"Kara Dawkins," Charlie said. She pulled out her phone and showed them a photo of Kara. "I was told she worked here."

Hovering over the screen, the bartender shook his head, but Charlie thought she saw a flicker of recognition flit across the girl's face.

"She a local? Goes to Salem High?"

"That's right," Charlie said, feeling suddenly hopeful.

"I thought so," Lindsey nodded. "She and my sister played soccer together back in middle school, I think. As for working here? No. Not since I've been here."

"And how long is that?"

"Almost two years. I train most of the new servers, too, so I would know if we'd hired her."

Charlie forced a smile onto her face and thanked both of them for answering her questions.

Feeling lost, she settled into her seat at the bar, glad for the drink in her hand. The Lakeside Tavern had turned into a dead end, and she had no idea where to go next. She stared at the hazy reflection of her own face in the polished surface of the bartop, trying to untangle all the loose strands from the case.

Kara had been sneaking out at night, but why? She supposedly had a job no one knew about, but where? Every answer seemed to lead to more questions.

Then there was the mysterious email containing the "white rabbit" riddle. Someone was trying to tell her something, but Charlie had no idea what it was.

"Hey, stranger," a voice said from over Charlie's shoulder.

Charlie spun around on her stool. When she saw that it was Zoe Wyatt standing there, she grinned.

Zoe was one of Charlie's oldest friends. With the last names Winters and Wyatt, Charlie, Allie, and Zoe had been assigned lockers side by side from sixth grade through graduation. It hadn't taken long for a friendship to develop between the girls.

These days, Zoe was a deputy at the local sheriff's department, so maybe the day wouldn't be a total bust after all. Charlie wasn't above prodding Zoe for inside information.

"What's up?" Charlie asked, picking up her drink and taking a sip.

The front of Zoe's uniform pulled taut as she crossed her arms. "I'll tell you what's up. I'm majorly pissed off at you."

"At me?" Charlie pointed at her chest with her free hand. "Why?"

"Uh, because I've been trying to get you to come out for drinks since you got back, and all I keep hearing is a crapload of excuses about how busy you are."

It was true. Zoe had invited her out at least three times now, and Charlie kept begging off.

"Now I walk in here and find you, alcoholic beverage in hand," Zoe went on, pretending to get choked up now. "Is it me? Am I not one of the cool kids anymore?"

"Zoe, I hate to break this to you, but neither one of us was ever one of the cool kids."

Zoe sniffed a half-laugh at that. "So what are you doing here? Meeting someone?"

"Nope. I was following a lead." She lifted her drink. "If you couldn't tell by the fact that I'm now sitting here drinking alone, it was a dead end."

"Oof. That sounds sad."

"Pretty much," Charlie agreed. "What are *you* doing here?"

"Celebrating."

"Celebrating what?"

"The end of another tedious workday. Turns out law enforcement work is about ninety-five percent paperwork, the bulk of it utterly unnecessary. The other five percent is comprised of listening to people complain. How society hasn't crumbled by now, I have no idea. Even so, another day is done. Let us celebrate with strong drink."

Charlie laughed. Signaling to the bartender, she ordered two bottles of Bell's Amber Ale. She waited until they were nearly through the first round before she started pressing Zoe for information.

"So speaking of work, I was hoping I could ask you a few questions."

Zoe made a *tsk* sound with her tongue.

"More work is no way to celebrate the end of a workday, Charlie."

"I understand, it's just I've really hit a wall," Charlie said. "Besides, the one bonus of moving back here is having an old friend in the sheriff's department. Makes me feel like a real big shot."

She nudged Zoe with an elbow before plucking a menu from a clear acrylic stand resting on the bar. "You want to order some food? I'm starving. Plus, beer always makes me crave something salty."

Squinting, Zoe took a slug of beer.

"Are you trying to bribe me with food now?"

Charlie glanced over the menu at her friend.

"Would that work?"

Zoe raised an eyebrow. "Maybe."

Charlie ordered a plate of nachos, one of the Lakeside Tavern's so-called *specialties*. When the chips came out piled high with cheese, guacamole, sour cream, and beans, they both dug in. After a few bites, Zoe swiveled her stool so she was facing Charlie more squarely.

"OK. You've managed to sufficiently loosen my ordinarily fastidious morals by plying me with beer and nachos. What do you want?"

Grinning, Charlie leaned an elbow against the bar.

"I was curious if you've heard anything about Kara Dawkins."

"Dawkins… Misty Dawkins' kid?"

"That's the one. She's missing."

"Ah. Right. I did hear some rumbling about that, now that you mention it. It's not really my beat, you know, but the general consensus is that she ran off." She shoved a chip loaded with guacamole and cheese into her maw and chewed. "So Misty hired you?"

"Yeah. She's pretty worried. Came into my office sobbing and everything."

"Well, I can tell you right now, we get one or two of these every month. Nine-point-five times out of ten, the kids are off somewhere, usually doing crap they're not supposed to be doing. They run out of either money or alcohol and they come a-crawlin' back."

"And what about the point-five times out of ten when it's something worse?"

Zoe gulped at her beer, finishing it off, and indicated to the bartender that she wanted another.

"Then we get involved. I'm just saying, a kid with that history? I mean, you heard about her getting arrested, right?"

"I did. But being troubled doesn't preclude her from foul play. In fact, it might increase the odds."

The bartender swapped Zoe's empty for a fresh bottle, and Zoe gave a nod of thanks.

"That's fair," she said, lifting the bottle to her lips. "I'm curious, though. Have you found anything that suggests foul play? Actual evidence, I mean."

"Maybe. She was supposed to meet a friend in Town Square Park. From their texting, it sounded like Kara showed. But when her friend got there a while later, she was gone."

Tipping her head to one side, Zoe seemed to consider this.

"It's kind of mysterious. I'll grant you that." Pausing with a chip halfway to her mouth, she added, "Town Square Park... Wednesday?"

"Yeah. Why?"

Zoe downed the morsel of food and licked a smear of sour cream from her thumb.

"We had some complaints from residents in that area about a black SUV speeding around, blasting music real loud, laying down rubber. More obnoxious than criminal, really."

"The same day Kara went missing?"

Nodding, Zoe said, "I was the unlucky S.O.B. that got to go investigate."

"What time was this?"

"Late. Between eleven and midnight."

Charlie slouched against the bar, cheek resting on her fist.

"That's several hours after Kara was supposed to meet her friend." She picked a black olive off the top of the nachos and ate it.

"I mean, I figured it was probably just a coincidence, anyway," Zoe said. "It came to mind because it was the same part of town and all."

Charlie could appreciate that. Zoe didn't have to give her anything, after all.

"Did you get a plate? Or a make and model?" she asked, more to show her appreciation at the tip than anything else.

"Nah. They'd moved on by the time I got out there. But there was one identifying detail on the vehicle."

"What was it?"

"A big sticker across the back that said *No Fat Chix*. That's chix with an X."

"Wow. Classy."

Zoe shook her head, chuckling. "Yeah. Probably not a Harvard grad."

CHAPTER THIRTEEN

As they finished off the plate of nachos, they reminisced about old times. The late crowd began to filter in, adding an ambient murmur of voices to the background of their conversation. Someone fired up the jukebox, playing "Don't Stop Believin'" by Journey. If Charlie was honest, her main motivation for staying for drinks with Zoe had been to question her about the Kara Dawkins case. But now that she was here, swapping nostalgic stories from their past, she was glad for it. Maybe that tingling swirl in her head of alcohol laying waste to brain cells was part of it.

The blonde waitress from earlier whisked past them with a tray full of cocktails. Zoe let out a heavy sigh.

"What?" Charlie said, sensing something odd in Zoe's demeanor.

"Nothing. She is gorgeous. That's all."

The waitress was cute enough, Charlie thought as she studied her. The girl had angular brown eyes and a smattering of freckles over her nose, but Charlie still wasn't sure what Zoe was getting at. Envy?

"The waitress? You're just as pretty as she is."

Zoe's gaze slid over to meet hers.

"I'm not jealous, Charlie. I'm gay."

"Oh."

Zoe took a drink, smiling around the bottle. At least she seemed amused and not offended. "Did you really not know?"

Shaking her head, Charlie fiddled with the corner of her cocktail napkin, folding it back on itself.

"Sorry. Does that make me a terrible friend?"

"No." Zoe laughed. "I just figured you would have heard by now."

"From who?"

"I don't know. You hear things."

"I don't talk to anyone from here."

Zoe waved her hand around, nearly knocking over her bottle, but caught it before any liquid spilled.

"Yeah, but Facebook…"

"Oh, I don't use Facebook."

"How is that possible?"

"OK, I use it plenty for work. You wouldn't believe the sensitive-slash-scandalous info I can dig up on social media." Charlie took a drink and wiped the corner of her mouth. "Probably why I don't use it personally. I know how very available that information is, and how easy it is to think you're only sharing with friends."

"You sound paranoid."

Charlie quirked one shoulder upward.

"It's like my uncle Frank says: a little bit of paranoia goes a long way."

Zoe's head tipped to one side as she peered over at Charlie. "Hey, how is your uncle, anyway?"

"Good," Charlie said, because that's what people wanted to hear. "You know him. He's not going down without a fight."

"Cancer's about to get its head kicked in." Zoe lifted her bottle high. "To your uncle. A tough old S.O.B. if ever there was one."

They toasted to Uncle Frank, and Charlie finished off her beer with one long pull.

After a moment she said, "It makes sense though."

"What does?"

"You being gay." She had a fresh bottle now, and rivulets of condensation ran down the glass. She poked at a particularly fat droplet. "That explains why you were the only girl in school who didn't think Chase Russell was hot."

"Ugh. No." Zoe made a face like she'd just eaten something bitter. "I didn't think Chase was hot because he looks like a lizard."

Charlie laughed, nearly choking on her beer.

Zoe gave her a few firm wallops on the back.

"Don't die on me, Winters."

It was a few seconds before Charlie was able to speak or even take a normal breath again.

"Was it hard?"

"Thinking Chase Russell looked like a lizard person?" Zoe asked, then shrugged. "I struggled with it sometimes. Tried to find meaning in an increasingly reptilian world."

Charlie shook her head, chuckling. "No, I mean being gay in a town like Salem Island. I mean, maybe now things are a bit more progressive, but back then? At the very least, I imagine it would have been shitty to feel like you had to keep that a secret from everyone."

"Well, not *everyone*."

"You told people? Back then?" Charlie asked, and she couldn't help but feel a twinge of disappointment. Like maybe Zoe hadn't trusted Charlie enough to tell her. Which was silly, because not only was it ancient history, it also wasn't Charlie's right to know.

"I told one person. And that's why—" Zoe stopped herself, seeming to change her mind about whatever she was going to say. "Never mind."

Charlie's curiosity was piqued. She stared hard at her friend, and a moment of silence stretched out between them before Zoe crumbled.

"Allie knew."

"Allie?" Charlie repeated.

Whatever she'd been expecting Zoe to say, that hadn't been it. Zoe had always been more Charlie's friend than Allie's, though her twin always had a way of charming Charlie's friends.

"I…" Zoe paused again, her cheeks flushing. "Jesus, this is so embarrassing. We were at a party once—I think it was at Cassie

Whindon's. We were both drunk. And for some reason I thought it would be a good time to tell Allie that I had a crush on her."

"Oh," Charlie said, suddenly understanding why Zoe had been so reluctant to talk about it. "What did she say?"

"In the moment she was totally cool about it. But when I woke up the next morning and remembered it all, I couldn't believe what I'd done. I was sure she'd tell someone, and then it would be out there for everyone to know. I was so terrified I stayed home sick from school for the next two days."

Charlie tried to imagine how much dread Zoe must have felt in that moment. She didn't know what to say, so she put a hand on her friend's shoulder and gave it a squeeze.

"Eventually my mom figured out I wasn't really sick and made me go back to school. And even though no one said anything, for at least a week I was still convinced everyone knew. I overanalyzed every look. Every word." She blinked and a sad smile spread over her lips. "When you're young you just assume that everyone is secretly judging you. Like you're constantly on everyone's mind, and they're just desperate to find your flaws. Truth is closer to the opposite. No one is paying attention. They're too busy thinking the world is watching *them*."

It was true, Charlie thought. She remembered a bad haircut in eighth grade, thinking everyone would notice and laugh and judge. But no one said a thing about it.

"Anyway," Zoe said, "that's the real reason I'm surprised you didn't already know. I guess I just figured you guys told each other everything sooner or later."

Charlie's smile faded some.

"Not everything."

She spun her bottle in her hands and wondered at the secrets we kept. Zoe's secrets. Allie's secrets. Kara's secrets.

Beside her, she heard Zoe swear under her breath.

"What?" Charlie asked.

"Leroy Gibbs just walked in," Zoe muttered, her voice still low. "Come on, we can go somewhere else."

She was already starting to drain her bottle, but Charlie stopped her.

"It's fine. Really. We can stay."

Zoe's forehead puckered into a series of concerned lines.

"Are you sure?"

"Yes."

Charlie watched him saunter over to one of the pool tables at the far end of the tavern, his eyes wild, his salt-and-pepper beard in its usual state of disarray, covering most everything from his cheekbones down to his shirt collar in messy tangles of hair. In all the many times she'd driven past his house over the years, she'd never seen him in the flesh. She knew what he looked like, of course. There'd been plenty of pictures of him in the paper when he was first arrested for Allie's murder. And again when the charges were dropped due to insufficient evidence.

But it was different seeing him now, in person. He was bigger, more imposing than photographs could accurately depict. Broad and burly with massive hands, fingers as thick as serpents.

She couldn't help but imagine the strong fingers wrapping around Allie's throat and squeezing. Constricting. Charlie's blood ran cold at the thought.

Pinching her eyes shut, she forced herself to look away. She drank, tried to wash down the dark thoughts. She'd told Zoe it was OK if they stayed. She needed to be OK.

She opened her mouth, about to ask Zoe how her parents were, when she was jostled by someone sidling up to the bar behind her. Charlie turned, annoyed, and found Will Crawford smirking down at her.

"Charlie Winters and Zoe Wyatt. Why do I get a nervous sloshing in my stomach when I walk in and see the two of you sitting together?"

Clutching the neck of her beer bottle, Zoe pointed at him with her pinky finger.

"Probably because of that time we put a giant inflatable penis in your locker."

Will blinked.

"That was *you*?"

Charlie slugged Zoe's arm.

"Damn it, Zoe. You shouldn't have told him." Charlie sighed and took a drink. "We could have kept him wondering for the rest of his life."

"I can't believe you let all this time pass without fessing up," Will said, shaking his head.

"That'll teach you to rig up a system to keep your locker permanently unlocked."

"A lesson you waited until the last week of my senior year to teach me?"

"Better late than never," Zoe said.

The bartender set down a tumbler of Scotch in front of Will, who paid and collected his drink.

"You ladies enjoy your evening," Will said before moving on.

Charlie watched him for a few seconds, still mystified that Will Crawford had become a Scotch-drinking, suit-wearing lawyer. When she swiveled back, Zoe had a stupid smile on her face.

"Didn't you have a thing for Will?"

Charlie scoffed.

"No."

"Liar. You totally did."

"Like a teensy little crush," Charlie admitted, rolling her eyes. "It wasn't a big deal."

Zoe snorted. "Uh-huh."

Across the bar, Charlie spotted two men drinking. They bore the telltale signs of the classic Michigan-man archetype. They wore flannel shirts and baseball hats—one Lions, one Red Wings—and both sported bushy beards. She couldn't see their feet, but they were almost definitely wearing chunky Dad shoes. They kept taking turns glancing over their shoulders at where Leroy Gibbs stood playing pool, scowling as they glared at him. Every once in a while, Charlie caught a snippet of what they were saying.

"It ain't right, him strutting in here like that. We all know what he done," the one in the Red Wings hat said. His voice was loud and slurred.

"Well then let's stop talkin' and *do* something about it," said Lions hat.

Charlie's gut tightened. She was starting to get a bad feeling. Everyone in town had an opinion on Allie's murder, with half the population seeming to think Gibbs had been railroaded by a police force eager to close the case and the other half believing that the rushed investigation had let the murderous Gibbs walk free. The two gentlemen across the bar seemed to fall in the latter camp.

She peeked over at Zoe, but she was going on about the time an unknown perpetrator interrupted their tenth-grade history class by throwing a tube of hemorrhoid cream into the room and shouting, "Anal relief!" before running off. She hadn't seemed to notice the two angry Michigan-men across the way.

Charlie watched Lions hat gulp down the rest of his beer. His empty mug thudded onto the bar, and then he pushed up from his stool.

"I still wonder who that was," Zoe was saying. "By the time Mrs. Gregson got to the door, he was just gone. Like the Flash. The joke I can still appreciate on a certain level, but it's the sheer footspeed that really stuck with me."

Lions and Red Wings stalked over to where Gibbs stood, chalking the end of his pool cue. Lions hat crowded closer to Gibbs, saying something low and giving him a rough push.

"Uh, Zoe?" Charlie said. "I think something bad is about to—"

She was cut off by the sound of a fully-grown Michigan-man being hoisted in the air by Leroy Gibbs and slammed onto the pool table like a child, pool balls clacking and rolling about, the Lions hat fluttering to the floor. The small crowd of onlookers all jumped back and groaned collectively.

Leroy Gibbs, having just dispatched one member of the two-man mob, lurched for the other. His hulking figure looked, in this moment, very apelike. Between his oddly animal posture and the unkempt beard crawling so high on his cheeks, Charlie couldn't help but think of him as a man about halfway through the transition to werewolf.

Zoe's head jolted toward the commotion.

"Ah, crap," she said, snapping for the bartender's attention. "Glenn, we got a situation. Do me a favor and call down to the station for backup."

Gibbs had his hands on the second man's throat, and Charlie found herself unable to stop staring at the way his knuckles flexed as he choked his attacker.

From behind, the now hatless Michigan-man rose from the pool table and sucker-punched Gibbs in the left kidney. Gibbs clutched his side instinctively, freeing Red Wings hat as he did. It was two on one now, about to get ugly.

"That's enough, boys," Zoe said, stepping into the scrum. "Break it up."

The hatless man ignored her, rushing Gibbs and swinging on him. But Gibbs sidestepped the blow and gave the man a shove, which sent him careening into Zoe. The two of them crashed into a nearby table, glasses and dishes and silverware clattering to the floor.

Seeing that things were only escalating, Charlie jumped down from her stool, intent on helping her friend, but someone caught her by the arm.

"I wouldn't," Will said, gesturing across the bar. "Glenn's got it handled."

The lanky bartender came around the bar with a shotgun in hand. He racked it once, the sound somehow rising over the din, and the brawl ceased, almost as if someone had pressed the pause button on the whole thing.

"You three are going to sit quietly until the police come, ya hear?" the bartender said.

While the two Michigan-men nodded with eyes wide, Gibbs said nothing, looking unperturbed.

Will let out a breath from beside her.

"Well, that was quite a show," he said with a smirk.

Zoe strode over to them, and Charlie noticed a wide gash on her arm oozing bright red blood.

"Zoe, you're bleeding," she said, pointing at the wound.

Lifting her arm, Zoe poked at the laceration and winced.

"Balls. That's deep." Zoe's voice was remarkably calm, and Charlie wondered if she was in shock or just that unflappable.

Charlie grabbed a stack of cocktail napkins and handed them to her.

"I should take you to the ER."

"Nah," Zoe said, waving her away. "I'll slap a bandage on it. I'm gonna have to go down to the station anyway to make a statement. If the bleeding hasn't stopped by then, I'll go get some stitches."

"Are you sure?" Charlie said. "It looks bad."

"This is nothing. Remember the time I biffed a hippie jump on my skateboard and landed on my chin?"

Just the memory of the row of black stitching along Zoe's jaw made Charlie grimace.

There was a commotion near the front door as four Salem County deputies filed in. Zoe waved them over with the hand not clutching a wad of bloodied napkins, and then her eyes flicked over to Will.

"Hello again, Will."

"Zoe."

With a look of mischief in her eyes, Zoe glanced from Will to Charlie, then back to Will.

"Do me a favor, Will?"

"Of course."

"See that Charlie here gets home in one piece?"

"It would be my pleasure."

Before Zoe turned to join her comrades in uniform, she winked at Charlie.

CHAPTER FOURTEEN

"It's still early," Will said. "You want to stay for another drink before we go?"

"Honestly, I don't know why she's making a fuss. I'm just down the street. I can walk."

"Then I'll walk you. I made a promise to Zoe, and truth be told, she scares me."

"Zoe scares you?" Charlie repeated.

"Oh yeah. She's got a wicked sense of vengeance." He pointed to a small mark on his cheek. "See this scar?"

"Yeah," Charlie said, then recoiled. "Zoe did that?"

"Hit me in the face with a rock."

"What? Why?"

"Well, I *might* have started it. But I was only throwing tiny stones at her. Pebbles, practically. But eventually she got annoyed enough that she picked up this massive, potato-sized rock and let it rip."

"Ouch," Charlie said, shuddering. "I don't know if I can ever remember seeing Zoe mad."

"We were young. I think I was twelve. Still... I make every effort to stay on her good side these days. In any case, we don't have to stay for a drink if you'd rather leave now."

"No, let's stay. Maybe you can help me with that University of Michigan law degree brain of yours."

Will sighed.

"You know, it's hard when women are only interested in you for your brilliant mind."

They sat at the bar, and since Will was drinking Scotch, Charlie ordered another Negroni.

"Well?" he said. "My brain is ripe for the picking."

"Does 'white rabbit' mean anything to you?"

He squinted, looking confused.

"When I was a kid, I had a pet rabbit that was white. Why?"

"I got this cryptic email today telling me to 'Follow the white rabbit,' and then 'Find her.'"

"'Find her?'" Will repeated. "Does this have something to do with Kara Dawkins?"

"That was my thought, but at this point, who knows? It could have been spam. Maybe white rabbit is the name of a boner pill."

Will smiled, sipping his drink.

"You don't actually think that, though. Or else you wouldn't be asking me if I know what it means."

"Truthfully, I thought I'd be done with this case by now. I figured it'd be like everyone said: I'd find Kara camped out on a friend's couch somewhere."

"I take it things aren't going well, then?"

"Just a lot of unanswered questions. I'm pretty sure she was sneaking out at night, probably had a fake ID, and one of her friends said something about her working at a club. This is the only club on Salem Island I could think of, but it didn't pan out. It's just dead end after dead end."

"What about the Red Velvet Lounge?"

"The what?"

"It's a strip club. Just outside of Port Blanc."

Charlie set her glass down.

"Well, shit. I hadn't considered that 'club' might mean a *strip* club," she said, suddenly wondering again about Kara's fake ID.

"It's the only one I know of that has a local connection."

"What kind of local connection?"

"The owner, Silas Demetrio, he's from here. He was, oh, probably five or six years ahead of us in school?" Will shrugged. "Anyway, there's also Little Angels in New Baltimore and Night Moves in Mt. Clemens. But they don't get quite the same local traffic."

"You seem to have an encyclopedic knowledge of the local strip clubs. That brilliant mind's been hard at work, I guess."

Will grinned and swirled his Scotch.

"Let's just say that legal issues arise wherever booze and nudity intertwine. For a small-town lawyer, it pays to know these things."

When they'd finished their drinks, they headed for the door, coats in hand. Will made a show of playing the gallant gentleman by helping her slip into hers.

In the parking lot, their footsteps crunched over a light layer of snow that had fallen over the course of the evening. It was a clear night, the stars shining bright against the ink-blue sky.

Cars whizzed past as they strolled along Main Street toward Charlie's place. Their tires made slushy sounds on the road, hissing and spitting.

"This is probably the Scotch talking, but I have an overwhelming urge to confess something to you right now."

"What's that?"

"I had a bit of a crush on you in high school."

Charlie choked out a disbelieving laugh.

"You did not."

"It's true. In fact, I know of several guys who had a thing for you."

"Uh… I think you're confusing me with Allie."

"Not at all," Will said, shaking his head adamantly. "Allie was an open book. But you… you were more mysterious. I spent half my senior year trying to work up the nerve to ask you out."

A giggle escaped Charlie's mouth, some combination of booze and Will's confession working together to make her giddy.

"You're full of it."

"Why?"

"Because you never said a word."

"Well, you were scary."

That got another laugh out of her.

"Scary? How am I scary?"

He shrugged. "You were… intense."

The laughter ceased, but a smile still played on Charlie's lips.

"That's just a nice way of saying I'm a bitch," she said.

"Maybe 'intense' isn't quite right." He thought on it for a moment. "Unapproachable. Maybe that's a better word."

She smirked and raised an eyebrow.

"So… a stuck-up bitch?"

Will pointed at her.

"You're twisting my words around on purpose."

He sighed, his breath coming out in a whirling cloud of mist.

"Do you remember our advanced biology class?" he asked.

"With Mr. Bates? Yeah."

"You'd sit in the back of the room, quiet as a cat, barely uttering a word. But you always had this look in your eye… like you were cataloging every little thing that happened."

"Like the time you raised your hand in the middle of a lecture about human gestation and asked if breast milk was two percent or skim?"

Will burst out laughing.

"See? That's exactly what I'm talking about. I don't even remember that, but you do." He chuckled again. "Did I really ask Mr. Bates that question?"

"Yep."

"Jesus, what a pain in the ass I must have been." As they walked on, Will's face turned serious, his eyes on the ground. "Anyway, my point is, I wanted to know you better. But I didn't know how to get past the walls."

The bluntness of his words caught Charlie by surprise. She stopped in her tracks.

"Wow."

Will blinked a few times.

"Sorry. I'm a bit drunk. I didn't mean to… dissect you like that."

Charlie craned her neck to look at the moon. It was huge, nearly full.

"No, it's OK. I suppose you're not wrong. Allie used to accuse me of being antisocial."

Charlie smiled faintly, remembering the time Allie told her she was going to turn into a dorky weirdo with no friends if she didn't quit reading all the time.

She scraped a patch of sidewalk clean with the toe of her shoe, and then glanced up at Will.

"So am I less scary now?"

"God, no."

She laughed and tilted her head to one side.

"Then why are you talking to me?"

"Because these days I have enough experience to know how to handle intimidating women," he said, his eyes locking onto hers.

"Do you now?"

Will nodded and took a step closer.

Charlie's heart fluttered against her ribcage like a trapped bird as Will bent down and kissed her. His lips were cold from the night air, but behind that was warmth. She gripped the lapels of his coat, pulling him closer.

Someone in a passing car—probably a teenager—called out, "Get a room!" as they passed by, breaking the spell. Charlie and Will pulled back at the same moment, laughing.

"Hope you enjoyed the show," Will yelled at the fading taillights.

Turning to her, he put out his hand.

"M'lady?"

Charlie took his hand, and they walked on, fingers intertwined. She felt a flush working up from her neck to her cheeks. This was not how she'd expected the night to end.

They continued down the sidewalk, taking the alley next to Charlie's office around to the back stairway that led up to her apartment. Charlie climbed the first step and turned back to face Will. They were close to level height now. He put a hand on either side of the wrought-iron railing and leaned in, kissing her again.

After a long moment, he stepped back, fingers brushing against her cheek.

"I hope we can do this again sometime soon."

"Ask him upstairs," Allie whispered. "You need human contact, Charlie. It's not normal, living most of your life alone like you do. Plus, you wouldn't shut up about his penis before."

Charlie nodded, wondering if he could tell she was blushing in the darkness.

"Me too," she said.

"Human contact. A person shouldn't primarily socialize with the voice of their dead sister. Invite him in. Now." Allie's voice was a hiss. "Don't you dare say 'goodnight.' I will revolt. I will spend all night singing a nonstop medley of annoying songs. I won't let you sleep."

Charlie sucked a deep breath into her lungs and let it out slowly.

"Goodnight, Will."

As her feet rang out against the metal steps, Allie cleared her throat.

"You asked for it, Charles. So would you rather hear 'Thong Song' by Sisqo or 'Who Let the Dogs Out' by the Baha Men? I'm taking requests."

CHAPTER FIFTEEN

Charlie woke the next morning with a throbbing headache. She made a pot of coffee and wondered if she'd dreamed the kiss with Will. All through her morning work hours, she pondered it, brief snippets of the night coming back to her, all of the memories strangely distant.

"No, the kiss was real," Allie assured her. "And it could have been so much more if you weren't so intent on living like a nun."

Charlie said nothing, trying to ignore her.

"Actually, that's not a bad idea, you becoming a nun. The fact that you'd live with the other nuns would be sort of like having friends."

"I have friends," Charlie said, counting them off on her fingers. "Zoe. Will. Frank."

Allie scoffed.

"You can't count Uncle Frank. He's family."

"Fine. Zoe and Will."

"Wow. You really got me there, Charles. Two friends. You think in maybe another decade you'll be ready for a third?"

Charlie rolled her eyes and sipped her coffee.

"Have you even considered what you're going to do when Frank's gone?"

Charlie stopped drinking.

"I mean, even if he beats the cancer, he's no spring chicken," Allie went on.

"Stop," Charlie said, her voice just above a whisper.

"What? It's true. He isn't going to be around forever, you know."

Charlie thunked her mug onto the counter.

"I said stop it!" Her tone was shrill, verging on panicked.

Allie took the hint and shut up after that, keeping silent for the next several hours.

But it didn't matter. Allie's words had done their damage, worming their way into her psyche. What would she do if Frank didn't make it? What if she did end up alone for the rest of her life?

The questions rang in her skull all through picking up Frank and driving him to the hospital, receding only slightly once they got to the room where he received his chemo treatments. She watched a nurse hook Frank up to his IV bag of meds and reminded herself that she had to have hope. She owed him that.

Frank settled back into his chair and closed his eyes. Charlie thought he might doze off, so she brought out her notebook and flipped through the pages, looking over her notes for the thousandth time.

"How's your case? The missing girl," Frank said.

Charlie glanced up. His eyes were still closed, but apparently he was in the mood to talk.

"Someone sent me a cryptic email yesterday. Anonymously."

"And what did this cryptic email say?"

"'Follow the white rabbit.'"

Frank's eyelids fluttered open. He repeated the words, frowning.

"Mean anything to you?" Charlie asked.

"Can't say that it does." He shook his head. "Bizarre."

"I know," Charlie agreed. "Like, if they actually want to tell me something, why not just say it?"

"The technology stuff is all over my head, but I got a computer guy you could talk to," Frank said.

"You have a computer guy?"

"Well, computers aren't my strong suit, you know that. He's great on the divorce cases. You should see the stuff he's been able to dig up from message boards and stuff. Solid gold," Frank said, shaking his head. "The things people post when they think they're anonymous."

"Well, that sounds promising," Charlie said. "How do I get in touch with this guy?"

"He prefers that clients go to him."

"OK. Does he have an office or what?"

"You know the place over by the river docks? In the old Sander's Dry Goods warehouse?"

It was easy enough to picture the place. The massive old building was situated right on the river and had been a major shipping hub in the early nineteenth century. Since then it had undergone a stint as a garden center, an indoor trampoline park, and a dinner theater venue. Charlie also remembered plans to convert the place into luxury lofts when she was in high school that never came to fruition. None of the ventures seemed to last long, but she'd heard the current owner was having more success.

"The marijuana dispensary?"

Charlie imagined a nerd camped out on the dispensary lawn, laptop on his knees, high out of his gourd.

"Yeah, that's it. The computer thing is sort of a side hustle."

"He *owns* the dispensary?" Charlie asked. That was almost weirder than her first assumption.

Frank nodded, and before Charlie could request more details, he said, "Ask for Mason, and tell him Frank sent you."

"Wait." Charlie held up a hand. "Mason *Resnik*?"

"Yeah. You know him?"

"We went to school together," Charlie said, chuckling to herself. Pot and computers. She should have known it'd be Mason.

Before Charlie could say more, Frank sat forward in his chair, nonexistent eyebrows all aflutter.

"A Volkswagen!" he said, jabbing a finger in the air. The words came out with an excited laugh.

Charlie was lost.

"A what?"

"Your white rabbit."

Charlie just stared, still not following.

"A VW Rabbit. What if the anonymous tip is about a car? It would make sense to follow a car, right?"

"That's not bad," she said. Considering it further, she added, "Actually, it's the only explanation that even half makes sense, so far."

Frank rubbed his hands together, a look of sheer glee on his face, and for a moment, the old Frank was there. The one who loved nothing more than solving a riddle.

"You clever old bastard," she said.

That only made him grin wider.

By the time she'd dropped him off a few hours later, Charlie's hangover was long gone. She left a message for Zoe, asking if she could track down any white VW Rabbits in the county.

With that taken care of, her focus shifted to something else: Will's tip about the Red Velvet Lounge. She looked the place up online, noting a Yelp review that praised the "hot girls and hotter wings!" Even though it was open during the day, she figured the evening rush would be a better time to scope the place out. The bigger the crowd, the easier time she'd have snooping around without attracting unwanted attention.

Charlie returned to the project she'd started that morning—creating a MISSING flier with Kara's name, age, physical description, and a large color photo. It was an old-school technique, but Frank insisted it worked for animals, so why not a girl?

Charlie added her phone number to the bottom of the page in bold text, then sent the file to the print shop down the street. Less than thirty minutes later, they had a hundred copies ready for her, hot off the press.

She spent the rest of the daylight hours plastering Kara's face all over town. The grocery store, the post office, and every lamppost in between. It brought back a lot of memories, most of them unpleasant. How many fliers had she posted when Allie went missing? Hundreds, at least. And where had that gotten her?

The stapler thumped as Charlie affixed another flier to a utility pole. She only hoped this time would be different.

CHAPTER SIXTEEN

As the sun cast a reddish light on the western horizon, Charlie's car juddered over the bridge to the mainland, tires thumping against the rough roadway as she left Salem Island behind. It'd been years since she'd rolled down this particular roadway. Even so, she recognized every barn, every truck stop, every bullet-pocked stop sign.

Once again, she found herself thrust into a slab of the rural Midwest. Woods occupied the roadsides most places, with the occasional corn or soybean field thrown in for good measure. Driving through it now was simultaneously novel and deeply familiar.

She made her way to a new place, however—the Red Velvet Lounge, the strip club of such seeming importance to the Kara Dawkins case.

The night settled over things, falling quickly. She flipped on the headlights. Pierced the darkness.

Finally, a neon glow in the distance announced that she'd found the place. The red sign shone bright, a brilliant, gleaming portrayal of a dancing cartoon woman with the club's name in gaudy letters forming a shallow arch beneath the female form.

Charlie slowed the car, turned into the lot. A buzzing energy sizzled in her head now, churned in her gut. Nothing to worry about, she knew. Anticipation had a way of riling her nerves. Always did.

Potholes scarred the parking lot, most of the open punctures in the asphalt half full of water. She weaved around them until she found a spot and parked, killing the lights and engine right away.

The quiet seemed to make that gnawing sensation in her gut churn harder. She waited a moment before exiting the vehicle.

Wanted to let her body settle, her nerves settle. Wanted to take in the scene before she walked into it.

The lot looked fairly packed, considering it was early in the evening. The three rows of parking spaces nearest the building were full, and a slow stream of traffic flowed in as she watched.

A bouncer sat on a stool near the front door, the muscular physique of his torso seeming almost comically bulky propped on the piece of stick-like furniture. In the cartoon version of this scene, the spindly legs of the stool would absolutely snap beneath him, the stool practically disappearing as he slammed straight down to sit on the sidewalk.

Finally, Charlie reached for the door handle, took one more breath, and opened the car door. As soon as she was outside, the overwhelming stench of fryer grease assaulted her nostrils. She remembered that a lot of strip clubs served chicken wings, and with the aid of this oily smell, she could already picture them congealing there under the sneeze guard, all slathered in that glowing orange paste of the buffalo sauce.

She strode between the parked cars, walking toward the big front doors framed so elegantly by the dead shrubbery. When she glanced up, she was surprised to see the bouncer staring at her. Was that wariness she read in the bunched skin along his forehead? She thought so, and that got her hackles up. Maybe something suspicious *was* happening here.

Most of these places would hump your leg to get you through the front doors and force you to buy your one-drink-per-hour minimum. She figured they'd be even more thrilled to have a real live woman coming in without getting paid for it. And yet, this particular club had a bouncer out here actually screening people, presumably turning some away? Yes. Something strange must be happening here.

She found herself moving the last few steps a touch slower, watching the muscle-bound bouncer, trying to read every quirk in his body language. She stopped shy of the velvet ropes. Locked eyes with the meathead defying gravity by balancing on this stool. The polo collar ringed around his beefy neck looked like it could burst open at any second.

There was a propane patio heater set up behind the guy, and she could feel the heat coming off it in waves. It ruffled the wisps of hair at the side of her face, made her blink rapidly against the dryness.

He squinted at Charlie, looking her up and down. Gestured at her with his clipboard before he spoke.

"You a cop?"

She put her hands up, trying a disarming gesture on him.

"Hell no."

He smirked. Apparently he hadn't been disarmed.

"Nah. Sorry lady. You look like a cop."

Then his expression changed, going from suspicious to curious. He sniffed the air a few times.

"Yep. Smell like a cop, too." He crinkled his nose. "I can smell 'em a mile away. Beat it."

His hand flicked at the air as though he were brushing her away, eyes going back to his clipboard.

She just stood there, dumbfounded. During the ride over, it'd never occurred to her even once that she might get turned away at the door.

After a few seconds, he looked up, eyebrows raised. He locked eyes with her, and after a pause, he waved her away again, tilting his head in a mocking pose.

CHAPTER SEVENTEEN

Confusion roiled in Charlie's head as she retreated from the velvet rope and walked back to her car, feeling numb. What the hell had just happened?

She slid behind the wheel and plopped the key fob into the cup holder, but something stopped her finger just shy of the start button. Some instinct grabbed her by the shoulders, whispered in her head in Uncle Frank's voice: *Better to give all of this a moment to digest before moving on.* Charlie worked herself through the steps again, hoping something would stand out this time.

She'd been turned away from a seedy strip club, of all places. Almost right away the bouncer had been suspicious of her, called her a cop, figured her for snooping around. Of course, she had, in fact, been snooping around, but there would be no reason she could think of for him to suspect that. She was usually pretty good at blending in. It was part of the job.

She came to the same conclusion she had on the walk up to the building, the gut revulsion she'd felt when she saw the bouncer's eyes narrow as they fell upon her: this place had something to hide. Probably something big, whether or not it had anything to do with Kara. Might as well stick around and watch the place for a while. She had nothing to lose but a bit of her time.

The dome light clicked off as if on cue, plunging her back into shadow.

Thankfully the stream of traffic into the lot would also obscure whether or not she'd left, though she doubted the bouncer was the meticulous type. Oh, he may be particular when it came to things like anabolic steroids and human growth hormone, but she suspected he was less so when it came to pesky little things like doing his job.

A few flecks of light snow fell on the windshield, melting quickly into water droplets. Charlie stared through the spatter.

The crowd trickled in, slowly but surely. Gentlemen of all ages and sizes stepped out of their cars, trucks, and SUVS and headed for the double front doors. The velvet rope swept aside for each and every one of them, allowing them entry. No one but her got turned away, from what she could see. That was curious, wasn't it?

"A place like this must have regulars," Allie said. "He probably knows damn near everyone coming up here on a weeknight."

"I was thinking the same," Charlie said.

Allie affected some kind of redneck accent then.

"Goin' down to the little strip club where everybody knows your name. A few wings. A few laughs. Don't get any better than that."

Charlie didn't respond. It only egged Allie on. Better to play possum. Just sort of play dead until the bad jokes stopped.

Charlie flicked her eyes toward the rearview mirror. She squinted as she gazed into the reflection there. Beyond the rear windshield, where empty asphalt had been the last time she'd looked, tightly packed sedans and SUVs now filled the mirror's frame.

A good time to make a move, she thought. She could take a look around the back and sides of the building, do some poking around now that things were in full swing.

Her gaze slid back to the bouncer out front, who now had his smartphone pressed against his ear. He spoke loudly into the phone, so loudly that she could hear him plainly in her car.

"So the other night, I'm home alone. Bored out of my skull, right? And I remember that my buddy Dennis got me a bottle of that Yippee Ki-Yay whiskey for Christmas—like the *Die Hard* thing, you know? So I drink a couple of glasses of that. Wind up getting the spins."

"This guy speaks in all caps," Allie said.

Charlie shushed her.

She listened for a few more seconds as the bouncer talked about getting so drunk that he somehow vomited into his dishwasher, and how "for some reason it looked just like eggnog." He couldn't be more distracted. Now was her chance.

Charlie slipped out of the car, quiet and slow, and closed the door behind her with a gentle push. She crept between vehicles, staying out of his line of sight.

His voice sounded even louder out here. Sharp. Like he was trying to damage the hearing of the poor soul on the other end of the call.

Soon she reached the edge of the cars. There was nothing to conceal her from this point forward.

She held her breath, counted to three, and darted into the open, scrambling around the side of the building. Based on the ongoing loud babble, he hadn't noticed. Good.

His voice finally cut out of her range of hearing as she rounded the corner to the back of the building. The sudden quiet was jarring. The dark didn't help either. A lone floodlight on the far corner provided the faintest yellow glow. Easier to stay hidden, at least.

Her eyes slowly adjusted to the lack of light, and at last she found what she was looking for. A fire door cut a rectangle in the stone facade, a slab of steel there. She lurked toward it. Tried it.

Unlocked.

Yes.

She slipped inside, careful to keep the door from making any noise behind her.

A dingy hallway took shape in the shadows. Brick walls painted white, gouged and scuffed and scraped. Thin industrial carpet, mottled gray with holes worn into it. It smelled like stale beer and must. She snapped a quick picture with her phone and moved on.

"Why take a picture of a beat-up hallway?" Allie said, at least having the decency to keep her voice low.

"So I can remember what everything looked like later."

She worked her way down the hall, peeking into a couple of doors. Snapping more pictures. It looked like storage, mostly. Boxes of restaurant and drink supplies. Straws. Napkins.

In the next room, she found a healthy stash of booze. A huge box of cheap-ass Five O'Clock vodka sat next to a rack of empty Grey Goose and Absolut bottles with a funnel resting nearby. So they were passing off swill as the top-shelf stuff. Nice. She snapped a photo of that as well. Could be used for leverage later.

Voices murmured out from behind the next door. Girls' voices. She moved closer, trying to listen through the heavy door, but she couldn't make out the words.

Her hand drifted to the doorknob. Fingers lacing around it. She turned it.

And then rough hands grabbed the backs of her arms. Squeezed. Lifted her off her feet.

"Busted!" Allie said, an annoying level of delight in her voice.

Charlie looked over her shoulder to see another muscle-bound hulk of a bouncer staring back at her. The human side of beef grunted, annoyed. He hefted her back toward the fire door like she was nothing.

The wad of muscles tossed her back out the way she had come, giving her a good shove that sent her stumbling over the asphalt.

"You must be the snooping bitch Rocky was telling us about. Well, consider this strike two. You try to get in here again, we'll call the cops. Trespassing."

He slammed the door before she could think of a witty retort. And then she heard the lock clank into place.

CHAPTER EIGHTEEN

Charlie trudged back to her car, gliding along the edge of the building toward the bright glow where the parking lot lay. Her jaw clenched in little pulses, falling in and out of time with her steps. Frustrated.

She rubbed at the sore spots on her arms where the meathead had grabbed her. She'd have bruises for sure.

It wasn't the pain that bothered her, though. It was being manhandled by some juiced-up moron who thought he had some God-given right to push people around.

"If it makes you feel any better, he probably has a tiny sack," Allie said. "You know, from all the 'roids."

Charlie didn't respond. No need to encourage her now.

"Someone's crabby," Allie said in a sing-song voice.

She took a deep breath and let it out slowly, tried to let the aggressive feelings go. This long, useless night was over. At least that was something.

Might as well head home. Get some sleep. She could look at the case with fresh eyes tomorrow. The club had been a bust for now, but there were other angles to work yet.

At last she reached the parking lot and veered to take a diagonal path toward her car. Almost there. Almost done.

A slow series of slaps caught her ear. She swiveled her head to find the bouncer out front standing, giving her a mocking golf clap as she left. He smirked and gave her a nod before going back to perching on his tiny stool, eyes going back to the stupid clipboard as always.

Now Charlie's jaw quivered from clenching as hard as she could, gritty sounds coming from her teeth.

"Careful with those choppers," Allie said. "I seem to recall the dentist giving you a stern talk about not grinding your molars."

Charlie put her head down and walked faster, finally reaching her car.

There. It was over.

Just as she put her hand on the door handle, though, she saw it: a black Cadillac Escalade with a "No Fat Chix" decal in bright yellow letters over the rear window. This was the vehicle Zoe had told her about—the one that had been driving recklessly around the park the day Kara disappeared.

Maybe her night wasn't over just yet.

CHAPTER NINETEEN

Charlie sat in her car, eyes locked on the SUV. The driver hadn't come out of the club yet, but he would. Eventually.

She poured coffee out of a thermos and took a drink. Bitter, but it was still mostly warm, which she was thankful for.

Snippets of the bouncer's loud talking came to her still. She didn't understand how anyone could talk so loud. He seemed to be making numerous calls, but from what Charlie could tell, it was always him talking. Whoever was on the other end of these calls didn't seem to chime in much.

"Almost seems like he doesn't need the phone," Allie said. "Surely these people can hear him wherever they are, anyway."

Just now he was going on about a documentary he'd watched about prisoners in solitary confinement.

"These guys are in the hole for weeks, sometimes months at a time. They start to go a little mental, right? And the only way they can rebel against the guards is to get naked and throw their food at the walls and stuff. Or take a shit on the floor and then shove it under the door."

There was a pause in the conversation, as though shoving shit under a door was finally something the other party deemed worthy of comment.

"Yeah, man. They pick up their own dook with their bare hands and cram it under the door like it's Play-Doh or something. All mushed up. Like a fine paste pushed under that tiny crack into the hallway. By the time they get to that stage, they look psycho, man. Wide eyes, pupils all huge and shit."

Charlie sipped her coffee again and tried not to picture human feces being finger-forced under a door. Harder than it might seem.

Her eyes swiveled back to the black SUV, the jagged letters of the ridiculous decal glowing bright under the sickly yellow street lamps. She'd called Zoe earlier and left a message with the license plate number. It was late, especially by Salem Island standards, so she didn't figure she'd get any kind of response until tomorrow morning.

In the meantime, she'd wait and watch. The driver had to come out eventually. The club was only open another hour or so. She could wait him out.

It occurred to her, not for the first time, that so much of the private detective business came down to patience. Discipline. Waiting for the right opportunity. Whatever obstacle a case presented you, whatever mystery you were trying to solve, it could generally be defeated with the sheer brute force of time and effort. Whoever got in her way, Charlie could outwork them, outwait them, or outlast them. She was confident in that. And in that sense, this driver was just another in a long line of foes for her to dispatch.

Time passed. Charlie finally ate the Snickers bar she'd bought at the gas station, more out of boredom than hunger. The peanuts were stale, but it was still decent.

The bouncer's flood of phone calls seemed to recede to nothing all at once. He was quiet now. Perched on his stool like an owl. His eyelids looked heavier than before. Saggy. Charlie watched as slow blinks assailed his face, each closing of his eyes growing just longer than the last, until his chin sank to his chest.

"Hilarious," Allie said. "Maybe he was talking so loud to keep himself awake. Like how they blast Metallica at prisoners in Guantanamo Bay. They should send this guy in there to describe some movies he's watched recently. The terrorists would start talking within minutes."

Charlie took another sip of coffee, and movement caught her eye. The first wave of patrons came streaming out the front door.

Good. She checked her phone. Only about a half hour until closing time now, so the exodus should be pretty steady from here on out.

Men of all ages poured out of the Red Velvet Lounge and stumbled over the wet asphalt of the lot—some clean-shaven, some bearded, a scant few with mustaches. One guy just had big mutton chops, which seemed to amuse Allie a great deal.

"'Ello, guvnah!" she said in a horrible British accent, guffawing at the end.

The men fanned out to reach their cars, most of them probably heading home to slide into bed next to a wife who had no clue what they'd been up to. A few came dangerously close to the SUV, getting Charlie's hopes up, but none of them went for it.

"Nada," Allie said. "You know this guy ain't coming out until the last possible minute, right? That's how this kind of thing works."

"Maybe. It's not much longer either way."

"Easy for you to say, guzzling coffee and wolfing down a Snickers and all. As it happens, I'm bored as hell, and it's past my bedtime."

"Oh, really? Big plans tomorrow?"

That shut her up.

The flow of foot traffic slowed some as the clock ticked down. The bouncer kept falling asleep and waking himself up again, shaved head sinking and jerking back up like a bobber at the end of a fishing line.

When the driver came out at last, he was alone. Charlie sat forward in her seat upon seeing him, fingers lacing around the steering wheel. Some gut instinct told her this was the guy. No doubt in her mind. Even Allie kept quiet as they watched him traverse the blacktop.

The shadows swirled around him in such a way that she couldn't see his face, but he looked tall and skinny—all shoulders and elbows. He looked younger than she'd imagined, too, an adolescent scrawniness still visible in the way his deltoids stuck out from the rest of his stick frame.

He veered around a couple of mud puddles as he got close, the crook of his jaw entering the light for just a second. Dark stubble shrouded the flesh there. Charlie couldn't make out much else.

He climbed into the SUV, the dome light glowing over messy dark hair. It looked like maybe it'd started out spiky but had gotten trampled over time. When the light clicked off, he shifted into gear and drove out of the lot.

Charlie waited a few beats and then followed, her heart picking up speed along with her car.

CHAPTER TWENTY

Charlie followed the SUV out into the sticks, going back the way she'd come. The lights winked out all around them as the vehicles wound their way deeper on the rural roads, leaving civilization behind. The traffic likewise died off until they were the last two vehicles on the road for mile after mile.

Her heart thudded along, a firm beat she felt in her neck. Steady for now.

She struggled to find a good balance here. She wanted to keep him in sight without getting so close as to be obvious. He opened up as they got out into the middle of nowhere, though, eventually creeping toward eighty miles an hour. When she almost lost him after the first big swell of speed, she decided she'd better stay closer. The potential upside made it worth the risk.

It became clear almost right away that they were headed for Salem Island. Nothing much else existed out this way, save for trees and soybeans. Anyway, it made sense, Charlie thought. This SUV had apparently been spotted tearing around town just the other night, and now he was headed back. Did that mean he was a local?

Just as they hit the outskirts of town, Charlie's phone rang. She pressed a button on the steering wheel to pick up via Bluetooth. Allie was aghast.

"You do know Oprah would be furious about this, don't you? The hands-free crap? Not good enough!"

Charlie ignored her. She focused on the voice coming through the speakers: Zoe.

"Someone's out late tonight, eh? I ran that plate for you."

"And?"

"Stolen."

"What the deuce?" Allie said.

"How often does that happen around here?" Charlie asked. She couldn't imagine Salem Island was a hotspot for that kind of activity.

"Almost never. We get the occasional joyride scenario, where kids steal a car for a few hours or a night. If they don't crash it, they usually abandon it somewhere. But this is obviously different. That car was reported stolen over two months ago, in Chicago."

"Well, I'm following him now, so we'll see where he goes next. I'll report back."

"Wait. I got something else for you. I searched the vehicle registry—no white Volkswagen Rabbits around here."

"Damn," Charlie said. Another dead end. "Thanks, Zoe."

"It's cool. You owe me."

As if on cue, the driver of the Escalade gunned it as soon as Charlie ended the call. The dark vehicle took off like a rocket. Faster than before.

"Well, well, well," Allie said. "Perhaps the post-boob haze of the Red Velvet Lounge finally cleared, and it dawned on this guy that you've been following him for the last thirty minutes."

Charlie gripped the wheel tighter with both hands now as she gave chase.

CHAPTER TWENTY-ONE

The SUV fishtailed as it veered right onto a dirt road, its attempt to dart away from her thwarted some by the skid. Charlie braked hard and then followed, heading deeper into the woods. Her heart hammered in her chest as the sound of the tires changed from the hum of asphalt to the grit of dirt flecked with gravel.

Clouds of dust billowed up from the rear of the vehicle in front of her like tan smoke flitting through her high beams. She needed to stay right on his bumper just to see him through the murk.

The trees flicked by faster and faster as they picked up speed again. She watched the speedometer creep up to seventy, then eighty, then ninety, turning that flicker of woods into a black blur on the sides of the road, the individual trees now indistinguishable.

The potholes throttled both cars, jamming them with more and more force as they accelerated. Charlie felt like she was getting tossed around on the back of a mechanical bull or something, her head going a little light. She pulled herself upright, holding her abs rigid to absorb the shock as much as she could.

The Escalade bounced hard to the left and then the right. The driver looked out of his depth, speeding down this kind of road—anyone would, really. She remembered how young he'd looked—those spindly arms and legs sprouting out of the long, slender torso.

Charlie focused on nothing but the SUV for the next couple of miles. Her pulse pounded, and her hands felt sweaty on the wheel. But she stayed on him.

When she finally looked down and saw the orange needle quivering at ninety-five miles per hour, she thought about giving up. One mistake at this speed could be fatal—even things she couldn't control, like deer, were potential threats on her life. She eased up on the gas pedal.

"Don't you even think about it," Allie said.

"What?"

"Giving up now? This dirtbag clearly knows something about Kara, probably has information that could lead us to her right now. Tonight."

She hesitated another second, the Escalade pulling away, the No Fat Chix decal growing blurry in the swirling, brown fog. Then she jammed the pedal again, felt the car stand up taller as it lurched forward with gusto. She started making up ground right away.

They hit an especially bumpy stretch—the road here washed out into grooves, rutted like a giant washboard made of packed sand. Both vehicles bobbed up and down, each timed to the opposite of the other.

THUMP. THUMP. THUMP. THUMP.

Charlie jostled in and out of her seat. Wrestled to keep a hold on the wheel. It felt for all the world like something had to give, something had to break. This couldn't go on for long.

And then the SUV careened, suddenly out of control. It juddered to the left, the rear end lurching behind the rest of the vehicle. Charlie could see the moment the driver overcorrected and jerked the wheel to the right.

The Escalade pitched into a hard-right turn and launched off the road. There was a terrible *crunch* as it slammed into a tree. The vehicle halted with sickening abruptness, its front end wrapped around the trunk.

It sat motionless for a split second. Still. And then black smoke fluttered up from the wounded front end, visible in the wedge of night still lit by the crooked headlights.

CHAPTER TWENTY-TWO

Charlie slammed on the brakes, skidding just past the wreck. In the rearview mirror, everything behind her car glowed red from the brake lights.

She held still for a second, craned her neck to get a better look. The world seemed impossibly quiet now, impossibly calm after all that rushing momentum. It made her skin crawl.

Nothing moved in the shadowy place behind the vehicle's windows. In fact, she could see nothing at all there—the glass looked utterly black just now. Inky like the bottom of the sea.

She swallowed. Felt the lump shift in her throat.

"Go on," Allie said just above a whisper.

Charlie threw the car into reverse and backed up, pulling off to the side of the road just behind the half-smashed vehicle.

Again, she hesitated. Waited. Watched. Still no movement.

Finally, she scooped her phone out of the cup holder, never breaking her stare from the Escalade, eyes opened wide. She'd call it in. Then she'd take a look for herself.

She gave the 911 dispatcher the closest crossroad that she remembered, mind never fully straying into the reality of the phone call, instead staying in the moment with the SUV. The dispatcher asked her to stay on the line, but she hung up without really thinking about it. Couldn't handle the distraction any longer.

She licked her lips. Tried to see anything at all beyond the thick black occupying the windows.

Her hand fumbled under the wheel and flipped the brights on, lighting up the inside of the SUV at last. The silhouette of the man inside was motionless, stark black against the white of the inflated airbag. His head cocked funny against the headrest, lolling off to one side. Probably knocked out, she thought.

She rubbed her thumb against her fingers. Thinking.

The police would be here soon, and he'd probably still be out. Was that a reason to stay put? Wait for backup? Or was it an even better excuse to get a look?

She should wait. She knew she should wait.

But no. She couldn't do that.

"Don't you want to see who he is?" Allie said, then cleared her throat theatrically. "I mean, uh, he could be hurt, right? Isn't it our duty to check? I'm just worried about the guy's health. That's all."

"Nice try."

"What?"

"Covering your curiosity under the guise of some good Samaritan crap."

There was a long pause before Allie replied.

"I have no idea what you're talking about."

Charlie took a breath. Cracked open the car door and slid into the night.

"Here goes, I guess," she said under her breath.

She'd grabbed her stun gun from her bag, just in case. Clasped it in her right hand. Then she withdrew the Maglite from her jacket.

Charlie swept her light over the vehicle as she inched forward, walking in slow motion. Listening. Watching.

And then a muffled sound erupted. Pattering of some kind. Gone almost as fast as it had arrived.

Charlie stopped. Glared. Aimed her light at the driver's side window. She saw no motion in the SUV, though at this angle she couldn't really differentiate his silhouette from that of the headrest.

Had the sound been from the vehicle? Or from the woods?

She raised the stun gun and the flashlight. Confused. Scanned the light over the perimeter of woods surrounding her. Nothing stared back but the trees.

Pins and needles climbed her spine now, and her pulse rippled in her ears. She wished she could turn the volume of it down. Needed to listen more than ever.

Silence.

Nothing.

She lowered the stun gun. Took a few deep breaths and moved one step closer to the door. She squinted, trying to see through the tinted glass.

"Hurry up, already," Allie whispered, a clear giddiness in her voice.

Charlie tucked the flashlight under her opposite arm and reached out for the handle.

There was a soft clunk and the door lurched at her, hard steel slamming into her ribs and knocking her off-balance.

She staggered backward, feet tangling in the underbrush as the driver burst out of the car.

"Hey!" Charlie shouted, but it did nothing to slow him.

He was out and off and running all in one motion, bounding into the pitch-black woods.

CHAPTER TWENTY-THREE

Charlie ran without thought, her flashlight cutting a narrow path in the darkness.

She hurdled some deadfall. Tried to keep eyes on him as she ran.

He flitted in and out of the foliage, disappearing and reappearing in her spotlight over and over. Part of her wondered if her light was helping him as much as her, lighting the way ahead for him, allowing him to find the openings in the dense growth.

At best he'd be woozy, though, she thought. Odds were high he'd make it less than a hundred yards before he bashed into another tree.

He was fast, though. Long strides.

"Dude runs like a gazelle," Allie said.

He was pulling away from her. Pressing into the darkness. She was starting to lose sight of him more and more of the time.

The woods seemed to be thickening around her. Trees clustering more tightly. Brush and deadfall packing more and more of the ground with obstacles. And yet his pace didn't slow.

She came down on a low spot and felt her right knee buckle. Staggering forward, unwilling to break her stride, she somehow managed to keep herself upright. But it didn't matter. She could hear his footsteps crashing ahead at the same breakneck pace.

Finally, Charlie gave up. Stopped. She shined the light after him one more second, watched him disappear into the gloom and leaves one more time, and then she circled back the way she'd come.

"Quitters never win," Allie said.

Winded, Charlie answered between breaths.

"I'm just calculating our odds here."

Breath.

"We'll never catch him out here. He's too fast. And the snow back here is mostly melted, so we can't even follow his footprints."

Breath.

"Better to take our golden opportunity to search his vehicle before the police get here, don't you think?"

"OK. Fine." Allie clucked out a little mouth noise. "That's smart."

Charlie hustled back through the foliage, more confident on the now familiar ground. When she reached the edge of the woods, she scrabbled up the shoulder, the dark bulk of the SUV taking shape there on the side of the road.

The driver's side door still hung open, and she aimed her light inside, illuminating the cracked dashboard and the spider-webbed windshield. The airbags were still deflating—two off-white puffs going saggy before her eyes, fabric puckering. Considering the damage the vehicle had taken, it was a wonder this guy was up and about, let alone sprinting away from the scene.

Charlie shined her light over the seats, front and back. Apart from bits of glass and crumpled fast-food wrappers, she found nothing.

She crept closer, tucking her hand in her sleeve to avoid leaving prints. OK. She needed to be quick about this.

She leaned over the driver's seat and reached out for the center console. Her sleeved hand found the latch and lifted the lid. Shit. Nothing but Kleenex and a small box of Luden's throat drops inside.

She squatted to look under the seat, skimmed her light at the shadows there. At first, she couldn't quite tell what she was looking at, the flashlight's glow somehow strange in the cramped space. She gave the sweeping of the light three passes before she saw it: a bundle tucked up against the metal runner for adjusting the depth of the seat.

"Looks like we got us a little goodie bag," Allie said.

It was a plastic brick of something, wrapped in shiny tape—clouded, partially translucent but not enough to see what was inside.

She jogged back to her car and fished a pair of nitrile gloves from the trunk. Gripping her flashlight between her teeth, she pulled them on, struggling some out of excitement. One of the gloves folded up on the heel of her hand, and she had to work it free to get it the rest of the way on.

Finally, she snaked her hand into that tiny cavern beneath the driver's seat. Grabbed the bundle. Pulled it free.

And now she turned it over in her hands. She thought she knew what was inside, but… better to know now.

She peeled one corner open. Saw it for herself.

Pills. Circular white tablets with some kind of indecipherable design on them. She was pretty sure it was ecstasy.

CHAPTER TWENTY-FOUR

"So that's when the, uh, subject took off sprinting into the woods?"

Charlie stood in a semicircle of law enforcement officers, Salem County's finest, not far from the SUV with its front end wrapped around a maple tree. She fielded rapid-fire questions from the uniformed officers, all of them standing in various poses that involved hooking their hands or thumbs into their gun belts. Another set of police donned nitrile gloves and searched the vehicle, a process Charlie watched out of the corner of her eye.

"Yeah. I tried to follow, but it's dark. Thought I might snap my ankle or something. End up with my face looking like the front of his SUV."

The officers exchanged glances. The bright flash of photography caught Charlie's attention over by the vehicle, blinding white light.

"He could know the area," one of the deputies said. "I mean, it could be just a straight-up panic type of situation, fight or flight or whatever, but if he knows the area, maybe knows someone who lives near here, he could have taken off with a game plan."

Another deputy nodded.

"Entering the woods right here? On foot? At night? It'd get pretty hairy out there if you didn't know the lay of the land."

Charlie pictured the driver running away again. The long strides. Darting movements to elude trees. He certainly ran with confidence, which could arise from either knowing the land or some kind of narcotic courage. She considered chiming in, but the conversation shifted topics too quickly for that.

"Oh yeah. That's ecstasy alright," the deputy searching the vehicle said. He jogged over to them, wiggling the plastic bundle, a giant grin on his face. "Quite a bit of it. This has gotta be our biggest drug confiscation in years."

The deputies murmured agreement, all of their voices tangling over each other for a second.

"Do you get a lot of that these days?" Charlie said. "Ecstasy, I mean."

All their heads whipped around, as though they'd momentarily forgotten she was there. The oldest of the deputies grimaced, disgusted. He adjusted his thumbs in his belt.

"Don't see a lot of it around here, no," he said. "A bit more lately, though. Some of the city stuff is starting to creep into Salem Island, just like pollution seeping into the water supply. These drugs, though, that culture finally arriving in our little town? Makes me sick to my stomach. Threatens our way of life here. This younger generation. Christ almighty. Don't even get me started about these millennials. No respect, for themselves or anyone else."

Charlie spotted Zoe's car parked in the distance and wandered over to find her. The old man's rant just kept rolling on, even with no one listening.

"I used to think the bums back in the seventies were bad. The patchouli people, you know. Peace and love and copious amounts of reefer and all. But the hippies were nothing compared to these young kids today. If the hippies were looking to expand their minds and live in a perpetual state of peace and love, the kids today want to get too fucked up to move. Just want to escape reality, I think. Detach all the freakin' way. Gonna be the death of this country, too. Makes me want to puke."

She found Zoe standing along the edge of the woods, shining her flashlight out into the murk. She wore sweatpants, and a long T-shirt spilled out from under her jacket—her pajamas, Charlie presumed.

"Took me a second to recognize you, all dressed up like this," Charlie said as she approached.

Zoe's eyebrow crinkled for a second, and then she looked down at herself.

"Oh. Right. I was just getting into bed when I got the call."

She swung her light around, and they both watched it in silence a moment. The glowing circle moved over the woods like a spotlight sweeping across a stage, flitting over tree trunks and glittering off the layer of frost and crusty snow adhered to some of the leaves.

No movement out there, of course. Just a bunch of trees with their arms perpetually outstretched.

At last, Zoe shrugged and clicked off her flashlight.

"So what do you think of all of this?" Charlie asked.

"Probably a small-time drug dealer. You said he seemed young, and this whole chase, running from a civilian vehicle like this… It just strikes me as… someone who lacks experience, I guess."

Charlie nodded, hesitated a moment before asking the question she really wanted to ask.

"You think this has anything to do with the Kara Dawkins case?"

Zoe frowned at that.

"It could, but I really hope not. At this point, it's better for everyone if Kara ran away, you know? That's the best-case scenario, I guess you could say. If that's the truth, I figure we'll hear that she's turned up within the next day or two. If not…"

They went quiet and stared into the darkness.

CHAPTER TWENTY-FIVE

By the time Charlie got back to her apartment that night, she was exhausted. And frustrated. There'd been the epic fail at the club, and then she'd let the mystery driver of the stolen black SUV get away. She'd been close to something tonight. Close to finally untangling some of this Kara Dawkins mess. But it had slipped through her fingers.

She brushed her teeth and washed her face, then climbed into bed. Despite how tired she felt, she lay awake for some time, staring up at the ceiling.

A long crack in the plaster ran from the light fixture in the center of the room to one corner. It reminded her of her childhood bedroom. A patched spot scarred the wall across from their beds, and Allie always claimed it looked like Homer Simpson. Charlie couldn't see it.

So one day, Allie took a permanent marker and filled in the details. The eyes, the nose and mouth, the squiggle of hair. Allie had been right. It *did* look like Homer Simpson. Their mother had been decidedly less impressed with Allie's artistic vision.

When sleep finally came, Charlie dreamed she was back in the woods. Allie ran alongside her this time, her pale face glowing against the darkness like a crescent moon. The woods rolled on and on, an endless black sprawl.

A strange burbling sound bled into the dream. Rhythmic. Like the sound of music from underwater.

Not music, though.

A ringtone.

Her phone.

Charlie shook herself awake, blinking up at the cracked white plaster. It was lighter in the room now, the morning sun beginning to filter in through the blinds. If anyone was calling this early, it'd be Zoe. Had they identified the driver already?

Squeezing her eyes shut against the light, she answered the phone with a voice command.

"Hello?"

"Is this Charlotte Winters?"

The voice was female, but it wasn't Zoe.

Charlie sat up and grappled for the phone. The number on the screen wasn't one she recognized.

"It is."

"Of A1 Investigations?"

"Yes." She propped herself up on one elbow, wondering what this was all about.

"You put these fliers up all over town?"

She heard the distinct rustle of paper over the line. The Kara fliers. Charlie sat up fully.

"Yeah, that's me. You have information? About Kara Dawkins?"

"Who? I... no. No, I don't. I'm calling about my daughter."

Charlie blinked and rubbed at the corner of her eyelid. It was too early for her to try to make sense of this on her own.

"I'm afraid I don't understand."

After a pause, the woman said, "My daughter... she's missing, too."

CHAPTER TWENTY-SIX

The second missing girl's name was Amber Spadafore. She was twenty, a Salem Island native who was now a nursing major at Michigan State.

Charlie headed to the office early to meet with the family. While she waited, she prowled through Amber's various online profiles, the same way she'd done with Kara's that first day.

There was a sudden commotion outside, a woman's sharp voice. Charlie looked up from the computer screen to find a cluster of people standing just outside the front door of the office. She couldn't hear what the woman was saying, but it was clear by her tone that she was upset. She spun around and grasped for the door, yanking it open.

The woman's face went from scowl to phony smile in the blink of an eye as she came through the door, followed by three men.

"Does she travel with an entourage? Or is this her harem?" Allie asked.

"Are you Charlotte? The one I spoke with on the phone?"

"That's me," Charlie said. "You're Amber's mother?"

"I am." The woman put her hand out. "Sharon Ritter."

Charlie took her hand and shook it briefly. She was the kind of woman who made Charlie feel like she was a grubby little kid and not an actual adult. Perfectly manicured nails. Makeup applied to complement her natural features. Hair styled but not overly so. She wore a gold necklace with an ornate key-shaped pendant studded with diamonds.

Pausing to take in her surroundings, the woman's eyes searched the room. Charlie couldn't help but imagining she was silently judging all of it: the shabby carpet, the ancient second-hand office furniture.

Sharon gestured to the man beside her, who stepped forward to shake.

"This is Amber's father, Ted Spadafore. We're divorced," Sharon explained.

He was exactly what Charlie imagined when she thought of all the rich people from Grosse Pointe and Bloomfield Hills who owned vacation homes on the island. Overly tan, bleached teeth, expensive watch. He'd attempted to dress casual, but his jeans were just a smidge too perfect, straight off the rack.

Glancing at the other two men, Charlie tried to fit them into the picture. The older of the two she figured to be Sharon's new husband. The other looked to be around the same age as Amber. Her brother, most likely.

When it became clear that Sharon wasn't doing any further introductions, the older man cleared his throat.

"Todd Ritter," he said. "I'm Amber's stepfather."

He instantly struck her as a discount version of Ted Spadafore. They were dressed in the same dorky dad chic. They had the same sandy hair. But Todd was shorter, a touch paunchier. Hairline starting to recede. Above all, he was plain. Unremarkable.

"Even his name," Allie said. "Tahhhhd."

She drew the vowel sound out, adding a little extra Midwest twang.

Sharon rounded on him, teeth flashing in a snarl.

"Oh, for crying out loud. Not *everyone* has to be formally introduced," she snapped, and then she pointed at Todd and her son and rattled off an introduction. "Todd, my husband. Jason, my son. Can we move on to something more productive?"

"Why don't we all sit, and I can ask a few preliminary questions," Charlie said, nodding to the leather couch.

The space on the couch was soon filled by Sharon, her ex-husband, and their son, leaving Todd to perch awkwardly next to his wife on one of the arms.

Charlie hadn't expected quite such a full house.

"I can go grab an extra chair," she offered.

Todd started to nod and said, "That would be——"

But he was quickly cut off by his wife, who waved a dismissive hand in the air.

"He's fine. Can we please get started? Or am I the only one here who's actually concerned about my daughter being missing?"

"Honey, she was only trying to be polite. I think we're all plenty concerned," Todd said, his tone placating.

Charlie held up a hand to interrupt and hoped her polite smile would break the tension.

"Why don't we start with something simple?" she said. "When was the last time anyone saw or spoke to Amber?"

"Last Monday. We think." Sharon flicked a gold-bangled wrist in the air. "She's on holiday break, so she's been home. But she left to go back to school on Monday. She's very active in her sorority, and they've been planning a pancake dinner for the children's hospital. She went back to do some work on that for a few days. It wasn't until yesterday we even figured out that anything was wrong."

The old sofa creaked as Amber's father shifted in his seat, uncrossing his legs.

"I still don't understand how you could have possibly missed that she was gone until yesterday," he muttered, balling his hand into a fist. "It's been a week!"

Nostrils flaring, Sharon pursed her lips and said, "You've got a lot of nerve, lecturing me."

Ted Spadafore glared over at his ex-wife.

"Yeah? And why is that?"

"If we could get back to—" Charlie tried to break in, but they weren't listening.

Sharon scoffed. From the corner of her eye, Charlie noticed Todd wince. A Pavlovian response to that noise coming from his wife?

"What? You think you're father of the year? After you ran off with that tramp secretary of yours and abandoned your family?"

"Don't call her that. And I didn't *abandon* anyone!"

Ted's face went from sun-bronzed to the red of an uncooked hot dog. By comparison, Sharon remained remarkably cool, running a hand through her hair.

"You did, and I'll call her whatever I want."

"Maybe if you weren't such a controlling shrew, I wouldn't have—"

After sitting on the far end of the couch in utter silence, Jason Spadafore suddenly leapt to his feet, landing in a sort of karate stance.

"Will you both just shut the fuck up?" he bellowed loudly enough to drown out his parents. "All you ever do is argue—everyone is sick of it! Amber probably ran off just to get away from you."

Mouth agape, Sharon looked like she'd been slapped.

"What a disgusting thing to say."

He shook his head.

"You know what? I'm out of here," he said, turning on his heel and heading for the door.

"Jason, don't you—" Sharon started to stand, presumably to chase after her son, but Ted stopped her with a hand on her arm.

"Let him go."

The door slammed behind Jason, and his mother settled back into her seat, blinking.

Allie let out a nervous chuckle.

"Holy shit. For a second there, I thought the kid was going to roundhouse kick his dad in those big white horse teeth of his."

With both parents shocked into an awkward silence for the moment, Charlie seized on the opportunity to get back to her questions.

"OK, so you saw Amber last Monday. Could you tell me what time?"

Sharon's gaze moved from the door to Charlie. She folded her hands in her lap, regaining her composure.

"She left in the morning to meet up with some old high school friends for brunch. But she came back in the afternoon to grab her things."

"And you saw her then?"

Sharon shook her head.

"No, but we have a doorbell camera. It showed her returning around two thirty and then leaving again around seven."

"And no one else was home at that point?"

"I was at a real estate conference in Ann Arbor." Sharon fiddled with a diamond earring. "Todd was working late, and Jason was out with friends. They didn't get back home until after she'd gone."

Charlie could see the muscles along Ted Spadafore's jaw clench, and Charlie forged ahead in an attempt to curtail further bickering.

"Can I ask what you do, Mr. Spadafore?"

His brow furrowed at the sudden change of subject.

"I own a financial consulting firm."

"And what about you, Mr. Ritter?"

"Ritter Custom Installations, owner and operator. We do dock installations. Boat lifts. That kind of thing."

Charlie made a pleasant face as she jotted this down, hoping her positive attitude might rub off on the family.

"Tell me about yesterday," Charlie said. "How did you discover Amber was missing?"

"She'd wanted to invite a few friends from her sorority to stay for Christmas. Girls from out of town that aren't going home for the holidays. I wanted them to feel included on Christmas morning, so I asked Amber to think about a few small gift ideas for them. I kept texting her about it, and she kept not responding. I finally called and got her voicemail. That was Friday. Yesterday she still hadn't gotten back to me, so I called the house and talked to one of her sorority sisters. She told me no one had seen Amber since the start of break."

Amber's father broke in.

"That's when Sharon called me, and I reminded her that Amber's car has GPS tracking. I called up the company and got a location on it."

Charlie glanced down at her notes.

"And it was in a park-and-ride lot just off the island, is that right?"

Ted nodded.

"We drove out there straight away. The car was there. But…" Eyes filling with tears, he shook his head.

"How was the car when you found it? Locked? Unlocked?"

"Unlocked."

"Were any of Amber's things inside?"

"All of her school stuff was still in the car," Sharon said, clasping her fingers so tightly that her knuckles blanched white. "Laundry, overnight bag. But her phone and purse and keys were gone."

Charlie set her notebook aside, folding her hands together.

"Well, I can tell you right now that I've already spoken to the police. With two girls going missing in such a short period of time, they're making this investigation their highest priority. But if you still want me looking into things, the first thing I'll need is a list of Amber's friends. A contact at the sorority house would be a great start. And I'd really like to talk to the people she met up with the day she disappeared."

"I think it makes sense," Sharon said, glancing at her ex-husband. "Since you're already looking for the other girl, I mean, it seems like we could pool our resources, so to speak."

"Absolutely," Ted agreed.

Charlie noticed Todd nodding along with this, as if he were part of the conversation.

She wheeled her chair back from the desk and stood.

"Let me go grab a service agreement for you to sign. I'll be right back."

Ducking into the back office, Charlie grabbed one of the pre-printed contracts Frank kept in a filing cabinet. She went over the form, filling in the blanks, pausing when she reached the space for the client's name.

"Decisions, decisions. Do you put down just one of the parents? Both parents, but leave off poor Todd? List all three?" Allie asked. "Tricky situation."

In the end, Charlie put down all three names: Ted Spadafore, Sharon Ritter, and Todd Ritter.

Charlie fixed the papers to a clipboard before returning to the main office. She passed it to the family and returned to the chair behind her desk.

"Our rate for this kind of investigation is seventy-five dollars an hour. We'll also require a thousand-dollar retainer at the time of signing."

Ted Spadafore nodded along with this as he scribbled his signature at the bottom of the contract.

"I can write you a check right now," he said, handing the clipboard to his ex-wife and getting out his checkbook.

Sharon signed her name like she did everything else: with a fierce efficiency. The pen scratched over the paper like a sharpened claw.

Todd took the clipboard last. Where the other two had simply signed it after a cursory glance, he was apparently intent on reading it in full.

Amber's father slid a check across the desk to Charlie.

"The*odore* Spada*fore*!" Allie chuckled, then repeated it several more times in a sing-song. "No wonder he goes by Ted."

"If we're finished here, I've got a meeting I have to get to," he said, getting to his feet.

"Typical," Sharon said, muttering under her breath.

"Excuse me?"

"Oh, nothing. Write your check and then slither back to your bimbo. That's what you do, isn't it?"

He bared his teeth, on the brink of responding, then seemed to decide he'd had enough for one day.

"I don't have time for this," he said, spinning on his heel to face Charlie. "You'll keep me in the loop?"

"Of course."

With that, he grabbed his coat from the rack and left.

Sharon watched him go, letting out a small puff of breath. Then she turned her sharp gaze on Todd, pen in hand, his eyes scanning the lines of legalese printed in black ink. With his face buried in the contract, he didn't realize his wife was staring him down.

"What are you doing?"

His eyes flicked up briefly, and he flashed an awkward smile.

"Reading the contract."

Thrusting her lower jaw out and rolling her eyes, Sharon shook her head.

"For the love of God, Todd. Will you just sign the damn thing?"

He looked at her in earnest now and tapped the top page with the tips of his fingers.

"I'm just looking it over, honey. I think it's always wise to—"

"Look, I appreciate the overly concerned stepfather act you're putting on, but she isn't your daughter. I don't even know why your name is on the contract, frankly."

Todd's face tightened. He glanced at Charlie, then back at his wife. Charlie cringed inwardly.

"Honey, why would you say that?"

Sharon pinched the bridge of her nose.

"Here we go. Mr. Sensitive! I didn't mean anything by it, Todd. It's just a simple fact. You are not Amber's father." Finished with him, her focus shifted to Charlie. "Now I expect you'll get started on all of this immediately?"

"Absolutely. I'll be—"

To Charlie's surprise, Todd interrupted.

"Excuse me, Sharon, but I'm the one who noticed the flier for the other missing girl in the first place."

Sharon sighed heavily and rolled her eyes.

"Jesus Christ, Todd! My daughter is missing. Do you think you can put your hurt feelings aside until our next therapy session and focus on that, please? We're wasting this poor woman's time."

Face flushing the shade of raw ground beef, Todd blinked down at the clipboard.

"You're right," he said, quietly. "I'm sorry."

He signed the contract and handed it back to Charlie. Sharon was already on her feet and slipping her coat on.

With one final disdainful look around the grungy office, she wrinkled her nose and muttered, "I need some fresh air. I'll be outside."

Todd stared after her for a moment, then reached for his own jacket. Zipping it, he turned to Charlie.

"I don't know if we said thank you, but… thank you." He made eye contact briefly, then looked away again. "My wife isn't always able to express her true feelings. She can be… brusque sometimes to hide her vulnerability. Underneath that tough exterior, she loves her daughter more than anything. She's terrified, and it means the world to have you out there looking for our girl. It really does."

CHAPTER TWENTY-SEVEN

After the Ritter-Spadafore party had departed, Charlie sat at her desk, absently bouncing a pen against her cheek. Two missing girls. Were the cases related? There was no proof yet, but Charlie's gut said yes.

Based on what the family had just told her, Amber Spadafore had gone missing first—a full two days before Kara Dawkins. That was probably significant. And it meant Charlie was already a week behind on Amber's case. She swallowed in a dry throat. Pressure.

She knew the police had Amber's car. She needed to talk to Zoe, see if they'd found anything of interest. But she hated to ask for another favor so soon. She didn't want Zoe thinking she only ever called when she wanted something.

She pulled out her phone and the list of Amber's friends Sharon Ritter had written down for her. The name on the first line was Julia Prior. She was Amber's roommate and sorority sister.

When Charlie explained who she was and why she was calling, the girl let out a squeak of distress.

"I can't believe this is real. None of us can. We're in shock!"

"How well do you know Amber?"

"We're both nursing students, so we've been in all the same classes together since we were freshmen. So yeah, I'd say I know her pretty well."

"And how would you describe her?"

"Oh, Amber is smart as hell. She's the only girl who aced our big pharmacology test the first time through. If it weren't for her, I don't know if I would have passed that class."

An achiever, Charlie thought. Book-smart. It fit with everything else she'd found online. Quite the opposite of Kara Dawkins when it came to type.

"What about socially? Does she have a lot of friends?"

"I mean, I think everyone in the house would consider her a friend. Everyone loves Amber."

"And outside of that?"

"Nursing school isn't really like other programs. We have our standard course load, plus clinicals. Our nursing class alone accounts for twenty hours every week. It's basically a part-time job in addition to our other classes. And then we have the house activities. Volunteering and whatnot. My point is, we don't have quite the amount of free time other students do."

"So would that mean a boyfriend would be out of the question?"

"Not necessarily. We do a lot of the house activities with the Zeta Psi guys. So we're friendly with a lot of them. Amber has a few admirers. But nothing serious."

"Admirers?"

"Let's just say I know of at least one Zeta Psi who would love to date her."

"But she's not interested?"

"I don't know if I'd say that. It's not like he's a creepy stalker or something. They're friends. But I can tell by the way he looks at her and how he is around her that he's, like, totally infatuated with her."

The word set off alarm bells in Charlie's head.

"What does Amber think of that? Or hasn't she noticed?"

"Oh, she's definitely noticed. I don't think you could ignore it. I think she likes it. The admiration. I mean, who wouldn't?"

"What's his name, this admirer?"

"Paul… shoot, I can't think of his last name right now. I think it starts with a T, though."

"Would you happen to have his phone number?"

"I think I do. Hold on."

When Julia returned, she rattled off the digits, and Charlie copied them down in her notebook. She thanked the girl for her time.

"You're going to find her," Julia said. "If something had happened to her, I think I'd know it. Amber has that kind of energy, you know? It'd be like a light went out in the world or something."

After Charlie hung up, she said to herself, "I hope you're right."

CHAPTER TWENTY-EIGHT

Charlie's next call was to Paul T., Amber's not-stalker. He sounded genuinely upset to hear of Amber's disappearance, though Charlie wasn't willing to stake an entire investigation on the shakiness of his voice.

"When was the last time you saw or spoke to Amber?"

"We hung out a few days before break started. That would have been the last time I saw her in person. But we texted a few times after that. I sent her a picture of me in front of the castle at Disneyland. She's a Disney freak."

"I see. So you're in California right now?"

"Yeah. My family does it every year for Christmas break. My grandparents all live out here."

"Could you do me a strange favor? Could you text me a photo of you standing in front of a palm tree when we're done?"

"Uh… sure?"

"Thanks. And I appreciate you taking the time to answer my questions."

"Any old palm tree?" Paul asked.

"Any old palm tree."

"OK."

They hung up, and a few seconds later, the requested photo of Paul and a palm tree appeared on Charlie's phone.

"What was all that about?" Allie asked.

"I wanted to make sure he was where he said he was. If we had Amber's phone, I could have checked for the Disneyland text he says he sent, but we don't, so…"

"You think he could come up with a lie that quickly?" Allie shook her head. "Boys his age aren't that clever."

"How would you know?"

Allie shrugged.

"I'm just saying. Boys are dumb."

The front door opened then. Charlie spun around in her chair and was surprised to find Zoe entering the office.

"Are you psychic?"

"What?" Zoe shrugged out of her police-issue parka and tossed it on the couch.

"I was just thinking about calling you, but you beat me to it."

Zoe gave a quick half-smile, but Charlie could tell her heart wasn't in it. Her voice sounded strange, too. Charlie studied her friend's face, trying to place the odd look she found there.

"What's up?" she asked when Zoe didn't say anything.

"Well, I guess I should start out by apologizing," she said finally, falling back onto the old leather behemoth.

"For what?"

"Everyone was so dismissive of the Kara Dawkins thing, even me. I guess maybe it's sort of contagious. It's easy to convince yourself everything is just fine when that's what everyone else is saying. But now, with this second girl going missing, the whole department is really feeling like they screwed the pooch." She sighed. "No. Not they. *We.*"

Charlie clicked and unclicked her pen.

"Did you really come all the way over here to tell me that?" She pointed at Zoe's uniform. "While you're on duty?"

Zoe glanced down at the khaki-colored uniform. She'd never been good at lying or hiding things, and Charlie could sense there was something Zoe wasn't saying.

"Or did they send you over here to copy my homework?"

Zoe sighed.

"Pretty much."

With a grin, Charlie leaned back in her chair. If she played her cards right, this could be very good.

"Is this a quid pro quo arrangement? I tell you what I know, and you tell me what you know?"

"I have been authorized to share certain information."

Charlie rolled her chair forward.

"Can I see Amber's car?"

Zoe shook her head.

"They already towed it to the crime lab on the mainland." She pulled a tablet out of her bag and handed it to Charlie. "But I have pictures."

Charlie swiped through the photos of Amber's car, an ice-blue Hyundai Elantra. There were several shots of the exterior of the car. It was in good condition—no dings or scrapes, recently washed. The next set of photos showed the interior of the car. Again, it was spotless. No dust or random bits of trash. An air freshener hung from the rearview mirror. Charlie brought the screen closer to her face and zoomed in on the photo.

"Is that a *Little Mermaid* air freshener?" Charlie asked, remembering Paul's comment that Amber was a Disney fanatic.

Zoe leaned in to get a better view.

"Looks like it."

Charlie continued flipping through the photos.

"What do you suppose that smells like?"

"Hmm…" Zoe considered it. "Seaweed and fish?"

Photos of the backseat showed an overnight bag and a basket of laundry, already neatly folded.

It was clear Amber had left the house in her own car, intending to drive back to East Lansing. What had happened after she left the house? Was she meeting someone at the park-and-ride? Or had she been taken somewhere along the route, and the kidnapper abandoned her car there?

Outside again, the next photo was a shot of the open trunk. There were a pair of boots, a snow brush, and a portable air compressor, still in the box.

Charlie went back to one of the first photos, a shot of the driver's side door open.

"This is before anyone touched the car, right?"

"Yeah."

"How tall is Amber?"

"Five foot six."

"That's about my height." Charlie tapped the screen. "And the seat looks pretty far back to me."

Squinting, Zoe studied the photo.

"It does," Zoe agreed. "You think that means something?"

"Yeah, but it only really confirms the obvious."

"What's that?"

"That by the time the car was parked in the commuter lot, someone else was driving. Someone taller than Amber."

"A man."

"Most likely. And she was alone when she left the house, so that means she stopped somewhere between here and the park-and-ride. It's the only explanation. Otherwise, how does someone else end up behind the wheel?" Charlie snapped her fingers. "What about the GPS on her car?"

"We checked it. The history shows her pretty much driving straight from the house to the lot, though she did stick to the back roads, for some reason."

Charlie tried to make sense of that. Again, she wondered if Amber had been meeting someone at the park-and-ride. Her finger swiped over the screen, absently sifting through the photos again.

"How long until they process the fingerprints?"

"Few days. They got lots. And we already took prints from the whole family so we can rule them out."

Finally, Charlie handed the tablet back to Zoe.

"Well, I'll put together what I have on Kara Dawkins and send it over," she said. "You'll keep me updated on the official investigation?"

Zoe slid her coat back on and fastened the zipper.

"Where I can."

CHAPTER TWENTY-NINE

Charlie spent the rest of the morning digging through Amber Spadafore's background. She also got in touch with one of the girls Amber had brunch with the morning she disappeared, who agreed to gather the rest of the crew together to meet with Charlie for a brief interview later in the day.

Around noon, Charlie took a break. She walked to Town Square Pizza and ordered two meatball subs. Since she had some time to kill before the interview with Amber's friends, she figured she might as well take Frank lunch. He didn't have chemo today, but he still had to eat.

When he answered the door, he was in his robe. It wasn't like Frank to not get dressed in the morning. He was an early riser, a wake up at 6 a.m. ready to kick the day in the face kind of guy. Now that she considered it, Charlie wasn't sure she'd ever seen him in pajamas. His face was puffy and gray, and his eyes looked bloodshot and yellow.

She forced herself to smile and held up the plastic bag printed with the Town Square Pizza logo.

"I brought lunch. Meatball subs."

Frank winced.

"I'm not hungry just now," he said. "You can just put mine in the fridge."

She wanted to argue that it wouldn't be good later, but she could tell he was feeling pretty miserable and didn't want to push it. Doing as he asked, she put his sandwich in the fridge and left her own on the counter. She was starving, but the face Frank had made when she'd mentioned the subs made her think that just the sight and smell of her food might make him ill.

"There's been a development in my missing girl case."

Frank eased himself into his trusty chair, grimacing as he settled into the cushions.

"Oh yeah?"

"A second girl is missing."

That got his attention. He sat up straighter and stared at her intently.

"See? This is what I was saying before. Here, the police have been dicking around for what, a week? Ignoring the fact that a young girl has disappeared. And now there's another? Luckily, you've been out there, keeping the trail fresh."

"I guess so," Charlie said.

"You don't have to guess. It's the truth. Every cop worth a damn will tell you that the first seventy-two hours is the most critical period in a missing persons case. It's the best chance they have at finding a lead, in part because people have short memories. And you were the one out there, gathering that evidence before it faded, while the cops sat around with their thumbs in their asses. So don't give me any of that 'I guess so' garbage."

Charlie couldn't help but smile at his passion.

"Any advice, oh wise one?"

"I assume you're looking at ways they might be connected somehow?"

"Yeah, but so far, I haven't found much to link the two girls. Kara's seventeen. Still in high school. Amber is twenty and in college."

"Do they look alike?"

"Not really. Kara is blonde. Amber is a brunette," Charlie said. "They're both pretty, though."

"What about the families?"

"Both sets of parents are divorced, but that's about where the similarities end. Misty and her husband live over in the Mill Creek subdivision. The Ritters have a house on Outer Drive."

"Ah. So the new girl is a cake-eater."

It was an old name the locals used for the rich city people who owned vacation homes on Salem Island. Charlie thought it had something to do with Marie Antoinette, but she wasn't sure.

"Yes, but they do actually live on the island."

"What'd you get from the family?"

"A whole lot of drama."

"Oh yeah? Who with?"

"There was major tension between Amber's mom and dad." Though now that Charlie thought about it, Sharon Ritter had sniped at everyone during the interview. "Actually, the mom is just generally kind of a pain in the ass."

Frank nodded.

"At one point, the parents started bickering, and Amber's brother totally blew up," Charlie explained. "Screamed at them and then walked out."

"That's interesting." Frank stroked the stubble along his jawline. "I'd start there, then. Give them a real good look, find out what they're hiding. But be… discreet."

"You think the family is involved?"

"Not necessarily. But with the level of turmoil you described, I'd want to know more. If they carry on like that in public, then what goes on behind closed doors?" Frank asked, bobbing his head up and down. "The secrets. The family secrets often lead you where you need to go. Someone has to know something."

"What are you suggesting?"

"Nanny cams."

Charlie blinked.

"You want me to spy on my own client?"

"There are two girls missing," Frank said, and she thought he had a point. He went on. "Besides, it's in the contract."

"It is?"

"I set up hidden cameras all the time in divorce cases. If anything, this is much more serious than that, isn't it?"

He was right. There were two girls missing. Amber's parents had hired Charlie to find their daughter, and she intended to do it, by whatever means necessary.

CHAPTER THIRTY

After bidding farewell to Frank and making him promise to call if he needed anything, Charlie headed back to town for her meeting with Amber's brunch posse. Starving now, she unfolded the paper swathing her sub, the sandwich perched in her lap like a swaddled baby. It was cold. Probably going to be horrid, but she was starving. She took a bite.

"Good God. First you eat a whole pizza alone in your car, now a cold sub? This situation is declining rapidly."

"It wasn't a whole pizza," Charlie said, chewing. "And the sub's not so bad, actually."

"Will you listen to yourself? This is just pathetic."

"I didn't want to eat it in front of Frank when he's not feeling well. What was I supposed to do?"

Allie scoffed.

"You're supposed to, I don't know… have a life? Some friends? Someone to talk to other than your dead sister."

Charlie ignored her, finishing the sub just as she arrived outside Cafe Fina. She wadded up the wrapper and tossed it back in the paper bag the sub had come in. She hoped Frank would manage to eat something today. She hated seeing him with no appetite. It was very un-Frank.

As she climbed out of her car, she caught sight of the soup bench across the park. She thought back to when she'd talked to Kara's friend Maggie. It had been just a couple days ago, but it seemed longer now. She'd still been holding out hope that Kara had run away back then.

A cloud of coffee bean smell hit her as soon as she opened the door. She picked out the group of Amber's friends and went over to their table.

"Sarah?"

One of the girls raised her hand. She was very pregnant—probably seven or eight months, judging by her girth.

As Charlie slid into a chair, a waitress came to take her order.

"I'll have a chai latte, please."

When the waitress left, Sarah introduced the other two girls, Sophie and Jennifer.

"We were just talking about how we're so blown away by all of this," Sarah said. "I mean, we saw Amber last week. How can she be missing? I can't wrap my head around it."

"How did she seem that morning?" Charlie said, the scream of the espresso machine's milk steamer almost drowning her out.

"Fine. The same old Amber. Just super thoughtful and gracious. It was such a wonderful surprise."

"What was?"

"The shower? Oh, I probably forgot to explain that part," Sarah said and stroked her belly. "I'm pregnant. Obviously. Amber had organized kind of a mini shower. A surprise. She'd even gone to the restaurant ahead of time and put out decorations on the table and everything. It was just… so sweet."

Sarah started to tear up, and Sophie reached over to pat her arm.

"Amber's always been good at organizing things," Sophie added. "She has this way of pulling a group of people together and getting the best out of them. She was the captain of our dance team in high school. That's how we all know each other."

The waitress returned with Charlie's drink.

"So you didn't notice anything unusual at brunch?"

"Definitely not," Sarah said. "It was just a really pleasant morning. Hard to believe things could go so terribly wrong just after."

Charlie nodded, took a long drink of tea. She knew the feeling well.

"Did Amber mention where she was headed after the brunch?"

"Back to East Lansing," Jennifer said. "She said she had a mountain of laundry to do before she left."

The same frustration Charlie had felt at the beginning of her search for Kara Dawkins resurfaced. Asking the same old questions and getting nowhere.

Sarah glanced at her watch.

"Oh shoot! I have a doctor's appointment to get to. Are we almost finished?"

"We're done, actually," Charlie said. "Thank you all for coming down here."

Tucking her notebook into her bag, Charlie scooted away from the table and left a few bills to pay for her tea. As she headed for the door, Jennifer and Sophie were helping Sarah maneuver into a fluffy down jacket.

Charlie pushed outside, a burst of icy air ruffling her hair. She took a deep breath and hoped the Ritter house was ready to give up its secrets.

CHAPTER THIRTY-ONE

By the time Charlie arrived at the Ritter house that evening, the family was just sitting down to eat. Todd Ritter, the stepfather, led her toward the dining room, stopping just shy of the doorway. Charlie could see Amber's mother and brother seated at the table in the room beyond, both of them noticeably quiet compared to earlier. She sensed an awkward tension in the air.

"You're sure you're not hungry?" Todd said. "You're more than welcome to eat with us. Chicken parm tonight. Made it myself. Not to brag or anything, but it's sort of my specialty. Secret's all in getting a good crispy texture."

"No thanks. I just wanted to get a look at Amber's room, if I could."

"Her bedroom?"

"Yeah. You never know what little detail might help."

Todd nodded, gave a shrug. Charlie couldn't help but notice the contrast between his relative level of nonchalance and the family's demeanor in the next room, which seemed somber. Choked. Tight.

"Sure. That makes sense," he said. "It's just upstairs. Second door on the right."

He waved his finger at the staircase, pointing like an air traffic controller waving in a 747.

"You need anything, just give a shout. We'll be down here digging in."

"This guy seems way too much like a sitcom dad or something," Allie said, keeping her voice quiet, as though he might hear.

Charlie climbed the stairs and found the door to Amber's room—white paneled wood with a Winnie-the-Pooh sticker just above the doorknob. The edges of the yellow sticker had been peeled back, some of the white papery layer underneath exposed. Maybe Amber had put this here as a kid, and years later, embarrassed, made some half-hearted attempt to remove it. Funny how that worked, Charlie thought, how we always tried to erase our pasts. Opening the door, Charlie's eyes snapped to the corkboard on the far wall with photos pinned to it. She crossed the room to get a closer look.

Snapshots. The pictures all featured Amber and her friends at a variety of wholesome locations: the school cafeteria, an amusement park, even one of a big group at the bowling alley, everyone giggling.

Now Charlie's eyes latched onto a picture of Amber and another girl smiling at the old Poseidon's Kingdom amusement park. They were seated high up in the Ferris wheel. She'd heard about people climbing it to sit in the very topmost cars, but Charlie had never had the guts to do it.

At last she took a step back to get a look at the rest of the room. There was certainly more of a traditional girly feel here than she'd found in Kara Dawkins' room. Pinks and purples dominated the area around the bed. That region almost seemed trapped in little-princess mode to a creepy degree.

The rest of the room spoke more to the twenty-year-old that Amber truly was.

Posters of various pop and rock stars coated most of the walls, spanning multiple genres and eras. Adele. Beyoncé. Kurt Cobain. Jim Morrison.

She picked up a music box from the high closet shelf, turning it over and over in her hands. She wound it up, opened the lid, and it tinkled out its melody—the theme from *Swan Lake*.

When the box stopped turning in her hands, she saw it—the seams slicing a rectangular slit into the wood on one side.

She dug a fingernail into the gap and slid the drawer open. Inside she found a single cigarette, the tangy tobacco smell rising up to meet her nostrils. Beside the white tube sat a black matchbook.

She picked up the matchbook, thinking it might contain the detective novel cliché of a phone number written inside, but plain white cardboard stared back at her when she flipped it open. Then she turned it over and read the business logo printed on the other side.

She gasped so hard she almost choked.

White text and red graphics gleamed against the glossy black. Stark and bright. A cartoon of a dancing girl twirled about the curved lettering of the logo:

The Red Velvet Lounge.

CHAPTER THIRTY-TWO

It took Charlie a second to get her breath back. She stared down at the logo quivering along with the matchbook in her hand.

The Red Velvet Lounge—the filthy strip club that reeked of fryer grease—could now potentially be tied to both girls. This was huge.

Part of Charlie wanted to rush straight to the club now. Kick down the door. Tear the place apart searching for anything. But she knew that wouldn't do. The bouncers knew to look for her.

She needed to be strategic. Patient. Needed a plan.

In the meantime, there was still work to be done here at the Ritter house. Frank's gut said the family knew something, and Charlie planned to find that out here and now.

She tucked the matchbook into her jacket pocket and stood on tippy toes to slide the music box back on its shelf in the closet. For now, she'd keep this little tidbit from the family. Just in case.

She thought back to her visit with Uncle Frank, his words echoing in her head: *If her family carries on like that in public, then what goes on behind closed doors? The secrets. The secrets often lead you where you need to go.*

Charlie snaked a hand into her bag, pulled out a small, white cube. A nanny cam. She'd hide it here in Amber's room, see if maybe someone came in after she left.

She tucked the camera in a scarf on the dresser, propped it up behind the jewelry box. Then she moved to the hall.

Peeking out of Amber's doorway, she held her breath and listened. Faintly she heard what sounded like a fork tinkling against a plate. They were still eating. Good.

Working quickly, she checked the other rooms in the hall, identified two bedrooms. She entered the master bedroom first, scanned it in the half-light streaming in from the hall. Her heartbeat thrummed in her ears, the notion that she might get caught sending a thrill through her.

She nestled the second camera among the Spanish moss in the pot of a fake ficus in the corner. She didn't love the angle—about half the room would likely be cut off—but as hiding spots went, faux plants were among the best. They didn't have to be watered.

"You're really doing this, huh?" Allie said.

"What?"

"Spying on these people."

"I'd be willing to do a whole lot more than this to find those girls." A memory of the day the police came to tell her parents what they'd found on the beach flashed in Charlie's mind. She could still hear the low moan of anguish her mother made when the deputy told her they were reclassifying Allie's case as a homicide. "All that matters is finding the truth."

Next she went across the hall to the other bedroom, presumably that of Amber's brother—the dirty clothes on the floor and multiple bottles of Axe body spray on the nightstand seemed to verify that.

Allie read off the varieties of Axe, amused.

"Ice Chill, Apollo, Anarchy for Him. Oh my God. Smell the Anarchy one. Please."

"No time," Charlie said.

Charlie chose a bookcase to house the camera. The lens would peek out from one side of a Bluetooth speaker, nicely concealed from most angles. It was perfect.

With the camera in place, she hurried back into the hall, slowly shutting the door behind her. Again, she listened. This time no fork sounds tipped anything off. She wanted to place one more camera, but it would be a risk.

"Where's that last camera going?" Allie said.

"Basement."

"Yeah?"

"Just a gut feeling. There's probably a rec room or something down there. Maybe a home theater. We've got the bedrooms covered. That'd be another place someone might expect privacy."

She dug another camera from her bag and placed it in her jacket pocket. Better to have it close.

She took a deep breath and started her descent. If the family were still eating, her path should be clear—that window of opportunity had to be waning by now, though.

At the bottom of the staircase, she went left, working her way around the dining room to the kitchen, figuring that to be the most likely place for a basement entrance.

She passed through a living room with a blocky-looking wood coffee table and tufted leather furniture in the exact shade of a Tim Hortons coffee with two creams. The floors were some kind of polished stone, and Charlie had to be extra careful because her feet made a tap-dancing sound with every step if she moved too fast.

The Christmas tree stood in here, festooned with silver and red. She'd never seen such an anally decorated tree outside of a magazine. The trees they'd had growing up had always been a mishmash of ornaments, many of them made by her and Allie in school: a googly-eyed felt Santa, a pine-cone reindeer with lopsided antlers, a snowman made from pompoms and pipe cleaners.

At last she stepped into the kitchen. Stainless-steel appliances. White shaker cabinets. Marble-look countertops. Mason jars wrapped in burlap and baker's twine. A suburban cliché.

There were two doors on the back wall of the kitchen. One of them had to be for the basement stairwell.

"It's definitely the left one," Allie said.

Charlie chose the door on the right, twisting the handle and pulling the door free without a sound. The distinct smell of rotting produce wafted in her face, a wedge of light from the kitchen pendants illuminating a broom closet with a stainless-steel garbage can inside.

"Ha! Told you," Allie said, her voice annoyingly smug.

Just as Charlie eased the closet door shut, she heard a chair scrape over the dining room floor. She had to hustle.

The next door revealed what she'd been looking for: carpeted stairs leading down. She could only see the first four steps before darkness blotted out everything beyond, but she could hear the telltale sound of a handful of silverware clattering on top of a plate. Whoever was clearing the table would probably enter the kitchen any second now.

Charlie stepped into the dim stairwell and shut the door behind her, sealing herself into the pitch-black space. She felt around on the wall for a light switch. There was a long beat after flicking it before the fluorescent lights below shivered to life.

Her shoes whispered over the carpeted stairs as she descended. She had been right about the basement rec room idea. A huge flat-screen was mounted in one corner with every video game console imaginable sitting in the entertainment center underneath. At least ten controllers cluttered the coffee table in front of yet another tufted leather sofa, this one the color of a Spanish peanut.

But the real centerpiece of the room was a huge train set. It dominated the basement, covering more than half of the floor space. It was set up in a large rectangular loop with a hinged section at one end that could be lifted out of the way like a drawbridge. A miniature village huddled at one end, with tiny buildings and roads. At the other end, there was a mountain with a tunnel and rolling hills flocked with some kind of green fiber to mimic grass.

Charlie bent closer, admiring the level of detail on the train depot, right down to the arrival and departure times posted behind the ticket window. She imagined how much fun she and Allie would have had with a giant playroom like this.

"Playroom? Are you kidding?" Allie said. "This is all Tahhhhd's. Guarantee it. Look how fussy it is. How clean. Everything in its place. They probably don't even let the kids down here at all."

Charlie nestled the final camera behind a bundle of wires to one side, angled to stare out at the rest of the room.

At the top of the stairway, she turned off the lights and listened, holding her breath in the dark. When she was as confident as she could be that no one was outside the door, she went for it. Slipping out of the basement, she glanced around, finding the kitchen empty.

The door closed with a soft click, and just as Charlie's fingers released the handle, she heard a noise behind her. The soft scuff of feet over tile. She turned and found Sharon Ritter staring at her from the kitchen doorway. Eyebrows scrunched. Lips pressed into a thin line.

"Sorry, I was looking for a bathroom?"

The woman's face softened.

"I always say this house has too many doors," she said and gestured over Charlie's shoulder. "Go all the way through the dining room and there's a powder room off the entryway."

Charlie thanked her and ducked through the doorway she'd indicated. Entering the small bathroom off the foyer, Charlie was practically punched in the face by the overwhelming odor of pine. As she closed herself in, she spotted the can of Glade in a wicker basket on the back of the toilet.

"Sparkling Spruce," Allie said, reading the label. "This family is obsessed with artificial smells."

Charlie made a show of flushing the toilet and washing her hands.

"It's almost as if they're hiding something, you know?" Allie arched an eyebrow. "Air fresheners. Body spray. It's like underneath the picture-perfect family, they know there's something stanky they have to cover up."

Charlie was eager to see what the cameras would show her. She hoped Frank was right, and that the secrets she found here would be the key to finding the girls.

CHAPTER THIRTY-THREE

Charlie lounged in her car across the street from the Ritter house, computer sitting open on her lap. Now, thanks to the nanny cams, she could get a deeper look inside the Ritter household—as close as someone could get to peeling off the roof and seeing the family secrets laid bare.

Her gut told her that something she found tonight would lead her to the girls, one way or another. Amber had gone missing first. Someone in the family had to know something. Had to.

Four miniature screens filled her monitor. Most were inactive at the moment, and the basement screen was pitch-black with the lights off. So far the only notable action had been a black-and-white cat sauntering through the master bedroom.

A light snow began to fall, peppering the windshield with random flakes. Charlie popped open a bag of Doritos and a Fresca and waited to watch the family in their natural habitat. They'd creep into their private areas sooner or later. In any case, it was better to have a snack with this kind of thing, she thought, or else the restlessness could wear your nerves down quickly. Even in a best-case scenario, a surveillance session like this was a tedious task. Lots of downtime. Lots of staring into a blank screen or watching nothing through binoculars. Food made it borderline tolerable.

Charlie nibbled on another chip, this one inexplicably lacking nacho cheese dust. So far something like every other one had been like that. Had she gotten a bad bag?

It was inane details like this that often came to the forefront of her thoughts only in the midst of this part of the job. Bored and listless, suddenly every nacho cheese detail tapered into a sharp focus.

After they'd been sitting in silence for some time, Allie spoke up.

"You know what your problem is?"

"This should be good," Charlie said.

"You're aloof."

"Aloof?" Charlie snickered. "I guess somebody's been leafing through a thesaurus."

"You make no effort with people. No attempt to be part of the group."

Charlie let her head fall back against the seat and stared up at the ceiling.

"Sorry I was never Miss Popular like you."

"I'm just saying. If you don't learn to open yourself up to people, you'll end up a bitter old hag who collects creepy dolls because she has no friends or family."

Charlie snorted. "That's oddly specific."

"Life is so beautiful, Charlie. We are surrounded by mysteries, miracles, wonders, and love. A universe populated with details that are striking, strange, vexing, haunting, moving. It's everywhere. All around us. You just have to reach out. Connect with something outside yourself. Try."

Allie sighed. Then she went on.

"You stopped believing in it, I think. Life, I mean. You could be out living it instead of what you're doing, which mostly involves eating in your car alone, from what I can tell. Not all of us get to do that, you know? Live our lives. We don't get to love or share our passions or fight for what we believe in. It got taken from us. Anyway, it's not for me to tell you what to do, I guess. It's your life."

She was quiet for a moment, and Charlie thought that was the end of it.

"Just remember, I'm not always going to be here. What will you do then?"

The smirk on Charlie's face vanished.

"What the hell does that mean?"

Allie shrugged.

"Just saying. I could disappear at any second." She snapped her fingers. "Like that. Poof. Gone."

"Shut up," Charlie said.

What was Allie's obsession with this lately? First she'd gone on and on about Frank, and now this.

Charlie tried to focus on other things, but her mind kept wandering back to the idea of Allie being gone. She couldn't imagine what her life would be like without her sister constantly in her head.

Over an hour passed before anything on the screens moved. The basement lights clicked on, the one dark screen going to a blinding bright white. As the camera adjusted, the picture seemed to fade into view, and then a figure appeared, moving down the stairs.

"Activity in the basement," Allie said, as though reporting it over a police radio. "Looks like the patriarch of the house, one Todd Ritter, is heading down to his man-baby room. Over."

"Man-baby room?"

"Yup. He's going down to his basement to play with his trains. Like a freakin' baby."

Sure enough, Todd Ritter moved to the train set. He leaned down and flipped a hidden switch under the table. Tiny lights flicked on in the model buildings, and the little steam engine raced around the track, taking a winding path over a bridge and through the mountain tunnel. The chugging of the train sounded tinny over the laptop speakers. When the steam engine's whistle blew, it was quite shrill.

"See? Man-baby."

Charlie crunched another chip before she answered. She tried to chew as obnoxiously as possible, knowing that Allie had always hated that when they were kids.

"I guess."

Todd fiddled with train bits and changed some of the cars for the next few minutes. Watching this was somehow duller than watching blank screens, Charlie thought, and she tore into the Doritos pretty good.

Another forty minutes went by before one of the upstairs cams came to life. Charlie's eyes snapped to it as Allie narrated once again.

"Activity in the master bedroom," Allie said. "Looks like Sharon Ritter... and... an unidentified male subject?"

Charlie squinted at the screen. Most of the man's body was cut off the left edge of the picture, but he was too tall to be the brother, Jason. Before she could think much about it, the guy ripped his T-shirt off.

"Holy shirtless!" Allie said. "We've got man meat."

The pants came off next, one leg and then the other. He hopped off-screen. Then Sharon passed through the frame, stripped down to her underwear. She, too, exited stage right, the last visible bit of her body language seeming to suggest she was climbing onto the bed.

Now even Allie was speechless.

"Hurry," Sharon said, her voice hushed. Within seconds, soft moans came through the laptop speakers over the train whistles in the other room. Even with the action happening off-screen, the sound made it too intimate, so Charlie turned it down to a level that was just barely audible.

She struggled to process what she was witnessing. Sharon Ritter was having an affair? With Todd in the house? She slid her eyes back to the basement camera feed. Todd was still playing with his trains. Oblivious.

"Yikes," Allie said. "You wanted to know what the Ritters might be hiding? Well, there's a family secret for you."

"Yeah," Charlie agreed.

They fell quiet. Charlie couldn't pry her eyes away from the feed showing the blank slab of wall and a window in the master bedroom. After a second she noticed that shadows flitted against the wall, presumably from the doings on the bed.

"Just reading the shadows here, but if I'm not mistaken, is that reverse cowgirl I'm seeing?" Allie said, laughing to herself. "Go Sharon. For an older gal, I'm sort of impressed."

Charlie closed her eyes, thankful to see the screen disappear for a second.

"Shut up. You can't tell that."

"Can if you use your eyeballs."

When Charlie opened her eyes, the dark forms on the wall were still undulating, but she couldn't make out anything in the shifting shapes.

She crunched another Dorito to distract herself.

"Wait. Wait a minute," Allie said. "We've been sitting here the whole time, and this guy wasn't at dinner, was he?"

Charlie pictured the table as it had been earlier.

"No. It was just the family. Todd, Sharon, Jason. And the chicken parm."

"And we've been out here watching pretty much the whole time since then. Would've seen any cars parking, anyone going to the door."

Charlie thought back. Not a single car had passed through the cul-de-sac loop since they'd been out here.

"Yeah. Right."

"So how'd lover boy get in?"

Charlie's thoughts stopped dead for a second. How *did* this guy get in?

"He would have had to sneak in somehow, to get past Todd. Probably a back door."

"That *would* line up with my reverse cowgirl theory."

Charlie didn't take the bait this time.

"Either way, he would have had to come up to the house through the backyard on foot. Any other way, we would have seen him."

"And you checked the whole house, essentially? Between going through the bedrooms and getting down to the basement, you got eyes on every room?"

"Yeah. I mean, it's not impossible that he was hiding somewhere, but I kind of doubt it."

"Besides, if he'd seen you planting the cameras, he probably wouldn't be doing what he's doing now, would he?"

They both stared at the shadows again.

She closed her eyes, felt the laptop radiate warmth against her legs. Not unpleasant on such a cold night.

"Question," Allie said. "Do we think this guy, our Don Juan, could be in any way linked to Amber's disappearance?"

Charlie opened her eyes. The shadow puppets on the wall seemed to have finally gone still.

"Maybe. With the infidelity, hiding it could be a motive."

"Like if Amber found out about her mom and what's-his-face."

"Right. If he wanted to keep her quiet…"

"We'd still need to connect him to Kara Dawkins."

"True."

"Movement," Allie said. "In the… which room is this?"

"The brother's room."

Charlie watched as Jason Spadafore's stocky form paced across the room, something aggressive in his movements, in the set of his shoulders. And then he started screaming into the iPhone pressed to his ear.

Charlie turned the volume on her laptop up. There was music on in the background, loud enough that it was blowing out the crappy nanny cam mic.

There was a brief moment, between songs, when Charlie made out a snippet of the tirade.

"—a lying bitch—"

"Real smart setting up the camera right next to that speaker, dingus," Allie said.

Charlie shushed her, leaning closer to the screen, as if that might make it easier to decipher Jason's words, but all she could hear was more distorted gibberish from the speaker, throaty and strange. It almost sounded like a record playing backward.

Jason punctuated the end of his call by holding the phone out in front of his face like a rock singer's microphone and screaming into it, something apelike about his body language, the arched upper back, the neck jutting out. Then he hurled the phone at the wall, where it splintered into pieces and sank to the floor.

"Someone's in a bad mood," Allie said.

"His sister is missing. I'm sure the whole family is a little tense."

Amber's brother stood over the broken gadget for a second, shoulders heaving, arms parted in some pose that made Charlie think of a professional wrestler. In one motion, he turned to his right and used both hands to sweep everything off the top of his dresser into a pile on the floor, yelling at no one.

"What next?" Allie asked. "Foot through the door? Blunt object through the TV screen? Haven't seen that one in a while."

Instead of committing further violence against the decor, Jason tugged on a hoodie and stormed out of the room. Charlie's eyes scanned all the feeds, hoping to pick him up on one. Nothing.

Moments later, he burst out the front door, elbowed through the screen door, and stumbled down the front steps. He picked up speed, racing down the walk, through the gate, over the sidewalk into the street. He was headed right toward her car.

"Uh-oh," Allie whispered. "Do you think he spotted the camera?"

Charlie shrank low in her seat as though to hide. Braced herself.

As he drew in line with the hood of her car, he suddenly changed direction, veering toward a truck parked across the street.

He climbed inside, slamming the door shut with a loud *clunk*. The engine roared to life, a violent sound in the quiet, and the headlights clicked on to spear the darkness.

Charlie exhaled. Relief flooded her body, letting all those tense muscles in her back and shoulders relax again. She wasn't sure exactly what she had been scared would happen, but the kid seemed to be coming unglued. Better to stay out of his warpath for the moment.

The truck tore out of its parking spot, sliding on the packed snow. Red taillights flared for a moment just before they disappeared around the corner, tires squealing all the way around the bend.

"Shouldn't we follow this maniac?" Allie said.

"I'm not sure. I'm curious where he's headed, but I kind of think we should try to get a look at the dude up in the bedroom, you know?"

"It's a tough call, but yeah. I think getting a look at the outsider makes sense. Like as a priority, I mean."

Charlie nodded.

"So we wait."

CHAPTER THIRTY-FOUR

With the carnal shadows still fresh in her mind, the thought of eating any more Doritos made Charlie squeamish. She folded up the top of the bag and placed it in the backseat, out of sight.

The Fresca still seemed OK, at least, if a little warm now. She sipped it, wanted to make it last. Room-temp Fresca—the nectar of the gods.

"Jesus. How much longer can this go on?" Allie said.

"What?"

"Whatever prolonged sex act we've got going in the bedroom. It's been a while, right? This guy's got the stamina of a bull or something."

Charlie chugged some Fresca to avoid responding to that, remembering after a second not to polish it off.

"No question about it," Allie said. "We've got a thoroughbred stallion on our hands. I can see what Sharon sees in him."

"Stop."

Charlie went back to watching Todd Ritter in the basement. He was playing video games now. Possibly *Minecraft*, but she didn't have a good enough angle of the TV screen to be sure.

"This guy is fiddling down in the basement while Rome is burning up in his bedroom. Good God," Allie said.

"Not like it's his fault."

"I guess that's one way of looking at it."

"What's that supposed to mean?"

"I mean, he's pretty disengaged. I'm not saying he's to blame, necessarily, but what we're witnessing here is a high level of checked out. He's playing with his trains. Clueless. At the very least, if he were more tuned in, he would have an inkling of what's happening. You've got to figure this is a regular thing, right?"

Charlie sighed.

"Probably."

"And we're on the same page that our boy Todd Ritter is oblivious to all of this, yeah? Unless he and his wife have some kind of *arrangement.*"

"I suppose that's possible," Charlie said. "Except that Sharon told the guy to hurry. Back when they first started, I mean."

"She could have meant like, 'Hurry up because I'm so hot for you.'"

Charlie drummed her fingers against the steering wheel.

"Maybe. But we also figure he must have snuck into the house. Why sneak in if there's some sort of agreement between them?"

"Yeah. You're right. I guess I was holding out hope that our good buddy Todd wasn't getting cuckolded quite so hard. I don't mean to judge the man. It's a sad situation."

They fell quiet after that. Todd moved blocks around on the screen. It had to be *Minecraft.*

"OK, here we go," Allie said.

Charlie's eyes flicked to the upstairs feed. Solid shapes moved there instead of shadows.

The mystery man strode through the frame, putting his T-shirt back on. He'd somehow timed it perfectly to cover his head with fabric as the camera might have gotten a look. However, an identifying feature did come into focus. A tattoo on his inner left forearm—it looked like a skull with some kind of symbol growing out of the base of it.

"Almost looks like a Dark Mark tattoo," Allie said. "From Harry Potter, you know?"

Charlie squinted. Looked closer. It did look a lot like that.

"Think we can get a look at him on the way out?" Allie said.

"Maybe. If we figure he's going out the back, we can try to get out there. Cut him off. Take a look."

"Better hustle."

"Yeah. Just a second. Let's make sure he's actually leaving."

With his T-shirt now on and back to the camera, he stretched for a moment, arms out wide, spine elongated. He had a slender build. Wiry. Sinewy. It was hard to say for sure, but he looked on the young side, at least compared to Sharon.

Before Charlie could react, he tore open the bedroom window and started climbing out in one motion, one leg and then the other into the breach. A practiced move. His upper body descended a fraction of a second later. He disappeared through the hole there in the window frame. Just gone.

Allie swore.

"He's bolting. Go!"

Charlie scrambled to find the door handle, and her feet were clumsy beneath her as she stepped onto the asphalt.

She ran for the backyard.

CHAPTER THIRTY-FIVE

Charlie crashed through the front gate, picking up speed. When she drew near to the house, she veered off the flagstone path and into the snow. The white crusty stuff grabbed at her ankles, tried to slow her, but she bounded through it, picking her knees up higher.

She rounded the first corner to the side of the house. Trudging past the dining room and kitchen windows, Charlie ducked low to avoid being seen by anyone inside. Just as she reached the rear of the house, she spotted movement near the far end of the backyard. A dark figure vaulted the privacy fence and disappeared into a copse of spruce trees.

If she didn't hurry, she was going to lose him completely. She pushed herself harder, sprinting now. Halfway across the yard, her right foot hit a slippery patch which sent her careening off her intended path. Off-balance, she stumbled a few strides, falling forward more than running. She put her arms out, certain she was going down, but with one final, lurching step, she managed to right herself.

When she drew near the fence, she slowed. It was too tall for her to peer over, and the gaps between the slats were too narrow to see much. As for climbing it, the planks of pale wood were bare on this side, nothing to grip. How the hell had Sharon's mystery lover gotten over it so quickly?

She gave it a shot anyway, fingers clawing at the smooth surface, trying to find purchase. When that failed, she wrapped her hands around the top edge and hauled herself up just high enough to peek over the other side.

The densely wooded acreage beyond the fence lay dark and motionless. He was gone, and the trees back here had shielded the ground from snow, so he hadn't left a trail.

Charlie eased herself down to the ground, thinking. She turned back to the house, studying the trellis he must have scampered down. Her gaze followed the wooden structure up to the still open window above.

Sharon Ritter appeared there—a dark silhouette backlit by the glow inside. She cupped a hand over her brow, staring out into the backyard.

Charlie ducked behind a shrub near the fence and froze there.

After a second, Sharon called out in a whispery voice, "Hello?"

Charlie's heart thudded in her chest. She tried to keep her breathing quiet, but it was difficult after all that running through the snow—it seemed easier to lose your breath in the cold. She closed her eyes, focused only on the air flowing in and out of her.

Finally, she heard the window slide closed.

CHAPTER THIRTY-SIX

Cold and dejected, Charlie eased her car door open, still panting for breath. She plopped into the driver's seat and slid the warm laptop back onto her lap, pressed her frigid fingers against the vents where the heat seeped out of the machine.

She'd missed her chance to identify Mrs. Ritter's side piece. If she'd gotten out of the car twenty seconds earlier, she might have scored a look at his face. Still, she reminded herself, the tattoo gave her a starting point. She pictured it again—a skull with some swirling shape sprouting out of the bottom of it, almost like a twist of vines. Identifying marks like that could be searched in the databases of most jails and prisons, so she could have Zoe take a look. If he'd ever run afoul of the law, they might have something. She couldn't help but imagine that the type of guy who climbed a trellis to sneak in and out of a second-story window to commit adultery had, perhaps, little respect for legal matters or rules in general.

As she got her breathing back under control, activity caught her attention on one of the feeds. Sharon flitted through the master bedroom with what looked like her pajamas on. After a second, the lights went out.

"I can imagine ol' Sharon is downright exhausted," Allie said. "Dude just plain wore her out."

Charlie picked up the empty Fresca can and pretended to drink out of it rather than respond. She could just faintly taste some citrus vapor.

"I'm talking about how they did it for like four hours or something," Allie said. "I mean, it was probably more like forty-five minutes, but that's like four hours in sex time, especially with the husband just down two sets of stairs. Might even be five hours."

Charlie's phone rang, mercifully interrupting Allie's rant. It rumbled against the smooth plastic of the cup holder, startling both of them. She knew based on the *Cops* theme song ringtone that it was Zoe.

"Hey."

"Just wanted to give you a heads-up," Zoe said. "Since you added the Amber Spadafore case to your load today, it just so happens we've got a Spadafore down here."

Charlie struggled to process this concept, and then the meaning hit all at once.

"Jason?"

"Yep. He got hauled in for causing a ruckus down at O'Malley's Pub."

"What kind of ruckus?"

"Broke a pool stick over some dude's head, apparently," Zoe said. "The victim's name is Seth Martin. He's a local, and before you ask, he's been out of town the past two weeks on a ski trip."

"Meaning he couldn't have been involved with either of the missing girls," Charlie said.

"Right. Anyway, after Jason dispatched Mr. Martin with the pool cue, he swung the splintered butt at anyone who tried to get close. When the deputies arrived, they said it looked like he was trying to stake vampires or something, waving this sharp wooden stick around, you know."

"Wow. I watched him storm out of his house a while ago. He seemed upset, but I wasn't sure what to make of it."

Zoe sighed.

"Yeah, well, it could be more trouble for a family who already has more than their fill of the stuff at the moment. He thunked the guy pretty good over the noggin. Concussed him. He seems OK for now. Awake, alert, at the hospital for observation, but you never know. I've read about cases where someone goes home from a fight, after getting hit in the head like that, and they end up dying like eighteen hours later or something."

"God, I hope not." Charlie closed her eyes and pinched the bridge of her nose. "The family already has enough on their plate, like you said."

"You just never know when it comes to head wounds like that. Either way, you've got to figure this guy, the victim, he'll want to press charges. The attack was supposedly unprovoked."

"Have you given Jason his phone call yet?"

"Nah. Chief wants to let him stew for a while. Think on his actions."

Charlie nodded, though she knew Zoe couldn't see her.

"Well, thanks for letting me know."

"Yep. Catch you on the flip-flop."

"Later."

Charlie went back to staring into the laptop monitor. By this time, there was only one person still awake. Her eyes once again focused on Todd Ritter in his playroom. He was back at his train set, fiddling once again, removing a piece of track to replace it with another. She watched him through slitted eyelids, unblinking.

"God, how could he be so oblivious to what's going on in his own home?" Allie said, voicing Charlie's precise thoughts at the moment.

Charlie didn't answer, though she couldn't disagree.

"I mean, I can't help but feel bad for the guy. But what are you going to do? There are a lot of suckers like him in life. They never get a clue as to what people are really like."

Confident that the excitement in the Ritter house was mostly over for the night, Charlie closed the laptop and set it in the backseat. She flipped on her headlights and put the car in gear.

"Where are we headed?" Allie asked.

"To bail out Jason Spadafore."

CHAPTER THIRTY-SEVEN

"You sure you want to do this?" Zoe asked, moving behind the front desk of the police station and plucking a large set of keys from one of the drawers.

"Yep."

"It's your five hundred bucks," Zoe said with a shrug. "I'll be right back."

Charlie milled around the waiting area, arms crossed. A few moments later, Zoe returned from the holding area with Jason in tow. When he saw Charlie standing there, he scowled.

"What are you doing here? Where's my mom?"

Uncrossing her arms, Charlie spread her hands wide.

"She's not here. It's just me."

"She sent you?"

"Not exactly."

"Not exactly," he mocked her. "What the hell does that mean?"

"Hey, pal, you should watch your tone," Zoe said. "This lady just did a nice thing, bailing your ass out. If it wasn't for her, you'd be sitting in that cell until morning."

Charlie appreciated Zoe jumping to her defense, but if she wanted Jason to talk to her, she needed to find a way to de-escalate the situation.

"It's OK, Zoe. I've got this."

Stepping closer to Jason, she tried to steer him away from the front desk with a gentle hand on his elbow.

"Could we talk a minute?"

He jerked away from her.

"About what?"

"About Amber. You didn't have much to say today, but I imagine you're close, being only a year apart."

He angled his chin away from her, staring at an empty corner of the room.

"I guess."

"So why don't you tell me about her? Did you know if she had any plans to meet up with anyone aside from her old school friends while she was here? An old boyfriend?"

He shook his head.

"She didn't say anything like that." His eyes squinted as he studied her. "You know my parents only hired you for appearances, right?"

"What do you mean?"

"I mean no one takes you seriously. My dad says your whole business is a racket. But the other family had already hired you, so my mom said it would look like they didn't care as much about *their* daughter if they didn't hire you too. The whole thing is a fucking joke."

Charlie felt her hackles rise at the insult and then realized that was exactly what he wanted. He was trying to bait her.

"OK. If you don't want to talk about Amber, then why don't you tell me about tonight?"

"Tonight?"

"Yeah. The fight at the bar. How did that start?"

Jason's brow twitched.

"Didn't like the way some townie trash was looking at me."

"That's it? A look?" Charlie blinked. "You're sure there wasn't something that set you off?"

"Like what?"

"I don't know. You were on edge when I saw you this morning. And then I watched you storm out of the house tonight. An hour later, you start a brawl at O'Malley's. Is there something other than the stuff with Amber that's bothering you?"

Jason wasn't making eye contact, but she could see the muscles of his jaw tense. There was something. The question was, how far could she push him?

"Maybe you had an argument with someone? Your mom? Or maybe a friend or girlfriend?"

His neck swung around as he turned to face her, and for a moment she thought he was going to tell her. But then his expression clouded again. Pivoting away from her, he addressed Zoe.

"Am I free to go?"

"You need to sign for your personal effects." Zoe held up a plastic baggie containing his wallet and keys. "And honestly, I think you ought to hear—"

Jason stalked over and scribbled his signature on the clipboard before yanking the baggie from Zoe's grip. As he strode to the door, Charlie hurried to step in his path.

"Jason, wait."

He paused and leaned in close enough that she could smell the beer on his breath.

"My parents are rich idiots who think they can solve every problem by throwing money at it, so this is between you and them. Leave me out of it."

The door slammed behind him, and Charlie watched him stalk out of the station.

"You think he knows something?" Zoe asked. "About his sister's disappearance, I mean?"

"Maybe. Or it could just be that he's a spoiled kid with no coping skills. I don't think he has the best role models at home, to be honest."

Zoe nodded.

"That stuff about his parents solving all their problems by throwing money at them? You should have heard the dad down here this morning, going on and on about how much money he's donated to the police fundraisers over the years."

Charlie's mind wandered back to searching Amber's pretty princess room. But there'd been secrets underneath the sugary sweetness, hadn't there? The cigarette she'd found in the music box and the matchbook from the Red Velvet Lounge.

"What do you know about the Red Velvet Lounge?"

"The strip joint?"

"Yeah."

"I hear there are scantily clad women who will dance for money."

"There were apparently rumors around school that Kara was working at a club, and from the sound of it, the Red Velvet Lounge fits the bill. Then I found a matchbook for the very same club in Amber Spadafore's room."

Zoe raised an eyebrow.

"I hate to say this, but that is some extremely weak sauce."

"I know, but it's the only thing I've found so far that might connect the two girls."

Zoe reached up to adjust her glasses, then folded her arms over her chest.

"So go over there and check it out."

"I already did." Charlie leaned one shoulder against the wall. "They wouldn't let me in. They figured me out for a snoop, somehow."

"Or they thought you were a jealous girlfriend or wife. A lot of clubs don't let women in if they're not with a man."

Charlie cocked her head to one side.

"You know this from experience?"

"Actually, yes. It's not really my scene, personally, but I dated a chick who was all about it. We were denied entry at several clubs because we weren't escorted by a man."

"Interesting."

Charlie had been operating under the assumption that the bouncers knew she was there looking for dirt. Maybe they'd simply been worried she was there to stir up other kinds of trouble. If that was the case, there might be a chance she could still get in. She just had to find a man willing to *escort* her.

And she knew just the one.

"Whoa," Zoe said.

"What?"

"You had this look on your face. It… reminded me so much of Allie. It was just eerie."

CHAPTER THIRTY-EIGHT

In bed, Charlie drifted toward sleep. A warmth settled over her body, starting in her core before spreading to her limbs and, finally, her cheeks. A kind of calm seemed to accompany this swell of heat—the weight of the blanket, too, bringing her some deep sense of peace and tranquility.

Still, one little niggling voice stayed active in her mind. Allie's voice. Her sister kept probing, kept talking, kept replaying the various dramas that had unfolded tonight in and around the Ritter household. The family had certainly packed a lot of excitement into one evening. Allie laid it all out again.

"First, there's the affair—Sharon Ritter sneaking a man into her bedroom while her husband plays with trains in the basement."

She clicked her tongue, as though checking a box before moving on to the next item on her list.

"Then there's the brother's outburst—after a tumultuous phone call, Jason Spadafore smashes his phone before rushing off and getting into a brawl at a local bar. Beating some guy's head in with a pool cue."

Another tongue click.

"Finally, the man who'd lain with Sharon in the biblical sense climbs out the second-story window, scampers down a trellis, and hops an eight-foot privacy fence, managing to narrowly avoid your eyeballs in the process. So yeah. Big night at the Ritter house."

She was quiet for a second.

"Am I forgetting anything?"

Charlie sighed. She'd have to talk to Allie or this could go on all night.

"The tattoo," she said.

"Right. Good call. Lover boy has a Dark Mark or something similar inked on his inner arm. A skull and a vine or some snakes or something."

Charlie drifted again as her sister finally went quiet. She inched out toward sleep, the room around her seeming to fade into the black nothingness of unconsciousness. Then Allie started at it again.

"We need to identify lover boy. Then we need to find out what Jason's mixed up in, what that call was about. To me, those are two legitimate leads that need to be explored."

"Agreed."

"And poor Todd Ritter, seemingly oblivious to everything down in his toy chamber. He makes the trains run on time, I guess."

"He's 'poor Todd Ritter' now, huh? I thought you said all of this was partially his fault."

Allie huffed.

"False. I said it's partially his fault for not knowing what's going on—not that I typically blame infidelity victims, mind you. But if you live the bulk of your adult life in a basement playroom... well, some of the not knowing is on you. In any case, toy obsession aside, he and Amber might be the only normal ones in the family from the looks of it. By comparison, anyway."

"I guess I can agree with that," Charlie said.

"The only one we didn't get a good hard look at tonight was Amber's biological dad. Theodore-dore-dore Spadafore-fore-fore." Allie added a false echo to each name. "But you said his alibi was pretty rock-solid."

They fell quiet for a beat, and then Charlie spoke.

"Isn't it strange to get these glimpses into other families? To see how they really live? It's like peeking behind the doors and windows of each home, you find a completely different world, foreign to your own. These families are nothing like ours, you know?"

"Yeah," Allie said. "Definitely not."

"If I think about it long enough, it makes me think that no 'normal' exists when it comes to families. There is no ideal. No right answer. Each one creates its own tangled web of relationships, too complex and sophisticated to be copied elsewhere."

"That's true," Allie agreed. "Take the Dawkins family, for example. The parents seem utterly normal, utterly stable, and the daughter is the troubled one. Meanwhile, the Ritters are, to some degree, the opposite—the daughter is the normal one and the mom is the one breaking social norms; maybe the brother, too, I guess."

Charlie rolled over. Stared up at the ceiling shrouded in darkness. Allie's voice punctured the silence again.

"And after all of that, even a dysfunctional family like the Ritters can't compare to our fractured family—broken forever." Her sister sighed. "Or at least, they aren't that way yet. Maybe it depends on what happens from here. With the girls, you know."

Allie's words hit Charlie like a punch in the gut. If she didn't solve these cases, if she didn't find the girls…

Immediately her brain whirred to life. Poring back over the facts, the files in her mind opening wide. She mentally dug through the information again.

She sat up. Reached for the nightstand. Opened the drawer. Inside, in a plastic baggie, she found what she was looking for.

She spun the Red Velvet Lounge matchbook in her fingers, the one she'd found in Amber's room. It was the one thing she had that tied these two girls together. And she knew what she had to do next.

CHAPTER THIRTY-NINE

The next morning, there was an email waiting in Charlie's inbox from Ted Spadafore's assistant. She'd attached Amber's cell phone records for the past two months.

"I can't believe he passed you off to an assistant," Allie commented.

Charlie only shook her head, snatching up her computer and heading downstairs to the office to print out the call records. She took the warm pages from the printer tray and settled into her work, color-coding the numbers the same way she'd done with Kara's calls. When that was finished, she compared the two lists, hoping to find a number in common between the girls.

After poring over the numbers for what seemed like hours, Charlie was forced to admit defeat. The call records didn't share a single number in common.

Charlie shoved the pile of papers away in disgust. She was sick of dead ends. She wanted to feel like she was making progress for once. With that in mind, she got out her phone and called Will.

"I was just thinking about you," he said, not bothering with *hello*. "I want to see you."

She felt a thrill in her gut at that but forced herself to stay focused on the task at hand.

"Good. Because I have a favor to ask."

"What kind of favor?" he asked.

"I need you to get me into the Red Velvet Lounge."

"OK," he said. No hesitation.

"Really? No argument? What kind of lawyer are you, anyway?"

"Hey, if a lady demands I take her to a venue where other ladies are removing their clothes, I don't ask questions, and I certainly don't argue."

They made plans to meet up around eight—Will assured her the place would be busy that time of night—and said their goodbyes. Charlie ended the call, feeling giddy at the thought of seeing Will again.

Charlie climbed the rickety metal staircase back up to the apartment.

"You realize you always think of it as the apartment?"

"What?"

"*The* apartment. Not *your* apartment. Like you've still got one foot out the door. Ready to flee Salem Island if things get too intense or something."

Charlie ignored this. Who cared what she called the place or how at home she felt… or didn't? She was here, wasn't she?

Besides that, she had bigger things to worry about, like how to disguise herself so the bouncers at the Red Velvet Lounge wouldn't recognize her.

An hour before Will was scheduled to pick her up, Charlie started to get ready. She showered, shaved her legs, and slid into an old gold dress of Allie's. Hair hanging in wet ropes, she stared at herself in the bathroom mirror for a long while, trying to figure out what to do with it. Allie flitted around in the background, full of nervous energy.

"Go big or go home," she said. "That's my motto."

Charlie pulled out a blow dryer, curling iron, hairspray, and a comb and got to work. Every time she paused in the process of teasing and spraying, Allie said, "More."

When she finished, her hair was arranged in a wavy cloud that flipped to one side. She leaned forward and pinched a tuft of hair sticking up in the front. It was crispy from all the hairspray she'd used to plaster it in place.

"You look like you should be backstage at a Mötley Crüe concert," Allie said. "Trying to blow, like, the guitarist or something."

The description was accurate enough, Charlie thought. Between the dress, hair, and makeup, she was looking particularly late eighties or early nineties at the moment—a ploy she hoped would help her get past security at the club, especially with Will at her side as her fake date. She thought back to the last bit Allie had said.

"Wait. Why the guitarist?"

"I don't know. He's the least famous, I think. Don't even know his name. Let's be real. You're not Nikki Sixx material, Charlie."

Charlie looked at herself in the mirror again. She thought she looked sufficiently unrecognizable, though it was hard to be certain. The makeup probably disguised her the most. She'd applied the foundation in a thick enough coat that she could have spackled over a hole in a wall. It gave her face an overall plastic look. Fake and airbrushed.

A few minutes before eight, there was a knock on the door. Charlie snatched up a pair of heeled boots on her way to answer it.

Will stepped back from the door at the sight of her, eyes wide.

"Well, hello there."

She spun in a circle.

"What do you think? Am I incognito?"

"Yeah, I don't think we have to worry about you being recognized. The bouncer is going to take one look at you and think, 'Paid company.'"

"Nice," Charlie said, tugging on one of the boots. "Hooker chic. That's definitely the look I was going for."

"Whoa there, don't sell yourself short. You don't just look like any old hooker. You look like a very *expensive* hooker."

Charlie rolled her eyes.

"Oh, that's so much better. Thank you."

When she had squeezed into the second boot, Will grasped her by the wrist and pulled her closer, pressing his mouth to hers. Her pulse sped up as his hands slid around her waist. She pressed her body against his, and for a moment she was tempted to yank him backward onto the mattress.

But eventually, something jolted her back to reality, because she caught herself taking a step away from him, breaking the spell.

"You're going to mess up my makeup," she said, wiping her lips. "I appreciate that you're doing this, though. It's a big help."

"Hey, taking a beautiful woman on a date in the name of truth, justice, and the American way? Not a problem."

CHAPTER FORTY

A little thrill of excitement ran through Charlie as she crossed the parking lot to Will's Lincoln. The club would have answers. It had to. And this time, she'd actually be able to get inside.

But almost as soon as Will steered the car onto the main road leading off Salem Island, Charlie's confidence began to wane. The bouncers had caught her sneaking in. What if one of them recognized her, even with the disguise?

She flipped down the sun visor and checked her reflection in the small, lit mirror. Maybe it was the change in lighting, but her makeup was even more ridiculous than she remembered. Still, she barely recognized herself, so hopefully that meant the bouncers wouldn't either. She folded the visor up and settled into her seat.

As they pulled into the lot of the Red Velvet Lounge, Charlie plucked a pair of sunglasses from her purse, trying to decide if wearing them at night would make her more or less conspicuous to the bouncer.

"Aw," Allie said. "Seems like a waste to cover up your handiwork. I've seen you spread peanut butter on a sandwich more conservatively than the raccoon-looking crap you smudged around your eyes."

"Shut up."

Will whipped his head toward Charlie.

"You say something?"

"Hm? No. Did I?"

"I don't know. It sounded like you were sort of whispering something."

"Thinking out loud, maybe," Charlie said, managing to talk through Allie's giggling. "I guess I'm kind of nervous."

Will parked the car as he answered.

"Nervous? About going into this stinkhole?"

He killed the engine and rotated in his seat to face Charlie directly. Will waited until her eyes met his.

"We'll have no trouble whatsoever. Trust me."

"He seems pretty confident, Charlie," Allie said. "I don't know about you, but I'm reassured by a man who knows his way around a seedy strip club."

Shut up. Charlie thought it with the sharpness of a knife's edge.

When she glanced over at Will again, he was studying her intently.

"How are you handling all of this, anyway?" he asked. "The case in general, I mean. It must feel a little personal for you, considering…"

He trailed off, but the implication was clear. *It must be personal to be working a case about two missing girls after what happened to Allie.*

Charlie looked away, staring out her window at the neon glow of the club's sign.

"I know what's at stake. That's for sure."

"It feels kind of like a nightmare, doesn't it? Like history repeating itself in the worst way possible," Will said. "I know the girl's dad, you know? Ted Spadafore."

That got her attention. Charlie swiveled to face him.

"You do?"

"He's my financial advisor."

"What's he like?"

"Like the kind of guy you'd trust with your 401K. Solid, but boring. Anyway, we're not exactly buddies or anything, but it's a reminder of what a small damn world it is. We're all attached by these invisible strings, it seems like."

Charlie nodded, thinking he was exactly right. Her whole job was to find those invisible strings and pluck them one by one to see where they led. With any luck, she'd find a few fresh strands tonight.

"Well," Will said. "You ready?"

Charlie took another deep breath and reached for her door handle.

They climbed out of the car and started making their way across the wet asphalt. And there was the bouncer, the same one from her last visit here, as bulky as ever. Perched on his stool like a bear performing in a circus. His phone was jammed to his ear again. Maybe that was good. Another potential distraction.

She clutched at Will's arm as she laid eyes on the bouncer, an instinctive move, done without thought. If he minded a grown woman pawing at his arm like a frightened child, however, he showed it not at all. He looped his elbow inside hers as though they were square-dancing partners.

As they stepped up onto the sidewalk and took the final paces to the velvet ropes, Charlie's anxiety intensified by an order of magnitude. Weird things lurched in her belly with great violence—sea creatures, she thought. Like two large frogs were fighting to the death in the pit of her stomach.

She tried to plan what she would do if the bouncer showed any sign of recognition. How she might try to seem nonchalant about it. Confused. Tilting her head to one side like a dog out of its depth.

Instead the bouncer seemed to recognize Will. He gave the faintest nod and waved them through without much thought. Once again, he was loud-talking on the phone, this time about different small dog breeds. They got an earful as they passed through the gap where the velvet rope had swung out of the way.

"Thing about pugs is their respiratory problems, bro. Real serious probs on account of their flat snouts. Me, I'm more of a Min Pin guy. Real regal breed. Prancing around everywhere like they own the whole world, you know?"

She kept expecting his words to cut off all at once. Surely he'd notice her. Surely they'd get turned away, just like before. Instead he went on about dogs.

"Oh, no way. You gotta clip the ears and dock the tail, bud. Now I know the AKC no longer requires it, but let's be real. That's how it's always been, and that's how it'll always be. Nuh-uh. Don't want 'em. Just snip 'em off."

Will pushed open the door, held it for her, and Charlie pressed forward into the forbidden realm beyond.

CHAPTER FORTY-ONE

The sleazy club was pretty much exactly what Charlie expected—right down to the stench. Bad cologne intermingled with the greasy food in the buffet, all of it tinged with just a hint of body odor.

Topless girls gyrating? Check.

Liquor? Check.

Sweaty losers ham-fisting dollar bills into G-strings? Check.

A couple of men in sweatpants camped in the corner near the buffet, their plates piled high with bright orange chicken wings? Check.

Charlie reminded herself of the plan as she crossed the room toward the seating. Settle in. Observe. Then look for openings to ask some of the girls about Amber and Kara.

Gaudy lights swung around the room before refocusing on the breasts center stage. Soloing guitars blared over the speakers, music from the dreaded 1987 to '89 era when the only thing bigger than the guitars was the hair. At least Charlie's disguise wouldn't seem out of place.

She followed Will across the room to a table in the darkest corner, where they'd be able to watch from the shadows. A swiveling strobe light passed over them periodically, but other than that they were well hidden.

"This is weirdly like the cantina scene in *Star Wars*," Allie said. "Except, you know, filthy."

"And sort of pathetic," Charlie said.

"You pass through these doors, and it's like a different universe exists within these walls. Totally foreign to ours, bustling with strange life and customs."

A waitress in a Red Velvet Lounge branded tank top and black booty shorts came over to take their mandatory drink order. Her top was slit down the front, revealing lots of cleavage and just a hint of black lace bra.

"Jim Beam, neat," Will said.

The waitress turned her gaze on Charlie and smiled.

"What about you, hon?" Her voice was high-pitched and soft like a little girl.

"I'll have the same," she said.

The lights went down across the room, and there was a moment of quiet as the darkness caught everyone's attention. A single spotlight flared on the stage, and out came a dancer with a snake draped over her shoulders—a python, if Charlie wasn't mistaken. The men in the front row grew rowdier as she emerged. Hooting. Hollering.

The waitress returned with their drinks. Charlie sipped at her glass, dabbing at the droplet of watered-down bourbon that clung to her lip.

"So are you less nervous now that you see how ridiculous this place is?" Will asked.

"Well, yeah," Charlie said.

She thought about launching into Allie's *Star Wars* cantina observation but held her tongue. Allie hated when Charlie stole her material.

Just as quickly, Charlie's mind snapped to the idea that Will had come here before. There was something disorienting about that—here he was making fun of it, conspiring with her as if they were both outsiders observing this strangeness, and yet the bouncer out front had recognized him.

She looked Will up and down, let her eyes scan the room again. She couldn't picture it.

"You're wondering if he's more of a wing guy or a breast guy, right?" Allie said.

The image flashed in Charlie's head of Will pulled up next to the buffet, loading fiery orange wings onto his plate, rapid-fire tapping the tongs excitedly between wings as though applauding with the kitchen tool. She cringed and took another drink.

"I'm curious about something," Charlie said, waiting until she had Will's full attention. "Correct me if I'm wrong, but you said you come here, didn't you? Like on a regular basis. You knew exactly what club I was talking about when I was still sort of grasping around for the place. Like no hesitation, you knew. Immediately."

He laughed.

"Oh, I come here alright. Not on my free time, though."

Charlie felt her brow crinkle.

"What does that mean?"

"It probably sounds weird, but it's a work thing. Certain clients are more comfortable meeting in places like this, believe it or not."

"Like who?"

He shrugged and took another sip. She'd thought about telling him the drinks were all the cheap stuff, but he'd surprised her by ordering Jim Beam in the first place—a fairly cheap, if well-regarded, bourbon.

"Oh, I represent all kinds of people," he said. "Everyone from local ministers to factory workers to people like the owners of clubs like this one. Take a step back and think in general terms. Imagine, say, pro athletes, rock stars, that kind of thing. You can imagine Dennis Rodman or Gene Simmons wanting to meet in a strip club, right?"

"Yeah, I guess so."

"Well, a lot of guys in the business world are in a sort of equal state of arrested development, even if they wear a suit instead of face paint and piercings. Bottom line: everyone needs a lawyer at some point. It's my job to accommodate all of them. In some cases, that means going into their worlds, into the places where they're comfortable, and I don't mind it a bit. You get to see all the different hues and tones when you go out among the people."

Charlie glanced at the dancer, who was still gyrating onstage with the snake strung across her shoulders, though she'd lost some of her clothing along the way.

"And who are you to judge if the people you're among just so happen to be half-nude and dry-humping a metal pole, right?" she said dryly.

Will shrugged.

"All of life is light and shadow, right? Well, I'd rather have more colors than fewer in my life. I know other people don't see it that way, and that's fine, too."

He tipped his head back and finished off his bourbon before he went on.

"It strikes me that a lot of us live in a sort of echo chamber these days. We surround ourselves with people who agree with us on everything— politics, art, entertainment. A lot of people might say a place like this is offensive on multiple levels, and I might even agree on some points. But who am I to impose my ideals on someone else? And what a boring, monotonous world it would be if I could."

Charlie eyeballed Will as he waved over their waitress and ordered another drink. His answer made sense. There were even qualities in it she found charming, and yet… well, Will had always been good with words. Had he merely found a way to make frequenting a strip club sound like some noble cause? Maybe he'd told a partial truth, concealed the ugly parts and played up the pretty ones.

"Dude's too damn slick for his own good," Allie said just above a whisper, as though Will might hear her.

"A lot of fancy talk, but I know why you really come here," Charlie said once Will was looking her way again.

"What's that?" he said.

"The wings."

CHAPTER FORTY-TWO

Having spent some time in the club, Charlie could see that her original plan would never work. It was too busy. There was no way she could walk up to any of these girls and ask them about Kara and Amber. The bouncers had eyes on the girls above all—protecting the merchandise.

Plan B it was, then. She'd need to sneak into the back, and she'd need Will's help to do it. At least she'd had the foresight to prep him for the possibility. He'd be going above and beyond to help her on this one.

Charlie downed the last of her drink and felt a rush as the alcohol entered her bloodstream. The top of her scalp tingled ever so slightly, and a numbness grabbed at her cheeks. A little liquid courage could help with this next step.

She met Will's eyes. Leaned in close to him.

"You ready to do this?" she asked.

Nodding once, he turned to face the crowd. Scanning. Picking out his target. She liked that he was being this strategic.

Part of her had expected some nerves from him when the moment arrived. He was about to tangle with security at a strip club, probably get a whole slew of people paying attention to him in the process. A smidge of stage fright would be normal as far as she was concerned. Instead, he seemed cockier than ever.

He strutted across the room, taking a sip of his drink along the way. She could see him making a show of scanning the room, his expression conveying how utterly unimpressed he was by everything around him. It occurred to her that this kind of thing must be fun for him. Manipulating people. Playing a role. Maybe that made sense. He'd described the courtroom as a kind of theater himself. Maybe he honed his swagger there, refined it into something he could turn off and on with the flick of some mental switch.

Along the far wall, he conferred with one of the bouncers, gesturing wildly. The bouncer leaned his head back and roared out a laugh she could hear over the music.

"He's way too good at this," Allie said.

"Yeah, maybe."

Now Will's body language changed again. He tightened up. Hands coming up as though to defend himself.

The bouncer roared out another guffaw, again tipping his head all the way back as though to point the laughter at the ceiling. Charlie realized that Will was acting out some joke. The bouncer wiped tears from his eyes and waved over another bouncer who was standing guard at the back hallway.

That was Charlie's cue. She rose from her seat, straightened the spangled skirt of her dress, and pressed forward into the crowded main floor. She crossed through the throngs of men crowding around the smaller stages where girls disrobed and gyrated.

At last she reached the clearing before the back hall. She tried her best to look nonchalant, to channel whatever cool indifference Will had going for him as he'd made his way up to the bouncer. And she resisted the urge to glance over her shoulder at him now, to check his progress with the second bouncer in particular. She thought maybe she could hear the three of them laughing, but it was hard to be sure over the blaring music.

She stepped into the hall, into the shadows. It was much darker here. Her eyes opened wide, trying to make out her surroundings.

She pushed through another set of doors, and there she saw it. The room she'd gotten to last time just before the bouncer grabbed her—the place where she'd heard girls' voices just beyond the door.

CHAPTER FORTY-THREE

Charlie eased open the heavy steel door, trying to get a peek as the slab of metal glided away. At first, she could only see the bright light shining in the growing slit of the doorway.

Then she saw the girls—six of them huddled before a pair of vanities, barely dressed, caking on makeup in the mirrors. They seemed younger than the dancers she'd seen on the floor. Fresh-faced and innocent-looking.

They all glanced up at her, gone quiet for a second, but their previous conversation resumed after the hitch. They weren't exactly surprised to see her, she thought.

"Anyway… What was I just saying?" a redhead with a long face and neck said, smearing more eyeliner around her fake lashes.

"You were talking about this stupid smoking law stuff," another girl said. This one had dark hair in a frizzy mess of crinkles atop her head.

"Right. Yeah. See, everything they do to try to restrict it just makes smoking seem cooler. Rebellious, you know? Vaping, too. When you outlaw something and try to repress it, you only make it more appealing."

"It's the forbidden fruit," Frizzy said.

"What?" Red said, turning her head. "Oh, right, yeah. That's it exactly. 'Tastes better 'cause it's stolen' is what I always say for that, but I can respect your, uh, biblical reference."

Charlie approached slowly as the two kept talking, almost like she was creeping up on a pack of small woodland animals, worried she might spook them into bolting.

A mousy girl turned to Charlie as she got close and spoke to her in a low voice. "Are you the new girl?"

Charlie hesitated a second before she answered, instantly falling into the suggested role. "Yeah. Sorry, I'm nervous. Not sure how all of this works. I mean, I guess I've never done anything like this. You know?"

The other girls all turned now, cooing and offering support. Comforting phrases peppered at her from all angles, the voices tangling over each other.

"Don't worry. You'll do great."

"Aw, you'll get the hang of it."

"Just stay strong."

"Thanks," Charlie said, wiping a fake tear from the corner of her eye. She took one of the seats near the left vanity, which one of the girls gave up for her.

"Jesus. Dial it back a little," Allie whispered. "You maybe don't remember what it's like to be young anymore, but these troubled youths have finely tuned bullshit detectors. They'll sniff out your waif act from a mile away if you lay it on too thick."

Charlie noticed that instead of standard stripper garb—like the schoolgirl outfit and leopard-print ensemble she'd spotted onstage—the girls back here all wore more traditional lingerie. Corsets and garters and other items that took more effort to remove.

"So could I maybe ask you some questions about what to expect?" Charlie said, turning to face the group. "It might help me calm down, I think."

They all nodded and vocalized various terms of agreement.

"What kind of stuff do you usually do?" Charlie asked.

Now they all fell quiet.

Red shrugged.

"You know," the long-faced girl said, turning back to the mirror. "Depends on what the guy wants, I guess."

Charlie licked her lips. She'd suspected something more than stripping since she walked through those doors. Now she was on the verge of confirming it.

"Like lap dances? That kind of thing?" Charlie said, keeping her voice small and tight.

Red chuckled at that.

"Well, no. Not like that. Maybe the occasional hand job if you're lucky. But typically… it's the other… the usual thing men pay girls like us for."

Charlie looked around the room as Red talked. It occurred to her that this was nowhere near the backstage area—that'd be on the other side of the building. This was like a separate operation from the strip club, essentially—prostitution being run out of the back of the building. Probably exactly why they kept such a discerning bouncer out front.

"I have another question, actually," Charlie said, pulling out the pictures of Kara and Amber. "Have any of you seen either of these girls before?"

The pictures changed hands, all of the faces in the room going somber. It was so quiet, Charlie could hear the light bulbs buzzing along the tops of the mirrors.

The other girls exchanged glances that Charlie read as frightened, but the mousy girl's eyes went wide, locked on the face in one of the photos.

"Her. It's been a few weeks now, but I seen her around a few times a while back."

Her index finger extended, its tip landing on Kara's chin in the photo. Just as the skin made contact with the glossy photo paper, the door behind them burst open, the steel slamming against the doorstop and reverberating like a tuning fork.

All heads turned to watch the bouncer enter the room. He did a double-take when he saw Charlie, stopped in his tracks.

His eyes narrowed, beady black marbles that made her intensely uncomfortable.

She tucked the photos away and grabbed a makeup poof from the table, dabbing powder at her nose, trying to play it cool. She could feel her pulse quicken in her neck, heart knocking in her chest.

The bouncer chuckled behind her. Came up beside her. Rolled his eyes once she made eye contact.

"Nice try, cop."

Then he grabbed her.

CHAPTER FORTY-FOUR

The bouncer lugged Charlie down the dark hallway to the door on the opposite side. She squirmed, struggled against his grip, but he had pinned her arms down, making her effort useless. It felt like trying to fight a sequoia.

She screamed for help, but the bass from the main stage area was so loud, she doubted anyone could hear her outside of this corridor.

Balancing her over his shoulder, he pulled at a retractable key ring attached to his belt loop and unlocked the deadbolt. The big steel door glided out of the way.

Inside they went. Charlie craned her neck to get a look at the room. Shadows everywhere. Too dark to make out much, save for some shelves along the back wall and some kind of large bulky thing just in front of them—probably a desk.

He flipped the light switches just inside the door, and after a moment of hesitation, the overhead bulbs flickered on.

It was an office of some sort, the middle of the room occupied by an old metal desk with drawers on either side. Bookcases along the wall were piled with three-ring binders and cardboard file boxes.

The bouncer plopped her down in one of the chairs facing the big desk, then went back to lock the door behind him. She noted that it was the kind of lock that required a key on either side.

She'd just dug her phone out of her purse when he ripped both out of her fingers, phone then purse.

"I don't think so," he said, holding her things out of reach.

He moved to the other side of the desk. Dug around in the drawers. Eventually he pulled free a set of keys.

"Don't think I'll be leaving the spares for you to dig out, either."

He scurried over to the door, surprisingly light on his feet for such a big piece of meat. Agile and quick.

"I'll be back, so behave yourself," he said over his shoulder.

He stepped through the doorway, his bulky form disappearing behind the steel. The last thing she heard was the telltale rattle and snick of the key turning the deadbolt before the room went silent.

She rushed to the door to try the handle. It was firmly locked, just as she knew it would be. She pounded on the door a few times with the heel of her hand, knowing it was useless. No one would hear it over the Mötley Crüe and Poison medley blaring out there.

She was trapped.

CHAPTER FORTY-FIVE

Charlie stood motionless with her hands still pressed on the locked steel door. *Now what? Think.*

She wheeled around, eyes scanning the desk. No landline there. No phone. No way out. She blinked, going still again, mind oddly blank.

"Don't just stand there, dummy," Allie said. "That blockhead just locked you in a room full of evidence, didn't he? Make yourself useful."

Allie was right. Charlie was trapped, yes, but not helpless. Who knew what information might be right here in this dingy office?

She lurched into action and began searching the room. The binders and boxes that filled the shelves along the wall were full of spreadsheets. Numbers. Dollars and cents.

"Paper copies of all of this?" Allie said. "Why? Someone tell these people about Excel and cloud storage already."

Next she rifled through the desk drawers. Two staplers. Paper clips. A pile of pens and pencils. More sheets of financial reports, this time in manila folders. Nothing of use.

She closed this last drawer. Took a breath. What to do next? Her eyes remained on the desk. Fixed on the drawer handles. Some itch in her hand told her to open them again. To be thorough.

After the briefest hesitation, her fingers obeyed. Clasped around the bottom right drawer handle. Peeled it open.

Still nothing. The same pile of writing implements as last time. But something was off.

She looked at the face of the drawer and then inside again. It was too shallow.

She pulled everything out and threw it on the floor. Some of the pens skittered and rolled along the tile floor, a strange sound in the quiet.

Her fingers splayed along the wooden bottom of the drawer. Scrabbling over it. Searching. She felt it along the back seam—the minor indentation that she knew must be the fingerhold. Her suspicion had been correct.

She pulled up the false bottom, a thin veneer of wood. It let out a little cracking sound as it scraped out of the drawer.

At last the light revealed what lay beneath.

Several bundles wrapped in layers of clear plastic and sealed with packing tape. The package on top was open. Charlie picked one of the pencils off the floor and used the tip to drag out some of the contents without touching it, though she already had a pretty good idea of what was inside. Out came a tiny Ziploc baggie filled with white pills, each one stamped with a strange design. Just like the ones she'd found under the driver's seat of the No Fat Chix SUV.

CHAPTER FORTY-SIX

By the time the heavy footsteps in the hall announced the bouncer's return, the desk drawer was in order once more—untouched so far as he'd be able to tell. He fumbled at the door audibly, zipping that key ring out from his belt, the key twitching at the hole before finding its way and entering the lock, the doorknob squeaking as he turned it.

Charlie rushed back to her chair and fished a hand down into her boot, seeking the hard object nestled there. Her fingers clasped the one thing the bouncer hadn't confiscated—the mini stun gun snugged against her ankle. She pulled the weapon free and had everything ready just as he barged into the room.

As soon as she could see his shadow falling over the floor, she moaned and pretended to pass out. Her back arched, her whole body going slack and sliding down the chair onto the floor, eyes closed.

The bouncer gasped. It was such a ridiculous sound coming out of the big brute that Charlie almost laughed, fighting to keep the twitch of a smile off her lips.

His feet pattered over the floor in an odd shuffle. She could hear the concern in his steps, some telltale worry conveyed in the staccato rhythm.

The footsteps drew right up on her. He stooped. Brought his face so close to hers that she could feel his breath on her cheeks and across the bridge of her nose. He reeked of sweat and some kind of musky aftershave.

No hesitation. Charlie jammed the stun gun into his neck. Heard the crackle as it sent a few thousand volts into the meat of him.

He stiffened. Spine going ramrod-straight as though the electricity were pulling taut all the strings of this meathead puppet. She searched his face, saw the light go out in his eyes.

And then he came crashing down on top of her, the dead weight of his bulky upper body draped over her face and most of her torso.

All of the breath heaved out of her on impact. His weight settled on her, hard and heavy. It felt like a tree trunk had just fallen onto her.

"Timber!" Allie shouted.

Charlie squirmed, legs kicking, hips bucking. Shifting his bulk was like trying to move a side of beef.

She worked her arms free and tried to push him off of her. She caught a glimpse of the office ceiling as his hulking form moved enough to unblock the light. Her fingers mashed into his wide and fleshy cheeks, and she lifted his slack face above hers. His head quivered before flopping back down when she lost her grip.

Charlie rested a moment. Took a few deep breaths. Working this way, the most she could manage was shoving his head around on his limp noodle neck. She needed to change tactics, get at the torso, shift the bulk of him to get out from under.

She slid her hands to the place where the shoulder and chest met and rolled him aside enough to shimmy her hips and then legs out, slithering back and forth like a snake. The removal of the pressure made her feel strangely weightless as she got to her feet, the sense of freedom light and airy.

The door lay open before her. She rushed out of the office, into the dark of the hallway. The girls' room was straight ahead, the main floor to the right. Both ways looked clear.

She headed back toward the club. Best to get Will and slip out. They'd figure out the next step once they were away from this place, probably call in Zoe and the cavalry.

The pulse of the bass in the next room swelled as she neared the door. She could feel the rattle of it in her sternum.

That was when the euphoria hit. Roiling on her scalp. Tingling in her chest. Some floating, soaring feeling stirring in her skull. She felt incredible. That airiness persisted, an astounding physical sensation. She was free. Escaping.

Then she heard the bouncer call out from behind her. It sounded like the big lug had peeled himself off the floor, and now he was screaming into a phone or walkie.

"She's headed for the main floor now. Grab her!"

CHAPTER FORTY-SEVEN

As soon as she slipped through the door onto the main floor of the Red Velvet Lounge, a crew of bouncers closed in on her. An angry mass of deltoids, traps, and pecs twitching their way across the room.

The strobe effect of the lights made them look like stop-motion animation, hunks of chiseled clay encroaching. Every blink advanced them closer. Closer. Closer.

Will lunged into the picture then, his movements also lurching in the pulses of light and darkness. He tried to intervene, putting himself between her and the closest bouncer, his arms raised in a disarming gesture—his body language akin to a hostage in a bank robbery. Hands up. Head shaking in that slow-motion *we don't want any trouble* way.

The bouncer hurled a meaty paw at him, the right cross almost too fast to see. Everyone heard it, though. The punch cracked audibly, even over the blare of the hair metal.

Will's skull snapped straight back. His hands flew up to cup at the point of impact as he bent at the waist.

Charlie shot forward with her stun gun, zapping the bouncer under the chin. The weapon sizzled against his flesh and released the faint odor of ozone.

He went limp and belly-smacked the floor, convulsing a few times before going still.

Charlie whirled to face the circle of others closing on them. Too many. This wasn't going to work. She and Will backed up toward the crowd huddling around the bar.

The next bouncer advanced, thick arms splayed at his sides. To her surprise, Will once again stepped forward to protect her. No hands up, though. This time when the bouncer swung at him, he ducked.

The haymaker swooped over Will's head and caught an unsuspecting drunk sitting at the bar flush on the temple. The impact sounded like two coconuts smacking together.

The drunk went down, managing to rake a couple of beers out of other patrons' hands on his way to the floor. It set off a chain reaction of pushing and shoving that worked its way down the length of the bar.

Beer went flying in all directions. First, spatter flung everywhere in roping tendrils, then a mist of it. Foam slopped to the floor and bar, and a couple of unlucky dudes sporting silk shirts now found themselves plastered with Pabst Blue Ribbon. Charlie watched them glance down at their sodden clothes with expressions of disbelief.

Two mugs shattered on the floor, glassy explosions that got all heads turned away from the boobs. That was when the pushing and shoving escalated.

Confusion.

Aggression.

Something wild rippled through the crowd all at once. Some switch flipping the mob mentality for violence on. Even Charlie could feel it.

Everyone went apeshit.

The pushing and shoving turned to kicking and punching, headbutting and stomping, elbows and knees flying, bodies flinging at each other. The brawl was underway.

An older man in denim overalls aimed a punch at the throat of one of the bouncers. The meathead dropped to his knees, hands clutching at his inverted Adam's apple, eyes watering.

Will kept shoving the Goliaths away from them, directing the big sides of beef into the mosh-pit-type area near the bar. The violence swirled there like a turbulent sea.

Charlie watched a man clamber up onto the bar, swinging a glass vodka bottle like a baseball bat. He shattered the bottle over a behemoth's head, and when the impact didn't seem to faze the brute, he thrust it forward to try to stab him with the broken edge. The bouncer dodged the jagged weapon, surprisingly agile for his size.

And then Charlie was being swept away, caught up in the jostle of the crowd.

The lights came up. The music cut out, the MC's voice demanding that everyone "Break it up!" over the PA. But it was too late for that. Even the strippers retreated now, tripping over the stage in their haste to disappear behind the curtains.

Charlie found Will's eyes in the chaos. They needed to get out of here.

CHAPTER FORTY-EIGHT

Outside the club, Charlie held Will's phone to her ear. The dispatcher had told her to stay on the line until the police arrived, and so she did, pacing among the parked cars. She couldn't pry her eyes away from the stone facade of the Red Velvet Lounge, however.

The yelling and smashing of glass could be heard from outside. Violent sounds, stark and striking against the quiet.

"Here we go," Will said, breaking her concentration.

Somewhat reluctantly, Charlie shifted her focus from the building to see what he was excited about.

The police lights crested a hill in the distance, red and blue twirling over the snowy asphalt, lighting up the trees along the side of the road. No sirens, Charlie noted. Out here in the sticks, they probably didn't need them too often.

Three state police cruisers knifed into the lot, bounding up the ramp onto the blacktop, front ends bouncing up and down, almost bottoming out. Their tires squealed as they veered around the rows of cars and skidded through that final sharp turn to angle themselves toward the front door.

The first car jerked to the left and then stopped abruptly. The others followed its lead, parking just shy of the front walk, one after another, each car diagonal to the building.

"They're here now," Charlie said into the phone, suddenly remembering the dispatcher on the other end.

"You're confirming that police have arrived at the scene now, ma'am?"

"Yep. Thanks for your help."

Charlie hung up and returned the phone to Will, the night air cold against her palm, which had gone clammy keeping the thing pressed to her ear. She rubbed her fingers into the heel of her hand a couple times, as though that might help dry the dampness. Then she turned back to watch the stunning conclusion of the night.

A total of just four Michigan state troopers climbed out of the three vehicles, all of them sporting military-style crew cuts. They convened for a moment, the tallest of the men gesturing toward the door, probably laying out some basic tactical approach. The others all bobbed their heads as he talked.

Part of Charlie wondered if they shouldn't wait for more officers to arrive, but there was no reason to believe anyone inside was armed. It was just your standard barroom brawl. Between their guns and whatever other gadgets the state troopers had handy, the officers would likely gain control of the scene quickly and without incident.

Finally, the men drew their weapons, all of them aiming them at the ground, and charged the building, the tall guy in front. Even something about the way they moved seemed military now—a uniformly stiff jog that carried them over the cement. The lead officer wrenched the door open, and one by one they disappeared through the opening.

"Ready to watch the show?" Will said, cackling. He once again rested his butt on the front end of his car. "Can't wait to see this parade of ogres hauled out in cuffs."

Charlie thought he seemed a little too giddy about all of this—but then he didn't know about the girls in the back room yet, or even about the ecstasy. To him, this was all a bit of vengeance for the vicious punch to the eye he'd taken from the bouncer.

She turned again to look at him, to really look. His eye was swelling, seeming to bulge and grow before her eyes. It already looked a shade darker, and she knew the appearance would deteriorate by tomorrow morning.

"Your eye looks terrible," she said.

He smiled again, gesturing at the side of his face.

"This? Ah, but chicks think this kind of thing is cool, Charlie. They see a guy walk in with an eye swollen and purple like a ripe plum, and they're all like, 'Who's *this* guy?'" He gave one of his characteristic shrugs. "Anyway, it's only my eye. I have another one."

Charlie chuckled a little at that.

"You should see the other guy, too," Will said. "After the police beat the shit out of him, I mean. I've seen up close the damage they can do with those nightsticks, and I imagine they don't care too much for the Muscle Beach types. It ain't going to be pretty."

His eyes went wide then, and Charlie followed his gaze back to the front doors of the club.

Word must have spread quickly about the police being on the scene, as a bunch of patrons spilled out through the doors now, a trickle and then a steady flow. A couple of opportunistic types had taken care to loot a few bottles of expensive booze during the riot, hugging them in their arms like precious treasure, but Charlie knew that they were really getting the cheapest of cheap swill dressed up in fancy bottles.

The stream of people kept coming, so many that Charlie began to wonder if the cops had opted to primarily clear the place out and only arrest the most egregious offenders. That didn't bode well for the guy who'd smashed a Belvedere bottle over a bouncer's head, but it was probably the most efficient way to end this mess—more like clearing out a keg party than anything.

Additional police vehicles arrived in the minutes that followed: three black Salem County sheriff cruisers, a dark blue Michigan state police truck which matched the first three cruisers on the scene, and a couple of smaller white cruisers belonging to the nearest police department in Port Blanc, a tiny rural town that probably barely even needed their own department, truth be told. Maybe the Red Velvet Lounge kept them busy, though.

Charlie spotted Zoe among the cluster of law enforcement officers and waved from across the parking lot, but Zoe was too focused on doing her job to notice.

By the time the last pair of officers entered the building, the trickle of foot traffic coming out had all but stopped, and the building had gone strangely still. The anticipation built. Charlie felt goosebumps plump along her forearms.

The door burst open as though kicked, and out walked one of the muscle-bound leviathans, his arms pinned behind his back. He scowled, bottom teeth bared, swiveling his head as though expecting a crowd and finding none. A state trooper filed along behind him, looking strangely small and old behind the big brute.

"Finally," Will said. "I thought they were going to let everyone off with a warning or something dumb like that."

Charlie puffed something of a laugh from her nostrils.

"Weren't you the one railing on about how local law enforcement is out of control the other day? Story changes pretty quickly, doesn't it?"

"Whoa, whoa, whoa. Now hold on. That was different." Will aimed a finger at her. "None of the cops punched me in the face or put their hands on you. These juiced-up apes deserve whatever they got coming to 'em."

The stream of perp walks continued, building up some speed now—a parade of bouncers with black eyes and bloody noses, each of them sporting cuffs. The loudmouth from the front door detail came out looking like he'd had a nose job performed by way of fists, his schnoz all dented and crooked and swollen. Charlie started to slow clap the way he'd done the first time she'd gotten caught snooping around, adding in a thumbs up when he scowled in her direction.

After the bouncers, a pair of polo-shirted guys exited. Charlie figured they must be the managers or owners. While they lacked the musculature of the security guys, they still looked imposing in their own way, a strange and dangerous energy in their eyes.

Charlie watched Zoe file out of the building and load one of the meatheads into a cruiser. With her cargo secured in the backseat, she rounded the rear of the car and headed to where Charlie and Will stood observing the scene.

Zoe held something in her hands awkwardly, and as she got closer, Charlie realized it was her purse.

"Should have known you'd be all mixed up in this," Zoe said, handing the bag over. "Thought you might want this back."

"Thanks," Charlie said, peeking quickly inside to check that everything was there.

Zoe's gaze fell on Will and his eye, which was now partially swollen shut.

"Yikes. Nice shiner."

Will grinned.

"Pretty cool, huh?"

Satisfied that the bouncers hadn't pilfered anything important from her bag, Charlie slung the handle over her arm and focused on Zoe again.

"Did you search the office yet?"

"We did. Found the drugs just where you said they'd be. Port Blanc PD is gonna wanna throw a parade in your honor. They've been trying to find dirt on these guys for years, and you just served it up on a silver platter."

"And what about the girls? At least one of them recognized Kara Dawkins, and said she'd been around up until a few weeks ago."

"We'll get official statements from them before they're released," Zoe assured her.

"Kara's only seventeen, you know," Charlie reminded Zoe. "I wouldn't be surprised if some of the others are underage."

"It'll be handled. Trust me." Zoe snapped her fingers. "Oh hey, I forgot to tell you. We solved the Jason Spadafore mystery."

"Mystery?"

"You know… how he bashed that guy over the head for what seemed like no reason?"

"Oh, right. So there was a reason?"

"Yeah. Turns out Jason and his girlfriend split up recently. I guess he was holding out hope for a reconciliation, but she has moved on to greener pastures."

Charlie could see where this was headed.

"And Jason decided to wallop the 'greener pastures' in the skull with a pool cue?"

"Yes, ma'am." Zoe's head bobbed up and down. "That's about the long and short of it."

Charlie remembered Jason's angry phone call and the one snippet she'd been able to make out: "a lying bitch." Well, that certainly fit. She wasn't sure she'd ever considered Jason a true suspect, certainly not after what she'd found in the club tonight. Still, she hated unanswered questions, and now she had one less on her plate.

Glancing back at the building, Zoe tucked her thumbs in her belt. "I better head back inside. The ladies started getting antsy once they saw their bosses being led out in handcuffs."

"You'll let me know what you find out?"

Already trudging toward the front doors of the Red Velvet Lounge, Zoe spun around and walked backward a few paces.

"Yeah. I'll call you tomorrow."

"You're the best," Charlie called out.

Zoe gave a dismissive wave.

"The way I see it, you owe me like a dozen apple fritters at this point."

Zoe disappeared through the open front doors. At the sound of the police truck's engine roaring to life, Will turned to Charlie, pushing himself to his feet.

"Well, that was eventful." Will spun his keys around his index finger. "Should we call it a night?"

"I guess so," Charlie said. "Only I think I should drive."

"Why?"

"Because I have two good eyes and didn't just take a blow to the head."

"Fair enough," he said, tossing his keys over to her. "My head is starting to throb a bit. Is it just me or was that guy's fist the size of a honey-baked ham?"

Will said little on the drive back to Salem Island, and by the time they reached the parking lot outside Charlie's apartment, she could tell by the grimace on his face that the pain was starting to get to him.

"Why don't you come up and get some Tylenol? I probably have something we can put on your eye, too."

She expected some kind of quip from him, but he only nodded, looking miserable. Their feet drummed against the metal steps as they climbed up to the apartment. Will paused inside the door.

"I forgot to ask before," he said, his gaze lingering on the blank walls, meager furniture, and a stack of yet-to-be-unpacked cardboard boxes against one wall, "but who did your decorating?"

Charlie pointed at the mattress, secretly glad that he was making jokes again. She'd started to worry there for a minute.

"Sit."

Will obeyed, lowering himself to perch on one corner of the bed. In the kitchen, Charlie snatched a bottle of acetaminophen from a drawer and then filled a glass of water at the sink. When Will lifted his arm to down two of the tablets, her attention was suddenly drawn to a dark red spatter on his sleeve.

"There's blood all over your shirt."

Will tilted his arm to see.

"Huh," he said, totally nonchalant. "I don't think it's mine."

"I might be able to rinse it out if it hasn't set. Gimme," she said, waiting while he unbuttoned and removed the shirt.

She filled the sink with water to wash Will's shirt, then dug out a bag of frozen peas from her freezer and handed it over.

"Lie back and put this on your eye," she said.

Sprawling out on the bed, Will rested his head on one of the pillows and let out a sigh of satisfaction. He squinted over at her through his good eye.

"You know, if this was a thinly veiled attempt to get me into your bed, it worked."

Charlie scoffed and rolled her eyes.

"Oh yeah… every time I look at that puffy saddlebag of an eye you've got, I get the strongest urge to just tear off my panties."

"I don't know," Will said, yawning. "You might have to take a number. Did you notice Zoe checking me out?"

"She's gay."

"I know. But that's what I've been trying to tell you. This black eye magic is no joke. No woman is immune to its powers."

Charlie shook her head, dousing the stains on Will's shirt with dish soap.

"This is it, Charles," Allie said. "You've got him right where you want him."

"Don't start up with this again."

"Oh, please. Don't tell me you brought him all the way up here, and *now* you're going to chicken out. You've been fantasizing about this since you were sixteen."

"I have not. You were the boy-crazy one, not me."

When Charlie glanced over her shoulder at Will, his eyes were closed. She took the opportunity to study him openly. His face. His lean chest. His long arms folded over his bare stomach. OK, she probably *had* fantasized about a Will scene like this a time or two—maybe without the pack of frozen peas draped over half of his face.

"Ha! I knew it," Allie said.

Charlie swallowed. She left the shirt to soak and took a step closer to where Will lay. She knelt next to the bed, watching his chest rise and fall. Slowly. Rhythmically.

"Will?"

He didn't answer.

"Oh, come on," Allie moaned. "He fell asleep?!"

Smiling to herself, Charlie carefully removed the bag of peas from Will's face and returned them to the freezer. Then she climbed in beside him and closed her eyes, waiting for sleep to overtake her.

CHAPTER FORTY-NINE

Charlie awoke the next morning to a knock at the apartment door. The clock on her phone said 8:12 a.m. She slid on a pair of sweatpants as she stumbled to the door.

The lock rattled as her sleep-stupid fingers struggled to unlatch the deadbolt. Finally, she opened the door.

"Gooooooood morning," Zoe said, mysteriously full of energy at this unholy hour.

Charlie pawed at the corner of her eye with a knuckle.

"Can I help you, officer?"

"They're interviewing the owner of the Red Velvet Lounge in a bit. Sheriff said it'd be OK if you came down to observe the interrogation."

That got Charlie's attention.

"For real?"

"Wouldn't be much of a prank, would it?" Zoe crossed her arms. "Everyone's so darn pleased with the bust that I guess they're feeling mighty generous. Also, your good friend Zoe Wyatt might have put in a good word for you. Reminded them all that it was you who called it in."

"This is gonna cost me, isn't it?"

"Oh yeah." Zoe nodded. "You owe me big time."

The hinges on the door squeaked as Charlie threw it wide and stepped back, waving her friend inside.

"Come on in. It'll only take me a minute to get dressed."

Zoe's eyes swept the apartment, and she raised her left eyebrow.

"I love what you've done with the place." When her gaze fell on the bed, her right eyebrow joined the first. A devilish smile spread over her lips. "Hello, Will."

A shirtless Will sat half-propped against a pillow in Charlie's bed, blinking groggily. He raised a hand in Zoe's direction.

"Morning, Zo."

"What have you two kids been up to?" Zoe asked, and Charlie could hear a ridiculous level of glee in her voice.

Charlie swiped a key from the bedside table and tossed it into Will's lap. He picked it up and examined it as if it were some mysterious artifact he'd never seen before.

"Spare key," Charlie explained. "So you can lock up when you leave."

Will closed his fist around the key and shook it, a child's look of awe still occupying his features.

"With great power comes great responsibility," he said, staring into the middle distance. "I will guard it with my life."

Zoe tittered. She seemed to be highly amused by the whole scenario, standing in the doorway with that Cheshire Cat grin on her face. Charlie nudged her out the door.

Zoe waggled her fingers at Will.

"Goodbye, Will."

Charlie pulled the door shut behind her. The metal stairs down to the parking lot sounded like a steel drum under their collective footsteps. Zoe beamed all the way down to her car, shooting Charlie periodic glances.

"After all that business where you tried to deny totally having the hots for him in school," Zoe said. "How full of shit are you?"

"Nothing happened, if you must know."

"Uh-huh. Riiight."

Charlie grumbled something unintelligible and climbed into the car. They rode a while in silence before Zoe started in again.

"Hey, man, I'm happy for you. You're cute together."

Allie made a disgusted, gagging sound at the same moment that Charlie said, "Oh, barf."

"What?" Zoe asked, taking a right.

Charlie gestured to the Salem County jail, which had come into view on the road ahead.

"Can we maybe put this on hold until later? I'd rather not walk in here looking like a total amateur."

Zoe pointed at Charlie's legs.

"That why you wore sweatpants?"

Charlie glanced down at herself. In her haste to leave, she'd forgotten to change.

"Why didn't you say anything?"

Zoe shrugged.

"I thought it would be funny?"

Allie cackled.

Charlie crossed her arms over her chest and glared out the window.

"I hate you."

CHAPTER FIFTY

The owner of the Red Velvet Lounge was Silas Demetrio, a swarthy little man with thick eyebrows and a permanent sneer. Acne scars pocked his cheeks, evenly divoting his skin like hammered metal. Despite the circumstances, the guy didn't look frightened in the slightest.

Charlie watched from the observation room as he mostly declined to talk, deferring questions and waiting for his attorney to arrive.

"Robbie Turner. That's all I'm saying. He's the one that brought the girl around, OK? Said he was her… *manager*, I think he called it. That's about all I know. Want to know more? Talk to him."

A detective named Peterson wiped at the corner of his mouth.

"By manager, you mean to imply he was Kara Dawkins' pimp, correct? On your property?"

Two lines formed between Demetrio's brows as his scowl deepened.

"No. We don't allow nothing like that." He held up his hand like a crossing guard halting traffic. "No way. She wanted to dance? Fine. But that was the end of it. We run a pretty tight ship, I think."

A slight smile formed on Peterson's face.

"A tight ship, eh?" he repeated. "So the fact that she was under-age, that would be representative of this 'tight ship' that you run?"

Demetrio's thin lips practically disappeared as he pressed his mouth into a tight line.

"All I would have known was the ID she showed me, OK? The ID says eighteen and up, then as far as I'm concerned, it's all above board. Not like I'm running deep background checks on every girl who shows up looking for a job. Someone shows me convincing forged documents, how am I responsible?"

Still smiling, Peterson nodded.

"Yeah, well, the court will have their say."

"Perfect. In the meantime, you can direct all questions to my attorney when he gets here. I'm done talking."

"No need to get testy," the detective said, backing off the pressure. "We're just talking here."

Demetrio just shook his head. When he spoke again, he did it through a predatory smile.

"Lawyer."

Detective Peterson gathered his papers, tucked them in a folder. He pushed his chair out from the small table and stood.

"Robbie Turner, eh?" he said.

"That's right. Robbie. Turner. Other than that?" Demetrio leaned back in his seat. "Lawyer."

Charlie and Zoe studied the club owner through the two-way glass.

"What do you think?" Charlie asked.

On the other side of the window, Silas Demetrio drummed his fingers on the table, tapping out a random beat.

"He seems remarkably calm for a guy who's got a one-way ticket to prison," Zoe said, crossing her arms. "We've confirmed that at least two of the other girls from the club are underage. Combined with the drugs we found in the office, they'll get shut down for sure. He can blame this Robbie Turner all he wants. The fact is, he's the captain of this ship, and it's going down."

"But what about Kara and Amber? Is Demetrio tied up in all of that?"

Zoe gestured at the man in the next room.

"He already admitted that Kara Dawkins worked there."

"But no one from the club remembers seeing Amber?"

"None of the girls who work there now," Zoe said. "Amber's been away at school for a couple years. So maybe she *used* to work there."

"Maybe."

"I mean, you found that matchbook for the club in her room, right?"

"Yeah."

Zoe spread her hands as if to indicate that this was proof of a solid connection between Amber and the club.

"Before you said that was—and I quote—'extremely weak sauce.'"

"Yeah, well… that was before we knew how scummy the place was."

The door to the observation room swung open, and Detective Peterson poked his head in.

"Demetrio's lawyer just got here, but I thought you might want to see this," he said and handed Zoe a printout of Robbie Turner's criminal record.

They scanned the first page. Robert Turner, Jr., was a twenty-two-year-old Caucasian male with a history of arrests going back to his teen years for shoplifting, possession, retail fraud, drunk and disorderly conduct. The list went on.

"Looks like we have ourselves a budding small-time criminal," Zoe said. "He gets around, too. He's got busts spread over several counties. Salem, Washtenaw, Kalamazoo."

Zoe tilted the page and squinted at the grainy driver's license photo.

"Yeah, you know, I think I kinda know this guy."

"Really?" Charlie asked, intrigued.

"I mean, just a vague familiarity. We see so many run-of-the-mill delinquents like this, they all kind of bleed together. But he's got kind of a squirrelly look to him that makes me think I've seen him come through a few times. I think maybe his hair is different now."

Zoe flipped the page, revealing a section with the heading "SMT," which stood for scars, marks, and tattoos. It noted a scar on the left hand and a tattoo on the left forearm. A black-and-white photo of the inked arm showed a skull and dagger, with a banner wrapping around both that read, "Death Before Dishonor."

"Holy shit," Charlie said, staring at the photo, remembering now. She could see the blurred shape in her mind's eye. The undulating shadows on the wall. A chase through the snow.

She pointed at the page in Zoe's hands.

"That's the dude who's nailing Sharon Ritter."

CHAPTER FIFTY-ONE

Back in Zoe's car, they zoomed toward the east side of town. It was time to pay Robbie Turner a visit.

As they drove, a discussion with Will from a couple days earlier suddenly sprang to Charlie's mind.

"Did you hit Will in the face with a rock when you were kids?"

Zoe adjusted her glasses, eyes on the ceiling.

"I thought he'd duck."

"What?"

"When I threw the rock," Zoe said. "I faked him out a few times, and he kept ducking. So when I actually threw it, I thought he'd do the same. Instead he just stood there like an idiot and got hit in the face."

"I see. So it's *his* fault the rock hit him."

"That's not what I'm saying," Zoe insisted, her cheeks flushing. "I felt horrible about it, by the way. It was a big rock and it hit him—BAM!—right below his left eye. But you don't know what it was like growing up next door to him. He was like Bart Simpson. One time, he melted a hole in one of my Barbie dolls with a magnifying glass. And do you remember that summer they had to close down all the beaches because of high bacteria levels?"

"Yeah, sort of."

"I was seven. Will convinced me the bacteria story was a lie to cover up the real reason they'd closed the beaches. A shark was loose in Lake St. Clair and several kids had gone missing."

Charlie chuckled.

"I didn't dip a toe in the lake that summer. I was terrified."

They reached the address on Robbie Turner's driver registration, and Zoe parked across the street from the crumbling old apartment building.

"So we can tie Robbie Turner to Kara Dawkins, since he was the one who brought her in to the Red Velvet Lounge," Zoe said.

"Correct."

"And we can tie him to Amber Spadafore through her mother, whom he is—as you so eloquently put it—nailing."

"Also correct."

"But what about Amber herself? You think he's nailing her, too?"

"Ugh," Charlie said, grimacing at the thought. "I hope not."

Zoe unbuckled her seatbelt and opened her door.

"Ready?"

Charlie shadowed her down the snowy sidewalk, eyeballing the brick building Robbie Turner called home. The whole place looked like it might cave in on itself in a strong wind.

Zoe held the front door aside, and Charlie entered a dank foyer ahead of her. In its prime, the building had probably once been quite lovely, with cove ceilings and arched doorways, but now it was in a state of decay. Cracked plaster. Peeling paint.

At the end of a dim passage that smelled of stale cigarette smoke and wet dog, Zoe paused before a door. A brass plaque marked this apartment as 1F.

"This is it," she said with a nod.

She lifted her fist to knock, but Charlie stopped her before her knuckles made contact.

"Wait."

"What?"

"Are you gonna do the standard cop knock?"

"The what?"

"Cops have this way of knocking. Very aggressive. Like, 'Open the door, or we'll kick it down.'"

Zoe's lips quirked up on the right side. It was clear she wasn't amused.

"I'm just saying, with Robbie Turner's history, he probably knows the knock."

With a melodramatic roll of her eyes, Zoe stepped back and tumbled her hand toward the door, giving Charlie leave to do the knocking herself.

Charlie gave the door four light taps. A neighborly knock.

Noises came from inside the apartment. Shuffling footsteps. Groaning floorboards.

The door swung aside, revealing a middle-aged man in a red plaid bathrobe. Two pale stick legs protruded from the bottom hem and disappeared into a pair of ratty slippers.

He sniffed and said, "Hey," smirking slightly at Charlie in a way he probably thought was charming but wasn't. Then his eyes slid over to Zoe, and he stood up straighter.

"What is this?" he asked. "If that old hag upstairs is saying I got the stereo on too loud again, I wasn't even playing music."

"We're looking for Robbie Turner," Zoe said.

The man relaxed at that, propping one shoulder against the door frame.

"Ah. Shoulda known." He ran his hand through his thinning hair, stirring it into a shaggy mess. "What'd the little punk do now?"

"Is he here?" Zoe asked.

"Nah. Kicked his ass out a couple months ago."

"And your name, sir?"

Even though Zoe was the one asking, he stared at Charlie when he answered.

"Wayne Kelly. And who might you be?"

He adjusted his stance, revealing quite a bit of one thin, pasty thigh. Between that and the triangle of sparsely haired chest, Charlie began to feel more than a little uncomfortable.

"I think we all know that Wayne here isn't wearing *anything* under that robe," Allie said.

"I'm Deputy Wyatt." Zoe pointed a thumb at Charlie. "And this is my colleague, Miss Winters. Have you seen or spoken to Robbie since he moved out?"

Pursing his lips, Wayne fiddled with the tie of his bathrobe. Charlie winced. That tie was the only thing standing between her and him.

"We ain't exactly on speaking terms. Little fucker owes me three months of rent."

"I see."

"When he left, he stole my guitar and a whole rotisserie chicken I had in the fridge."

"He stole a chicken?" Zoe asked.

Her eyes flicked over to Charlie, who had to bite down on her cheek to keep from smiling.

"Yes, ma'am. A rotisserie, like I said."

"Surely the fact that it was a *rotisserie* chicken bumps this up from a misdemeanor to a felony," Allie said.

Zoe hooked her thumbs around her gun belt.

"Any idea where he might be living now?"

Wayne scratched the week's worth of stubble on his chin.

"Nope."

Producing a card from her pocket, Zoe handed it to Wayne.

"Well, we appreciate your help today, Mr. Kelly. If you do hear from Robbie or get an idea of where he might be, I'd appreciate it if you'd give me a call."

Wayne's bloodshot gaze ogled first the card, then Charlie.

"What about you? *You* got a card?" Wayne twirled the bathrobe tie the way a burlesque dancer might spin the end of a feather boa.

"Fresh out," Charlie said, backing away.

She followed Zoe out, feeling Wayne's creeping gaze on her back as she went. Once outside, they both took in deep breaths of fresh air.

"So, do we believe him? Or is he covering for Robbie?"

"Only one way to find out," Charlie said, scampering down the front steps and skirting around the corner of the building.

The dumpster positioned near the back of the building was overflowing with trash. Beside it, a hideous couch with orange upholstery was propped against the wall. Charlie lowered it to the snowy ground, getting a whiff of cat piss as she did. She scooted the sofa closer to the wall of the building, just beneath one of the last two windows on this side.

Scrambling up onto one arm of the sofa, she cupped her hands around her face and pressed her nose to the scuzzy glass.

"This is… I can't be doing this," Zoe said.

"*You're* not doing this," Charlie said, squinting to see through the haze. "I am."

This window looked in on a small bedroom. Charlie spotted a Playboy Playmate calendar from 2016 tacked to the wall. On the bed, a pair of plaid flannel pants that matched the bathrobe Wayne had been wearing sat in a heap.

Bouncing across the length of the sofa, Charlie moved to the next window. Another bedroom. This one was empty aside from a stripped mattress on the floor and a Pepsi bottle that looked suspiciously like it was filled with piss. On the wood frame over the door, something familiar caught her eye: a bumper sticker reading, "No Fat Chix." Robbie was absolutely passionate about that, it seemed. The corner of this decal was torn and rumpled, like someone had tried to scrape it off and quickly gave up.

Hopping down to the snow, Charlie dusted her hands.

"Shockingly, I think dear Wayne was being truthful with us. Robbie's room looks abandoned."

"Well, crap," Zoe said.

As they trudged back to Zoe's cruiser, the radio on her belt blipped out a mishmash of cop jargon that Charlie didn't understand.

Zoe picked up the handset.

"Ten-four, on my way," she said, then turned to Charlie. "I gotta head back to the station. I'll drop you at your place?"

Charlie nodded and kicked at a loose stone. It went skittering over the blacktop.

Zoe must have sensed the frustration she was feeling, because she reached out and clapped Charlie on the back.

"Robbie may not be here, but we'll find him. He's gotta be panicking at this point. He wrecked his car. His boss got busted. He'll screw up somewhere, and we'll get him."

"I'm sure you're right," Charlie said, but the words sounded hollow in her ears.

CHAPTER FIFTY-TWO

Charlie schlepped up to her apartment, trying to shake off the funk that had settled over her. Zoe had continued trying to cheer her up on the ride, reminding her that there was an APB out on Robbie Turner. But Charlie couldn't stop thinking about how she'd almost had him—he'd been literally within arm's reach the night she'd chased him through the woods. So damn close.

She unlocked the door to the apartment and dropped her bag inside. There was a note from Will on the bed.

C-
Call me when you want to stir up more trouble.
-W

It brought a brief smile to her face before she went back to brooding about losing Robbie Turner. She dropped onto the edge of the bed and hunched forward, propping her elbows on her knees.

He got kicked out of his apartment. Where would a twenty-two-year-old in trouble go?

Charlie's head snapped up, and she hustled into the kitchenette, where her laptop sat open on the counter. She typed in "Robert Turner Salem Island" and hit the enter key. The second result was a local address for Robert and Felicia Turner. Young Robbie's parents lived on the island.

*

Robbie's parents lived in a single-story ranch house bordered by a row of skeletal lilac bushes. A pontoon boat covered with a tarp squatted next to the garage. Charlie peeked into the garage as she passed. It was empty, but that didn't necessarily mean no one was home.

The driveway and sidewalk had been freshly shoveled, and crystals of rock salt crackled under her feet as she approached the front door. She knocked against a steel screen door, the metal cold against her knuckles.

Through a small pane of decorative glass on the door, she spied an L-shaped beige sectional taking up most of the floor space. Flat-screen TV mounted on the wall. A china cabinet in the corner filled with some kind of small figurine collection. Angels or fairies, she thought.

Charlie listened while she waited, hoping to hear a muffled voice or the faint sound of a TV in another room. She heard nothing and sensed no movement.

She knocked again to be sure, but after a full minute, she was forced to concede that no one was home.

Treading back to her car, she considered whether she should sit on the house for a while, figuring that either Robbie or his parents would have to turn up at some point. The prospect of watching an empty house for hours on end didn't exactly sound appealing, but she couldn't think of what else to do.

She opened her car door and climbed in, glancing back at the house in hopes of seeing some sign that someone was inside: the flutter of a curtain, a light turning on. But there was nothing. Charlie sighed.

The moment she pulled her door shut, she sensed movement. A flash of something metallic near her right eye.

Cold steel pressed against her neck, just above her larynx. Holding absolutely still, Charlie's gaze snapped to the rearview mirror, where a pair of wild brown eyes stared back at her. Above them, a scraggle of dark hair.

Robbie Turner crouched in her backseat, holding a knife to her throat.

CHAPTER FIFTY-THREE

Robbie jerked forward, his torso pressing into the back of her seat, something twitchy and animal in his movements.

Charlie gaped. Frozen. Breath heaving into her open mouth.

Her eyes whirled in her skull, trying to watch both him and the knife against her throat, somehow not able to look directly at either.

"Don't move," he said, his voice low and menacing.

Charlie swallowed, wincing when the blade dug a little harder into the skin. She had to think. Had to be smart.

It was a struggle to speak, to keep her voice from trembling with the knife brushing her carotid artery.

"OK, Robbie. You're in control here. Tell me what you want."

"What I want?" His eyes stretched wide in the rearview mirror. "I want you to stop snooping around after me. I want you to leave me the fuck alone."

Charlie tried to nod, but the edge of the knife stopped her.

"Alright. But I don't know if that's going to help you all that much anymore."

"What do you mean?"

"The cops busted the Red Velvet Lounge last night."

His face went hard, eyes flashing.

"So what?"

"So the owner, Demetrio? He gave you up. Said you were the one who brought Kara Dawkins in. I'm not the only one looking for you now."

That rattled him. She watched his face contort in fear as his mind connected the dots. It was a gamble, laying it all out like this. If he was thinking rationally, he might be willing to let her go. He could take her car and her phone and run. If not... well, then she might end up like Kara and Amber.

"Fuck. Oh fuck."

The blade began to shake, nudging uncomfortably against Charlie's larynx.

"The police know that I'm here, Robbie. If anything happens to me..."

The knife glittered where it caught the dome light as the blade sliced the air again. Away from her this time.

She gasped as the blade flopped onto the empty passenger seat. It bounced twice, and then it settled into one of the grooves in the upholstery.

They both stared at the spiky metal for a moment, shocked silence filling the car. Charlie's chest quivered, sucked in a fresh breath.

Then Robbie's hands shot up as though Charlie had pulled a gun on him. Palms out. Arms shaking. Fingers trembling.

"I'm sorry," he said in a wavering voice. "I'm sorry, OK? I thought I could scare you off. I didn't know what else to do. Everything's gone to shit, and I panicked. But now..."

She turned to face him fully, found the expression of a frightened child staring back at her. Eyes wide and wet.

He cleared his throat.

"Look, I don't want to hurt you. Don't want to hurt anybody. I just... want to tell my side of the story."

Charlie wasn't sure what to make of his sudden shift in demeanor, but she wanted to keep him talking.

"I'm listening," she said.

"I didn't kidnap Kara or anyone, OK? But I know how the cops think around here. They'll pin it on me anyway. Maybe even off me and plant a weapon on my corpse or something. An easy way to make all of this go away. I've seen the stuff about Jeffrey Epstein on the news. I know how the real world works."

He was talking too fast, rambling. He'd dropped the knife, but his pupils were huge, which meant he was probably on something. Charlie needed to redirect him, but her instincts told her to be delicate about it. Gentle and soothing. She didn't want to spook him.

"I understand, and I promise you that I only want the truth. Why don't you try starting at the beginning?"

He gulped, his Adam's apple rising and falling at the front of his neck. A quirk played at his mouth, and Charlie thought he was about to talk again, perhaps finding a calmer tone than before, starting from the beginning like she'd said. Instead his bottom lip broke into a full-on tremble.

Robbie burst into tears, sobs racking his torso, throttling him with rough hands. The sounds torn from his throat were not the soft whimpers of a child. They were the anguished, awful sobs of a full-grown man.

"Kara," he said, unable to go on for a moment. Snot dripped down from his nose.

Charlie thought about saying something but decided it was better to wait. Let this play out on his terms. No need to rush him.

He finally broke his hands-up pose to smear his thumb and index finger at his eyes, the sobs receding and then cutting off. Removing his hand, he blinked a few times, tears gleaming in his eyelashes like crystals.

"I guess you could say we had an on and off thing, me and Kara. Probably doesn't sound like much, I guess, but I care about her. Shit, I'm worried sick about her. I'd never hurt her. Nothing like that."

"And you had her dancing at the Red Velvet Lounge?"

For a second, a hard look flashed across his face, but his eyes went soft again just as quickly.

"That was her idea, I swear. She thought she could make a fortune up there, and she was right. I just helped her make it happen."

"It's funny," Allie said. "He didn't seem so broken up the night he was getting it on with Sharon Ritter."

"You said you and Kara were on and off," Charlie said, choosing her words carefully. "Were you two seeing other people?"

He rolled his eyes.

"Yeah, I figure you know plenty more than you're lettin' on, so let's just get it out there. I been fu— uh, seein' Sharon Ritter on the side as of late. And I get how bad that looks. Tyin' me to both girls, but… that one is just a physical thing. Not like with Kara, I mean."

He blinked a few more times, staring off at nothing.

"Wouldn't you know Amber Spadafore from school as well?"

"No. I mean, yeah, I knew who she was and all that. Small town. But we didn't cross paths much. She always ran with a different crew. No. More than that. Like, she lived in a different world from me. Bunch of achievers with their advanced algebra and extracurriculars. Only math I know intimately is to do with, like, the number of grams in an eighth, you know? Anyhow, I always thought she was stuck up. Maybe that wasn't fair. I guess I know how people judge people and all now, don't I? Now… Shit. I guess now White Rabbit's about to ruin my life, so what the fuck difference does it make, right? Just another small-town loser going off to do time."

Charlie flinched.

"Wait. Back up. You said White Rabbit is ruining your life? What does that mean?"

"The pills. You're the one that found 'em in the Escalade, right? Even if I clear my name on this kidnapping shit, avoid getting railroaded and snuffed by some ambitious deputy or something, I'll still get six to eight years for the pills. Intent to distribute or some garbage. Plus there's the stolen SUV." He groaned. "Maybe I can get out early for good behavior or some shit. I don't know."

Charlie remained quiet. Follow the ecstasy. That was what the anonymous email had been trying to tell her. Well, she had followed it, and it led her to Robbie. So now what?

"So the ecstasy. That's White Rabbit?"

"Yeah. They got all different names for the different production runs or some shit. Had some Green Nintendo a while back. Orange Pineapple. Blue Dolphin. Shit like that. Mostly named after the color of the tablet, I guess. Sometimes the shape, too. The little pineapples were cool. Or, like, funny, you know? More funny than cool maybe, but yeah."

"OK," Charlie said. "One more question. How is it that you know Sharon Ritter in the first place?"

Robbie ran a hand through his hair, looking uncomfortable. "She... wanted to buy some stuff."

"Sharon Ritter bought ecstasy from you?"

He nodded and flung himself backward in his seat. "I know how this looks, OK? But here's the thing: I got an alibi. When Amber went missing, I was locked up over in Livingston County for two days. Public intoxication and assault. Spent the first night in the drunk tank." Robbie sat forward again, clinging to the headrest of Charlie's seat. "Look that shit up, and you'll see. I couldn'ta done it. It's, like... what do you call it? Airtight."

CHAPTER FIFTY-FOUR

To Charlie's surprise, Robbie agreed to turn himself in to the authorities, but only if she'd come with him to the sheriff's department to speak on his behalf.

"You gotta be my advocate," he kept saying, latching onto a word she'd used. "You have the words to do it, to make 'em listen. They'd never listen to me. Buncha cops? No way."

She drove slowly and carefully as though any jolt might spook him into bolting. Even as they pulled into a parking space in the lot, she half-expected him to run for it. Instead, he blubbered softly in the backseat with his head down—a broken thing. Once the levee broke and he let those tears flow freely, he was done for. Charlie had seen it happen before, even to hardened criminals, let alone a kid mixed up in trouble bigger than himself.

They climbed out of the car, her and then him. She started toward the glass door, but he didn't follow. He stood next to the car, frozen in place. When she turned back, the look in his eye reminded her of a startled rabbit. She decided she better buoy her efforts to reassure him, just to be safe.

"You're doing the right thing," she said, trying to match her reassuring words to the most recent worry he'd expressed. "I have friends here. I'll make sure this all gets straightened out. You'll have a chance to tell your side of the story."

He followed after a second, walking slowly. They pushed through the door and in.

The deputy behind the desk gave them a look, lips pursed, eyebrows shooting straight up—but Charlie shook her head discreetly, and the mustached officer picked up her meaning. His face went blank.

"I'll get Deputy Wyatt for you, then. You can wait here."

As he disappeared around a corner, Charlie aimed a reassuring smile at Robbie. He could only stare at her, dazed.

"I think I'm gonna throw up," he said a moment later.

Charlie took his arm and steered him toward a row of chairs along one wall of the waiting area. There were beads of sweat on his upper lip, and his face looked pale.

"Sit here. You're going to be OK."

When Zoe came out, Charlie darted forward to intercept her. Zoe hissed, "Where'd you find him?"

"He found me, is more like it. Look, can we put him in an interview room for a minute so we can talk?"

Zoe nodded, her mouth hanging open slightly.

"Yeah, sure. Is he gonna come willingly? He looks pretty cagey."

Charlie glanced over at him.

"He'll come. He's just scared." She bent down next to where he was sitting and spoke softly. "Robbie? This is my friend, Deputy Wyatt."

His eyes flicked from Charlie over to Zoe then back to Charlie.

"We're going to take you back to an interview room, where you can give a statement. Is that alright?"

She watched his chest rise and fall once, twice, three times before he answered with a nod.

"Follow me, then," Zoe said.

With Robbie deposited securely in an interview room, Charlie had a chance to bring Zoe up to speed on everything he'd told her. When she finished, Zoe crossed her arms.

"You're not buying his sob story, are you? I mean, come on. He admits to having a relationship with Kara Dawkins *and* Amber Spadafore's mother, not to mention the drugs."

"Depends on whether or not his alibi checks out," Charlie said, looking through the window at the slumped figure in the interview room. "Do you still have that printout of his criminal history from this morning?"

"Well, if the arrest was that recent, it probably isn't on there." Zoe squinted, thinking. "But I can pull up the arrest record manually if you know which department."

"Livingston County, he said, but I don't know if it was sheriff, local, or state police."

"Let's go do some digging, then," Zoe said, leading Charlie down the hall to her office.

Zoe slid into her chair and brought up a database for the Livingston County Sheriff's Department on her computer. She typed in Robbie's name and birthdate.

"Nothing for the sheriff's department," she said. "Let's try the state boys."

The keyboard clattered as her fingers struck the keys.

"There it is. December twelfth. Citation for public intoxication and assault." Zoe stared at the screen for a moment. "Can't believe he was telling the truth."

"We can't rule out his involvement in Kara's disappearance," Charlie said. "But it doesn't feel right to me."

"If I'm being totally honest, I have to agree with you." Zoe swiveled from side to side in her chair, lips pursed. "Robbie doesn't seem like our guy."

"And unfortunately, that means we're back at square one."

"Yeah," Zoe said. "It also means someone has to tell the families that we found our so-called prime suspect and then cleared him."

Charlie straightened in her chair.

"You told the families?"

"It was the sheriff's call. He wanted them to know we were making progress."

"Well, don't look at me," Charlie said, scoffing. "I'm the one who brought Robbie in. I'm not delivering the bad news for you, too."

"I was afraid you'd say that." Sighing, Zoe pushed herself to her feet. "Now if you'll excuse me, I have some very awkward calls to make."

When Charlie got back to the office, she went straight to her laptop to update her master file with what she'd learned. She'd now confirmed that Kara had indeed been sneaking out those nights to go to the Red Velvet Lounge. She'd also learned that both Kara and Sharon Ritter were in some kind of relationship with Robbie Turner. Those facts alone made Robbie the ideal suspect. He was a criminal connected to both victims. And yet he had a rock-solid alibi for the night of Amber Spadafore's disappearance.

Charlie had pasted photos of both Kara and Amber into the file, and she stared at the faces of the two missing girls now. How long did they have left? Charlie felt the pressure rising, a tightness in her gut as the clock ticked down.

She turned away from the screen, closing her eyes. Ruling Robbie out as a suspect felt like starting over, but it wasn't. Not really. She just needed to incorporate the new information with what she already had and go over everything with fresh eyes.

Taking a deep breath, she swiveled back to the computer and started at the beginning.

She pored over the notes for hours, trying to find something she might have missed. A pattern. A dangling thread. Anything. At one point, she was startled to glance up from her computer and find herself sitting in the dark. Night had fallen without her even noticing. She reached for the switch on the desk lamp and turned it on, illuminating the desk but not much else. A small island of light in the pitch-black around her.

She got back to work on her current task—she'd started sifting back through all of Kara's and Amber's social media posts, trying to find some connection there. A shared friend. A day they might have crossed paths somehow. So far, she'd found nothing.

Charlie kept scrolling, certain there was a connection between the girls somewhere, if she could only find it. She came across a photo from Halloween on Amber's Instagram feed: Amber wearing a long red wig, purple seashell bra, and a green sequin skirt. Beside her, there was a girl dressed as a Playboy Bunny—black satin bodysuit and matching rabbit ears. And that was when she remembered the White Rabbit email.

She knew what it meant now that Robbie had told her White Rabbit was a nickname for the ecstasy he'd been peddling. The problem was, following the White Rabbit had led to Robbie, and Robbie had an alibi.

Charlie frowned. And then it hit her: when she'd asked how Robbie met Sharon Ritter, he said she'd bought ecstasy from him.

White Rabbit.

Her connection to Amber was obvious. But she could also be tied to Kara. They were both seeing Robbie Turner. Could Sharon have found out about Kara and Robbie and wanted to rid herself of the competition?

Charlie's heart began to race. She fumbled back through her notes, trying to find Sharon's alibi for the days the girls went missing. She said she'd been at a conference somewhere, but what was it called? There. Charlie's finger landed on the letters scrawled in her own handwriting: the Southeast Michigan Real Estate Conference and Expo.

Had Sharon lied about going to the conference?

Charlie searched the conference name plus Sharon's name. The Facebook page for Sharon's real estate business came up. Charlie clicked on it, her eyes flicking rapidly across the screen. Her gaze froze on the top post. There was Sharon Ritter in front of a podium, leading a session about online marketing techniques. Further down the page she found photo after photo of Sharon at the conference—handing out promotional tote bags from her booth, seated onstage for a panel, clinking champagne glasses with another woman at the closing night party.

Shoulders slumped, Charlie flipped the laptop shut. The defeat she'd felt earlier in the day rushed back at her tenfold. She didn't know why she'd even considered Sharon Ritter as a suspect, now that she thought about it. There may have been a motive for abducting Kara, but why kidnap her own daughter?

After a few moments of sitting in the silence of the office, Charlie stood, tucking the computer under her arm, and turned out the light.

"You're giving up?" Allie asked. "Just like that?"

"No, but I'm running in circles at this point. I need sleep."

On the walk up to the apartment, Charlie could only hope tomorrow would be more fruitful.

CHAPTER FIFTY-FIVE

Charlie woke before dawn, some remnant of a dream still twitching in her skull. A gasp parted her lips. It was the sound that woke her, she thought. The hiss and the harried breath that followed.

Her eyes snapped open. Shadows blanketed the apartment, the predawn gloom still ruling this space.

Her heart punched in her chest. Flexing. Squeezing.

Everything seemed in order, but the warning signal going off in her head remained even after the waking world had vanquished the dream threat, whatever it might have been. She must have had a nightmare—that seemed obvious enough—but she couldn't remember.

Her mind groped after any small detail, but it had fled her mind. In any case, she found herself awake now. No use fighting it, even if the clock showed an absurd pre-7 a.m. hour.

She sat up, swinging her legs out from under the covers. The cold wood planks of the floor assaulted her feet, the chill swarming over her flesh. She slid on a pair of slippers to block it out.

Then she shuffled over to the kitchen area, the soles of the slippers scuffing along. Sleep still possessed her legs to some extent, kept her wobbly atop them.

By the dim glow of her laptop screen at the end of the counter, she put on a pot of coffee. Some kind of autopilot kicked in, moving her arms and feet as necessary to grind the beans, fill the machine with water, turn it on.

Her eyes only half-watched what she was doing, her thoughts roaming elsewhere. First she tried to remember the dream one more time. Then, giving that up as a lost cause, she played back some of the recent discoveries in her case: Kara working at the Red Velvet Lounge. Robbie Turner peddling White Rabbit ecstasy.

The coffee machine gurgled, hollow sounds stuttering out now and again. She couldn't see the stream of brown fluid cascading down into the carafe in the half-light, but she could watch the rising tide as the pot filled.

The aroma of fresh coffee slowly permeated the room and made Charlie's mouth water. Made her feel a little warmer out of sheer anticipation. She pictured the black fluid swirling down into the cup, sloshing and tilting toward the rim as she leaned in to drink it.

She couldn't wait for that first sip, then that first cup, and then the second. And, hey, perhaps the third. Why not? It was early as hell, right? That made for as good an excuse as any, as far as she was concerned.

Her phone rumbled, rattling hard against the nightstand across the room. The sudden noise in the quiet made her jump.

She reached it just as the screen went dark again. Waking the screen and squinting against the bright glare, she saw the notification was for a new email and opened it.

All caps. Choppy fragments. And again, it appeared as if Charlie had sent the email to herself.

PACKAGE FOR YOU.
HARBOR BEACH.
BENCH ON THE BLUFFS.
YOU KNOW THE PLACE.

A cold feeling snaked around her, her skin pulling itself tight.

Her eyes locked on that string of capital letters, scanning the words over and over, backward and forward.

She did know the place. She knew it too well. Still dreamed about it often. The exact spot on the beach where Allie's foot had washed up all those years ago.

And part of her wondered, with a lump swelling in her throat, if that was what she'd dreamed last night. The park bench along the water's edge. Was it possible?

The coffee machine coughed a few more times and then fell silent.

Charlie barely heard it. Didn't bother pouring herself a cup. She dressed quickly and headed out the door.

◄

CHAPTER FIFTY-SIX

Charlie parked in the lot next to the public beach. She'd passed a few cars on the ride over, headlights gleaming in the dark of the morning, but this area, out near the water, was utterly dead at this hour. Empty. Motionless save for the water lapping at the sand.

It was a gray morning. Misty and murky. The predawn twilight was just poking its head over the horizon.

Down the beach, she could make out the rusting hulk of the Poseidon's Kingdom Ferris wheel. The skeletal metal thrust up from the land, its rounded top reminding her of a skull.

The cold breeze rolled off the water to nip at her as she climbed out of the car, reaching right through her jacket as though it had punctured the fabric. She hugged her arms around herself, wishing she'd thought to wear a heavier coat, not to mention a hat and gloves. She'd forgotten how much colder it felt down here by the water. At least she still had a touch of sleep warmth in her core to help fight it off.

She walked north, crossing the parking lot and moving away from the swimming area where she and Allie had spent hours of their childhood collecting shells, sea glass, Petoskey stones. Her trajectory pointed her toward the secluded area beyond the sand, where the rolling dunes extended to within just a few feet of the shore.

That was where the bench was. That was where, she supposed, the package would be. Whatever it was.

Her mind fumbled at the possibilities as she traversed the asphalt parking lot. She kept picturing a small cardboard box there on the bench, perhaps wrapped with twine. But what lay inside?

A clue. It had to be a clue, didn't it? That was all she could think of.

Whoever was sending these emails clearly knew she was working the case of the missing girls. But if they were trying to help, they were being awfully cryptic about it. First the White Rabbit riddle and now this.

And yet the White Rabbit message *had* been a clue, one that pointed to the drugs, to the club, to Robbie. And even though they'd ruled Robbie out as a suspect, all of those strands still led back to Kara Dawkins and Amber Spadafore. It was a piece of the puzzle, if not the solution.

And if that logic held up here, the mystery package would be the same. She hoped.

Then again, who was to say the person sending the messages was trying to be helpful?

She stepped off the concrete and onto the moist sand along the shore. The tides kept the beach clear of snow, mercifully leaving her a path to walk. She passed a stand of windswept pines, their craggy trunks jutting up from the banks of sand.

A big gust of wind ripped off the water and gave Charlie a stiff shove. The force made her feet stutter-step beneath her. Almost like the wind meant to stop her progress, keep her from whatever lay ahead.

Then the cold rushed over her, clutched at the fleshy parts of her, penetrated the skin to touch her cheekbones and chin and knuckles. Goosebumps fattened everywhere, but they were no help in warming her, no use.

She pulled her hands up into her sleeves, hugged herself tighter, and pressed on, shivering. The wind didn't let up. A constant gale blew into her face now, swirled a frigid mist at her. The breeze fluctuated, growing stronger and weaker by the second but never really stopping.

Charlie didn't let up either. She leaned into it, fought through it. Persisted. Even with the wet and cold seeming to accumulate on her skin and clothes, she kept going.

The sky gradually lightened as she progressed, but she could sense no warmth accompanying the rising sun. If anything, the day seemed to grow colder.

The bench emerged from the void, taking shape little by little as she descended the slope toward the low point where the water and land meshed. Soon she could see the details of the steel bench, the outline of the concrete bed below.

She squinted as she got closer. Tried to see anything sitting on the bench. She was looking, she realized, for that cardboard box she'd pictured, the one with the twine coiling around it, the one that surely held some clue.

Instead she saw nothing. An empty park bench.

She stopped beside it. Brought her hand down, rested it on the back of the seat, touching it as though to reassure herself that her eyes weren't betraying her somehow. It was really there and really empty.

That didn't make sense.

She remembered the words of the email. Pictured the all-caps text in her head.

PACKAGE FOR YOU.
HARBOR BEACH.
BENCH ON THE BLUFFS.
YOU KNOW THE PLACE.

Part of her wanted to sweep her arm across the seat, to verify once again by touch that there was no package there. Nothing at all.

The cold seemed to sharpen then. A bitter chill sinking deeper into her flesh. And she realized that a creeping awareness accompanied this fresh sense of the cold. Something that left her feeling vulnerable and violated.

Her skin crawled. The goosebumps refreshing themselves.

She swiveled her head. Eyes scanning everywhere. Was someone watching her?

She saw no one. Not even so much as traffic lights or noise in the distance. No movement beyond the churning of the water and the shivering of the dry beach grass.

The goosebumps only intensified as she took in the desolation. She felt alone. Very alone.

The shadows elongated around her, their forms somehow turning sinister and strange. She swallowed.

Why had someone summoned her at this hour? Alone in the gloomy light of the morning.

Just as she turned to leave, she spotted it—the pale bulk lying on the sand in the distance—even if it took her eyes a moment to fully process what was there.

She swiveled her head back. Froze. Stared.

She felt something brush her bottom lip, realizing only after that she'd brought her hand to her mouth. It trembled there just shy of her face.

The hairs pricked up on the back of her neck, one by one. Quivering with some pulsing energy.

The bulk lay motionless. Sprawled and pallid.

Charlie's shoulders heaved up and down with her breath now. Wind sucking in and out with a grating scrape.

The color around her shifted, all the drab gray going a couple shades brighter, as though she could instantly see the results of her pupils dilating.

She had to get closer. Had to know for sure.

She put one foot in front of the other, shoes sinking into the sand with each step.

The camera in her mind seemed to zoom in on the mass laid out on the beach. Naked and gray and lying right on the border of where the waves reached their apex and rolled back.

The details filled in one at a time.

Hair fanned out on the ground. Wet. Moving along with the water lapping up and retreating every few seconds.

Skin leached of color. Faded. Bleached. Gone so dull it almost seemed milky, save for that ashen tone underlying it all.

Eyes closed, the lashes thatched and dark and delicate. Some ephemeral beauty still present there.

Just focusing on the eyes, Charlie could almost believe the girl was sleeping. Almost.

And then her gaze drifted lower. Where pieces were missing.

The sorrow grew too big then. Swelling until it burst in Charlie's skull. Somehow overtaking the shock. Throttling her.

Pain.

It grabbed Charlie by the shoulders, fished an icy hand into her ribcage to grasp after her heart. The impact made her whole body shake.

Pain.

Tears budded and overflowed at the corners of her eyes. Muted whimpers spluttering from her lips.

And suddenly she felt far away from here. Thrust back into the past. All those old feelings flooding through her again. Losing Allie.

Pain. Familiar pain.

How could this make any sense?

Life. Death. The universe. Any of it?

How?

The body of Amber Spadafore lay strewn on the beach. Both feet had been cut off.

CHAPTER FIFTY-SEVEN

Charlie huddled in her car, sheltered from the wind and the chill. Still, she trembled, teeth chattering.

She stared through the windshield. Part of her trying to remember what she was in the middle of doing. The rest of her mind gone blank.

Gray clouds scudded out over the water. Brighter now as the daylight began to seep into the world in earnest.

Her eyes drifted down the beach. Glided toward that place just past the crest of the hill, where the girl lay. From here, she couldn't see the body, and that felt wrong.

She couldn't just leave her out there. Couldn't abandon her.

Alone. All alone. Vulnerable. It was wrong, even if there was nothing to be done.

She blinked. Refocused on the world within the car, on the task at hand.

Her phone perched in her right hand. The screen gaped at her. Ready. Waiting.

Charlie moved a shaky finger to the phone. She needed to call it in. Tell Zoe what she'd found. That was all.

She scrolled to Zoe on the contact list. But her finger hesitated shy of hitting the call button. Something stopped her.

She blinked again. Why was she waiting?

She turned her head. Coughed into her fist. The sound was unpleasant. Dry and throaty. Flecks of spittle spattered her fist.

She waited for Allie to chime in. To make some joke like, *Cough it, don't spray it.*

No joke came. It occurred to Charlie that Allie had been awfully quiet all morning.

She coughed again, and some distant part of her mind prickled with childish fear. *What if I never stop coughing?*

She pinched her eyes shut. Hot tears streamed down her face now, rivulets of wet tracing lines down her cheeks. Her throat felt raw.

The coughing turned suddenly to something more like choking.

Charlie panicked.

She couldn't breathe. Couldn't move. Could only retch and gasp for air.

Hyperventilating. She needed to relax. Needed to—

A voice in her head spoke to her then. Calm. Strong.

Not Allie's voice. It was her own.

Stop fighting it. Just relax.

You've just seen a dead body—a murder victim—and you are in shock.

She rested her forehead on the steering wheel, the tears now spilling down to the floor instead of her cheeks. And the coughing slowly retreated.

She leaned there a long time, even after the attack had passed. Breathing. Wiping the wet from her eyes and face.

The puzzle pieces clicked together at last. If Charlie found Amber's killer, she might be solving Allie's case as well. The fact that the killer had mutilated Amber's feet suggested a connection to Allie's case, didn't it? It was almost undeniable.

Right away her mind snapped to Leroy Gibbs, the suspect who was never charged all those years ago. His picture bloomed in her head, the shambling weirdo with the crazy eyes and unkempt beard.

Her mind reeled. Lightheaded. A little dizzy.

Could this really be the lead she had searched for all this time? Charlie's heart thundered at the prospect.

She lifted her head and blinked again, the last of the tears falling away.

At last, she pressed the button to dial Zoe's number and brought the phone to her ear.

CHAPTER FIFTY-EIGHT

A small group of observers, almost exclusively law enforcement save for Charlie, huddled in the observation room. The sense of anticipation was palpable: bouncing legs, trembling fingers, twitchy movements, picking at imaginary fuzz on their shirts and pants.

Across from them, visible through a pane of two-way glass the size of a big-screen TV, the interrogation room waited for the main event to begin—a dingy-looking affair, Charlie thought. Drop ceiling. Cinder-block walls painted eggnog yellow. In the center sat the star of today's show.

Leroy Gibbs hunched over a glossy tabletop, gouged and scraped by years of use. His forearms rested on the edge of it, the tips of his gnarled fingers brushing the veneer.

His beard covered most of his face like frizzy gray ivy, reaching up almost to his cheekbones. The hair atop his head was a messy salt-and-pepper tangle matted over his forehead, strands reaching down to partially obscure his eyes.

Charlie could see enough in those eyes to get a sense of the faraway look in them. The man struck her as bewildered, perhaps a little confused. Like a hermit pried out of his cave, aghast to see the daylight after so long alone in the dark.

An image of Amber Spadafore's closed eyes surfaced in her mind then. Dark tendrils of her hair undulating with the movement of the waves. Charlie kept getting these flashes of what she'd seen that morning on the beach. Snapshots burned into her memory that she'd never be able to unsee.

She hugged the hoodie Zoe had let her borrow tighter around herself. Hours had passed since she'd first discovered the girl's body on the beach, the bureaucratic machine of the Salem County Sheriff's Department working at the speed of a glacier, and still Charlie couldn't seem to get warm. Even after forcing down a cup of coffee and a stale donut from the station's break room, she remained chilled to the bone.

She turned to Zoe, her mouth etched into a frown.

"So your tech guy wasn't able to trace the source of the email at all?" Charlie asked.

"Nope." Zoe shrugged. "He said it isn't even that hard, sending an anonymous email like that."

The sheriff's department had been all too eager to see the mystery email that led Charlie to Amber Spadafore's body, and she'd hoped they'd have the resources to figure out who sent it. Apparently not. Another dead end.

Charlie balled her hands into fists at her sides, her mind tumbling the same thought around over and over: only Amber's killer could have told Charlie where to find the body. He was taunting her.

Zoe leaned in, her voice low.

"You need anything? A bottle of water or another coffee, maybe?"

Charlie shook her head.

"I'm fine."

It was starting to drive Charlie crazy the way Zoe kept fussing over her. Zoe wasn't the mother hen type, but every time she thought Charlie wasn't looking, she gawked at her with a nervous expression on her face. All the worrying made Charlie feel like a helpless child.

She stepped closer to the glass, her focus on Leroy Gibbs. He squirmed in his seat, seemingly unable to get comfortable, still waiting for his lawyer to arrive. He looked older than when she'd last laid eyes on him. Grayer. Face and torso starting to go gaunt. Something sallow in his complexion that hadn't been there before.

Had he done it? Killed Amber, then sent her that email?

She saw Amber again, unbidden. White sand against whiter skin. Flecks of dirt dotting her cheeks like freckles. Everything mottled and ashy in the dawn light.

Charlie dug her fingernails into the flesh of her palms as she pushed the ghostly vision away. She needed to concentrate on Gibbs. He was what mattered now.

Gazing through the window, Charlie tried to get a read on him. Above all, he seemed a blank figure to her—expressionless face, monotone voice. He rarely even made eye contact with anyone. During the whole preamble to the interview—the reading of his rights, the testing of the mic and camera—Gibbs just seemed disengaged. Aloof.

He was like a specimen of some kind, she thought. A test subject kept under glass. Observed and experimented on in his little cage.

Earlier Charlie had overheard one of the detectives suggest in a hushed tone that this was all an act, that Gibbs' behavior was a calculated effort, the first step in making a play at an insanity plea. Watching him with her own two eyes, she didn't think so.

A murmur spread through the observation room, traveling faster as it went like a cresting wave building up momentum. Finally, the accused's lawyer had arrived, the whispers reported. He was on his way into the interrogation room now.

The door jerked open on the other side of the glass, and a tall man wearing a suit moved across the screen, slapping his briefcase on the table as he took a seat next to Gibbs. Charlie recognized him straight away, but it took three full seconds of staring at his face for it to register, and when it finally did hit, it came with a shudder.

Will. The lawyer representing Gibbs was Will Crawford.

CHAPTER FIFTY-NINE

Charlie's chest tightened. Her face felt flushed and hot.

Will was representing Gibbs. How did that make any kind of sense? Why would he do it?

She needed out of the crowded observation room. Needed somewhere she could breathe and think. Fumbling with the door handle, she escaped into the hallway.

Fluorescent bulbs buzzed overhead. She blinked against the sudden brightness, but the air out here felt better. Cooler. Less stuffy.

She shuffled toward the drinking fountain down the corridor as her thoughts tumbled. Of course, she knew Will was a lawyer, that he represented people from all walks of life, but Gibbs? Leroy Gibbs? The man most people presumed had killed Allie for all these years?

She stooped and thumbed the button on the fountain. Took a sip of water.

Just then a door opened behind her. She turned.

Will poked his head out of the interrogation room, his eyes locked on a deputy standing just outside the door.

"Can I get a Pepsi for my client?" Will said, his voice low. Then his eyes shifted up. Met Charlie's. He flinched. "Charlie."

He stepped out into the hall as the deputy went off for the beverage, and the two of them were suddenly alone.

"Charlie. I was hoping I'd get a chance to talk to you. To explain."

"Explain what?" she asked, her tone bitter.

"OK, look. I know you're probably upset, and believe me, I wish I wasn't in this position, but—"

"Oh, you mean the position where you're representing the guy who killed my sister? *That* position?"

He reached for her, but she dodged his grasp.

"Come on, Charlie. He didn't kill Allie. And he didn't do this."

"How do you know?" Charlie asked, crossing her arms.

"Because there's no evidence. None. Even you have to see that."

"No evidence? I found a girl's body today with her feet chopped off. If that's not evidence, then what is?"

Will sighed, his shoulders slumping.

"Leroy is my cousin, Charlie. I felt a duty to make sure he gets a fair shake."

She frowned.

"You never told me that."

"I didn't think it was important. If I'd known this was coming, of course I would have mentioned it. I imagine you're feeling blindsided by all of this."

"You think?" she said, not able to hide the venom in her voice.

"Look, we're not close. But he is family. You have to understand my dilemma."

Charlie felt her hackles rise at that. She leaned closer, her voice practically a hiss.

"You don't get to talk to me about family. Allie was my sister. My best friend." She reached out and jabbed him in the chest with her finger. "You're representing the man who took her from me."

She turned, heading back for the observation room.

"Don't be like this. I'm a lawyer. This is what I do."

She pushed through the door, not turning back. The closing door mostly swallowed Will's voice, which had gone soft.

"I'm sorry, Charlie. I really am."

Charlie clenched her molars so tightly that her jaw was starting to ache, but she didn't even notice until Zoe tapped her arm.

"Are you OK?"

Forcing her jaw to relax, Charlie gave a curt nod.

"I'm fine."

"I'm sure Will felt like he had to do it," Zoe said. "Represent Leroy, I mean. For the family."

Zoe was using her mother hen voice again, her tone sounding like someone trying to soothe a child after a nightmare.

When Charlie didn't answer, Zoe went on.

"He changed a lot after his mom died, you know?"

Charlie remembered dully that Will's mom had died when he was quite young—twelve or thirteen, before Charlie had known him well. Representing Gibbs made sense on that level, she supposed, though it wasn't any easier to stomach.

"Anyway, I can imagine him feeling some sense of obligation because of all that," Zoe was saying, but Charlie was only half paying attention now because Will had re-entered the interrogation room.

"I've advised my client not to answer any questions," he said as he sat down. Several people scoffed or clicked their tongues in the observation room before Will went on. "But he's made it clear to me that he wants to cooperate and is doing so of his own volition, despite my protests."

Charlie couldn't help but notice the homogeneous body language being presented on the police side of the glass, the uniformed officers mostly tucking their thumbs in their belts while the suits—detectives and various administrators—had to sweep back the sides of their jackets to rest their hands on their hips instead.

In any case, all eyes latched onto the mirrored glass pane like it was a flat-screen at a Super Bowl party.

The detective seated across from Will and Gibbs fingered a manila folder open and slid out a photograph. It was one of Allie's senior pictures, the one where she was sprawled on her stomach in the grass, clutching a handful of dandelion seed heads.

Charlie felt her insides twist into a knot.

"Do you remember being questioned about the disappearance of Allison Winters, Mr. Gibbs?"

Will sighed.

"I hope you didn't drag us down here just to bring up ancient history, Detective Siebold."

"Are you gonna let him answer?"

Rolling his eyes, Will waved his hand.

"Go ahead, Mr. Gibbs."

"I remember. But I didn't…" Gibbs broke off and lowered his head.

"Didn't what?"

"I didn't hurt her," he muttered.

"But you knew her, didn't you?"

After a long pause, Gibbs nodded. The knot in Charlie's middle squeezed a little tighter.

"In fact, the weekend before Allison Winters disappeared, she and some friends chartered a boat that you captained, isn't that right?"

His fingers twitched and fidgeted, squeezing into fists and then releasing.

"Yes, sir."

"And what did you think about Allison when you saw her?"

"I didn't think nothin'."

"No? You didn't think anything of this beautiful eighteen-year-old girl in a bikini?" Detective Siebold held up the photo again, almost daring Gibbs to look at it.

"There was a bunch of 'em. They all were."

Detective Siebold frowned, confused.

"All were what?"

"All the girls were in the bathing suits. Wasn't just her. They all wore 'em."

Charlie got the sense that Gibbs didn't fully grasp what was happening here, as though he was distant not just from social normality but from actual reality.

"I told you, guys," one of the men in the observation room grumbled. "He's just laying the groundwork for an insanity plea. Wait and see."

The detective in the next room laced his fingers together on the table and looked Gibbs in the eye.

"Yes, but you took particular notice of Allison, didn't you?"

Gibbs shook his head.

"You didn't ask her if she wanted to steer the boat?"

Charlie watched the man's chest move up and down as he breathed. He murmured something unintelligible.

"What's that?"

"I thought she was pretty," Gibbs said.

Charlie thought he sounded sad when he said it. Like it was some great sin to have thought her sister pretty.

"Sick fuck," one of the observers said in a low voice.

Gaze flitting about the observation room now, Charlie noted the way almost everyone leaned in toward the glass. They were enjoying this, she thought, the way one might enjoy a movie or a play. Stimulated. She felt a pang of pity for the man on the other side of the window, and then, almost as quickly, a wave of disgust. Was she really feeling empathy for the man who had very likely murdered her sister?

"You thought she was pretty," Detective Siebold repeated. "That's right. And then what?"

Staring blankly, Gibbs said nothing.

"What happened after the boat ride ended? After you realized you probably wouldn't ever have a chance to talk to Allison again? Did you start thinking of ways you might see her again?"

Gibbs shook his head again, and Detective Siebold angled his chin a notch higher.

"So just to be clear, you didn't kidnap Allison Winters? You didn't kill her and dismember her body?"

The palm of Will's hand came down on the table.

"Look, Mr. Gibbs has agreed to talk with you. But this is the same line of questioning my client went through back then. You had nothing then and you have nothing now. Either give us something new, something you haven't already asked him a hundred times, or this interview is over."

The detective nodded and pulled two new photos from the folder—snapshots of Kara Dawkins and Amber Spadafore. Smiles on their faces. Eyes twinkling.

Charlie visualized Amber Spadafore laid out on the coroner's table, her porcelain skin fish-belly-white against the hard steel. She tried to stop herself from imagining the scalpel slicing into the pallid skin, peeling it away to reveal the red underneath, but the images came whether she wanted them or not.

She closed her eyes and heard Detective Siebold ask his next question.

"Have you ever seen either of these girls?"

Eyes darting from one grinning face to the next, Gibbs looked bewildered.

"Never seen 'em."

"No?" The detective's eyebrows crept up his forehead. "Not even around town? Maybe at the supermarket or the gas station?"

Gibbs moved his head from side to side.

"You didn't—"

"Come on, Jerry," Will said, interrupting. "I won't sit here and allow you to badger him like this. You asked if he knows or has seen either girl, and he said no. Twice. Move on."

The detective nodded, his mouth a tight smile. His fingers snaked into the manila folder a third time and came out with a photo of Amber Spadafore's body on the beach. It was a particularly grisly shot—a close-up of the mutilated legs ending in bloody stumps.

Gibbs recoiled, sliding back in his chair and shutting his eyes tight. Charlie couldn't help but think of a child turning away from a particularly gory scene in a horror movie. Was it an act, or was he genuinely that repulsed by the image?

Will was on his feet in an instant, red in the face, shouting about shock tactics.

Charlie's attention was diverted from the spectacle by Zoe taking a firm hold of her arm and pulling her toward the door.

"What are you doing?" Charlie hissed.

"I need to talk to you for a minute," Zoe said. "Outside."

"Can it wait?"

"No."

The hallway was bright compared to the dimmed lighting in the observation room. Charlie blinked a few times, waiting for her eyes to adjust.

"So…" Zoe said. "They're going to be in there for a while."

"Yeah."

"Like, probably for a few more hours, at least. Accounting for bathroom breaks, meal breaks, and all, I'd say this interrogation will stretch deep into the night." Zoe spoke pointedly, her eyes going wide as if there were some second meaning Charlie was supposed to catch onto.

"That's generally how it works, right? You can keep him for forty-eight hours without charging him."

Zoe nodded, still giving her that penetrating look.

Charlie just shook her head, baffled by Zoe's demeanor.

"It's just too bad that someone couldn't, you know, go peek in the windows of his house while they know he's tied up here. Poke around for some physical evidence." Zoe shrugged. "That's all."

Charlie blinked slowly, her eyes narrowing.

"So you want me to go snoop around Gibbs' house?"

Hand to her chest, Zoe gasped.

"I'm merely making casual conversation with a friend. An offhand comment, if you will."

"Right," Charlie said, still squinting at Zoe.

"I mean, even if you found something, it wouldn't be like you could act on it," Zoe said. "The most you'd be able to do would be to call in an anonymous tip."

"What happened to your fastidious morals?"

Zoe's face went hard.

"Kara Dawkins is still missing. We have to proceed as if she's still alive. He could be holding her somewhere, as we speak. Besides that, Leroy Gibbs already got away with murder once. I won't let that happen again. He killed Allie, and we're going to prove it."

Charlie swallowed, startled by Zoe's passion. Lost in the shock of finding Amber's body, Charlie had almost forgotten that Kara was still out there. After a moment, she nodded.

"You're right," she said, already beginning to formulate a plan. "Give me a call if anything happens. If they let him go, I mean."

"I will. But he's not going anywhere, trust me. Like you said, we'll keep him here long into the night."

As Charlie turned to go, Zoe caught her arm and gave it a squeeze.

"Be careful."

CHAPTER SIXTY

Charlie drummed her fingers against the steering wheel as she waited at one of Salem Island's three traffic lights, just two blocks from her apartment. The reality of what she was planning to do was finally sinking in.

The Gibbs house. Tonight. As soon as the dark fully settled, she would push through that door. She would see what there was to see. And everything would be different after. Everything.

The strange numbness from earlier had faded, replaced by restlessness. The anticipation made her skin crawl, as though fingertips lightly brushed down the lengths of her arms, swiped at the soft flesh just along her throat, tickled the backs of her knees.

So many times Charlie had wondered what she might have found in the Gibbs house if she'd been given a chance to poke around. The police had searched the place back then, of course. And they'd uncovered nothing. No hair. No blood. No fibers. No evidence that Allie had been there at all.

Still, Charlie could never let go of the idea that they might have missed something. That if only she'd had the opportunity to peek inside the ratty old house, she might have discovered something they'd missed. Allie was her sister, after all. Her twin. Charlie knew her better than anyone. Maybe she could have recognized some tiny detail that proved Allie had been there. Had died there.

The light turned green, and the car lurched into motion again. It felt strange to move just now. As though time itself should stand still as one approached the major events in life. Turning points.

Crossroads. The thresholds we passed over and through, the lines that divided our lives into before and after.

A flood of images came to her. Memories of Allie's investigation rendered in a jumbled montage of flapping police tape, whirling lights, the detectives sitting in the living room trying to talk to the family while her mom kept bursting into tears, clips from the local TV news reports. They fought to take her out of the moment, but Charlie pushed them away. The memories never helped anything.

Charlie pulled into the lot outside her apartment then, snow rasping under the tires where the plow had piled it along the sloped entrance. She parked near the stairs. Killed the engine. Sat in the quiet.

The wind howled as it blew over the hood and windshield. Shrill. Almost whistling.

Charlie had studied Allie's file, of course. She'd read the interviews, pored over the photos of the Gibbs house. But it wasn't the same as seeing it all with her own eyes.

Her hand clasped the door handle, hesitating a moment before pulling it.

Tonight, all of that would change. She knew it was unlikely that she'd find any trace of Allie there now. She was too late on that. But there was still a chance of finding justice for Amber and Kara. And she refused to give up hope that Kara might still be alive.

Charlie climbed out of the car and traversed the icy path. The wind ripped across her face, cold and dry, blasting her hard enough that her eyelids fluttered. The soles of her shoes skidded with each step, the ice preventing any real traction, making progress slow.

At the top of the stairs, she unlocked her door and stepped out of the wind. Shook the dusting of snow off the ankles of her pants.

She glanced around the room. She'd need to pack some supplies. There'd never be another chance like this, and she had to make it count.

She crossed the room and squatted beside the bed. Rooted around under it until she found the duffel bag. One good tug pulled it free of the mess. Then she slapped it on the mattress and unzipped the thing so its flaps hung open like a dog's loose lips.

In went a pair of heavy-duty Maglites the size of nightsticks—a primary flashlight and a backup. Zoe always praised this particular brand for its reliability, as well as its ability to bludgeon if and when necessary.

Then her lock pick kit went in the bag. Probably less than five minutes at the back door would be enough to get her in, which was a good feeling.

Next, she tossed in a ski mask to hide her face as she crept up to the house. Around here, a ski mask wouldn't look out of place at all this time of year. She'd look like an ice-fisherman headed home for the night.

She rifled through her toolbox and loaded a few of her tools into the bag, figuring that even with her lock pick stuff already in tow, she'd want options. Better to be prepared for whatever she might encounter.

She zipped the bag shut and lifted it, the tools inside clanking together. Placing the bag beside the door, Charlie peered out the window to gauge the level of daylight. The fact that the sheriff planned to hold Gibbs well into the night meant that she had the luxury of waiting until nightfall before attempting her little break-in.

She went to her laptop to check what time the sun would set, but the screen froze. Charlie drilled her fingers against the keyboard and swiped at the touchpad. Nothing happened.

For an anxious moment, she worried over the fate of her master case file if her computer finally bit the dust. Then she remembered it was backed up on her cloud drive. The file would be safe.

With the machine still frozen, she forced a hard reboot. The laptop went quiet, and Charlie was suddenly struck by how silent it was in the apartment. Allie hadn't uttered a single word since Charlie had found the body that morning.

A chill ran up Charlie's spine.

Was that right? She ran through it all in her mind: finding the body, calling Zoe, waiting for the police and the coroner to show up, watching them hoist the stretcher laden with the body bag into a van. Allie had been mute through all of it. Then there'd been everything at the station: hauling Gibbs in, Will showing up to represent him, the start of the interrogation. Nothing from Allie. Not a peep.

Charlie considered calling out to her, and then felt silly. Most of the time she couldn't get Allie to shut up. Maybe she should count this as a blessing. With what she had planned for tonight, there was enough on her plate.

The login screen for Charlie's computer came up. She typed in her password and signed in. Everything seemed to be in order. She opened her browser. It wouldn't be dark for another two hours.

She sighed, tapping her toes in a rhythmless beat. There was no way she could stand sitting around the apartment for two hours. The stillness would be unbearable.

Her eyes fell on a calendar she kept pinned on the wall next to the kitchen cabinets, which she mostly used for keeping track of Frank's chemo schedule. He didn't have chemo today, but there was another reminder scrawled under yesterday's date.

Refill Frank's RXs.

Her mouth dropped open. Frank's prescriptions. She'd forgotten to pick them up from the pharmacy.

A surge of guilt welled in her belly as she realized that she'd been so wrapped up in the case that she hadn't even checked in with Frank for several days.

Hurrying to the door, Charlie slid her shoes on and grabbed her coat. There was still time to drop off Frank's meds before her other plans for tonight. The hard part would be not telling him what she intended to do.

CHAPTER SIXTY-ONE

Frank's face looked drawn and tired when he answered the door. Charlie had hoped the fried chicken she brought along with his freshly refilled prescriptions would perk him up, but after making a show of eating one drumstick and half a biscuit, he pushed the rest away. This would have been a sacrilege to the old Frank. He didn't believe in leftovers.

Charlie spotted a pan of brownies on the kitchen counter as she put away the uneaten food.

"Who made the brownies?"

"Oh, those are from Tootsie," Frank said, lowering himself into his trusty recliner with a groan. "You know, from down the street? You should have one. They're a delight."

Mouth watering, Charlie helped herself to one of the fudgy squares. She chewed, studying her uncle. His posture seemed especially stiff today, and he kept reaching up to massage his neck.

"Are you feeling OK?" she asked.

"Eh, just my neck. Must have slept wrong or something. It's so stiff I can barely turn it."

Charlie grabbed a paper towel to use as a makeshift plate and went over to sit on the couch.

"You fell asleep in that chair again, didn't you?"

"I can't help it. Half the time I can't sleep for shit because of the chemo. But when I do doze off, I'm out," he said. "Dead to the world."

He watched her take a bite of brownie.

"I ever tell you about the time I accidentally ate half a pan of magic brownies?"

Charlie laughed.

"Explain to me how someone 'accidentally' eats half a pan of brownies."

"Well, OK. The eating of the brownies was intentional." He held up a finger. "I didn't know they were pot brownies, though. That was the accidental part."

"How'd that work out for you?"

"I was high for a good twenty-four hours. *Extremely* high. Practically hallucinating. And I had the worst case of cotton mouth. At one point my throat felt so dry, I actually started to think I might die from it."

That got Charlie giggling.

"It's funny now, but back then? Harrowing."

She finished off the brownie then licked the crumbs from her fingers.

"How's the case going?" Frank asked then. "Your missing girls."

Charlie had skirted the topic, hoping to avoid the subject altogether. She should have known better. Frank had a sharp mind. Gears always turning. She wondered if he sensed that she was holding something back.

"I've got a few leads," she said. "Avenues I haven't explored yet."

Even though she had no intention of telling him about her plot to snoop around the Gibbs property, she hadn't planned on withholding the information about finding Amber Spadafore's body. But now, seeing how tired and frail he looked today, she couldn't bring herself to tell him. It was too much. Too connected to the past, to what happened to Allie. He was fighting his own battle with the leukemia, and this seemed like too great a burden to put on him now.

When Charlie looked up at her uncle again, his head was tilted back against the chair, and he was snoring quietly. She figured that was her cue to leave.

The springs of the old plaid couch squeaked as she pushed to her feet, but Frank didn't stir. She gave him a light peck on the cheek, let herself out through the front door, and locked it behind her.

*

On her drive back home from Frank's, the sky began to darken, and with nightfall came a steady flurry of snow. A cloud of flakes followed Charlie inside when she unlocked the door to her apartment and pushed it open.

She hovered there on the doormat for a moment, feeling a sense of unease that she couldn't pinpoint. Her eyes scanned the space, landing on where her laptop sat open on the counter. Her gaze moved on to the bed, rumpled and unmade. Nothing new there.

The lamp on the bedside table caught her attention next. It was on. Had she left it that way?

She took a step toward it, tripping over the duffel bag of gear she'd left near the door. She caught herself on the corner of the bed, narrowly avoiding falling flat on her face. She waited for some comment from Allie—a quip about Charlie's natural grace and poise—but there was nothing.

In any case, her stumble had jarred her out of her previously paranoid thoughts. In approximately half an hour, she'd be trespassing on the property of one Leroy Gibbs. That was enough to make anyone jumpy.

She snatched the duffel bag by the handle and took it down to the car, skittering over the ice to where she'd parked. She tossed the bag in the backseat and climbed the stairs again to get the rest of her stuff. Back in the apartment, she took down a lockbox and holster from a shelf in the closet and strapped on her Glock 43. Next, she slid her phone from her pocket and turned it off. It was probably an overly cautious move, but phones could only be tracked when they were on. Should things go south on her little excursion onto the Gibbs property, she'd be better off not offering up evidence that could prove she'd been there.

Finally, Charlie tugged on a hat and gloves and gave one last look around the apartment to make sure she wasn't forgetting anything. Satisfied, she pulled the door shut behind her.

She took a breath. It was time.

CHAPTER SIXTY-TWO

The snow picked up as Charlie drove out toward the Gibbs house. The flakes glittered in the glow of the headlights, twisting into spirals here and there like the wind was trying to braid it on the way down.

How many times had she driven this route for no other reason but to drive by the home of Leroy Gibbs, dreaming of getting a peek behind that darkened door, behind all those windows with the shades drawn tight? She'd wondered countless times what might lie inside the ramshackle farmhouse, wondered whether or not the man who lived there had been the one who killed her sister.

Now, after all these years, she was about to peel the place open like prying the top off a can. She was about to get her look inside. It didn't feel real.

She rounded a curve in the road, taking it slow because of the snow, but also because she was close. And there it was, a dark, huddled shape in the distance, partially hidden by overgrown shrubs and some rough-looking pine trees. She closed in on it. Almost surprised to find no additional twinge of nerves coming over her.

She pulled into the driveway. Wheeling her head around, she glanced back down the drive. The pines blocked her view of the pavement, and she figured that would work both ways, hopefully keeping her car hidden.

She let the headlights shine on the Gibbs place for a few seconds. The run-down farmhouse looked like it would surely drop into a heap of rubble before another decade passed. Everything about the structure sagged, dipped, bulged, slumped, or drooped. Green paint peeled everywhere along the home's exterior, the exposed bits of weather-stained wood looking like rotting flesh somehow just now. Gray and bare. Gleaming some in the glow of her lights.

She swiveled in her seat, wanting to take in all of her surroundings before she made her move. The fields beyond the house, once producing crops, were now largely overgrown and wooded. It'd been a generation since any of this was farmed. Maybe two.

Finally, she killed the engine and cut out the lights. Her scalp prickled in the quiet.

She reached into the back and unzipped the duffel. Her fingers felt around for the knit material of the ski mask. Found it. The acrylic fabric scratched as she pulled it over her head. Leaning so she could see her reflection in the rearview mirror, she straightened up the eyes in the strange green glow of the dash lights.

Next, she reached back into the bag again. Pulled out the lock pick kit.

Her mind was strangely blank. Some hyper-focus whittled her thoughts down to just the next step and rendered it in images rather than language, omitting all those needless words that usually flowed through her skull.

With the lock picks stowed in her coat pocket, Charlie zipped the duffel up. She climbed out of the car, feet trampling through the crusty snow in the driveway, and hauled the bag out of the back. She didn't really want to tromp around to the back door, leaving prints in the snow, but it'd be better than trying to unlock the front, where a passing driver might see her.

The snow squeaked and cracked under her feet, and she moved out of the area lit by a distant streetlight and made her way around the side of the farmhouse. The shadows swallowed her little by little, and she was glad for the darkness that wrapped around her like a cloak.

A narrow walk led from the back door to a pile of firewood. It had been shoveled recently. Probably how Gibbs heated the place. Chopping wood all year round to get through the winters. He'd never had steady employment, as far as she knew, certainly nothing since Allie went missing. He'd mostly kept to himself in the years since. Perhaps he always had.

She pictured him again as he'd looked in the interrogation room: a bewildered man who seemed out of place under the bright lights. Frail and old. On the other hand, she'd seen the way he'd manhandled the two men at the Lakeside Tavern a few days ago. He hadn't seemed nearly so feeble then.

Her boots pounded up a set of concrete steps as she made her way to the door, footsteps echoing funny in the quiet. She squatted and brought her tension wrench to the deadbolt. With that in place and providing torque to the plug, she raked the tumblers with the tool in the opposite hand, slowly getting all the pins out of the way.

When Charlie felt the last pin give up, she twisted the tension wrench, and the bolt snicked out of the way. She pulled on a pair of gloves and wrapped her fingers around the doorknob. The warped door resisted slightly as it released from the jamb and then swung inward. This was it.

Pushing to her feet, she felt woozy, as if reality was just catching up with her. Now that she stood staring through the doorway into the dimly lit kitchen, her heart began to race. She swallowed hard and braced herself to cross the threshold. Hands and arms tingling. This time she couldn't push the feelings away so easily.

She hung there for a moment, waiting. It seemed like the perfect time for Allie to return, to squeal with delight at the dangerous, illegal thing Charlie was doing. Instead, there was only the silence of the empty house laid out before her. Eerie.

Duffel bag dangling from her outstretched arm, legs feeling strangely numb, Charlie stepped through the open door.

CHAPTER SIXTY-THREE

The hinges on the door squealed as Charlie shut it behind herself. She hesitated there on the rubber mat, taking in her surroundings while her heart chugged away in her chest.

She swept her flashlight across the kitchen, the circular glow revealing the room's details a little at a time. Junk covered every surface. Dishes and cereal boxes and catalogues clustered on the counters. An overflowing garbage bin huddled near the sink.

She knew she should get started, but the stillness made her chest flutter, made her nerves twitch. It felt like being at church or at a funeral, some hushed space. Reverent and strange.

Finally she willed herself to take one step, and then another. Even though she was moving lightly, the sounds echoed in the space.

She checked the cabinets—the upper ones first and then the lower. Opening doors and peeking inside, she found the standard stuff: Ajax under the sink. Cans of Hormel chili and Campbell's condensed soup in the cabinets. Drawers full of mismatched silverware and ancient coupon mailers. Nothing suspicious here.

Something screeched in the dark to Charlie's right. Shrill and wavering.

She froze. Listened. Chills rippling up her spine.

When it screeched a second time, she understood. The wind was scraping a tree branch against the window, that was all. She took a breath, gathered her nerves, and moved on.

She stepped into a formal dining room, though Leroy Gibbs seemed to use it for junk storage exclusively. Stacks of paperback books intermingled with rows of empty beer cans on the old farm table.

On her way to the living room beyond, she paused in front of a series of family photos hung on the wall. Judging from the hairstyles, they were from the seventies or eighties. In the half-light, the faces looked strange. Ghostly. Milky-white. Charlie aimed her flashlight at the nearest photograph, noting the haze of dust coating the glass.

There was just enough space cleared on an ancient, floral-print sofa in the living room to seat one person. The rest was piled high with a mishmash of dirty clothes, board game boxes, and more books. Across the room, an old CRT model TV squatted beside a tower of VHS tapes. The machine was bulky and huge, the likes of which Charlie hadn't seen in decades.

She used her flashlight to nudge the door leading to the small half-bath. She took one look and decided to let the beam of her light do the searching here. There was no way she was stepping inside the filthy space. Every surface had either yellowed with grime or been splotched black with mildew. Missing tiles stood out from the wall like knocked-out teeth. Water stains mottled the floor around the toilet. An inch or so of murky water sat in the clogged sink basin.

With a shudder, she moved to a stairway ascending to the second floor, her sense of dread only intensifying. Halfway up, one of the stairs let out a groan as she stepped on it, and she stopped dead. Waited. Let the silence fall around her again. Her breathing seemed impossibly loud as it heaved in and out, hitching funny in her throat.

Even though she knew she was alone here, every sound felt wrong in the hushed space. She couldn't get used to the quiet.

Finally, she pressed on. Though she stepped lightly the rest of the way up, the wood still moaned in protest, every sound making her wince.

The first door at the top of the steps led to another disgusting bathroom and two garbage-cluttered bedrooms. She peered into closets and trained her flashlight on the few swaths of dingy carpet that lay bare, hoping for something obvious like a bloodstain or a hidden wall panel leading to a secret dungeon. The kind of trace evidence she'd fantasized about on her way here would be nearly impossible to find among this mess, at least by herself.

The door to the last bedroom stood slightly ajar. Charlie elbowed her way in, eyes scanning all around her.

A shape stood there. A silhouette backlit by the moonlight filtering in through the open curtains.

Someone was in the room.

Charlie choked. Breath caught in her throat.

She stumbled backward, bashing into the wall behind her. Shoulder blades jabbing into the wood paneling.

She fumbled with her flashlight. Brought it up to illuminate the person before her.

The shape lost its detail. Morphing to a blankness under the light's touch. Then it lost its menace.

A mannequin was propped in front of the window. Probably used by a dressmaker in the Gibbs family decades ago. Tattered gray fabric showed the thing's age.

Charlie let out a shaky breath. The tightness in her chest wouldn't quite recede.

She tried to laugh it off as she pressed back into the room, but she couldn't deny the fact that the Gibbs house was doing a number on her nerves. She didn't like the quiet. Couldn't shake the feeling that she shouldn't be here. The way the house was frozen in time made her feel like a trespasser in an arcane realm.

She made her way back to the ground floor, wondering if anything in the place had been updated in twenty or thirty years. The wallpaper looked like it was from the sixties, the appliances the eighties. The most technologically advanced thing in the whole place was probably an electric razor she'd seen in the upstairs bathroom. Gibbs didn't even seem to have a computer.

Back downstairs, Charlie returned to a door off the kitchen she'd decided to save for last. The basement.

If she was honest with herself, she didn't want to go down there. She couldn't stop imagining the door slamming shut behind her the moment she entered the stairwell. But she had to be thorough. Had to make sure she checked every square inch of this house.

Charlie's heart thudded again as she took the first step down. Breathing seemed difficult in this moment. Her chest wanted to race through the motions, fluttering like a moth adhered to a screen door, the breaths coming too shallow to count for much. She had to concentrate to draw full breaths, fight the pulsating muscles along her ribcage, hold each lungful of air for a beat before she breathed out again.

The stairs creaked beneath her. The old wood straining and moaning.

Her flashlight shone down into the dark below. One lone spotlight surrounded by shadows. The glowing circle twitched on the concrete floor as she struggled to still her trembling hands.

Could this be where he hid the girls? Could Allie's remains be down here even now? Her bones tucked in some cobwebbed corner, sprawled on the floor. Waiting. Waiting for all these years.

As she reached the bottom of the steps, her light caught on a string hanging down from the ceiling. She pulled it. An overhead fluorescent bulb flickered to life.

The room seemed a little less scary once illuminated. It looked like a normal basement with poured concrete walls painted a pale gray, same as the floor, quite smooth in texture. More junk cluttered much of the floor space down here. Milk crates full of odd collections—old glass bottles, yarn, hundreds of warped records. Charlie flipped through a few of the albums. Big band stuff from the forties, mostly. Tommy Dorsey and Benny Goodman. They must have belonged to Gibbs' parents. Maybe even his grandparents.

She waded through the narrow path between the stacks of milk crates and found more rubbish still. A heap of empty beer cans crowded one corner. A few boxes of clothes even older than those she'd found in Gibbs' room. An old stove, crusted with grease.

When she finally reached the farthest wall from the steps, she stopped. Turned back. Looked over all that she'd made her way through.

It seemed obvious enough, even doing a cursory search. There was nothing here. The worst she could say about it was that it was messy and smelled like radishes.

She started back through the basement, returning the way she'd come, twisting sideways at times to squeeze through the sliver of an opening. Nausea creeping its way into her middle.

She paused a moment at the bottom of the steps, one hand resting on the rail. She reached up and pulled the string again, the room going full dark around her. And for just a second she didn't turn on her flashlight. She just stared into the abyss, into the vast black nothingness that seemed to fill all of the universe around her.

If she didn't find anything here, then she really was headed into the abyss, wasn't she? Nothing left to guide her. A cannonball plunge into the endless deep.

But no. She shouldn't think like that. She had to keep looking.

She clicked on her light again, shined it up the incline of the steps. Again she wished that Allie would speak. Would say something to reassure her or crack a joke to break the tension. Before she reached the top of the stairs, however, another thought occurred to her. What if Allie was gone for good?

CHAPTER SIXTY-FOUR

After poking through Leroy Gibbs' random junk collections one more time and finding only more garbage, Charlie went outside. She tromped through the snow toward the back of the property. The beam of her flashlight bounced along in front of her, following the up and down movement of her steps.

She thought about saying something to Allie, attempting to engage her or spur some conversation out of her, but she dared not risk it. What if her sister said nothing back? The notion of confirming this mounting fear, that Allie wasn't here with her now, was too much to bear.

The cold gripped her again within those first few steps out of the house. Harsh and dry. It numbed her face right away, reaching right through the acrylic fabric of the ski mask. For this moment she was glad for the chill, for the numbness, for all of it. In some way, the physical anesthetic slowly taking over her body kept the emotions at a distance along with the rest. She needed that now, a dulling of her feelings, because of all the possible outcomes of this search, the idea of finding nothing had never really occurred to her.

A structure took shape at the back edge of what was once the yard: a steel-sided barn crouching in a snarl of overgrown sumacs. The building stood out as blacker than the rest in this black-on-black night. As she trudged closer, she could see that it was a ramshackle thing, just like the house—rusted siding, peeling paint, and what looked like a pretty good-sized hole in the roof where the weather had invaded, peeling back the shingles and slowly but surely softening the wood to mush.

She had the hammer with her, expecting to find some kind of padlock out here, but the door was unlocked, already open a crack, in fact. The barn door groaned as she slid it a few more inches to the right, just enough to sidle through the opening.

At first, she could only see the bare dirt floor decorated with small clumps of straw. The beam of her flashlight illuminated yet more clutter here. An old claw-foot bathtub. A tangled heap of rusty bicycles. Pitchforks, shovels, rakes. A pyramid of paint cans.

Swinging her light to the right, though, she found something more interesting. A bulky form bungeed under a blue tarp. Lumpy in some places. Smooth in others. It wasn't the body she was half-expecting to find, however. It was a boat.

She swept the flashlight over the vessel, examining the exposed hull. It was made of wood with metallic-looking paint the color of copper. A motorboat, she realized. Old and dirty. It looked like it'd been trapped in this barn, swaddled beneath this very tarp, since about 1957.

She walked around the vessel, shining her light into the stalls on the other side. Empty. Nothing but more bare dirt and clumps of straw.

The nausea lurched in Charlie's gut. She lowered her light. Tried to think.

No girl. No evidence. Just the signs of a hermit, perhaps a mentally ill one at that. The reality that she couldn't prove Gibbs was the guy had started to seep in along the way, and the aftereffect was settling over her now, seeming more and more undeniable.

She swallowed. Not ready yet to face what these conclusions meant. Not ready… for what? Not ready to give up on Allie.

She swung her light up onto the boat again. The entire tarp was covered in a fine layer of dust, except for one spot. She could almost see where someone's hand had smeared the grit away. Loosening a few of the bungee cords, Charlie peeled back one side of the tarp and clambered up the wooden side.

She spotted more places where the dust had been disturbed on the deck, and she followed the trail to a small compartment near the motor. This place had been almost completely cleared of the grime that covered the rest of the boat.

She knelt. A seating pad covered the compartment, attached to the lid, and she slid her gloved fingers into the seams to remove it. The hinged lid popped as she pulled it free.

The smell hit her first. Like the time they'd lost power for a week in July when she was a kid, and fifty pounds of ground beef in their chest freezer had spoiled.

Her breath ceased as she gazed down into the chamber, the hollow place under the bench seat glowing under the glare of her flashlight. The package was irregularly shaped. Neatly wrapped in black plastic. Red-and-white baker's twine crisscrossed the bundle, looping into a precise bow on top.

Charlie's hand trembled as she reached for one loose end of the knotted twine, already certain she knew what was inside.

She tugged at the knot. With the bindings loosened, the wrapping opened and fell away like a flower blooming and withering in fast motion.

Nestled in the wrinkled sheet of black plastic, she found a pair of severed feet.

CHAPTER SIXTY-FIVE

Charlie jerked backward, gagging.

She couldn't breathe. Couldn't think. Swirls danced along the edges of her vision, and a woozy feeling came over her, made her certain she was about to faint.

She closed her eyes. Forced a big breath into her lungs. Held it, then let it out. She repeated this three times and felt the dizziness recede, even if her body still trembled.

Her eyelids fluttered open, and she stared down at the grisly bundle again. The cuts were neat. Precise. Much more surgical than what she remembered from Allie's case all those years ago.

And the nausea reeled in her belly again. Sickness. Anxiety. Dread.

She sat back from the gory package shoved down in the storage compartment and stared hard at nothing. Eyes going out of focus. Blinking in fast motion. She thought back over her search of the house. The filthy bathrooms, the junk piled everywhere, the dust that puffed up from the carpet with each step she took. The barn was no different. Messy and dirty and disorganized. Every corner filled with clutter.

And yet the feet had been wrapped so carefully. Neat and precise. Like a Christmas present from a department store. Even the grime around the area had been cleared away, as if the person who'd planted the feet here couldn't resist tidying up along the way.

Charlie froze.

Planted. The word had bubbled up from her subconscious all on its own, answering the question for her. Because that was what was wrong with the scene, wasn't it? It felt fake. Staged.

Someone was putting on a show.

She refocused on the reality before her. Leaned forward and placed the lid back over the compartment.

She stood. Moved to the edge of the boat. All these thoughts spiraled in her head. Overwhelming.

It was a staged scene, and Charlie knew what that meant. Someone, Amber's real killer, was trying to pin everything on Gibbs.

The implications grew so heavy that she buckled at the knees just as she was trying to climb out of the boat. She tumbled to the dirt floor of the barn. The straw and dirt seemed to leap up to slam into her, a heavy thud as her core connected with the hard, frozen ground. It knocked the wind out of her.

She lay there, prone, for a time. Staring at the dirt close up. Waiting for her breathing to come back to her.

At last the thought broke through to her conscious mind, the one she'd been trying to block out: if Amber Spadafore's murder and Kara Dawkins' abduction had nothing to do with Allie's disappearance, she would never solve her sister's case.

She would never find Allie now. She would never dig up her bones.

It occurred to Charlie that she was utterly at the whim of a cruel world. A killing, raping, awful world. She was useless. Powerless. She couldn't save Allie. She couldn't save Amber. Couldn't save any of them.

She whispered into the ground, her voice small.

"Allie. Are you there?"

She held her breath as she waited. Listened for that familiar voice, her heart thudding in her ears.

No response.

She spoke louder this time. Full volume.

"Allie. Please say something."

Nothing.

Allie wasn't there. Not anymore.

CHAPTER SIXTY-SIX

Charlie picked herself up off the barn floor. She batted at the dust and flecks of straw now clinging to the front of her coat. Little gray puffs rose from where her hands made contact. Her arms felt heavy, the cold sinking deeper into the flesh of her, leaving her numb.

And a movie opened in her head as she stood there halfheartedly dusting herself off.

She saw Misty Dawkins sitting across from her desk. The girl she'd known from school had grown older, a little thicker, and now she was crying. A Kleenex clenched in a fist in front of her face. Muffled sobs leaking out. Strained. Like she was trying with all of her might to hold it all in but couldn't do it. Couldn't contain the way she felt inside. It'd built up and up until it all came pouring out.

Charlie remembered snippets of what Misty had talked about. Little things about Kara being gone, about how she'd taken off before but this time she was scared, truly scared, for the first time she could remember. That sometimes moms just know this kind of thing.

And then Charlie remembered a picture of Kara, her younger brother wrapped around her piggyback-style, the two of them holding their hands up and giving the camera a peace sign.

Kara Dawkins. Kara was still out there.

That was why she couldn't give up.

Maybe Allie would never have justice, never have closure, but that only showed how much people needed it, how much people like Misty Dawkins and Amber's family needed it even still.

Charlie fled the barn, not bothering to close the door behind her. She swam back through the snow, disoriented at seeing everything from the opposite angle. She followed her tracks back until she could see the house, and then she picked up speed. Hurrying.

Her brain seemed to pick up momentum along with her feet. She ran back over the details, seeking out the missing pieces to this story. If it wasn't Gibbs, someone was deceiving her and everyone else. She had been missing something. Overlooking some piece to the case that hadn't fit the Gibbs angle but might point to Amber's real killer.

Her mind snapped to it as she neared the car: the emails. The emails didn't fit.

The first email had told her to follow the White Rabbit, which was pointing to Robbie and the ecstasy. Once Robbie had been ruled out as a suspect, the email had pivoted. It had directed her to the beach where the body was found. Whoever sent the email knew the severed feet would steer the investigation to Gibbs and the planted feet in his boat. These were both methods of throwing her off a trail—the real trail.

She ripped open the car door. Flung herself into the driver's seat. Started it. The car groaned like it always did in the cold.

The headlights shined on the dilapidated farmhouse, once again lighting those rotted pieces of wood where the paint had peeled away. Her thoughts were going so fast now that for a moment she just stared at the house, trying to untangle at least one of the strands in her head.

Charlie needed to… needed to… She put her hands on the wheel. Needed to think.

Zoe. She needed to call Zoe. But she needed to get off of Gibbs' property first.

She backed out of the driveway, tires squealing as the car swerved onto the road. A few miles from the house, she veered onto the shoulder.

She tore off her gloves and patted her coat pockets until she felt her phone's bulk. Nothing happened when she tried to wake it. Because she'd turned it off, she remembered suddenly. When it was finally powered up and ready to use, she struggled to get to the contact list with numb fingers.

By the time the phone was ringing against her ear, she had to remind herself what she was even going to say. The feet. She'd found the feet, but they were almost definitely planted. And not almost. Just definitely.

"Charlie, thank God," Zoe answered. "I called you like eight times. Where the hell are you?"

"Zoe, I'm… I just left Gibbs' house, and—"

"Charlie. Listen to me. It's Frank. Something's happened."

"Wait," Charlie said, her mind struggling to catch up. "What?"

"Your uncle. The paramedics are rushing him to McLaren Hospital, but I don't know anything more than that."

"But…" Charlie searched for the words. "Is he going to be OK?"

Zoe was quiet for what felt like a long time.

"I talked to the neighbor who found him. Mrs. Humphrey? She said it looked bad."

CHAPTER SIXTY-SEVEN

Frank lay in his hospital bed. Eyes closed. Motionless save for the inflating and deflating of his chest.

Wires and tubes circuited from machines to his hand and wrist. A monitor over the bed displayed Frank's vitals, green for heart rate, red for blood pressure, and on and on.

Charlie watched him through a pane of glass with chicken wire strung through it—the observation window, the nurse had called it. Visiting hours wouldn't resume until morning, but the small woman in pale purple scrubs had said it was OK for her to look in on him for the moment, at least until they turned out the lights in this hall. Then she went to fetch Frank's doctor.

Frank's fingers twitched, just once. Charlie leaned forward, waiting for some other sign of life, but Frank lay still again. His existence reduced to breathing. Nothing more.

Charlie hated seeing him like this. Hated that he was in this place with the strange, jittery energy echoing down the halls and the harsh fluorescent reflections sheening off tile and quartz veneer. Shiny and neat and orderly and utterly fake.

Death surrounded everything in a hospital, but it was always tucked somewhere behind closed doors. Out of sight. Out of mind.

Scrubbed. Sanitized.

A doctor in a white lab coat approached, followed closely by the same nurse from before. The pair paused in front of her, waiting for Charlie to turn her gaze away from the window looking in on Frank's room.

"You're the niece?" the doctor asked, putting out a hand for her to shake. "I'm Dr. Anagonye."

"You're not his normal doctor," Charlie said. "His oncologist, I mean."

"No, ma'am. I'm an internist here in the ICU, but I have been in touch with Dr. Silva. She's being kept abreast of Frank's condition."

"So is it the cancer?" Charlie gripped a fistful of her coat, as if holding onto herself for dear life. "Has it spread?"

The doctor looked confused for a moment before shaking his head.

"No, no. Your uncle was brought in with bacterial meningitis."

Charlie, who'd been expecting the worst, didn't know what to make of that.

"But he was fine. He's been fine."

"No neck pain or headaches?" the doctor asked.

Charlie remembered then how Frank had rubbed at his neck and commented about sleeping wrong.

"Yes, but—"

"It can come on incredibly fast. And it's not uncommon with chemotherapy patients. The fact that their immune system is weakened puts them at higher risk for infections like this."

Staring through the window at her uncle, Charlie felt a surge of hope. This whole time she'd been expecting them to tell her the cancer had progressed, that his diagnosis was no longer treatable. But it was only an infection. They'd pump him full of antibiotics, and he'd be back on his feet in no time.

"When will he wake up?"

Charlie didn't like the way the doctor glanced over at the nurse, his jaw tensed.

"I can't say for sure. Meningitis patients that present with a minimal score on the Glasgow Coma Scale have a significantly higher rate of morbidity and mortality," he said.

Charlie only understood about half of the doctor's words, but she was pretty sure she knew what "morbidity and mortality" meant in this context. Her eyelids blinked open and shut slowly. It was several seconds before she realized the doctor was still talking and had asked her a question.

"What?"

"Do you know if your uncle has an advance directive?"

Charlie shook her head.

"I don't know what that is."

"A living will? It would specify what medical action your uncle would want taken in the event he was unable to make those decisions himself."

The pause after that stretched out, emptiness swelling to fill the space in the stark hallway. Like those vast black seas of space out there. Nothingness that stretched out eternally, infinitely. When Charlie said nothing, the doctor continued.

"If there's no living will, as his next of kin, it would fall on you to make the… final decisions."

Final decisions. Meaning Charlie would have to be the one to decide when to "pull the plug," so to speak.

The doctor said more, but Charlie couldn't seem to get her brain to focus on the words. Instead, she found herself staring at a small food stain on the doctor's lab coat, a smear just left of his sternum. Spaghetti sauce? Maybe chili.

His speech ended then, and she did manage to catch the last sentence, her mind suddenly seeming to snap to attention.

"He's stable for now, but if his condition worsens…"

As the doctor turned to go, the nurse reached out and squeezed Charlie's arm.

"The lights will be on for another few minutes. Take your time."

Charlie hovered there before the window, frozen. The chicken wire embedded in the glass divided Frank and the room into tiny squares, like a mosaic.

Her phone buzzed. Without even looking to see who it was, Charlie reached into her pocket and turned the phone off. People had been calling and texting regularly since she got here, wanting updates on Frank. But she couldn't deal with that just now. Didn't want the responsibility of either delivering bad news or trying to bolster someone else's hopes.

Movement caught her eye through the glass. Frank's eyelids lurched. The skin shifting.

Dreaming, Charlie thought. *He must be dreaming.* That was good, wasn't it? But somehow, she didn't want to get her hopes up.

As if on cue, the lights in the hall snapped off. All the bulbs up and down the corridor blinking out one after another.

That was it, then. There was nothing left to do but go sit in the waiting room and… wait.

CHAPTER SIXTY-EIGHT

Charlie wound her way down the darkened hallways, the distant glow of the nursing station lighting her path. Familiar faces occupied the waiting room, three of Frank's neighbors. Betty Humphrey from next door, Linda Markowitz from down the street, and the one Charlie had only ever known as Tootsie.

She flinched as she came around the corner and saw them there, and words flung at her from all sides, buffeting her like a strong wind. *How is he? What did the doctor say? Do they know what's wrong?*

They meant well, she knew, but it didn't help. Not here and now. Her shoulders hunched out of reflex, head angled down to stare at the floor. Like maybe she could flinch back from all of this human contact.

Instead one of the women pulled her into a hug, arms coiling and flexing around her like constricting snakes.

Panicky feelings churned inside of her. Too many people. Too much stimulation. All of the contact made her feel separate. Strange and numb.

She withdrew then into herself like a snail retracting into its shell. Some defense mechanism overtaking her. Keeping her distant from the physical world. All the nerves deadened. Semi-catatonic.

The camera looking out from her eyes zoomed out, shifted its angle, pointed itself inward. Like she was looking at reality out of the corner of her eye now, never straight on.

Someone steered her onto a cushioned bench. They held her hand, talking right in her face. But it sounded like they were underwater. The words all muffled and swirling. Meaningless.

Charlie tried to focus on the face before her, but her body tingled with alienation, the throb of pins and needles rippling over her skin, until she could feel the sweat sliming her shirt under her arms. A slick membrane of dampness. It made her shudder.

And the words catapulted at her. All the faces pointed at her, jabbering away. Conversations she couldn't quite keep up with, even if she was a participant in many of them.

She didn't dwell on it. Didn't focus on it. Detached from the present. Let the time drift past. Her mind going all the way blank, eyeballs staring out at the TV on the wall or the beige ceramic tiles beneath her feet.

It felt, in many ways, like she was floating above this scene. Looking down on the waiting room from afar, from above. Apart from it. Apart from all the people. Focusing, somehow, on her two black shoes resting on that khaki floor.

She drifted like that for what felt like a long time. Gliding. Apart. Alone again, even in the crowd.

She remembered feeling this way at Allie's funeral. Empty and separate from everything. She wondered sometimes if she would have stayed that way, in a semi-catatonic state, had Allie's voice not beamed into her head and jolted her back to reality.

"This is going to sound egotistical, complaining about my own funeral," her sister had said, "but I kind of thought there'd be a better turnout, if I'm being honest. The demographics alone… lotta white hairs, am I right? We're like a couple boxes of wine away from a full-blown lemon party in here."

"They did a thing at school. For the kids," Charlie had explained. "Mom wanted to keep the actual ceremony to blood relatives, not have it, you know, overrun with a bunch of kids. Her words."

"Nice. Better for my funeral to look like a Cialis commercial or something, I guess. There are twelve guys here who look exactly like Mitt Romney. And those are the youngsters, relatively speaking."

Charlie had laughed at that. Gotten a few dirty looks from the geriatric funeral crowd.

"I wonder if the mortician was disappointed."

"Disappointed?"

"I mean, there wasn't much for him to do, right? Usually there's a whole procedure. Draining the blood and pumping in the pink embalming goo. Reconstructing any broken bits with various epoxies and putties. It'd take quite a bit of putty to reconstruct this one, I'm afraid." Allie sighed. "One closed casket to go, thank you very much. It's really a shame they don't make shoe-box-sized coffins, now that I think about it. All that wasted space. You think they put the foot up on the pillow, where my head should be? Or is it down at the bottom, where my feet would normally go?"

When Charlie hadn't answered, Allie continued her monologue.

"I feel like that's probably an underserved market. Single-serving caskets. Someone should get on that. Make a bundle."

Something jarred Charlie out of the daydream and back into the hospital. She was somewhat startled to find herself in a different seat than she remembered originally sitting down in. Now she was hunched in a remarkably uncomfortable chair—a wood-framed thing with tacky upholstery that reminded her of a school photo backdrop option called "Laser." And she faced a TV screen with the sound turned off, half-watching a seemingly endless stream of renovation projects on HGTV.

Allie's absence jabbed at her like the tip of a knife. Her sister hadn't said a word since Charlie found Amber's body, and she didn't understand why.

Allie? Are you there? Charlie thought, shaping the words in her mind.

Silence.

Worse than silence. A void. Like a piece of her was missing. A gaping wound.

She swallowed, struggling to get the saliva over the lump in her throat. Her neck constricted. Didn't want to obey.

It wasn't simply that Allie didn't speak or respond.

Allie was gone.

CHAPTER SIXTY-NINE

Hours had passed—at least Charlie thought it had been hours. Between the artificial lighting in the waiting room and the endless loop of HGTV shows flickering on the screen in front of her, it was hard to tell.

She glanced around and noticed that Linda Markowitz and Tootsie had gone. It was now just Charlie and Betty Humphrey, the one who'd found Frank.

"I was bringing him a tuna casserole. That's how it happened," she said.

Her eyes locked onto Charlie's when she spoke, cornflower-blue and bulging with strange stimulation, pupils all swollen in a way that Charlie associated with drug use. She seriously doubted, however, that the seventy-five-year-old woman with white hair and a flower-print dress had snorted any rails of crank of late.

"Did I already tell you?" Betty said. "How it happened, I mean."

Charlie shook her head. She had a feeling that she *had* heard the story already, but the night was mostly a blur of murmuring voices and a series of kitchen renovations on TV that all seemed to morph together into one gargantuan kitchen.

Betty's eyes burned brighter still once Charlie gave her the go-ahead to launch into her spiel again. Must have been a big night for her.

"So I was bringing him a tuna casserole—Frank's the kind of man who loves home cookin', and I know he can't do as much for himself these days, so I try to get over there a couple times a week with some grub."

Her hands clutched in front of her chest as she spoke, twitching there like squirrel paws, fingers wrapping over and over each other. The wrinkled skin rasped like sandpaper.

"I knocked on the door. No answer. Thought that was funny, because the lights were on. Whole mess of lights, you understand. Now, I wasn't worried. Not at first. But I felt like I should check to make sure because of, you know, Frank's condition."

She cleared her throat. Two little thrusts of air forced through the gullet. The strange sound of phlegm shifting scraped out of there, like something slimy and crackling at the same time.

"I started around the garage to the deck, you know? Figured I'd take a peek through the sliding door. And I'm bein' all careful, seein' as it's icy out, and I'm luggin' a pipin'-hot casserole pan. About halfway across the deck, I seen him through the window. Frank. Poor Frank. Lyin' there on the kitchen floor. Face down. And I just thought he was dead. Straight away. That was my gut reaction. *Oh, God. Frank just dropped dead in his kitchen.*"

Charlie noted the remnants of some accent creeping out as the story heated up—"his kitchen" coming out closer to "hees keetchen."

"So I gasp. Just about drop the casserole then and there. I hustle to the sliding door. Try it. Locked. And I see his cat there, perched on the arm of the sofa, and I remember wishing the darn cat could come unlock the door."

Marlowe. With Frank laid low, Charlie would have to remember to stop by and feed him.

Two more thrusts of air shot through the woman's throat, more mucus stirring inside.

"So I set the casserole pan down on the wooden bench there, and I called it in. Felt like the ambulance took forever to get there. And I'm just standing on my tiptoes, peeking inside, trying to get a better look at the body and what have you."

Body. That pushed Charlie over the edge. This old woman was talking about all of this like an exciting thing that had happened to her, a juicy piece of gossip she could prattle on about to all of her friends, like she'd found a dead body—just like a scene in one of her Agatha Christie novels or something.

But she wasn't talking about some bullshit whodunit here. She was talking about Frank, her uncle Frank. The man laid out just down the hall, looking gray and gaunt and just barely hanging in there.

And Allie was gone. And the case was careening away from her.

And now this old bag just wanted to talk about herself, about her thrilling experience. Brag. Dish about the big scandal, the big scoop.

Charlie gritted her teeth. Tried to stop herself from saying something cruel.

Betty went on.

"It was a lot of commotion, you know. Really rattled the neighborhood. The ambulance coming down the street, lights spinning, siren blaring. Everyone—all the neighbors—come out on their stoops to see what was going on. That's because of Frank, though, you understand. We all love Frank. Everybody. He's just adored by the whole neighborhood."

Charlie swallowed, the mean words seeming to disappear down her throat unspoken.

Betty's eyes didn't look quite so bright when she spoke again. A kind of sadness softened the skin around them, that excited bulge dying back, a wetness rising to take its place.

"Guess he just feels like a protector, you know? A watcher. Looking out for all of us, all our families, for all these years and years. It's like he's the police without the politics of all that. Maybe better than the police in a lot of ways. More pure, somehow, if that makes sense."

Charlie swallowed again. Throat going tight. Her guilt swelled some for insulting the woman, even internally.

Betty stared off into the middle distance, her voice getting quieter.

"I always wondered why he never started a family of his own, but maybe that's how it has to be for a watcher like him. They're so busy taking care of everyone else, they can't do all the domestic stuff for themselves. It's like a price he had to pay, maybe. For us. For all of us." Then Betty aimed a smile at her. "Of course, he always had you girls. Talks about you like you're his own."

Charlie burst into tears. All of the hurt rushing to the surface. Face going hot.

The water in her eyes blurred the room around her, and the hospital felt more and more distant. Like she was sinking into herself again. Drowning in the depths.

Betty clenched Charlie's hand in hers. She spoke comforting words, even if Charlie couldn't make them out specifically. She could hear the soothing tone, the reassuring lilt in the soft coos and mutters, and it helped, she thought, if only a little.

CHAPTER SEVENTY

Charlie woke just after sunrise, the first rays beaming through the windows of the waiting room and sweeping her eyelids. She squinted against the bright light. It took several seconds of rapid blinking before she could fully open her eyes and look at the clock.

It was still too early for visiting hours, but Charlie slipped down the hallway to peer through Frank's window. He looked the same. Frail. Ashen. Much older than his sixty-two years.

Charlie put her hand on the glass and tried to beam a thought into her uncle's head the same way she'd sought out Allie last night.

Hold on, Frank. Hold on, and don't you dare give up.

She spun on her heel, heading back the way she'd come. She needed to go home. Needed to feed Marlowe and take a shower and maybe sleep for a few hours in an actual bed. She'd be back, though. This afternoon, she'd return during visiting hours, and she'd finally have a chance to hold Frank's hand and tell him to his face that she expected him to put up one hell of a fight.

She pushed through the back door, stepping into the hush of Frank's house. The weight of his keys tugged at Charlie's hand as she pulled them from the deadbolt. Somehow it already seemed so vacant with him gone, even as she took just one step into the kitchen.

The quiet was unsettling. It made her chest go tight, made her eyes open a little wider, seemed to still her thoughts. She suddenly found herself conscious of the void, the sense of empty space that always accompanied silence, surrounded it.

Shadows shrouded the room, not a light on in the house, and Charlie couldn't help but wonder if it was Betty Humphrey or the EMTs who had turned them off. Probably Betty, she thought. It seemed like the kind of detail she'd consider, even in a crisis.

She flicked on the lights, and the sudden flare stung her eyes. The bulbs gleamed off the counter and the tile floor. Maybe her eyes were tired—a flash of the scene in the waiting room replayed in her head, the tears, Betty Humphrey squeezing her hands, cooing at her.

Something thumped in the next room. Charlie stared into the dark doorway beyond the kitchen. Held her breath. Listened.

A tiny patter pelted over the wood floor. Different from the earlier sound. Getting closer.

The black cat came trotting out of the darkness, crossed the threshold into the bright light of the kitchen. Marlowe. Already purring. Making eye contact with her. Tail curled at the top like a furry question mark extending from the cat's body.

Charlie couldn't help but smile at the creature. He seemed to be smiling back. Lips turning up. The tips of his top fangs exposed as always.

Frank always said Marlowe only came out like that for a small, small group of people. Always knew who was in the house, even several rooms away—by smell or by sound, he wasn't sure. That he was affectionate but very shy, and mostly hid from guests.

Charlie couldn't help but feel proud—a little special, even—to have curried the cat's favor. Of course, maybe he was just hungry.

He trotted over to his bowl and sat down, like a gentleman at a fancy restaurant, waiting patiently for his meal to be served.

Charlie dug in the cupboard. Plucked out a can of food. Read the label.

"Looks like our special this morning is turkey and giblets served in a light gravy of congealed fat," she said, eyeballing the can and then the cat. "I hope that's acceptable."

She popped the can open, dug about half of it out with a butter knife, presenting it to the beast in a stainless-steel bowl.

He sniffed it a couple times, head bobbing over it. Then his tongue flicked out, cupped a morsel of the pâté. He began to eat.

Charlie knelt and stroked the top of Marlowe's head a few times.

He closed his eyes, pleased. Though not pleased enough to stop eating, which Charlie was fine with.

She pictured Frank again, laid out in the hospital bed, body almost motionless. His eyes swiveled again beneath his eyelids, that protruding lens wandering, searching for something, pointing everywhere and nowhere.

And she couldn't help but wonder if Marlowe would be hers before long. Made her responsibility. A cat, a living being, inherited like a prized pocket watch being handed down to the next of kin.

Wasn't that the most likely outcome here? And how long would it be?

She teared up a little at the thought.

Soon. Too soon.

CHAPTER SEVENTY-ONE

While Marlowe continued mowing down his turkey and giblets, Charlie slid her phone from her pocket and turned it on. There were fourteen missed calls and five messages waiting for her.

She stared at the screen, and part of her wanted to turn the phone back off immediately. It had been refreshing to detach from everything for a while. To not be bothered with the concerns of other people's lives.

She waited, thinking this would be a perfect moment for Allie to interject with some snarky comment about Charlie's antisocial tendencies, but the only things she heard were the tiny wet noises of the cat eating.

Charlie wondered how long Allie would stay away. On the heels of that thought, a second question, worse than the first: what if she never came back?

Heaving a sigh, Charlie listened to her voicemail. All of the calls were from last night, and most of them were Zoe, trying to get in touch to notify her about Frank. But there was also one message from Will.

"Charlie, it's Will. Zoe called and told me what happened… about your uncle. I just wanted to see how you're doing. I… I'm sorry. About everything. Please call me."

Charlie held the phone in her hand for several seconds, debating whether or not she should call him. She dialed Zoe instead.

"I'm so glad you called," Zoe said after three rings. "I've been worrying about you all morning. How's Frank?"

"Not great. I haven't even been able to see him yet, except for through a pane of glass."

Zoe groaned.

"Are you still at the hospital?"

"No. I came to feed his cat, but I'm heading back to the hospital later." Charlie peeked over the counter to watch Marlowe lick the last morsels of food from the bowl.

"I'm gonna try to make it out there myself after work."

"I know that would mean a lot to him," Charlie said. "So what's going on with the case? Did they search the barn?"

"They did."

"And they found the... well... the feet?"

"Right where you said they'd be."

"And?"

There was a pause and then a rustling sound as Zoe sighed into the receiver.

"And they arrested Gibbs."

Charlie fell quiet for a few seconds. Her pulse throbbed in her ears.

"I see."

"The DA charged him with murder. They're searching the whole property right now, tearing it up, looking for any sign of Kara Dawkins, dead or alive."

"Zoe, I told you someone planted that evidence," Charlie said, then suddenly wondered if she had indeed mentioned that part. She didn't remember much of the phone call after Zoe had broken the news about Frank. But no, she was certain she'd emphasized that point.

"I know that, but look... it was already complicated enough, explaining that I got an anonymous tip on my personal cell phone. And I think you're forgetting, I'm a lowly street cop, not a detective. No one here cares what I think. Sheriff Brown is up for re-election this year. He wants an open and shut case. The last thing he wants is this dangling over his head while he's campaigning."

"It's not right," Charlie said. She wanted to say more, but the words wouldn't come. The pulsing in her ears seemed to grow louder.

"Charlie, this isn't—"

Charlie cut her off.

"Zoe, did you see the house?"

"No, I wasn't assigned to the search."

Charlie took a deep breath. The calmer she sounded, the more Zoe would have to take her seriously.

"It was a mess. Cluttered with all sorts of junk. I don't think Gibbs owns a vacuum or a broom or has ever heard of housework. But everything about the feet was neat. The way they were wrapped. Someone had wiped up the dust in the area, for crying out loud. The scene was staged."

"I hear you, but—" Zoe said, but Charlie interrupted. She wasn't going to accept any "buts" right now.

"What about the fact that the killer has been sending me emails since the beginning of all of this? There wasn't a computer in Gibbs' house. He still has VHS tapes, Zoe. *Tapes.* Leroy Gibbs has probably never sent an email in his life. There's no way he knows how to spoof an email address."

"I was there when they formally arrested him. Helped catalogue his personal belongings. He doesn't own a cell phone. Can you imagine? How is that even possible?"

Charlie gripped the phone tighter in her fist, praying that Zoe was on the path of listening to reason.

"It can't be him. None of it fits. Gibbs is not the guy."

Silence stretched out over the line. Charlie crossed her fingers.

"Bring me proof. Figure out who's sending you the emails, and I'll take it to the sheriff."

As Charlie ended the call, Marlowe strode over and wound around her ankle. She stooped to scratch the top of the cat's head.

Figure out who was sending the emails, Charlie thought to herself. Easier said than done, considering the police had already tried and failed on that front.

"What would Frank do in my shoes?" she asked the cat as she stroked the velveteen fur just behind his ears.

Marlowe didn't answer, but Frank did. Charlie stood. He'd told her what he'd do with the emails, back when she'd gotten the first one with the clue about following the White Rabbit.

"The technology stuff is all over my head, but I got a computer guy you could talk to," he'd said. "Ask for Mason, and tell him Frank sent you."

Charlie swiped her keys from where she'd dropped them on the counter and dashed for the door.

CHAPTER SEVENTY-TWO

Charlie stood for a moment in front of the huge industrial building, staring up at the sign out front. She'd assumed the dispensary was merely inside the former warehouse, perhaps one of many small shops. Now that she was here, it appeared—at least from the outside—that the dispensary occupied the entire space. The name of the place stretched from one side of the industrial facade to the other in bold white letters: Dank of America.

The front doors swooshed aside and Charlie found herself in a small anteroom. Behind a thick wall of glass—bulletproof, most likely—a man sat behind a desk.

"Good afternoon, ma'am. Have you visited us before?"

"No."

"OK. If you could just slide your ID through the slot there."

Charlie removed her driver's license and passed it through the small notch in the glass.

The man put her ID through a scanner, tapped a few buttons on his computer screen, and handed it back.

There was a subtle hiss as the inner doors of the dispensary swept open, and Charlie couldn't help but feel impressed by the level of professionalism. A dedicated security guard? Bulletproof glass? She'd been expecting something rinky-dink, a dim place lit with black lights that reeked of patchouli. Velvet posters on the wall and novelty bongs on the shelves. This seemed like a serious operation.

"You're all set."

"Thanks," Charlie said.

Stepping through the next set of doors, her wonder only increased. The interior brick walls had been painted white, giving the place a sleek, modern look. There was a row of what looked like old card catalogue cabinets from a library behind one counter. The other end of the space was set up like a small café, with the edibles displayed in glass bakery cases and apothecary candy jars. It was entirely more high-end than what she would have expected from a marijuana dispensary, especially one located on Salem Island.

Charlie approached the counter, where a woman with bright pink hair and a name tag that read, "Janice!" greeted her.

"What can I help you with today?"

"I'm looking for Mason?" Still stunned at the slickness of the place, it came out as half-question.

"One second," the woman said.

She slid a phone from a black apron at her waist and tapped at the screen.

"He should be right out."

A moment later, a man with black-framed glasses and dark hair stepped out from a door set in the back wall.

"Charlie Winters," he said. "I'd heard you were back in town."

"Hello, Mason."

Mason Resnik had been in the same class as Charlie and Allie all the way from second grade through graduation. He was so good with computers, even back then, that the school district had hired him to do tech support while he was still a sophomore. She remembered him getting called out of English lit more than once to troubleshoot for the principal.

He leaned his elbows on the counter.

"What's brought you to my humble establishment today? Business or pleasure?"

"Business, actually."

"Working for Frank, I hear."

"Yeah. I have a computer-related mystery I could use some help with."

"Why don't you come back to my office?" he said, gesturing that she should follow him.

He came around the counter and led her down a hallway. They passed a bank of windows on one side that looked out on a warehouse area. The huge space had been converted into a massive grow room—literally a forest of marijuana. At least half a dozen employees worked among the plants, all of them wearing lab coats, masks, and hair nets.

"Holy shit," Charlie said.

Mason turned and flashed a smile.

"What do you think of my empire?"

"You've come a long way from carving a bong out of a block of Cheddar cheese."

"I forgot about that," he said, chuckling.

His office was up a flight of open stairs that led to a second-floor loft space with exposed concrete walls and black steel beams. The entire back wall was glass. Through the paned window in Mason's office, Charlie watched a barge float past, being pushed upriver by a tugboat.

"Let's see what you've got," Mason said, pointing to an open spot on his desk.

"Someone sent me a couple of weird anonymous emails. I didn't take the first one that seriously, but… well, things have changed."

Charlie got out her laptop and opened the first anonymous email.

Wheeling closer, Mason studied the screen.

"'Follow the white rabbit. Find her,'" he said, reading the first message aloud. "Kind of creepy."

"Just wait," she said, pointing to the second email.

Charlie watched his eyes dart back and forth as he read.

"A mysterious package? This is some real James Bond shit. What was it?"

Chewing her lip, Charlie looked at him sideways.

"A body."

"Like a dead body?"

She nodded.

He leaned back in his chair, eyebrows just about touching his hairline.

"Whoa," he said, and just when it looked like he was going to say something else, he said it again. "Whoa."

"Yeah."

"I was going to ask what had changed to make you suddenly take these so seriously, but I guess I have my answer."

He gestured toward the laptop.

"May I?"

Charlie scooted it over to him.

"The police took a look and declared it a dead end, but... I guess I was hoping you might find something they didn't." Charlie pointed at the header of the email. "See here, how it looks like I sent the email to myself?"

"Spoofed," Mason said. "It's pretty common with scammers these days. They can do it with phone numbers, email addresses... an easy way to cover their tracks."

"Is there a way to find out who really sent it?"

"Let's see." Mason bent closer to the computer, fingers flying over the keyboard. "Well, the good news is that this isn't a very elaborate spoof attempt. You can see the original sender right here."

He pointed at a foreign email address on the screen, a Gmail address made up of a string of apparently random characters.

"And the bad news?" Charlie asked.

"The bad news is that you can't really trace Gmail addresses. The IP address just comes back as a Google server."

"I was afraid of that," she said. "So there's no way to find out who sent it?"

"Well, we could…" He started to type again, then paused, frowning. "Is your computer always this laggy?"

Charlie crossed her arms.

"No, but it has been kind of funky the last day or so."

Mason worked quickly, opening windows, typing commands. He was so fast that Charlie could barely keep track of what he was doing.

After a few moments, he stopped abruptly and asked, "Do you have kids?"

"No. Why?"

"Well, if you had kids, it might be a reason for you to install a keylogger on your computer."

"A keylogger?"

"Yeah, it's a program—spyware, basically—that keeps track of every keystroke. Everything you type, every password, everything—it logs it and sends it on to another computer."

"Right. I know what a keylogger is. But I didn't install it."

Mason tapped a finger against one of the icons on her computer screen.

"Well, whoever did messed up. Usually the programs have a way of hiding themselves from the user. Only the person who installed it has the password to access it. If this had been installed correctly, I probably wouldn't have been able to spot it. Not without a lot of digging."

"I think I already know what the answer is, but is there any way to figure out who installed it?" Charlie asked.

"Well, parents sometimes install it to monitor their kids' internet activity. Spouses might use it to spy on their significant other. Employers use it to find out what kind of personal browsing their employees are doing on the company computers. Criminals generally want to try to steal passwords and credit card information. Which one would best apply to you?"

"None. It sure as hell wasn't my mother. I don't have a significant other. Frank is technically my employer, but you know how he is. Even if he wanted to spy on me for some reason, he gets confused checking his email. And I don't know any criminals who would have had access to my computer, unless…"

Mason waited for her to go on, both eyebrows raised.

"What if it's the same person who's been sending the emails? What if the killer installed it so he could keep tabs on the investigation? Know where I was looking?"

Charlie's mind latched onto the idea, spun it around, considering every angle. It would explain why he'd been able to pivot so quickly once they'd ruled Robbie Turner out. If the killer was spying on her, he would have known he'd need to provide a new scapegoat. That was why he'd dumped the body that pointed to Gibbs as a suspect and planted the evidence on the Gibbs property. It all fit.

"Can you think of any times your computer would have been accessible?" Mason asked. "That might narrow it down."

"Yeah."

"When?"

"All the damn time. I have it in the office with me every day. The front door is open for anyone to come in. Any time I run upstairs for a cup of coffee or something, someone could slip in and out. And I'd have no idea."

"Well, I can try to remove it," Mason said. "It should only take a few minutes."

Mason's fingers moved to the keyboard again, but Charlie held up a hand to stop him.

"Wait." The plan formed in her head almost instantly. She could sense it there, a throb in her subconscious that occurred a beat before it came spilling out into her mind fully formed. "Don't remove it."

"Are you sure? They can literally see everything you type. Take screenshots. Some of them even let the hacker record audio."

Finalizing each step in her head, Charlie nodded.

"I'm sure. I have a plan."

If the killer was logging everything she typed, maybe she could use that to smoke him out.

CHAPTER SEVENTY-THREE

Charlie sat at her desk, the infected laptop screen staring back at her. She brought her hands forward as though to rest them in the customary spot, fingers splayed over the home row of the keyboard—but then she retracted them just as quickly. Crossing her forearms over her chest, she watched the computer out of the corner of her eye.

Why was she so reluctant to touch the thing? Was she afraid of it?

Her entire plan hinged on using the damn laptop, and the keylogger was the linchpin to the scheme. But she couldn't help it. The whole thing gave her the creeps. The idea that someone had come in here, invaded her space, installed spyware on her computer while she was away, and logged every single keystroke since. She shuddered just thinking about it, that vulnerable feeling crawling over her skin like pinpricks.

Her head swiveled to take in the room around her. She suddenly became quite conscious of the windows, the open blinds showing a clear view of the street, where anyone might look in on her. Just sitting near the glowing laptop screen made her feel like someone was watching her now.

She rose from her seat and closed the blinds. Shadows swelled to fill the room.

That felt better. Sort of.

That must be one of her phobias, she realized—to be watched without knowing about it. Rather ironic, considering her profession. Another perfect setup for an Allie insult that wouldn't come.

Charlie's eyes went to the screen again. She'd gone to see Zoe and set the rest of the plan in motion. All she had to do now was this last part.

She settled back in her desk chair. This time her hands didn't hesitate. She rested her palms alongside the touchpad, and her fingers hammered the keys now, typing a fast string of nonsense letters into the open text file before backspacing over all of them. That seemed to break the spell, the malevolent machine before her dying back to a normal laptop again.

She took a breath. She was just typing an email to Zoe, something she'd probably done a hundred times before without thinking about it. That was all. If it so happened this particular email was the bait in a trap, well…

The letters popped up on the screen as the keys clattered beneath her fingertips.

Zoe,

I found something in the Amber Spadafore/Kara Dawkins case. Something big.

I know this sounds paranoid, but I have reason to believe that someone has been listening in on my phone calls somehow. I'm worried that your office may likewise be compromised, so it's best if we talk in person. Somewhere safe. We need to proceed with absolute caution.

Meet me at the gazebo in the center of Ramsett Park tonight at 9 p.m.

Charlie

She looked over the email. It sounded a little cloak-and-dagger, but she worried that if she wasn't fairly obvious about it, the killer wouldn't take the lure. She needed him to be at the park.

She'd considered bluffing that she knew the real identity of the killer, but that could motivate him to kill Kara Dawkins if he hadn't already. Better to be cryptic. Tantalize. Try to draw him out of his hidey hole.

It was still something of a long shot, but as Allie had once told her, that was better than no shot.

CHAPTER SEVENTY-FOUR

Dusk had already faded to full dark by the time Charlie and Zoe arrived at Ramsett Park. They'd driven separately and positioned themselves at opposite ends of the L-shaped parking lot so they could keep an eye on all entrances.

Knowing her computer had been hacked, Charlie was worried her phone may be compromised as well, and she wasn't taking any chances. She and Zoe were keeping in touch via a pair of walkie-talkies Charlie had found in the back room of the office. She vaguely remembered her and Allie playing with them as kids, concocting make-believe spy scenarios and cop-and-bandit games.

"Nothing doing over this way," Zoe's voice crackled.

"Same," Charlie said back, holding the button with her thumb as she spoke. In this case, "nothing doing" meant literally nothing. Not a single car had passed Charlie's side, and she figured the same for Zoe's watch. That made sense to a large degree, especially on a cold night in the dead of winter such as this was. The park sat all the way on the east side of the island, not really a convenient traffic route to anywhere of import. The only people they were likely to see driving out this way were the people who lived in the immediate block or two, and maybe, just maybe, their killer. If her plan worked.

Charlie sipped hot coffee from the lid of her thermos, wanting to savor it before it cooled. Chances were they'd be here a while, she knew, and this coffee's current temperature stood almost no chance of holding out for the duration of the stakeout. She picked up her phone, wanting to double-check the time. She knew it'd been fifteen minutes tops since she'd gotten here, but some anxious part of her needed to verify that fact with her own eyes.

The white numbers came to life on the black screen, glowing for a beat before receding once more. It was 8:03 p.m. now, meaning they were still an hour away from the rendezvous time they'd set at the gazebo.

Her eyes flicked to the dark structure at that thought. Found it empty, of course. A spindly silhouette of stick-like beams with a wedge of darker, thicker roof hung above, the gazebo was a well-chosen stakeout location. Rising out of a clearing at the center of the park, they should be able to see anyone approaching it, even in the dark.

"You there, Aardvark?" Zoe's voice crackled again.

Charlie picked up the walkie, depressing the button on the side. "Aardvark?"

"I decided we needed code names," Zoe explained. "You're Aardvark. I'm The Jackal."

"Wait a minute. Why do you get a cool code name, but mine is super nerdy?"

"I don't make the rules, Aardvark. You and I both know this kind of thing comes from higher up the chain. Also, please keep this channel clear unless you have pertinent information. I don't think I need to tell you that this is neither the time nor the place for idle chatter. Over."

"I'm glad you're having fun with this," Charlie said. "I can tell you're really taking it all very seriously."

In reality, Charlie was glad Zoe had agreed to follow along with her ridiculous plan. She'd done enough work like this on her own that she knew having someone to talk to made it way less boring. Especially with Allie still out of commission.

On cue, Zoe's voice came over the speaker again.

"What was the name of the science class everyone had to take freshman year? It wasn't biology or chemistry or anything like that. It had some super generic name."

"Physical science?"

"Yes! I was just thinking about the time Mr. Olson had the class read this chapter about biomes out loud and then fell asleep. It wasn't the first time it happened, and we always liked to see how long we could go before he woke up. So the reading got around to Allie, and instead of 'organisms' she said 'orgasms.' There were a few chuckles, but we were trying so hard to be quiet, and I think everyone thought it was an accident, at first. A slip of the tongue, you know? But the word was in there like eight times, and she said it *every time*. With a completely straight face. Nelson Wong was next up, and he kept it going. Orgasm this, orgasm that. Then it was my turn, and I couldn't *not* do it. By the time the bell rang at the end of class, everyone was in on it. We were all dying."

A few puffs of laughter exited Charlie's nose. The influx of warm breath made her realize how cold the tip had gotten.

"Oh yeah. That's classic Allie."

As she spoke, some part of her thought that surely Allie would take the bait, come back to bask in the glow of her accomplishments. She couldn't resist, could she? But the lull when Charlie finished talking, the prolonged moment of quiet, did all of Allie's speaking for her.

"I've just been thinking about her a lot lately," Zoe said. "Probably because of Kara and Amber, I guess. More missing girls on Salem Island after all this time. It has a way of dredging things up. All the old memories come flooding back… That feeling probably never really goes away for you, huh?"

Charlie's throat tightened when she tried to answer, that pink flesh beyond her mouth constricting as though trying to choke her. When her lips opened, no words came out. She stared at the walkie-talkie clenched in her fingers, the black segmented panel where the tiny speaker lay beyond a thin layer of mesh seeming to stare right back at her. She wanted only to press the stupid button on the side, mumble some reassuring words into the thing, be a normal human being having a normal conversation, but she couldn't. Not now.

When the silence stretched out for too long, Zoe piped up again. "Charlie? You there?"

Charlie's eyelids fluttered. She cleared her throat. Pressed the button on the walkie-talkie at last.

"Yeah, I'm here. Sorry about that. Dropped my walkie there for a second and had to fumble around for it."

Zoe chuckled at that, and Charlie took another sip of her coffee, trying to wash that strange moment off her palate. It was starting to cool just the faintest bit, no longer the near-scalding temperature that she preferred. Hot enough to set her lips and tongue to tingling. Still, she couldn't complain.

Her eyes snapped back to the gazebo, the paranoid part of her once again expecting to see activity there. A shifting in the shadows. A silhouette. A flickering flashlight dancing over the snowy sidewalk. Something. Anything.

The octagonal structure stood as empty and motionless as ever. The park was as dead as the streets out here. Vacant and lifeless. Just a quiet, peaceful night on Salem Island, save for the murderer out there somewhere, and the girl he may be holding captive even still. Charlie imagined a spider wrapping a moth in its web, saving it for later.

She swallowed, something clicking deep in her throat. It occurred to her for the first time that she could feel the blood surging along in her neck. The veins punched at the muscles there with each beat of her heart, making the flesh twitch.

The mounting tension made sense, Charlie thought. One way or the other, this night would play out from here, probably within the next hour or so. The guy would show at the gazebo, or he wouldn't. They'd crack the case open like a hardboiled egg, or they'd fail.

Now or never.

When headlights glinted in her rearview mirror, her eyes flicked up to watch them. The car turned onto the street running alongside her end of the lot, slowing as it neared the park. Charlie held her breath.

CHAPTER SEVENTY-FIVE

Charlie ducked down in her seat as the car crept past her parking spot. Heart thudding. Eyes opened so wide they stung, staring into the dark through the windshield. She held her breath and listened.

The tires crunched over the snow in the lot, busting up the crusty stuff as they shambled forward. The engine's growl grew stronger, deeper. As the car drew alongside hers, the rumble rattled the floor of her car, sending strange vibrations into the meat of her feet and ankles.

Tilting her head up, she watched the shimmer of the headlights spread their glow over her dashboard. The lights moved like liquid, lurching and spilling onto the hood, sliding past along with the passing car.

The pitch of the grinding engine changed as the car cruised by her, and then the growl seemed to move forward no more. It held steady. Whirring along in place. Had he stopped? So close? Was he looking into the park now, studying the gazebo?

She waited as long as she could before she lifted her head to peer over the steering wheel. The bright flare of the brake lights glinted a bloody red over the snow. He'd stopped just a couple car lengths beyond her.

The car was a real piece of shit, she realized now. A small Toyota sedan with rusted-out fenders, old as hell. Probably a hole in the muffler, based on the sheer volume of the exhaust noise.

She squinted. Focused on the silhouette seated behind the wheel. Shadows flitted and fluttered like twisting smoke within the dark on the driver's side, but she couldn't make out what she was seeing.

The window slowly rolled down, buzzing a little as the pane of glass disappeared between the rubber lips there. He was putting his window down, trying to get a better look into the park. This was it. It had to be him.

Charlie held her breath again. Watching. Waiting. Knowing in her heart that something was about to happen here.

A half-wadded McDonald's bag flew out of the car window. It rolled like tumbleweed, skittering into the gutter. Based on the slight bulge to the thing, she could tell it was full of garbage. Probably your standard fry sleeve, burger wrapper, and waxed paper cup. Perhaps a cardboard nugget tray. The tip of a straw poked out of the top.

A couple of empty Sprite bottles followed that, making hollow thunking sounds that reminded her of ping-pong balls as they bounced along the asphalt and settled in the low spot near the bag. Then the window whirred to life again, this time going up.

It took Charlie several seconds to process what she was seeing. Littering. He was littering.

It wasn't the killer, she realized. This wasn't significant to their stakeout at all. It was just some dirtbag cleaning out his piece of shit car.

The driver's door cracked open, an ashtray appearing there in the opening, tipping over. Cigarette butts plummeted to the asphalt like raindrops, clouds of wispy ash mushrooming all around them.

Littering. Unbelievable, and somehow very offensive. So selfish. So vulgar. She could spot two garbage bins on the park premises without even turning her head, and this guy was just dumping his trash on the ground.

Charlie's mind raced to think of an insult. This guy was a… a… a litterbug. The insult felt anticlimactic. It didn't seem strong enough to describe how she felt about him just now. Too cutesy. She thought maybe Allie would have thought of something better. Probably something dirty and borderline inappropriate and awesome.

Charlie thought about confronting the guy. The car was still sitting there, brake lights shooting that red glare over everything. She couldn't risk it, though. She had to stay hidden.

Instead, she lifted her walkie to her mouth, felt the tremor in her hand from the spike of adrenaline she'd gotten when the car had first rolled up.

"Jackal, this is Aardvark. I just had some action over this way," she said. "A bit of a false alarm, really."

"I have to say, Aardvark, I appreciate your commitment to the code names. But go ahead. Whaddya got?"

"Oh, just some scumbag in a beat-up Toyota dumping his fast-food wrappers all over the street. The jerkoff is still sitting here now. Bold as brass. Probably trying to think of what other trash he can throw out his window."

"Nice. Well, give me his plate number, and we'll be sure he gets a little participation trophy for his efforts. Our lucky winner's ticket carries up to a $500 fine."

Charlie chuckled as she read off the plate number. That'd be a nice surprise for her new friend here.

The junky Toyota lurched to life at last, shuffling forward. The engine revved and popped, picking up speed before it veered out of the lot and disappeared.

"He just took off, so I'm back on my lonesome over here," Charlie said. "I'm so excited for him to get his ticket, though."

"Oh yeah. Nothing doing over here still," Zoe said. "I heard a car go by one of the side streets a while back, but it didn't come within viewing distance. Other than that, I've eaten like half a box of Cheese Nips."

Charlie smiled and leaned back in her seat, letting the headrest cradle her skull.

"Remember that time we snuck into the cemetery at night and tried to do a séance?" she asked. "You found some how-to thing online that suggested bringing along some kind of food or drink as an offering to the spirits, so we spent forever ransacking your parents' kitchen, trying to find just the right thing."

A bark of laughter came over the walkie-talkie.

"What'd we end up taking? I don't remember," Zoe said.

"Mountain Dew, gummy bears, and Flamin' Hot Cheetos."

"Nice. What about when Kyle Polarski shat on the skylight over the school cafeteria?"

"That was Kyle?" Charlie asked. "I thought it was Scott Bauman."

"Scott might have been there, but I think Kyle did the deed. You know, he's a gym teacher at the middle school now. I'll ask him next time I see him."

"Please do. I'm sure he'll love that."

Time seemed to speed up some as Charlie and Zoe reminisced. Was there something about conversing over these walkie-talkies that spurred the memories along? Charlie thought so. It was as though the little communication devices thrust them right back into childhood, set them jetting backward in time, boats against the current, borne back ceaselessly into the past and all that F. Scott Fitzgerald stuff.

The creeping gray of nostalgia snuck up on her, enveloped her, shook her out of that tense feeling she'd had when the litterbug had gone past, and shifted her into something of a wistful mood. Some longing feeling she didn't quite understand.

In any case, the clock moved faster. The coffee grew colder. But Charlie didn't mind any of it, even if this particular nostalgia maintained a distinctly bittersweet flavor. It was better to talk, to remember, to share these feelings with someone outside herself. Much better than facing it all alone, she thought.

She poured out the last of the coffee, the runnel of black growing thin as it descended from the thermos, receding into a few dark droplets. She sipped it. Just faintly warm now. Better than nothing.

She checked the time on her phone. The white letters glowed back 8:44 p.m. That made her lick her lips. Only sixteen minutes left on the countdown clock. Would he not show after all? She hadn't anticipated that possible ending, not truly.

But maybe it made sense. Nothing instead of something.

We never contemplate the empty spaces in life, she thought. *We see the walls and furniture and think of those as the room instead of all the space around them—the vast expanse of nothing that lies within the borders. Scientifically speaking, most of the universe is composed of nothing, right down to each of the cells that constructed our bodies. Why is that notion so hard to hold onto? We lack some kind of spatial awareness for it. So often we behave as though the objects around us comprise reality when most of the universe is empty. Nothing. Infinite black space flecked with relatively tiny stars.*

She swallowed the last of her coffee, feeling that little bit of grit in her throat, the sludge that had collected at the bottom of the thermos. As soon as the cup went all the way empty, a pang of regret welled in her, some grave concern that she'd have none left to sip at while she waited.

She lifted the phone again. Waited for the glowing numbers to appear. The time changed from 8:46 to 8:47 as she looked upon it.

Lights gleamed in the rearview mirror, and Charlie sat up straighter to watch. Headlights shining out from a dark sedan. This one seemed nicer than the litterbug's vehicle, even from a distance. It was newer and bigger—one of those boats that old, upper-middle-class people drove. A Cadillac or Buick, maybe. She couldn't quite tell with the clusters of snow hugging parts of the car.

The beams swiveled around the corner behind her and rolled right past. Charlie ducked again as it got close—watching, waiting for it to turn into the lot—but this car didn't slow. It zoomed on by. She tried to get a look at the license plate, but that too was largely tucked behind a crust of snow.

Oh, well. More nothing, she thought. Probably a resident of the area heading home.

"Just had a dark sedan zoom by," Charlie said into the walkie-talkie. "Didn't slow down or anything, so I figure it was nothing."

Zoe didn't respond right away.

"Yep. Yep. I've got eyes on him now," she said finally. "He just turned down this way."

"Yeah?"

"Well, this is interesting. He just took another right. I think he's heading back in your direction."

Another right. That didn't sound like someone who lived here. That sounded like someone circling the park.

She watched the mirror. Waited. Tried not to get her hopes up. Not yet.

A moment later, headlights flared in the corner of the mirror. As the vehicle got closer, she saw that it was indeed the same car.

"He's coming back," Charlie said.

This time he slowed and pulled into the park entrance. Charlie crouched down, trying to keep the car in view. Her heart punched at the walls of her chest like it was knocking on a door, asking to be let out.

The reflection of the brake lights tinted the snow scarlet. And then a bright white glow mixed in with the red—he had put the car in reverse.

Charlie whispered into the walkie-talkie, "He's parking. I think... I think it's really him."

The car's engine changed to a higher pitch and cut out then. The sudden quiet had an empty feeling to it. After a second, the red glow from the brake lights went dark.

A strange rush hit Charlie then, an almost overwhelming feeling of adrenaline flooding into her bloodstream. Her palms went icy-cold, and she had the sudden urge to burst into a fit of hysterical giggles. When she glanced up and caught a glimpse of herself in the mirror, she found she had gaping black pits for pupils.

When the car door slammed shut, she peeked out through the steering wheel again.

A dark figure stepped away from the car. A man bundled in a puffy coat, hat pulled down low over his brow. He hunched forward, something she interpreted as a reaction to the cold. His feet punched through the snow, taking slow steps at first and then speeding up as he made it to the sidewalk. After looking both ways, he veered into the park, not heading straight for the gazebo but instead making his way along a path toward the stream and trees on the east side of the park. If she remembered right, there was a place along the trail there that would be a perfect position for spying on the gazebo.

Charlie's breathing grew faster and faster, hitting top speed as the dark shape disappeared into the elongated shadows under the trees.

CHAPTER SEVENTY-SIX

With numb hands, Charlie thumbed the button on the walkie-talkie.

"Subject looks to be an adult male, around six feet tall. He just entered the park on foot," she said.

"Holy shit. This is really happening."

"Zoe, listen. This might be him, or it might be nothing. You stay there and keep watch in case it's the latter," she said. "I lost him in the shadows down along the stream, so I'm going in for a look. If I'm not back in, let's say, seven minutes, come in after me."

"Charlie, wait—"

But Charlie turned down the walkie-talkie before Zoe could finish her sentence. She needed silence now. No debates. No interruptions. Absolute quiet.

She stepped out of the car, closing the door behind her with a delicate touch. Then she shoved the walkie-talkie into her coat pocket and drew her gun.

She hurried across the street and into the park. Light on her feet. Soundless.

She slipped into the long shadows under the trees, all those limbs reaching out across the ground, blocking out the light. The dark place enveloped her, welcoming her. She knew he must be close. Closer than ever.

Her breath came soft and shallow. In through the lips and out through the nostrils. Trying to stay ever so quiet.

Her skin crawled as she pressed into the darkest of the gloom, and she slowed, no longer able to see much. Ambiguous shapes occupied the space ahead. Hulking contours blacker than the rest. Crooked. Fragmented. She knew she must be seeing tree trunks and brush and maybe some park benches or fencing, but her eyes couldn't make sense of any of them just now. She saw only sinister forms in the murk. Malevolent. Menacing.

The gun trembled at the end of her outstretched arm. She kept it angled down, the muzzle pointed toward the cement pathway sprawling out in front of her, the one thing she could still faintly see. The dark concrete aisle snaked through the snow, led her to wherever she was going.

Something writhed in the shadows to her left, and Charlie froze. Raised the gun. Squinted to try to make it out. Strange ripples stirring in gloom.

Her lips moved as though to call out, to ask whoever it was to reveal themselves. But she held her tongue. Something didn't feel right. Some part of her knew that she should know what she was looking at this time, something familiar in the way it moved.

Water. The fluttering she sensed was the trickle of the stream, not all the way frozen just yet. As soon as she recognized it for what it was, she could hear the little hiss it made. A whispered murmur without end.

And then she saw him. The figure. The man. He stepped out of the shadows and into the light, walking away from her, hands tucked in the pockets of his puffy coat. His back fully to her, an air of comfort about him, something confident in the way he moved. He didn't know she was there.

She followed, closing on him, still soundless. A crazy feeling came over her as she drew closer and closer. Half-terrified. Half-empowered. As though she were some lioness on the prowl just now. Hunting. Stalking another kill. Taking what belonged to her.

She got to within fifteen feet of him, and the details started to fill in on his person like a camera going into sharper focus. The texture and movement of the hair protruding from the back of his stocking hat. The stitched seams carving out the puffed bubbles on his jacket. The clouds of steam venting from his nose when he exhaled.

His head pivoted to look upon the gazebo off to their left, shadows of branches dappling over him as he moved. Chin tilting up and then down as he took it in, giving it a good, long look. Charlie's heart jumped at that. Further confirmation, wasn't it? This was the guy, staking out the place. Waiting for her and Zoe to arrive.

He moved into the clearing, finally out from under the last of the shadows, and in that moment, the distinct angle of his nose was cast in sharp relief against the moonlight shimmering down there. Light and darkness conspired to reveal that aquiline bump just lower than his brow. Charlie recognized the profile.

Will Crawford.

CHAPTER SEVENTY-SEVEN

Charlie's breath caught in her throat, some emotion reaching up to choke her. Clasping its crooked fingers so tightly that the sting brought tears to her eyes.

Shock. That's what this feeling was, some distant part of her knew. Shock and horror. That detached feeling came over her again, just like all those times before. Her legs tottered beneath her, deadened and numb. Somehow still holding her up.

And this strange sensation dislodged memories from way down deep, flooded them up from the darkness. She'd felt this before—an overwhelming disgust and loathing and disbelief—when Allie had disappeared. All those sleepless nights, lying in bed, staring up at the ceiling, inconsolable. All those eerie moments when she'd ventured into their empty bedroom, felt the absence in the hush of the space, felt the lack of Allie there in a visceral way like the hollow feeling she got after a punch in the stomach.

She focused on her breathing. Forced her throat to open, to let the wind in. It took a second to get the rhythm of it back under control.

Will. It was Will. How could it be him?

She ran the story of the missing girls back through her mind in fast motion, drawing the line between Will and the crimes. He'd known both of the victims, representing Kara Dawkins professionally and doing business with Amber Spadafore's father. Will had been the one who'd told her about the Red Velvet Lounge and had apparently frequented the place enough to be considered a regular. He would have had easy access to not only Charlie's office but her apartment, would know better than most when it was likely to be empty. And then there was the Leroy Gibbs connection. The falsely accused murderer was his cousin as well as his client, for God's sake. Will had access to Gibbs' property to plant evidence, and he knew the long-term history as well as anyone on Salem Island. Gibbs. Allie. He knew all of these people personally, rotated in the same orbit as everyone enmeshed in the crimes.

He'd been present at every step of the investigation, asking her questions about it, hiding in plain sight. A snake. A murderer.

Another thought struck her then. If Will was setting Gibbs up now, had he done it before?

She went over everything in her mind, the things Will had said to her about Allie.

Dear God. Had Will killed Allie? Was that why he'd been so certain that Gibbs couldn't have done it?

Nausea roiled in Charlie's gut. Lurching and spitting like a lantern. A twinge of sickness stabbed at her, so sharp in her middle that for a few seconds she thought she might vomit.

She swallowed a few times in a dry throat. Let the queasy feelings pass.

It made sense. Crazy as it seemed, it all made perfect sense. Will Crawford was the killer.

Charlie raised her shaking arms, pointed the gun at Will's back, tried her best to steady the weapon, to stop the muscles up and down her forearms and shoulders from twitching like mad.

When she spoke, her voice came out loud and sharp, ringing out over the empty park.

"Don't move."

CHAPTER SEVENTY-EIGHT

Will turned in slow motion. The furrow between his brows loosening when he saw it was Charlie behind him. For a split second, he looked pleased, a smile forming at the corners of his mouth. Then his eyes shifted down to the gun in Charlie's hands, focused on the black bulk of the weapon clasped between her fingers, and his eyebrows shot straight up.

"Charlie, what are you doing?"

"Put your hands up," Charlie said.

Her voice shook just a little. She hoped he didn't hear that.

All sound seemed to be whooshing around her now, the night air sibilant, whispering a string of nonsense syllables that seemed to fall in and out of time with the blood roaring in her ears. She swallowed and gave her head a shake. Tried to fight off the auditory hallucinations without effect.

Will's hands lifted up to near his ears, looking red from the cold.

"I don't understand what's happening."

"You've been spying on me," Charlie said.

His mouth opened and closed, as if he couldn't decide whether he wanted to try to deny it or not.

"You installed a keylogger on my computer."

"OK, look. I can explain." His shoulders came up in a shrug. "This isn't what it must seem like—"

"Quiet now," Charlie cut him off.

She wasn't interested in hearing his excuses just now. Didn't think she'd be able to process it all with the shock still running through her. She needed to focus on keeping the gun on him until Zoe got here. After that, there'd be time for talk.

Probing with her elbow, Charlie could feel the bulk of the walkie-talkie in her right coat pocket. She wanted to get the thing out, call Zoe, but she didn't dare take either of her hands off the gun, didn't dare take her eyes off Will. Not now.

Zoe would come. Soon. They'd made a plan, right? Seven minutes. That had to be coming up already. Had to. Any second now.

"Charlie, lower the gun at least. Please. I'm not dangerous. This whole thing is a misunderstanding."

"Shut up."

Will took a step forward, one of those elongated shadows from the branches above falling over his face for a second, blotting out one eye.

Charlie backpedaled several paces.

"Stay back."

She gestured with the gun as though to remind him that she had it. Any intimidating effect was likely undercut by the fact that her whole body was trembling.

The night whooshed louder. Flapping insects seemed to surround her, swooping ever closer. Her heart raced, more of a slurred murmur than the knocking beats that had pounded in her chest earlier. Some distant part of her thought she may be verging on a panic attack.

Where the hell was Zoe? She had to be here by now. Didn't she?

She took one hand from the gun and reached for her pocket. Her fingers clasped around the walkie-talkie, gave a pull. The bottom slid out easy enough, but the antenna caught on the edge of the pocket. Charlie glanced down, just for a second, only wanting to get the walkie unstuck.

And the next thing Charlie knew, Will was on her. The walkie-talkie spilled out of her pocket, striking the pavement somewhere in the shadows, but she was too focused on keeping her hold on the gun to think about that now. Will gripped her forearms, fingers as hard as steel. He threw his weight into her, his hip bashing into her abdomen. Knocking her back on her heels. Off-balance.

And then his hands were on the gun. Prying. Lifting.

She gripped tighter, but he was bigger, taller, stronger.

He ripped the gun away.

CHAPTER SEVENTY-NINE

Charlie gasped. A creaking sound torn from her throat. Lips parted. Jaw agape.

Her mind whittled down to a singular focus: her tunnel-vision view of her gun in his hand. The matte black of it partially concealed by his palm and fingers. It looked so much bigger now that he had it.

He didn't point it at her, though. Didn't even hold it by the grip. Instead, his bony fingers clasped around the top of the slide, barrel facing down toward the sidewalk.

"There. See? No one is in danger. Now, will you just listen?" His voice tried for a soothing tone. Soft and quiet, as if he could reassure her somehow.

But Charlie was beyond listening. Beyond reason. She was an animal trying to survive.

Her fingers stung. Raw and red from where he'd stripped the weapon away from her. The cold reached in to touch the wet in her mouth, in her throat.

Like a striking cobra, Charlie leapt forward and kicked him in the balls. The crack of her foot striking his groin sounded like a vicious helmet-to-helmet hit in a football game, the kind that put someone's lights out and brought out the stretcher and cart.

Will buckled over at the waist, hands cupping his crotch. One big breath huffed out of him, the steam coiling there before his bulging eyes. Coiling and disappearing.

His lips popped a few times. Little plosive sounds rendered as though he was trying to speak but couldn't. Stunned and hurting and speechless. This was her chance.

Just as she readied herself to snatch the pistol from his hands, the clatter of heavy footsteps on the pavement sounded behind her.

Zoe. Finally arriving to provide backup. Almost too late.

Charlie whirled around to face her friend.

"Zoe, I—"

The words died on her lips.

It wasn't Zoe charging toward her. Charlie froze, not understanding.

She knew him, recognized the face, but it took her frantic animal mind several moments to place him.

CHAPTER EIGHTY

Todd Ritter barreled straight past her as though he didn't see her. His eyes focused solely on Will, wide and wild and insane.

He rushed at the lawyer, launching himself like a torpedo. Will was still bent at the waist and didn't even see him coming. His feet lifted off the ground as Ritter's shoulder struck him in the chest, and both men went down in a tangle of limbs.

The men struggled, but in the darkness, Charlie couldn't make out who was winning. Still unsure of what was happening, she wasn't certain who she should even be rooting for.

She stepped closer, the writhing, grunting mass on the ground looking like a giant spider. Will bucked his hips, trying to throw the smaller man off. Todd straightened and drove his elbow into Will's stomach, putting his weight into it. Charlie saw Will's entire body spasm as the wind was knocked out of him.

In one clean motion, Todd's arm shot out and ripped the gun out of Will's hand without struggle.

Will held his empty hands out like he didn't know what to do with them. Dazed. Eyebrows lifted. Forehead wrinkled. Confusion etched into the lines up and down his face.

Without hesitation, Todd brought the butt of the Glock down on the dome of Will's skull with a sickening crunch. He moved with ferocity, hate, anger, aggression, decisiveness. All shocking to Charlie based on what she knew of the man. Hard to even believe. He looked like he was possessed.

Will's eyes rolled back in his head, eyelids fluttering over the exposed whites, and Todd brought the gun down again. Another crunch. Louder than the first.

Once more, Charlie couldn't believe the brutality of the act. The speed of it. The violence of it.

Mind whirring, she tried to make sense of it. Todd must have been following her, but why? And why attack Will so aggressively?

She supposed that if he'd witnessed their conversation and ensuing tussle over the gun, that he might have come to the same conclusion that Charlie had. That Will was the killer. Had the knowledge that this man murdered his stepdaughter sent Todd over the edge?

As Todd got to his feet in front of her, she thought he looked bigger than before. Something swollen-looking in the muscles of his upper back, some new thickness occupying his legs. All of him rippling, flexing, uncoiling as he rose to his full height. Towering over Will. Over her.

Charlie took a few steps back, suddenly wary of him. But why? He'd saved her… hadn't he?

Her eyes searched the ground for a frantic moment, trying to spot the walkie-talkie. But it was nowhere in sight.

She opened her mouth to speak, but no sound came out. Just the faintest wind on her teeth, on her lips.

Todd turned the gun on her as though he'd heard her, sensed her feelings, a smile playing along the edges of his lips. Something wolfish about it. Like a smile he was trying to conceal but couldn't.

He strode over to her, and she scrambled backward, but he was faster. On her in a split second.

When he spoke, his voice came out strangely calm. Perhaps even a little amused.

"I think we need to talk, you and I. So why don't we just do this the easy way?"

He lurched forward with another jolt of that unexpected savageness. A ripping, violent motion.

She only half saw the gun arcing downward for her head, a dark blur at the end of his arm. Slashing through the air.

Bright light flashed in her skull when it hit. Endless white that flashed and blazed and blotted out her vision.

And then everything went black.

CHAPTER EIGHTY-ONE

Charlie dreamed. Drifting.

She felt Allie there before she saw her. Her sister's presence was tangible here, as obvious to Charlie as heat or the color red. That familiar feeling of being with someone you knew so well, rich with all its nuances. You often only became aware of the feeling when they were gone, Charlie thought—the absence left a hole that showed you what you'd lost.

The dream images filtered into her consciousness a beat after that sense of Allie's presence. Flickering pictures that slowly strung themselves into a movie, like a flip-book animation from when they were kids. All the colors were saturated, exaggerated, hyper-real the way her dreams sometimes were.

She and Allie lay together in a field of soft grass. A simple wooden fence stood in the distance, but no other buildings, no other signs of civilization.

They ate popsicles from the ice cream truck—the usual bomb pop for Charlie and one of those disgusting Mario heads with gumball eyes for Allie. Allie's tongue was all red from licking Mario's hat. She currently tongued one of the jeweled eyes surrounded by flesh-colored ice cream, trying to pry the tiny prize free.

Charlie laughed at this visual. Then she stuck out her own tongue to confirm that it, too, had been dyed with food coloring—bright blue in her case.

They didn't say much. They didn't have to. They just ate their ice cream and looked up at the puffy clouds rolling by, finding animal shapes and cartoonish butts rendered in the white, vaporous mounds.

Nothing to worry about. Nothing to fear. Just a simple togetherness. One of life's many moments of joy—mild joy, but joy nonetheless. Profound in its own way.

Allie sat up, and the sun glinted down at just the right angle so that it looked like her hair glowed. Bars of bright light shooting through it. A gleam atop her head.

And in the distance Charlie heard the waves rolling up on the island. The smooth, wet churn of the water. The slap of the tide hitting the rock face of a cliff.

She turned to look toward the sound, but she couldn't see it from here. Couldn't see the water at all, but she heard the constant babble there in the distance. She stared out at the horizon for what felt like a long time. Listening.

And then something flicked her earlobe. She turned enough to see Allie out of the corner of her eye.

Her sister had moved closer. She lifted her hand again. Index finger catapulting off her thumb to strike the tip of Charlie's nose.

Charlie realized that Allie was muttering something as she did this, but she couldn't make out the words. She listened closer, turned to face Allie fully.

They made eye contact. Held it.

Allie flicked her finger again, connecting with Charlie's cheek. This time she understood what Allie said.

"Wake up, dummy."

CHAPTER EIGHTY-TWO

Charlie woke in stages, reality arriving in her consciousness piece by piece.

First, the sound filtered in. The faint purr of a car engine. The hum of the tires rolling over the pavement, a kind of white noise periodically broken up by the crunch of snow and the throaty grating as the tires touched the rough places where the snow plows had chewed up the top layer of the asphalt.

Then the throbbing. Sharp jolts of pain in her skull that flashed like a strobe light.

She remembered getting hit in the head—not the visual memory of the event happening. Just that piece of information, the knowledge that she'd been struck, the reason why her skull ached the way it did.

Fear came to her next. Made her skin crawl. A sense of danger without explanation. An amorphous thing, somehow undefined, that she couldn't understand just yet. She thought maybe that made it all the scarier.

Finally, her eyes peeled open. Just a crack at first. Trees flitted by on the side of the road. Dark shapes rising up from the ground. Hulking lines of black against the gleam of the streetlights. Crooked branches bending up toward the night sky.

Looking down, she saw that a zip tie bound her wrists. It was tight enough to crease the skin, two little bulges on either side of the plastic.

She sat in the passenger seat of a car she didn't recognize. It smelled vaguely of pine. She could see only a glimpse of the driver to her left, a tiny flash of the side of his face, lit in the pale glow of the dash lights. Not enough to recognize him. But rather than trying to get a better look, she closed her eyes again.

An urgent voice inside told her not to lift her head. Not to reveal her return to consciousness. To wait. To rest. To breathe. To think.

None of these pieces of reality added up to make any kind of sense. Not yet.

After a few breaths, she braved another look. Opened her eyes again. Tried to blink away some of the confusion.

Looking again out of the corner of her eye, she saw him. Knew him.

Todd Ritter. Amber's stepfather.

His head snapped in her direction, and she closed her eyes again. Waited.

He exhaled once. A vaguely aggressive sigh. Then he fell quiet again.

If he'd seen her awake, he gave no sign of it. Good.

Recognizing him jarred some of the memories loose: Todd tackling Will. Bashing him over the head. Doing the same to her.

She squinted her eyes to slits this time when she opened them. Looked out at the world through a thatch of eyelashes, through the tiny gaps between them, through the halos and smears of greenish light.

Todd faced forward. She could see the side of his face well enough to tell that much.

She took a deep breath, careful to keep it quiet. And the statistics of these kinds of situations came to her. Survival rates. Situational data.

The end result was simple: if you went quietly with the abductor, you died.

Better to make a stand. To fight. Make them drag you kicking and screaming, clawing and biting. Anything that might give you a chance.

And so she would.

She pictured it now, what she would do next. How she would go on the offensive.

Fog still roiled inside her skull. Murked up her thoughts. Fresh confusion coming in waves. But she pushed it aside, forced herself to focus.

She may not know exactly what was going on here, but she knew she wasn't going down without a fight.

She lurched for the steering wheel. Grabbed it and jerked hard to the right. The movement was abrupt enough to wrench the thing out of Todd's hands.

The driver sucked in a breath, spit hissing between his teeth.

His hands moved back to the wheel. Fought her for control. And then he slammed on the brakes.

Too late.

It all happened in an instant. A single heartbeat. Yet it felt like slow motion.

The tree seemed to fill the windshield like a movie screen. The camera zooming in and in and in. The big, dramatic close-up.

The front end slamming into the tree. Metal cracking against wood. Deafening.

The airbag inflating, a giant white pillow that engulfed her face.

The impact stopping their forward momentum dead, jerking Charlie so hard she could feel it in her teeth. The pressure.

And then everything going still. Quiet. Motionless.

Black smoke fluttered up from the wounded place where the metal meshed with the maple tree. Lit by the one flickering headlight somehow still glowing.

It took Charlie three shaking breaths to come back to herself. She glanced over at the driver. At Todd.

His face was squashed into the airbag, a smear of blood on the white of the material. From his nose, she thought.

Was he dead? Or just unconscious?

He stirred then, a groan escaping his mashed lips.

One word shivered in Charlie's head. Her entire reality reduced to three letters:

Run.

CHAPTER EIGHTY-THREE

Charlie burst out of the passenger door. Skidded down the banking shoulder, gravity pulling her into the ditch. Her feet gouged holes in the snow on the way down.

The bottom of the trench jammed her knees. One then the other. She stumbled. Balance teetering. Leaving her.

Some instinct waved her arms in front of her. Useless. Her wrists were still fastened together by the zip tie.

Falling. That weightless feeling sickening as the ground rushed up to meet her.

She landed on her side. Panicking. Thrashing at the snowy ground. Scrabbling like a crab stuck at the bottom of a bucket.

Then she rolled onto her belly. Pushed herself up onto her hands and knees. Climbed the other side of the ditch. Running.

Up onto the gravel. Across the street. Into the woods. Into the darkness.

The vast black swallowed her. Concealed her.

Instinct once again took over. No thoughts. No words. No strategy. Something animal inside that knew what to do here in the dark, in the wild. She trusted it. Let it take over. Somehow the animal self was able to see just enough to steer her away from the trees in her path, to keep her pressing forward.

She picked her feet up high. Bounding steps, each almost a small leap.

She banked hard to the left to run along a stream. Dared a look back as she made the turn.

Behind her, a flashlight bobbed along the surface of the snow. Lighting up pine boughs and glittering on icy branches. Todd was following her. And he still had her gun.

Forget that. Keep going. Keep running.

Run for your life.

She swiveled her head forward. Watched only the path ahead once more. The next few yards of the forest were the only thing that was real. A tiny reality that reset itself every few seconds. Erased all else but the next cluster of trees and bushes to avoid.

And some insane part of her, a detached part of her, observed all of this as though from a million miles away. Marveled at the notion that her whole life had led to this moment, this encounter with Todd Ritter. Everything she'd ever done and said and thought and experienced, it all delivered her to this run.

She would live or die based on how she handled this next little piece of time, this next little stretch of land. It seemed so absurd. Unlikely to the point that it verged on impossible. And yet all stories ended in death, one way or another, didn't they? Everyone's path surrendered them to that eventuality.

A lightness took shape up ahead. A clearing. At first, she could only make out snippets of it. The snow glowing brighter through the trees, reflecting back the moonlight no longer blocked by the shadows of the woods.

She crested a small hill, fighting the incline. Almost losing her balance as she battled through the steepest part of the slope just before the land leveled out at the top. And then she saw it.

The giant Ferris wheel towered over the horizon, lit by the moon, somehow hulking and skeletal at the same time. The sight stole her breath. Vacated her lungs. But only for a second, and then she was racing down the other side of the hill. She knew where she was now, and fresh adrenaline coursed through her system.

Hope.

She rocketed for the abandoned amusement park. Ran harder across the clearing before the park—the snow-covered parking lot that looked like some kind of frozen pond, empty like it was. Some lightness entered her body as she drew closer to the perimeter of the place. Familiarity buoying her spirit. Lifting her knees. Pressing her onward like a stiff wind at her back.

Glancing back, she saw the flashlight just reaching the top of the hill, appearing there, a flare rising up from the darkness of the hill as though it had just now beamed into existence.

She'd pulled away from Todd for the moment. Good. That'd give her options.

The front gates of the park loomed before her, but she veered away from them. They were boarded up, she knew. Reinforced with corrugated steel sheeting. Barbed wire spiraling over the top. But there were other ways in. Less obvious ways.

Perhaps ten yards from the edge of the parking lot, she spotted the gashed opening in the fence. The one all the high school kids had used to sneak in here to drink and smoke cigarettes for as long as she could remember. Still there after all this time.

She knifed through the gap, body angled sideways. She had to crouch, sliding one leg through at a time to avoid snagging on the slit links of chain. At last, she stepped into the darker terrain on the other side.

Now she was free to run again, and she did. But soon enough the running would stop.

It was here, in the park, that she'd make her stand.

CHAPTER EIGHTY-FOUR

Charlie shuffled out into the open space of the midway, skirting around the small trees and waist-high weeds that grew up from the cracks in the pathway. Adrenaline gushed all through her, making her movements jittery and jerky.

Abandoned food stalls squatted on all sides here. Fries. Funnel cakes. Italian ice. Elephant ears. Beyond the crumbling booths, a cluster of kiddie rides. The carousel with its rusting menagerie of mythological beasts: a unicorn, a dragon, a mermaid. A miniature rollercoaster, the cars done up to look like a sea monster.

She ran past them, knowing they weren't what she was looking for. Not this time. The idea of where and when to hide, to mount her attack, itched somewhere inside where she couldn't scratch it. She knew the idea, the perfect place was just there, out of reach, and she had to trust that she would know it when she saw it.

Her pace was slowing. She was jogging now more than running. Everything hurt, and the pain rushed in as the initial tide of endorphins began to recede.

Her side ached, a pair of machetes lodged in her liver. Each breath made her lungs burn. The wind scraped at the soft tissue of her throat on its way in and out, like the air had grown claws.

Still, she forced her feet to keep pounding their way over the asphalt. Even through the pain, she kept going.

Out in the open, away from the woods, the wind off the lake seemed to cut right through her coat and clothes. Digging into the flesh of her more deeply than before.

She pushed herself harder—mind still strong, still sharp—but the strength of her legs was dwindling. No longer accelerating the way she wanted, the muscles gone weak and shaky.

That hurt worse than all the physical pain, the betrayal of her body. She was so close. The end of all of this was so close. Right there. For better or worse. For life or death. The final battle loomed just ahead, and her mind was ready. But her flesh was giving out on her. Fading. Failing.

How could her whole life lead to this? Exhaustion defeating her. How could that be fair for her? For anyone?

She swallowed. Blinked back the threat of tears with fluttering eyelashes.

You can't run forever, Charlie. You knew that. It's time to choose a battleground. The place to make your final stand.

She swallowed again, and more words spoke in her head. A calm voice. A quiet voice. It was close, but it didn't quite sound like her own.

Brace yourself for the fight now. Give yourself an edge. Get the jump on him here and now.

Her eyes danced over her surroundings. Scanning. Weighing. Looking for answers. Potential. Possibilities.

She gazed up at the largest ride in the vicinity, The Kraken, with its eight curved metal legs of painted glossy black. Orange light bulbs protruded from each of the limbs.

The Ferris wheel stood taller still, dead ahead, all the way at the back of the park. All those struts and beams crisscrossing into the sky. A fossil of steel and rust-stained paint.

These metallic skeletons did her no good. Offered her no advantage.

Think smaller. Closer.

She looked over the smaller attractions that stood between her and the Ferris wheel. Considered each of them.

The ball pit in Triton's Playground caught her eye. She visualized herself hiding there, submerged among the rainbow-colored spheres. It could work, especially for a hiding spot, but it didn't give her any kind of advantage in the pending battle. Hiding only stretched out the timeline. She needed a fight plan, some kind of strategic gain.

Fight or die, the voice in her head repeated. *Fight or die.*

She spotted the familiar orange-and-yellow striped roof then. The dark of the open doorway, surrounded by the gaping mouth of the giant clown.

Zinky's Funhouse.

CHAPTER EIGHTY-FIVE

Inside the funhouse, Charlie slowed, waiting for her eyes to adjust to the darkness. She'd only ever been in here in the daytime, and it was unsettling to have to feel her way down the strange hallways. To trust her hands to guide her.

Even after her surroundings became just barely visible—everything shades of black on black—the bent corridors and narrowing walls played tricks on her.

She paused for a moment on the threshold of the Hall of Mirrors and held her breath, listening for him. But all of the outside sounds were muffled and stilled.

The mirrored walls gave the appearance of one long, endless hallway stretching out before her. Coupled with the utter quiet, Charlie felt her skin prickle with foreboding.

She crept forward into the dark, into the quiet. Moving slowly. With care. Looking for just the right place. No mistakes now.

She brought her face closer to one of the mirrored panels. Warped versions of herself stared back.

The hair on the back of her neck stood on end, a sudden preternatural feeling coming over her.

She wasn't alone.

There was a presence here, and it wasn't just the one hunting her either.

Something else. Something spectral but not altogether malignant occupying the space.

And Charlie knew that this was the place.

Just as she reached up to find the hidden latch, she caught sight of the faintest glow out of the corner of her eye. It came from just outside the Hall of Mirrors and slowly grew in intensity. A flashlight.

An icy feeling came over her. The bitter cold of adrenaline coursing through her hands, spreading up into her wrists. It pulled her skin taut as could be.

He was here.

CHAPTER EIGHTY-SIX

Charlie huddled in the dark. Waiting. Squatting behind the false wall among the mirrors. Biding her time until he was close enough.

A sensation like cold fingertips prickled against the backs of her arms. Up her spine and down her neck. A chill like no other she'd felt in all her years, not even when Allie had disappeared.

Allie said nothing. But Charlie could feel her there now. Could feel that they would be together in this moment, for better or worse.

Charlie's breathing had slowed, her body recovering some as she crouched here in the shadows. She could feel her heart pounding at her chest, at her ribcage. Firm now. A muscle once more. Not that fluttering, frightened hummingbird of a thing it had turned to out in the woods.

She adjusted her position, lowering her knees to rest on the concrete floor. The cement was like ice, but relief shrieked in her calves and ankles despite the cold. Euphoria expressed through a slowly dying soreness. The muscles giving thanks the only way they could.

She resisted the overwhelming urge to peer out from behind the pane of mirrored glass that concealed her. It was the only advantage she had. The optical illusion that made this wall look complete. Made someone unable to see the narrow gap in the mirrors unless they knew exactly where to look.

To peek her head out now would put her entire plan at risk. She couldn't do it. Not even for a second.

She would hear him coming. If she stayed quiet, stayed focused, she would hear. She had to.

But Todd's footsteps made no sound as he entered the corridor, creeping forward in slow motion like an assassin. His movements were smooth. Fluid. He was nothing more than a shadow.

Instead, she heard his breath. Loud panting, or so it seemed in this moment. Was the volume actually there, though, or were her senses heightened? Sharpened like the ears of an animal. That survival instinct helping her, guiding her.

She didn't know. Maybe it didn't matter.

He sounded more like a beast than a man now, and the visual part of her brain could not link this sound to the meek man who'd hung back to thank her in her office, to the nonchalant stepfather bragging about his chicken parmesan in the dining room of his home. Whatever he'd become, he was unrecognizable to her now.

She drew herself up, got her feet under her haunches again. Ready to strike.

The breath grew louder. Drew closer. Closer and closer still.

The reflection of the flashlight bouncing around came into view first, seemingly endless copies of itself rebounding from mirror to mirror, shooting everywhere like ricochets, shimmering a mess of partial beams back into her hidey hole, just for a second.

Charlie pounced.

CHAPTER EIGHTY-SEVEN

She tackled him at the waist, driving her shoulder into his gut. He grunted as the full weight of her struck him.

He stumbled backward, his shoes slipping beneath him as if he were on roller skates. She felt him struggling to remain upright, but she'd come on him too fast. Her momentum threw him off-balance, dragged him down, knocked him off his feet.

The pistol popped and flared and bucked in his hand, the sound of the gunshot impossibly loud in the confined space. One of the mirrored panels exploded into a thousand shards, tumbling down around them.

They hit the floor in one tangled heap with Todd taking the brunt. The impact tore the flashlight out of his hand, and the only source of light went spinning across the floor. Reeling.

Fifty versions of him and her struggled in the cracked mirrors. Endless reflections. Everything seeming to twirl along with the flashlight's movement.

Two silhouettes locked in conflict. Wild things. Savage. Muscles trembling. Eyes flashing.

And she couldn't tell somehow where he ended and she began. Their shadows seemed to weave into one another, connected like tendrils of smoke. Writhing with liquid smoothness in the strobe effect of the spinning flashlight.

She clawed at his hands, tried to peel his grip away from the gun.

But he fought her, wrenching the pistol away, clutching it close.

She took this chance to get her knees up onto his torso. Climbing him. Mounting him. Pinning most of his arm against his chest.

He shifted beneath her, trying to free himself, but she had the advantage now. The high ground. She got a hold on his pinky finger and wrenched it back. He threw back his head, and she could just barely hear the howl over the ringing in her ears.

Instead of loosening his grip on the gun, he changed tactics, swinging at her with his off hand, his free hand. He clubbed a fist at her head and neck. Landing blows over and over.

But they were awkward jabs, slaps at best. He could get no leverage lying on his back with her weight holding him down.

He wriggled again, bucking harder this time and throwing her off-balance just long enough that he was able to squeeze the trigger again.

The gun blazed and popped again. Thrashed in their hands like a fish.

More shards of mirror came tumbling down. Crashing like cymbals. Cracking and exploding all around them.

She paused only long enough to confirm she hadn't been hit, and then she was back on the attack. Clawing and scratching. Bringing her face in closer, which made his punching all the less effective.

She went for the hand on the gun, teeth bared. Her incisors grazed the edge of his knuckles as he struggled to move away, but a moment later she found purchase in the meat along the outside edge of his palm.

She bit down, sinking all those sharp points into his flesh. The skin resisted, holding tight. She pressed harder and the flesh suddenly gave, seeming to burst like a popping balloon, filling her mouth with the salty, metallic taste of blood.

He screamed. Shrill and thin. His voice cracked as it burst from his throat.

And he let go of the gun.

CHAPTER EIGHTY-EIGHT

Charlie snatched up the weapon. Pulled it back behind her ear. Brought it down as hard as she could. Swinging it like a hammer.

The butt of the Glock cracked as it collided with the space between his eyebrows. Hard. The back of his skull thumped into the concrete floor of the funhouse.

The reverberation of the impact stung all the way up to her shoulder. A kind of recoil.

All that force had to go somewhere. Some of it traveled up her arm. Jostled her joints as though trying to separate them from their sockets.

Thankfully, his face took the brunt of it.

After the briefest hesitation, a gash split his forehead open red, seeming to appear there in slow motion. Blood seeping out of the crease.

His eyes drifted. Stared out at nothing in particular. Something dim in them already.

But he was still conscious, at least part of the way. She could see it when his eyelids twitched.

She swung again. Again. Again.

Now she brought the gun all the way up over her head. Chopping down as though wielding an axe. His head just a chunk of wood in need of splitting.

Hatred expelled itself in each swing of the weapon. All her rage finding an outlet at last. A way out. Catharsis.

For Amber. For Kara. For Allie.

The cracks turned to wet slaps as the blood spread over his skin. Drained down over the eyes, spilling over the cheekbones. Bathtub sounds ringing out, echoing off the mirrors, off the concrete floor.

She caught one of the reflections of herself as she hoisted the gun over her head again. Froze with the weapon at the apex. Could faintly see the red spattered over her face.

From there, it was as though she took a step back, seeing all of the reflections instead of just one. All those versions of herself poised to bludgeon, fixing to kill. Warped versions of herself in all those cracked funhouse mirrors. Stretched. Widened. Bent.

Her lungs swelled as she sucked in a big breath. And she stopped herself. Let her arms go slack.

Her hands fell into her lap, folded over one another, the gun still clasped loosely in her fingers.

She wasn't a killer. No matter what happened, she wasn't a killer.

Todd was out. Unconscious. Eyes closed. Face all soupy with red. But still breathing.

She prodded him with the gun. Jamming the barrel into his neck a few times. Just to make sure he wasn't faking.

Then she moved, shuffled her weight off of his body. Knelt next to him.

He had a backpack looped around one shoulder. She stripped it from his limp noodle arm. Unzipped it. Peeled open the top like a mouth.

A nervous giggle spluttered out of her lips then. Involuntary. She just couldn't believe what she was seeing.

She shifted the bulk of the bag, angled the open flaps toward the glow of the flashlight. The objects inside slid, jostled, toppled over each other. Everything glittered faintly when the light touched it.

The collection of tools and supplies inside the bag could only be described as an anal-retentive kill kit—almost like Todd had been planning to go to serial killer summer camp.

Zip ties. Rope. Cuffs. A hunting knife. Glow sticks. Beef jerky.

Charlie cut her hands free with the blade, the knife's tip disappearing in the tiny gap between her wrists and re-emerging as it sliced through the thin band of plastic.

She rubbed at the red welts in her skin, the grooved places where the zip tie had pinched. Neat lines etched into her flesh.

Then she bound Todd at the hands and feet. Making sure his zip ties were nice and tight just like hers had been.

She stood over him then. Considered what she saw.

His face looked strange. Bloated and tired and a little sad, she thought. In the cold, the blood had already begun to congeal there in the folds separating his cheeks from his nose. Like ketchup going gummy and then crusty on the edge of the plate.

He'd probably be out a while after the beating she'd doled out. He'd have a nice headache too, but... something still bothered her.

It was the glass. All the broken shards of mirror. He could use those to cut his ties, maybe. Probably. If he tried hard enough, and he would.

She dug back in the bag. Got out the handcuffs.

Grasping him by the ankles, she dragged him back to the entrance of the Hall of Mirrors. Laid him out in that strangely tapering hallway. Slapped one side of the handcuffs around his wrist and the other around a metal handrail mounted to the wall.

There. Better.

The combination of zip ties and cuffs held both of his arms up over his head awkwardly. Made him look like someone in traction in a hospital, hands elevated due to some injury.

She smiled at that image. Her eyes lingered on the plastic bands pinching deeply into his flesh like a length of twine cutting into a pork loin, the meat bulging around them.

It was almost too bad, Charlie thought. Part of her wanted to watch him wriggle through all that broken glass like a worm, desperate to get a hold of one of the shards to cut himself free.

Now she dug his car keys out of his jacket pocket. Clenched them in her fist.

She zipped up the bag. Slung it over her shoulder. Maybe the serial killer summer camp kit would come in handy for her next task.

Because now she had to find the girl.

CHAPTER EIGHTY-NINE

Charlie stumbled down the steps of the funhouse onto the asphalt outside. She was too busy staring at the phone in her hand. Todd's phone.

She'd unlocked it by jamming his thumb to the screen.

Now the phone glowed in her hand, shining back at the stars above. Her fingers traced over the smooth surface. Dialing.

She brought the phone to her ear. Listened to the ringing.

Something about this felt like an out-of-body experience after the fight. Like it was impossible that she could be doing something so mundane as making a phone call after something like that. Like life should stop or change after the most dramatic moments. It couldn't just go back to anything resembling normal, could it?

Zoe answered. And Charlie got so excited she barked out a cough instead of words. She had to swallow before she could spit it out, but when the words finally came, they sounded normal. Too normal. Detached. Calm. Almost pleasant.

"Zoe. It's Charlie."

Charlie heard a faint click on the other line. For a second she thought Zoe couldn't hear her and had hung up. The thought brought a tinge of fear, of being forgotten here, lost, unable to make her way back to society somehow. A surge of that icy adrenaline feeling stung her hands.

But then Zoe did speak, urgency in her voice.

"Charlie, Jesus Christ! Where are you? Are you OK?"

"I'm fine. I'm at Poseidon's Kingdom. Standing outside the funhouse right now."

This time Zoe's words came out in a rush. "I don't know what happened, Charlie. I waited, like you said, and then another car came around the park, so I figured I should keep an eye on it. By the time I went in after you, you were gone. I couldn't find you, so I called in a team to search the park, but there was nothing there."

"Zoe. Stop," Charlie interrupted. "Ritter is the killer. Todd Ritter. I've got him detained here. Cuffed to a safety railing inside the funhouse. Face got busted up pretty good, too."

"Ritter," Zoe said, and Charlie could almost hear her brain trying to catch up. "Amber's *stepfather*?"

"Right. Just send a team out here to get him, OK? We'll figure out the rest later."

Zoe answered this, her voice shaky, but Charlie could only hear the first syllable before her finger swiped left and ended the call. It left a smudge of blood on the screen.

Charlie had an idea of what to do next, where to look. And it wouldn't wait.

CHAPTER NINETY

Charlie rushed back through the darkness, retracing her steps from earlier in the night. She ducked back through the slit in the fence, crossed that frozen pond of a parking lot.

Then she began mounting the hill in reverse. Slipping toward the top, slowing and kicking up snow just like last time. But then she was over it, building speed once again, gliding back the way she'd come.

Following the gashed tracks in the snow made the whole thing easier than her first go round with this terrain—that and the fact that she had Todd's flashlight now. Her hands not being bound by the zip tie was a nice bonus.

She pictured Todd as she'd last seen him. The blood-smeared face. The limp arms strung up above his sprawled form, linked to the rail by the cuffs.

And she remembered bludgeoning him, red spatter flying off of him with every stroke, the bloody gun still tucked in her belt even now. She gritted her teeth as she remembered, the savage part of her wanting to go back and finish the job.

But no. It was better this way. Better for her soul, she thought. And maybe better that he suffer a long while in prison. No parole. Death could be considered a mercy compared to that.

The light bounced along in front of her. Piercing all the dark it touched. Vanquishing the gloom one little slice at a time. The glow reflected off the branches, icy crystals sparkling everywhere.

Eventually she could see the hulking form of Todd's vehicle ahead. A dark hunk of twisted metal cast in silhouette, its front end bent impossibly around the trunk of the tree like some sort of modern sculpture.

She raced up to the vehicle. Opened the door. Slid the keys into the ignition.

The dome light came on, and she was thankful for that. The battery was still getting juice to the thing.

She tapped the screen in the center of the dashboard. Fingers flicking and pressing buttons. She picked her way to the GPS history. Scrolled through it. Skimming. Skimming.

There. A frequently visited location called "Ritter Custom Installations WH." Charlie thought WH likely stood for warehouse. A storage building for Todd's dock installation business. He'd been out there almost every day until two days ago, sometimes more than once a day.

She selected it. Eyeballed the little map the GPS screen kicked out. It was less than a mile, in a row of old industrial buildings that butted up to the back of the amusement park. Close enough to reach on foot.

A muffled noise caught her attention. The faintest thump.

She stopped. Held her breath. Listened.

Nothing.

Just her imagination, she thought.

She spotted Todd's keys nestled in one of the cupholders in the center console. Her fingers snaked into the opening and snatched the keychain. It was heavy, weighed down with over a dozen different keys.

Charlie took a breath and rushed into the darkness once more.

CHAPTER NINETY-ONE

Charlie's heart beat faster as she entered the narrow hall inside the warehouse, climbed down a few steps, and found another locked steel door. Heavy. Exterior quality.

This would be it. It had to be it.

She lifted the keys, hands and arms trembling badly now. The keys were labeled in true Todd Ritter style, but she had yet to figure out his code. There was a key named "Warehouse" but the one that actually opened the door out front had been called "Side door." It took her shaking fingers a couple of tries to pick out one of the keys and start the process of trial and error.

She listened as she worked, but she didn't hear anything inside. No voices. No stirring. Nothing at all.

And that silence dug at her as the seconds passed. Deeper and deeper.

What if… but no. Don't think now. Just do.

On her thirteenth try of the mess of keys on Todd's keychain, the deadbolt snicked out of the way. Unlocked.

She half-noticed that this key was labeled "Storage."

All of life snapped into slow motion again. Slower than the fight with Todd, she thought. Slower, even, than Allie's funeral.

She could hear her pulse in her neck. Wet knocking that seemed to echo in her ears.

Charlie shoved the big steel door. It scraped out of the frame, hinges squealing in the quiet. The keys jangled where they still hung from the deadbolt.

She watched as the door opened in increments. A wedge of pale light crawled over the cement floor of the room beyond, the glow from the floodlights outside spilling in from the glass blocks in the hall.

She swallowed. Felt a lump shift in her throat. Everything in her neck felt tight and dry.

The silence bloomed. Spreading. Growing. A deadness in the room before her. Her skin contracted as she stared into the dark there. Tighter across her chest, along her back.

Too quiet. It was too damn quiet in here.

She could already feel the tears bulging in the corners of her eyes. The salty water ready to spill.

She lifted the flashlight. Swept its shine across the room. Slow. Left to right.

Boxes filled in shelves everywhere. Stacked almost to the ceiling.

Spools of some industrial-looking materials huddled in the far-left corner—wire in various gauges and something that looked like heavy outdoor canvas.

The light crept over these things. Flitting up and down to illuminate each detail before moving on to the next.

Charlie squinted as though she were trying to peer through the cardboard, through the steel shelves.

When she'd gotten to about halfway through the room, the light started shaking.

She stopped sweeping the light. Paused her scan of the room. Tried to steady the involuntary movement of her arm.

The muscles fought her. Twitched harder.

And the negative thoughts pounced on the moment of weakness. Clawed at the vulnerability.

Because what if the girl isn't here?

What if I sweep this light all the way and there is nothing? No one? Or worse.

What if I'm too late?

She swallowed again. Closed her eyes for a second.

Breathe. Focus.

The breath rolled in and out of her now. Steady.

It was time to find out the truth, for better or worse.

She opened her eyes.

The light held strong now. She guided it the rest of the way.

Shined it right into the face of the girl in the far-right corner.

Kara Dawkins didn't move. Didn't blink. She just sat there. Slumped against the wall.

Eyes open wide. Staring at nothing. Glittering where the flashlight's beam touched them.

Purple bags formed semicircles beneath those eyes. Puffy and dark.

And Charlie could see, too, that her right wrist was held up. Frozen there above her head, dirt crusted around it. Cuffed to a pipe.

Charlie gasped at the sight. Shuffled back a few steps. Out of the doorway. Into the hall.

Her skin crawled when she thought about how similar Kara's pose looked to Todd's just now. Some strange symmetry there.

It was all wrong.

And then a dirty hand rose to shield Kara's eyes from the light. The girl blinked finally. Squinting and scowling. Peering out between her dirty fingers.

Charlie couldn't move. Couldn't breathe.

Kara tried to speak. Coughed a little instead. Throat sounding raspy. Harsh. Dry. She tried again. This time her voice came out as a croak.

"Are you… real?"

Charlie's lips popped, but no words came out.

With greatly delayed reaction, Charlie realized she was shining her light directly in Kara's eyes. She swung the beam away so it faced a wall away from them.

Charlie took a few steps into the room, her legs utterly numb beneath her. Dead stalks of meat and bone. Holding her up out of habit as much as anything.

The girl opened her eyes. Blinked up at Charlie. Something so tired in her expression. Hopeless even with hope staring her in the face.

And Charlie tried to think of what to say. How to tell Kara she was real. How to tell her that it was over now.

Mind blank. Hollow. Speechless.

And for a second, she stood there in the dark, in the quiet, just beyond arm's length away from Kara Dawkins. They looked at each other, neither one quite ready to trust reality in this moment, to believe that the other was all the way real.

Finally, Charlie knelt. Took Kara's free hand in hers. Angled the light between them, pointed it up at the ceiling so they could both see each other again. And she didn't think about the words anymore. She just let them come out on their own.

"The police will be here soon, OK? Your mom, she's been looking for you. She hired me to look for you. She's been worried sick about you, you know? And all your friends, too. Everyone's been so scared."

Kara's face wrinkled as though to cry, but no tears came.

Charlie stroked the girl's hair. Raked her fingers through the tangles.

In the half-light, Kara looked like a child.

She looked like Allie.

"All the people who love you are going to be so happy to see you, so happy to find that you're OK. You have no idea how much they love you, how badly they've been missing you. No idea."

They both burst into tears then. The world going into a kind of soft focus for Charlie, as though her mind zoomed out a bit, watched these events from some higher vantage point. Her tears blurred everything, distancing her from the moment some. A kind of mercy, she thought.

And they half-hugged the best they could with Kara still being chained to the wall. The girl pressed herself into Charlie's side and leaned her head onto her shoulder. Silent sobs shuddered through her body. Little shivers transferred from the girl into Charlie.

Even after they parted, Kara squeezed Charlie's hand tight. All through Charlie's phone call to Zoe, the girl clung to her like she thought they might drift apart if she let go.

CHAPTER NINETY-TWO

Police lights spiraled everywhere, the red and blue shining and spinning. Glinting off the snow, off the corrugated steel siding of Todd's warehouse.

Charlie stood with a blanket over her shoulders, watching the police funnel in and out of the door into the storage building. Some bagged evidence. Others followed with cameras, making sure to document everything. Cameras flashed here and there, bright bursts of white light.

An ambulance had come first and taken Kara away. The paramedics offered to take Charlie along, to get her checked out as well, but she declined. She wanted to stay. To see it through.

Another police cruiser rolled into the lot, pulling up alongside the building. Zoe climbed out a moment later, clad in her deputy's hat, hands stuffed in her pockets.

"Guess who we just pulled out of Ritter's trunk, hogtied like a... well, a hog, I guess?"

Charlie squinted. Her brain was too fried to even think about it.

"Will."

"Oh," Charlie said, realizing she'd completely lost track of him in all the chaos. "Is he OK?"

"The paramedics are taking him to the hospital. He looks like he went ten rounds with Mike Tyson."

Charlie went quiet, thinking back to the moment when she had recognized Will in the park. All the dark thoughts that had run through her mind.

"He was pretty shaken up," Zoe continued. "Confused. Wouldn't be surprised if he has a concussion. But he was adamant that I tell you that he's sorry. About the keylogger. It was him that put it on your computer."

"But why?"

"I guess he figured that, as Gibbs' attorney, he needed any information about the case that he could get."

After a few seconds passed, Charlie shrugged and said, "Win at all costs, right? That's his motto."

In a certain way, Charlie supposed she shouldn't have been surprised. And he *had* won, hadn't he? With Todd Ritter about to be charged with the crimes, Leroy Gibbs would be set free.

Something bitter rose to the back of Charlie's throat at that thought. She'd never know the truth about Allie. It could have been Gibbs. It could have been anyone. But now she'd never know.

She swallowed, though, and the bad taste went away. No use in dwelling on something like that. Life was short enough as it was.

"You sure you're OK?" she asked. "You've got quite the goose egg sprouting on your forehead. Not to mention the blood spatter."

"It'll wash off," Charlie said.

From where she was situated, Charlie could see the steel skeleton of the Ferris wheel against the moonlit sky. In a way, it felt like she was keeping an eye on both scenes. Todd had been apprehended at the park without issue, still right where Charlie had left him. According to Zoe, he'd said nothing as they cuffed him and hauled him off. Just stared at the ground.

And now a different set of police surely gathered evidence and filmed and flashed their cameras among the warped mirrors of the funhouse as well.

A kind of closure seemed to accompany actually being at the scene. Observing while the police sifted through what was left. When they were done, when all the evidence was sorted and logged and bagged and taken away, only then would it feel over—or at least as over as it ever could feel.

For now, the scene still swarmed with life. Crime scene techs worked every inch, inside and out. Scrutinizing. Analyzing. Recording.

And memories flared now and again. Little movies of the night's events playing in Charlie's head.

Waking in the car, the pale green light of the dash lighting Todd's profile.

The flashlight spinning around them in the hall of mirrors. All those reflections of the two shadows becoming one in the strobe effect.

The blood slowly seeping out of the crease in Todd's forehead where she'd bashed him. Thick red rising up from within.

And finally, the image of Charlie lifting the gun up over her head, her face and chest already spattered with his blood. Seeing herself. Stopping short.

Todd Ritter. Part of her still couldn't believe it was him.

Charlie had a gut feeling—a possible explanation for the crimes, for Todd's motive—but she didn't want to jump to any conclusions, not even in the privacy of her own head. She'd wait and see what he had to say for himself in the ensuing interrogation.

"You know I'm proud of you, don't you, Charlie?"

It was Allie. Charlie didn't say anything. Terrified she was imagining it, or that a reply might break the spell.

"You did good. Saved Kara. Brought Todd Ritter to justice. Best anyone could do, I think."

Charlie's eyelids fluttered.

"It's like Uncle Frank says, people need the truth," Allie said. "You may not be able to undo the worst of what happens in life. But what happened to Amber Spadafore, what happened to me. It leaves a wound on the world."

Tears came to Charlie's eyes then, blurring the twirling police lights. Bars of red and blue shone in her eyes. Strange jewels created where the light refracted through the lens of water.

"That's why we need people like you. Someone to come along to patch things up as best you can, you know? Stop the bleeding. Society needs that to keep functioning. Someone to set things right."

All of the shapes and colors shifted like a kaleidoscope when Charlie blinked.

"I know it's not an easy job. And I know it hurts sometimes. Because you can't bring back the dead."

She paused.

"But you can still try your best. You can fight for the victims. Stand up and make sure that justice is served. And you did a damn good job of that, I'd say."

"Thanks," Charlie said. She wiped at the corner of her eye and sniffed.

"Kicking Will in the balls was a nice touch, too," Allie said. "I mean, that was hilarious."

CHAPTER NINETY-THREE

Charlie and Zoe watched the interrogation through two-way glass.

Todd Ritter looked smaller in the orange county jail jumpsuit. There was a blank expression etched into the folds around his eyes as he hunched over the table.

Cuffs bound him at the wrists and ankles with chains looping through both, shackling him to the floor and interrogation table alike.

He sat motionless next to his lawyer. Completely still. He stared at nothing. Eyes piercing empty space. Glossy.

Everyone was waiting for the detective to show up. He was late. Probably wanted to let Todd stew a while. Keep him waiting. Uncomfortable.

"You really did a number on him," Zoe said, a note of pride in her voice.

"I kind of expected him to look worse, to be honest," Charlie said.

Gauze held a swatch of bandage to the center of his forehead. Charlie couldn't see even the faintest hint of blood showing through the white. Probably stitched up under there. Starting to heal already.

The other wounds, those lower on his face, had scabbed over. Dark splotches marring his complexion along his cheekbones and chin. Nothing serious.

Staring at the man she now knew to be responsible for abducting Kara Dawkins and murdering Amber Spadafore, part of Charlie wanted to believe she'd found Allie's killer as well. But the sheriff's department had ruled out that possibility—Todd Ritter had been in grad school in Texas at the time of Allie's murder. Once and for all, she had to admit that this case was in no way linked to her sister's.

Something stirred finally in the interrogation room, the door swinging open. The murmur of voices in the observation room went quiet.

"Here we go," Zoe whispered, standing up straighter.

The detective sauntered in. Slapped a manila folder on the table. The edges of some of the photos leaked out of the side. A ploy, Charlie thought. An implied threat, leaving them mostly to the imagination for now.

But Todd would know what they featured. The dead body of his stepdaughter, Amber. Naked. Laid out on the beach.

"Messed up this time, huh, bud?" the detective said, hands on his hips. "Messed up bad."

He reached for the folder of photos, hand moving quickly, snatching it up. It looked for all the world like he was going to deal them across the table like playing cards. Instead he neatened the stack, concealed the photos in the folder again, and set it down once more.

If Todd even saw the man, he showed no signs of it. He stared at nothing, same as before.

The detective probably wanted to startle Todd some with all of this. Shake him up. Get him emotional and get him talking.

Charlie couldn't get a read on Todd's demeanor, though. Was that a smile playing at the corners of his mouth just now? In any case, he bore little resemblance to the wild beast she'd fought a few nights ago.

Todd spoke then. Pulling her out of her thoughts.

"I did it," he said. "That's what you want to hear, right? I did it. I killed her."

His voice sounded clear and strong and utterly emotionless. Vacant. Haunted.

A cold finger smeared itself up Charlie's spine at the sound. She realized she was trembling and crossed her arms over her chest, obeying some instinct to shield herself.

The lawyer spoke up, tried to advise his client not to talk, but Todd shook his head. "Can't undo what's been done. Can't deny it, either. Shoot, everyone dies at some point, right? Everyone."

He looked up at the detective for the first time, his expression impossible to read. Was he making a joke with that last line?

The detective, frozen in place for all of this, quickly changed gears. He sat down, his body language shifting from confrontational to relaxed. Then he slid the folder of photos off the table, set it on the chair next to him, where it'd be out of Todd's line of sight. When he spoke again, his voice was softer than before.

"Let's, uh, start at the beginning," he said. "Tell me how all of this started."

Todd licked his lips, thought a moment. His eyes fell back to the middle distance.

"Amber was... I thought Amber was... coming on to me, I guess you could say. She gave me these looks, you know? Smiles. Rubbed my shoulders sometimes. For these past several years, I loved her as a daughter. Like any normal father would. But these advances, or what I thought were advances... over time, I guess they got under my skin."

He went quiet there. Eyes flicking around. Thinking. Remembering.

"You should understand, too, that things in my marriage weren't the best. My wife was... having an affair. A younger man. Maybe that got under my skin, too. In the end, I'm just a man, right? Just a man. A man wants to... express himself... wants to assert himself. Needs to."

His eyes flicked up to meet the detective's.

"I don't say this to make excuses. Just to explain..."

Again he trailed off to silence, eyes moving, searching through memories again.

The detective waited a long time before he came in with the gentle prodding.

"So things aren't going well with your wife. Any guy could understand that. And Amber, not even your real daughter, mind you, it sure seems like she's interested. Then what happened?"

Todd's eyes sped up as he talked, flicking back and forth.

"I came home early from work, and it was just Amber there in the house. Sharon had left that morning for her conference. It seemed like the perfect time to make my move. I'd been mulling it over for months, trying to work up the nerve. So I… put my arm around her. Kind of rubbed her shoulder in a way… a way where I thought she'd know what I meant, I guess. And she did."

His gaze snapped up to stare at the detective again.

"She laughed at me. She ripped away from my touch, and she laughed at me."

He pounded the table with the heel of his hand. A single violent stroke. Loud. It made everyone in both rooms jump.

Charlie tightened her arms against her chest. Tried to fight off that cold feeling slowly spreading over her.

Todd went on.

"And I guess something in me just… snapped. Rage like I've never felt before. I… strangled her. Don't even remember it very well. The memory is mostly of heat. And a red blur. It's like I put my hands on her, and she's dead… just like that."

He shook his head as he repeated it.

"Just like that."

When he spoke again, his voice went harder, colder.

"It felt good. Killing her. It's wrong, but when I first realized what I'd done, I felt… awake. Alive. More alive than I'd ever felt. People couldn't just walk all over me anymore, you understand? I could control the world around me. Put my hands on it and change it."

This time the detective didn't wait to prod. "What happened next?"

"When the first rush passed, I panicked. Went into self-preservation mode. Kind of made up the plan as I went along.

Everything was frantic, you know? Rushed and feverish. But I had to cover it up. Had to. So I took her car out. Dumped it."

"So the footage you gave us from your doorbell cam that showed Amber's car leaving," the detective said, seeming to put the pieces together as he spoke. "That was you driving?"

Todd nodded.

"What did you do with Amber?"

"Initially I had her in the trunk, but then I figured the police would check the GPS on her car once they found it. It was important to go straight from the house to the commuter lot. So I moved her to my car instead. When I got back from dumping her vehicle, I took her to one of my warehouses so I could give myself time to come up with a plan."

"How is it that none of that—either you coming back from dumping Amber's car or leaving in your car—is on the doorbell camera?"

"I erased it. I kept just the video of me returning from the warehouse that night, so it would look like I didn't arrive home until after Amber had already left. I'm sure all the deleted videos are stored on the cloud or something somewhere, but I only needed it to hold up long enough for you to have another suspect in custody."

Again, Todd seemed on the verge of smiling as he recounted this part of the tale. Amused with his bit of trickery.

The observation room went frigid, cavernous. The coldness gripping Charlie intensified. She wanted to look away, wanted to walk out of the observation room, but she couldn't. Her eyes remained fixed on Todd. Unblinking.

The detective lifted his chin and blinked across the table.

"Tell me about Kara Dawkins."

Todd closed his eyes for a moment. Licked his lips.

"I knew if it was just Amber missing, that I would be one of the first suspects. But if there was another… well, that would complicate things, wouldn't it? Suddenly the police would have to look at *her* family, at the possibility of a stranger abducting random girls from the street. It helped that Kara's disappearance came out first, before Amber's, but that was just sheer luck."

The Adam's apple in the center of Todd's throat bobbed up and down as he swallowed.

"Did you choose her at random, or…?" The detective let his question trail off.

"No, I'd seen her before with… with the man my wife was seeing. I followed him once, after, well… Anyway, I'd learned a little about him. About the drugs. I realized if Kara went missing, he would be a logical suspect. It was a simple matter of convenience."

Charlie wondered at the way he said it, almost apologetically. Like he worried they might think him petty or vindictive, of all things.

"I sent the email to the private detective about the White Rabbit," he continued. "I thought that would bring an end to all of it. But then you ruled Robbie Turner out as a suspect. So I had to change it up again."

"Think on your feet, so to speak?" the detective said.

Todd just glared at him for a long moment before he went on, and Charlie saw a vivid flash of the other version of the man, the aggressive version that lurked somewhere beneath the facade.

"I had to change the narrative. And there was one other person in town who seemed like an obvious fit for the abduction and murder of a pair of teenage girls. Someone who had already done it once and gotten away with it, depending on who you ask."

"Leroy Gibbs," the detective said, not bothering to frame it as a question.

Todd gave the briefest of nods before he went on.

"It meant further unpleasantness for me, of course. Had to take a hacksaw to my stepdaughter's feet. So I wrapped all of her in a vinyl tarp. Just her feet sticking out. Then maybe it wouldn't seem so much like her, I thought. The girl I knew. They were just feet.

And it worked, to some degree. Still, my hands shook the whole time. Felt like a, what do you call it… an out-of-body experience. But it had to be done. I knew the police would take the bait. Salem Island's ghost coming back to haunt them after all these years? With all that history, there was no way this place would allow a man to get away with something like that twice. No way."

"So what went wrong with the plan?" the detective asked. "Why attack and abduct Miss Winters?"

Ritter smiled a wolfish smile. Shook his head.

"I'd been watching her. Keeping tabs. It was helpful early on, to be able to know where she was in the investigation. Reassuring to watch her scurry after the breadcrumbs I'd left her. But even after the feet, even after Gibbs was arrested, she kept going. Still scrambling around like there was something else to find. She was the loose end, you know? Couldn't have that."

Charlie's hands and cheeks were numb now. She held her breath, afraid that if she exhaled, it'd come out as a visible mist. Still, she couldn't look away.

"I followed her to the park," Todd was saying. "Saw her getting into some kind of altercation with the lawyer. That was my chance to close the loop once and for all. Figured I'd take them both out, stage it to look like a murder–suicide. Pin everything on him. No loose ends. But it all spiraled away from me. Got out of control. And now it's all out in the light…"

The detective pursed his lips.

"Let's go back for a moment. When you abducted Kara Dawkins, did you plan what you would do with her?"

Todd's lawyer sat forward, tugging on his arm, whispering in his ear. After listening to him a moment, Todd answered.

"I planned to take her to one of my warehouses, if that's what you mean."

"But after that," the detective said, "what then? Were you going to kill her? Keep her for a while and let her go?"

The tip of Todd's tongue flicked out to wet his lips.

"Because a moment ago, when you were talking about setting up Leroy Gibbs, you said he was an obvious fit for someone who'd abduct *and murder* a pair of girls."

Todd's mouth opened, hanging agape for a second before he spoke.

"Yes. I had initially planned to kill her. But I couldn't do it."

His lawyer threw his hands up in disgust.

Todd shrugged, smiling again.

"It was something else with Amber. Something that happened to me as much as her. Some animal part of my brain taking over. I hadn't planned it. Hadn't looked at her and thought about how I was about to squeeze the life out of her. It just happened. I couldn't recreate it with Kara, even if I wanted to. Needed to."

Charlie thought back to the times she'd interacted with Todd before it had all come undone. How he'd thanked her in her office that day, or when he'd invited her to join the family for his "famous chicken parm."

She had to admit that she'd never suspected him, not even a little. And it wasn't only because he'd seemed to have an airtight alibi.

She'd never considered him because he'd been so... ordinary. So polite and meek. Somehow, listening to him now, that chilled her all the more.

Because what did it mean if someone like him could commit such heinous deeds?

He had done indisputably evil things, and still in most ways he looked and seemed just like anyone else. Her mailman. Her dentist. The guy who made her coffee or changed the tires on her car.

She shuddered at the thought.

And Charlie realized then that the creeping chill that had built throughout Todd's confession went back to Allie. For the first time, she was forced to consider that whoever killed Allie was probably every bit as ordinary as Todd Ritter.

Maybe it was easier to believe that all murderers were monsters. Somehow marked. That society could just weed them out and be rid of them, but reality was not so simple. The ones we call evil? The ones we label as monsters? Before that, they were our friends, our siblings, our co-workers. Husbands. Fathers.

They walk among us.

Lost in her thoughts, it was several moments before Charlie was aware that Todd was still talking in the other room.

"Before it got out, it didn't feel real. Felt like a dream, you know? Something that only existed in my head. But hey, everybody dies in the end. One way or another, that's how the story ends, so…"

The touch of emotion that had built in his voice over the course of the interview drained again as he said these last words. He drifted back to that weird half-amused tone, staring at nothing. Silent. Motionless.

The room held the quiet for a long time, not even the detective daring to break the spell. All eyes watched the subdued figure, perhaps all wondering the same thing, Charlie thought.

What was going through Todd Ritter's brain right now? Would it even mean anything to know?

When he spoke again, it was just louder than a whisper.

"This isn't who I was. Before, I mean. It isn't who I was, but it is now. Can't undo it, so what the hell?"

Charlie's phone buzzed, and feeling that the interrogation was winding down, she stepped into the hallway to take the call.

"Hello?"

"Charlotte Winters?" The voice was male with the slightest lilt of an accent.

"Yes?"

"This is Dr. Anagonye from McLaren Hospital. I'm calling in regard to your uncle."

Charlie readied herself for bad news about Frank. She reached out, bracing herself against the wall.

"He's awake."

CHAPTER NINETY-FOUR

Charlie looked in on Frank through the glass of the small window in the hallway. His eyes were closed, and for a moment, she worried he'd slipped away again in the time it had taken her to get to the hospital. But when she stepped through the open doorway and into the room, Frank's eyelids fluttered open.

Charlie's nose stung and then tears welled in her eyes as she moved closer and took her uncle's hand in hers.

Frank smiled.

"Hey, turkey."

Opening her mouth to respond, Charlie realized that if she tried to say anything right now, it would come out as a sob. She squeezed Frank's hand, taking a few moments to pull herself together. Finally, swallowing against the lump in her throat, she trusted herself to speak.

"Please don't ever do that again," she said.

Frank croaked out a laugh.

"I'll try not to."

Beside him, an IV pump softly whirred and clicked.

"So you found her? Your missing girl?"

"One of them. The other…" Charlie sighed, reliving the moment she found Amber's body on the beach. "She's gone. Was from the beginning. She never really had a chance."

Frank nodded, as if confirming something he already knew.

"Wait. How did you know?"

"Allie told me."

His tone was nonchalant, blasé even, but Charlie froze.

"What?"

"Don't worry. I haven't lost my marbles," he said, chuckling. "I dreamed when I was under. Not the whole time, I don't think. It's hard to say. It's all foggy. I don't even remember falling down in my house. The last memory I have is of you eating a brownie. And then…"

He shook his head.

"Anyway, what I can remember is all murky. Like I was surrounded by some kind of dark cloud. I could hear things, but they sounded garbled and far away, like when you're underwater. But there was one moment when the light pierced the haze. It was sunny and bright, and I could hear perfectly well. And Allie was there. She told me everything was going to be OK. That you'd solved the case. Found the girl."

Charlie stared at him, wondering how much of this could simply be explained away as a fever dream. The hallucinations of a very ill man on a cocktail of drugs, each one with its own jumble of bizarre side effects.

"You want to know the weirdest part?" Frank asked.

"What?"

"The thing that stands out to me most was that when she reached out to hold my hand, her fingers were all sticky, like she'd been eating an ice cream or something."

All the hairs on Charlie's arms stood on end, and her spine quivered. She suddenly flashed on the vision she'd had when she was knocked unconscious, of her and Allie eating popsicles.

Before she could say anything, a dark-haired woman in blue scrubs bustled in with a phlebotomy cart.

"Knock-knock," the woman said.

"Who's there?" Frank responded, looking far too pleased with himself.

Without missing a beat, the woman said, "Ivan."

"Ivan who?"

Affecting a Dracula-esque accent, the woman said, "I vant to steal your blood!"

Frank and Charlie laughed.

"Seriously though," the woman said. "My name is Marta, and I'm here for a blood draw."

Charlie made room at the bedside for the woman and her cart.

"Hey, turkey," Frank said. "Tomorrow's Christmas Eve, you know?"

"I know."

"Well, let's start the celebration early. I got a hankering for some fried chicken. Extra crispy. A breast, a thigh, and two wings. Maybe some mashed potatoes and gravy. All the fixins."

Charlie couldn't help but smile.

"Seriously?"

"Deadly. You wouldn't believe what passes as food in this joint."

"I heard that," Marta teased.

"OK," Charlie said. "As long as you promise to behave yourself while I'm gone."

"Me?" Frank asked with mock innocence. "I promise to stick to knock-knock jokes. Just good, clean fun."

"Yeah, don't pretend like you don't know half a dozen dirty ones." Charlie swiveled to face the phlebotomist. "If he tries to tell you one about 'Anita,' give him a good slap upside the head."

"Don't worry," Marta said, snapping on a glove. "I'll keep him in line."

Charlie exited the room and retraced her steps back to the elevators. As she passed by the waiting room, someone called her name.

She halted, turning to watch a tall form rise from one of the chairs. Will.

He had two black eyes now and a small line of stitches that ran from just over his right temple and disappeared into his hairline.

"Two shiners," she said. "Does that make you doubly irresistible?"

"You tell me," he said, a half-smile touching one corner of his mouth.

Charlie's eyes went down to the polished floor.

"You spied on me, Will. Do you expect me to just forget about that?"

"I know, and I'm sorry. I just wanted the truth. *Needed* the truth. I thought maybe you could understand that, of all people," he said. "Haven't you crossed a few lines on behalf of your clients?"

"Get a load of this guy. He violates your privacy and then tries to spin your question like a politician or something," Allie said, suddenly interjecting.

Charlie considered it and came to the conclusion that maybe they were both right. Maybe she was one of the few people who could appreciate what Will had done, in the name of pursuing justice. But he had broken her trust, something she had in short supply as it was. This wasn't something that could be repaired so quickly.

Charlie raised her eyes, meeting Will's gaze.

"You did what you thought you had to do to prove your client's innocence," she said. "On a certain level, I can respect it."

He pulled back, his expression softening.

"You and I both know, doing what we do, that no one can really be trusted. Not truly," Charlie continued. "So why would either of us be surprised by this type of thing? Why should it hurt us?"

His eyes went wide. Blinking.

"Charlie, you *can* trust me."

She shook her head.

"Can I? Because once I knew you were the one who'd installed that keylogger on my computer, it threw everything into question. I actually believed that you'd kidnapped Kara and killed Amber. I *believed* you killed Allie."

"Allie?" Will's eyelids stretched farther open still. "But you have to know I didn't—"

"Yeah," she said, nodding. "On some level, I do. But sometimes you think things you can't unthink. Not all the way. Some things you can't take back, maybe."

Will's shoulders sagged then, and she thought it was finally sinking in for him. Whatever there might have been between them was gone. Erased.

"Anyway, I forgive you," Charlie said, shrugging. "If that's what you want to hear."

She turned away, heading for the elevators. Inside, she jabbed a button with her finger, and the doors eased closed, sealing her away from the lawyer in the hallway.

"Damn. That was ice-cold, Charles," Allie said. "I kind of love it, but... *ouch*."

EPILOGUE

Two weeks after Todd Ritter entered his guilty plea, the snow that had blanketed Salem Island melted all at once. An unseasonably summery day descended upon eastern Michigan. It seemed to thaw the land itself.

The clouds parted, and the sun erupted in full force. The local weatherman, jubilant and almost breathless, made sure to use the graphic of the little sun cartoon character smiling beneath a pair of black sunglasses in every single one of his segments that day.

The first two days after the melt were a soggy mess. Every yard looked more like a swamp—brown grass swimming in a muddy soup. Standing water along most of the curbs, pools of it collecting atop the clogged storm drains.

But the sun remained. Persisted. Did its work. And on the third warm day, the ground dried out. The grass even started its journey back toward green.

When Charlie went for a walk that day, it felt like everyone in town was out and about. Enjoying the strangely pleasant run of weather. Most went without coats. The bravest of the lot even sported shorts.

"Actual sunshine on a January day?" Allie said. "What demonry is this?"

Charlie sniffed more than she laughed at the comment. Allie sometimes repeated jokes too often. She'd really run the "demonry" thing into the ground recently, slowly draining it of any comedic power.

Charlie fell in with the teeming masses out for a stroll. She walked down to the park, as did much of the crowd, it seemed.

Usually the bustle might kill the joy in a walk, but not today. Today it felt good to be out here no matter what. Maybe it even felt good to be with other people, instead of cooped up in a building by herself. Not apart from everyone like she so often was. Not alone.

Ramsett Park itself wasn't so busy, at least considering the crowd of foot traffic leading up to it and streaming past. Most of the picnic tables stood empty. All but one, in fact.

Charlie veered into the park when she saw who was there. She almost missed the turn, cutting off an older couple and apologizing as she stepped onto the sidewalk sloping down toward the trees.

She slowed as she drew closer to the two women occupying the picnic area, not wanting to get too close. Eventually she ambled out among the pines. Finding a spot where she could watch them among the boughs, for just a moment, without being seen.

Kara and Misty Dawkins ate sandwiches and talked. Mother and daughter reunited.

Charlie had visited Kara in the hospital, of course, and Kara and Misty had also stopped by Charlie's office to thank her for all she did. But this was different. Seeing them out in the world. Living their lives. Carrying on.

Together again. Made whole again. Their wound already healing.

Charlie watched for no more than a minute, seeing this tiny snippet of their life, this tiny moment of simple warmth, simple lightness. She witnessed the little smiles that passed between them. Saw Misty dig a bottle of Pepsi out of the cooler for Kara.

And then Charlie was moving on. Away. Picking her way back through the pines to return to the throng of people heading out of the park and moving toward downtown Salem Island.

Charlie thought maybe Allie would make some joke about the situation. Some sarcastic remark or non sequitur to take the air out of the moment somehow, to degrade the reverence of it just a bit. Instead her sister went the other way with it.

"That was nice," Allie said. "Seeing them together, I mean. A moment of light in a dark world, you know?"

Charlie could never have that with Allie. Justice. Reunion. The broken pieces made whole again. But she could help other people find it—not all, but some—and that seemed like something worth fighting for.

No one knew like her how badly people needed it.

She pressed back into the crowd, walked once more among the people. In some ways, she felt apart from them, but she wasn't alone.

A LETTER FROM L.T. AND TIM

Thanks so much for reading *First Girl Gone*. If you enjoyed it and want to hear about new releases in the Charlie Winters series, make sure to sign up to the Bookouture Vargus/McBain newsletter at this link:

www.bookouture.com/lt-vargus-and-tim-mcbain

We've put together a little bonus freebie for those who sign up to our personal newsletter, too: some deleted scenes from *First Girl Gone*. Curious about what Kara Dawkins was up to while Charlie searched for her? Now is your chance to find out.

ltvargus.com/winters

So what did you think of Charlie and Salem Island? What do you want to happen next for her? Let us know by leaving a review. It doesn't have to be anything fancy. Just a few words about your experience with the book. Reviews help authors so much, and we'd greatly appreciate it.

Charlie will be back soon, so be on the lookout.

L.T. Vargus and Tim McBain

ltvargusbooks
@ltvargus
ltvargus.com

Made in the USA
Las Vegas, NV
26 May 2022

49343598R00236